DANIEL SILVA

THE MESSENGER

A SIGNET BOOK

SIGNET
Published by New American Library, a division of
Penguin Group (USA) Inc., 375 Hudson Street,
New York, New York 10014, USA
Penguin Group (Canada), 90 Eglinton Avenue East, Suite 700, Toronto,
Ontario M4P 2Y3, Canada (a division of Pearson Penguin Canada Inc.)
Penguin Books Ltd., 80 Strand, London WC2R 0RL, England
Penguin Ireland, 25 St. Stephen's Green, Dublin 2,
Ireland (a division of Penguin Books Ltd.)
Penguin Group (Australia), 250 Camberwell Road, Camberwell, Victoria 3124,
Australia (a division of Pearson Australia Group Pty. Ltd.)
Penguin Books India Pvt. Ltd., 11 Community Centre, Panchsheel Park,
New Delhi - 110 017, India
Penguin Group (NZ), 67 Apollo Drive, Rosedale, North Shore 0632,
New Zealand (a division of Pearson New Zealand Ltd.)
Penguin Books (South Africa) (Pty.) Ltd., 24 Sturdee Avenue,
Rosebank, Johannesburg 2196, South Africa

Penguin Books Ltd., Registered Offices:
80 Strand, London WC2R 0RL, England

First published by Signet, an imprint of New American Library, a division of
Penguin Group (USA) Inc. Previously published in a G. P. Putnam's Sons
edition.

First Signet Printing, July 2007
10   9

For Phyllis and Bernard Jacob, for many years of guidance, love, and support. And as always, for my wife, Jamie, and my children, Lily and Nicholas.

The Saudis are active at every level of the terror chain, from planners to financiers, from cadre to foot soldier, from ideologist to cheerleader.

—LAURENT MURAWIEC, RAND Corporation

Unless the ideological roots of the hatred that led to September 11 are addressed, the war on terrorism will not be won. It will be only a matter of time before the next Osama bin Laden emerges.

—DORE GOLD, *Hatred's Kingdom*

We will control the land of the Vatican. We will control Rome and introduce Islam in it.

—SHEIKH MUHAMMAD BIN ABDAL-RAHMAN AL-ARIFI, Imam of the mosque at the King Fahd Defense Academy

PART ONE

THE DOOR
OF DEATH

1

LONDON

IT WAS ALI MASSOUDI who unwittingly roused Gabriel Allon from his brief and restless retirement: Massoudi, the great Europhile intellectual and freethinker, who, in a moment of blind panic, forgot that the English drive on the left side of the road.

The backdrop for his demise was a rain-swept October evening in Bloomsbury. The occasion was the final session of the first annual Policy Forum for Peace and Security in Palestine, Iraq, and Beyond. The conference had been launched early that morning amid great hope and fanfare, but by day's end it had taken on the quality of a traveling production of a mediocre play. Even the demonstrators who came in hope of sharing some of the flickering spotlight seemed to realize they were reading from the same tired script. The American president was burned in effigy at ten. The Israeli prime minister was put to the purifying flame at eleven. At lunchtime, amid a deluge that briefly turned Russell Square into a pond, there had been a folly having something to do with the rights of women in Saudi Arabia. At eight-thirty, as the gavel came down on the final panel, the two dozen stoics who had stayed to the end filed numbly toward the exits. Organizers of the affair detected little appetite for a return engagement next autumn.

A stagehand stole forward and removed a placard from the rostrum that read: GAZA IS LIBERATED—WHAT NOW? The first panelist on his feet was Sayyid of the London School of Economics, defender of the suicide bombers, apologist for al-Qaeda. Next was the austere Chamberlain of Cambridge, who spoke of Palestine and the Jews as though they were still the quandary of gray-suited men from the Foreign Office. Throughout the discussion the aging Chamberlain had served as a sort of Separation Fence between the incendiary Sayyid and a poor soul from the Israeli embassy named Rachel who had drawn hoots and whistles of disapproval each time she'd opened her mouth. Chamberlain tried to play the role of peacekeeper now as Sayyid pursued Rachel to the door with taunts that her days as a colonizer were drawing to an end.

Ali Massoudi, graduate professor of global governance and social theory at the University of Bremen, was the last to rise. Hardly surprising, his jealous colleagues might have said, for among the incestuous world of Middle Eastern studies, Massoudi had the reputation of one who never willingly relinquished a stage. Palestinian by

birth, Jordanian by passport, and European by upbringing and education, Professor Massoudi appeared to all
the world like a man of moderation. The shining future
of Arabia, they called him. The very face of progress. He
was known to be distrustful of religion in general and
militant Islam in particular. In newspaper editorials, in
lecture halls, and on television, he could always be
counted on to lament the dysfunction of the Arab world.
Its failure to properly educate its people. Its tendency to
blame the Americans and the Zionists for all its ailments.
His last book had amounted to a clarion call for an Islamic Reformation. The jihadists had denounced him as
a heretic. The moderates had proclaimed he had the
courage of Martin Luther. That afternoon he had argued, much to Sayyid's dismay, that the ball was now
squarely in the Palestinian court. Until the Palestinians
part company with the culture of terror, Massoudi had
said, the Israelis could never be expected to cede an inch
of the West Bank. Nor should they. Sacrilege, Sayyid had
cried. Apostasy.

Professor Massoudi was tall, a bit over six feet in
height, and far too good-looking for a man who worked
in close proximity to impressionable young women. His
hair was dark and curly, his cheekbones wide and strong,
and his square chin had a deep notch in the center. The
eyes were brown and deeply set and lent his face an air of
profound and reassuring intelligence. Dressed as he was
now, in a cashmere sport jacket and cream-colored roll-
neck sweater, he seemed the very archetype of the Euro-

pean intellectual. It was an image he worked hard to convey. Naturally deliberate of movement, he packed his papers and pens methodically into his well-traveled brief-case, then descended the steps from the stage and headed up the center aisle toward the exit.

Several members of the audience were loitering in the foyer. Standing to one side, a stormy island in an other-wise tranquil sea, was the girl. She wore faded jeans, a leather jacket, and a checkered Palestinian kaffiyeh round her neck. Her black hair shone like a raven's wing. Her eyes were nearly black, too, but shone with something else. Her name was Hamida al-Tatari. A refugee, she had said. Born in Amman, raised in Hamburg, now a citizen of Canada residing in North London. Massoudi had met her that afternoon at a reception in the student union. Over coffee she had fervently accused him of insufficient outrage over the crimes of the Americans and Jews. Mas-soudi had liked what he had seen. They were planning to have drinks that evening at the wine bar next to the the-ater in Sloane Square. His intentions weren't romantic. It wasn't Hamida's body he wanted. It was her zeal and her clean face. Her perfect English and Canadian passport.

She gave him a furtive glance as he crossed the foyer but made no attempt to speak to him. *Keep your distance after the symposium,* he had instructed her that after-noon. *A man in my position has to be careful about who he's seen with.* Outside he sheltered for a moment be-neath the portico and gazed at the traffic moving slug-gishly along the wet street. He felt someone brush against his elbow, then watched as Hamida plunged wordlessly into the cloudburst. He waited until she was gone, then hung his briefcase from his shoulder and set out in the opposite direction, toward his hotel in Russell Square.

The change came over him—the same change that always occurred whenever he moved from one life to the other. The quickening of the pulse, the sharpening of the senses, the sudden fondness for small details. Such as the balding young man, walking toward him beneath the shelter of an umbrella, whose gaze seemed to linger on Massoudi's face an instant too long. Or the newsagent who stared brazenly into Massoudi's eyes as he purchased a copy of the *Evening Standard*. Or the taxi driver who watched him, thirty seconds later, as he dropped the same newspaper into a rubbish bin in Upper Woburn Place.

A London bus overtook him. As it churned slowly past, Massoudi peered through the fogged windows and saw a dozen tired-looking faces, nearly all of them black or brown. *The new Londoners,* he thought, and for a moment the professor of global governance and social theory wrestled with the implications of this. How many secretly sympathized with his cause? How many would sign on the dotted line if he laid before them a contract of death?

In the wake of the bus, on the opposite pavement, was a single pedestrian: oilskin raincoat, stubby ponytail, two straight lines for eyebrows. Massoudi recognized him instantly. The young man had been at the conference—same row as Hamida but on the opposite side of the auditorium. He'd been sitting in the same seat earlier that morning, when Massoudi had been the lone dissenting voice during a panel discussion on the virtue of barring Israeli academics from European shores.

Massoudi lowered his gaze and kept walking, while his left hand went involuntarily to the shoulder strap of his briefcase. Was he being followed? If so, by whom? MI5 was the most likely explanation. The most likely, he reminded himself, but not the only one. Perhaps the German BND had followed him to London from Bremen. Or perhaps he was under CIA surveillance.

But it was the fourth possibility that made Massoudi's heart bang suddenly against his rib cage. What if the man was not English, or German, or American at all? What if he worked for an intelligence service that showed little compunction about liquidating its enemies, even on the streets of foreign capitals? An intelligence service with a history of using women as bait. He thought of what Hamida had said to him that afternoon.

"I grew up in Toronto, mostly."

"And before that?"

"Amman when I was very young. Then a year in Hamburg. I'm a Palestinian, Professor. My home is a suitcase."

Massoudi made a sudden turn off Woburn Place, into the tangle of side streets of St. Pancras. After a few paces he slowed and looked over his shoulder. The man in the oilskin coat had crossed the street and was following after him.

HE QUICKENED his pace, made a series of turns, left and right. Here a row of mews houses, here a block of flats, here an empty square littered with dead leaves. Massoudi saw little of it. He was trying to keep his orientation. He knew London's main thoroughfares well enough, but the backstreets were a mystery to him. He threw all tradecraft to the wind and made regular glances over his shoulder. Each glance seemed to find the man a pace or two closer.

He came to an intersection, looked left, and saw traffic rushing along the Euston Road. On the opposite side, he knew, lay King's Cross and St. Pancras stations. He turned in that direction, then, a few seconds later, glanced over his shoulder. The man had rounded the corner and was coming after him.

He began to run. He had never been much of an athlete, and years of academic pursuits had robbed his body of fitness. The weight of the laptop computer in his briefcase was like an anchor. With each stride the case banged against his hip. He secured it with his elbow and held the strap with his other hand, but this gave his stride an awkward galloping rhythm that slowed him even more. He considered jettisoning it but clung to it instead. In the wrong hands the laptop was a treasure trove of information. Personnel, surveillance photographs, communications links, *bank accounts . . .*

He stumbled to a stop at the Euston Road. Glancing over his shoulder, he saw his pursuer still plodding methodically toward him, hands in his pockets, eyes down. He looked to his left, saw empty asphalt, and stepped off the curb.

The groan of the lorry horn was the last sound Ali Massoudi ever heard. At impact the briefcase broke free of him. It took flight, turned over several times as it hovered above the road, then landed on the street with a solid thud. The man in the oilskin raincoat barely had to break stride as he bent down and snared it by the strap. He slipped it neatly over his shoulder, crossed the Euston Road, and followed the evening commuters into King's Cross.

2

JERUSALEM

THE BRIEFCASE HAD REACHED Paris by dawn, and by eleven it was being carried into an anonymous-looking office block on King Saul Boulevard in Tel Aviv. There the professor's personal effects were hastily inspected, while the hard drive of his laptop computer was subjected to a sustained assault by a team of technical wizards. By three that afternoon the first packet of intelligence had been forwarded to the Prime Minister's Office in Jerusalem, and by five a manila file folder containing the most alarming material was in the back of an armored Peugeot limousine heading toward Narkiss Street, a quiet leafy lane not far from the Ben Yehuda Mall.

The car stopped in front of the small apartment house at Number 16. Ari Shamron, the twice former chief of the Israeli secret service, now special adviser to the prime minister on all matters dealing with security and intelligence, emerged from the backseat. Rami, the black-eyed chief of his personal security detail, moved silently at his heels. Shamron had made countless enemies during his long and turbulent career, and because of Israel's tangled demographics, many were uncomfortably close. Shamron, even when he was inside his fortresslike villa in Tiberias, was surrounded always by bodyguards.

He paused for a moment on the garden walkway and looked up. It was a dowdy little building of Jerusalem limestone, three floors in height, with a large eucalyptus tree in front that cast a pleasant shadow over the front balconies. The limbs of the tree were swaying in the first cool wind of autumn, and from the open window on the third floor came the sharp odor of paint thinner.

Shamron, as he entered the foyer, glanced at the mailbox for apartment number three and saw it was absent a nameplate. He mounted the stairs and tramped slowly upward. He was short of stature and was dressed, as usual, in khaki trousers and a scuffed leather jacket with a tear in the right breast. His face was full of cracks and fissures, and his remaining fringe of gray hair was cropped so short as to be nearly invisible. His hands were leathery and liver-spotted and seemed to have been borrowed from a man twice his size. In one was the file.

The door was ajar when he arrived on the third-floor landing. He placed his fingers against it and gently pushed. The flat he entered had once been meticulously decorated by a beautiful Italian-Jewish woman of impeccable taste. Now the furniture, like the beautiful Italian woman, was gone, and the flat had been turned into an artist's studio. Not an artist, Shamron had to remind himself. Gabriel Allon was a restorer—one of the three or four most sought-after restorers in the world. He was standing now before an enormous canvas depicting a man surrounded by large predatory cats. Shamron settled himself quietly on a paint-smudged stool and watched him work for a few moments. He had always been mystified by Gabriel's ability to imitate the brushstrokes of the Old Masters. To Shamron it was something of a parlor trick, just another of Gabriel's gifts to be utilized, like his languages or his ability to get a Beretta off his hip and into firing position in the time it takes most men to clap their hands.

"It certainly looks better than when it first arrived," Shamron said, "but I still don't know why anyone would want to hang it in his home."

"It won't end up in a private home," Gabriel said, his brush to the canvas. "This is a museum piece."

"Who painted it?" Shamron asked abruptly, as though inquiring about the perpetrator of a bombing.

"Bohnams auction house in London thought it was Erasmus Quellinus," Gabriel said. "Quellinus might have laid the foundations, but it's clear to me that Rubens finished it for him." He moved his hand over the large canvas. "His brushstrokes are everywhere."

"What difference does it make?"

"About ten million pounds," Gabriel said. "Julian is going to do very nicely with this one."

Julian Isherwood was a London art dealer and some-time secret servant of Israeli intelligence. The service had a long name that had very little to do with the true nature of its work. Men like Shamron and Gabriel referred to it as the Office and nothing more.

"I hope Julian is giving you fair compensation."

"My restoration fee, plus a small commission on the sale."

"What's the total?"

Gabriel tapped his brush against his palette and resumed working.

"We need to talk," Shamron said.

"So talk."

"I'm not going to talk to your back." Gabriel turned and peered at Shamron once more through the lenses of his magnifying visor. "And I'm not going to talk to you while you're wearing those things. You look like something from my nightmares."

Gabriel reluctantly set his palette on the worktable and removed his magnifying visor, revealing a pair of eyes that were a shocking shade of emerald green. He was below average in height and had the spare physique of a cyclist. His face was high at the forehead and narrow at the chin, and he had a long bony nose that looked as though it had been carved from wood. His hair was cropped short and shot with gray at the temples. It was because of Shamron that Gabriel was an art restorer and not one of the finest painters of his generation—and why his temples had turned gray virtually overnight when he was in his early twenties. Shamron had been the intelligence officer chosen by Golda Meir to hunt down and assassinate the perpetrators of the 1972 Munich Massacre, and a promising young art student named Gabriel Allon had been his primary gunman.

He spent a few moments cleaning his palette and brushes, then went into the kitchen. Shamron sat down at the small table and waited for Gabriel to turn his back before hurriedly lighting one of his foul-smelling Turkish cigarettes. Gabriel, hearing the familiar *click-click* of Shamron's old Zippo lighter, pointed toward the Rubens in exasperation, but Shamron made a dismissive gesture and defiantly raised the cigarette to his lips. A comfortable silence settled between them while Gabriel poured bottled water into the teakettle and spooned coffee into the French press. Shamron was content to listen to the wind moving in the eucalyptus trees outside in the garden. Devoutly secular, he marked the passage of time not by the Jewish festivals but by the rhythms of the land— the day the rains came, the day the wildflowers exploded in the Galilee, the day the cool winds returned. Gabriel could read his thoughts. *Another autumn, and we're still here. The covenant had not been revoked.*

"The prime minister wants an answer." Shamron's gaze still was focused on the tangled little garden. "He's a patient man, but he won't wait forever."

"I told you that I'd give him an answer when I was finished with the painting."

Shamron looked at Gabriel. "Does your arrogance

know no bounds? The prime minister of the State of Israel wants you to be chief of Special Operations, and you put him off over some five-hundred-year-old piece of canvas."

"*Four* hundred."

Gabriel carried the coffee to the table and poured two cups. Shamron scooped sugar into his and gave it a single violent stir.

"You said yourself the painting is nearly finished. What is your answer going to be?"

"I haven't decided."

"May I offer you a piece of helpful advice?"

"And if I don't want your advice?"

"I'd give it to you anyway." Shamron squeezed the life out of his cigarette butt. "You should accept the prime minister's offer before he makes it to someone else."

"Nothing would make me happier."

"Really? And what will you do with yourself?" Greeted by silence, Shamron pressed on. "Allow me to paint a picture for you, Gabriel. I'll do the best I can. I'm not gifted like you. I don't come from a great German-Jewish intellectual family. I'm just a poor Polish Jew whose father sold pots from the back of a handcart."

Shamron's murderous Polish accent had grown thicker. Gabriel couldn't help but smile. He knew that whenever Shamron played the downtrodden Jew from Lvov, something entertaining was certain to follow.

"You have nowhere else to go, Gabriel. You said it

yourself when we offered you the job the first time. What will you do when you're finished with this Rubens of yours? Do you have any more work lined up?" Shamron's pause was theatrical in nature, for he knew the answer was no. "You can't go back to Europe until you're officially cleared in the bombing of the Gare de Lyon. Julian might send you another painting, but eventually that will end, too, because the packing and shipping costs will cut into his already-tenuous bottom line. Do you see my point, Gabriel?"

"I see it very clearly. You're trying to use my unfortunate situation as a means of blackmailing me into taking Operations."

"Blackmail? No, Gabriel. I know the meaning of blackmail, and God knows I've been known to use it when it suits my needs. But this is not blackmail. I'm trying to help you."

"Help?"

"Tell me something, Gabriel: What do you plan to do for money?"

"I have money."

"Enough to live like a hermit, but not enough to *live*." Shamron lapsed into a momentary silence and listened to the wind. "It's quiet now, isn't it? Tranquil almost. It's tempting to think it can go on like this forever. But it can't. We gave them Gaza without demanding anything in return, and they repaid us by freely electing Hamas to be their rulers. Next they'll want the West Bank, and if we don't surrender it in short order, there's going to be another round of bloodletting, much worse than even the second intifada. Trust me, Gabriel, one day soon it will all start up again. And not just here. *Everywhere.* Do you think they're sitting on their hands doing nothing? Of course not. They're planning the next campaign. They're talking to Osama and his friends, too. We now know for a fact that the Palestinian Authority has been thoroughly penetrated by al-Qaeda and its affiliates. We also know that they are planning major attacks against Israel and Israeli targets abroad in the very near future. The Office also believes the prime minister has been targeted for assassination, along with senior advisers."

"You included?"

"Of course," Shamron said. "I am, after all, the prime minister's special adviser on all matters dealing with security and terrorism. My death would be a tremendous symbolic victory for them."

He looked out the window again at the wind moving in the trees. "It's ironic, isn't it? This place was supposed to be our sanctuary. Now, in an odd way, it's left us more vulnerable than ever. Nearly half the world's Jews live in this tiny strip of land. One small nuclear device, that's all it would take. The Americans could survive one. The Russians might barely notice it. But us? A bomb in Tel Aviv would kill a quarter of the country's population— maybe more."

"And you need me to prevent this apocalypse? I thought the Office was in good hands these days."

"Things are definitely better now that Lev has been shown the door. Amos is an extraordinarily competent leader and administrator, but sometimes I think he has a bit too much of the soldier in him."

"He was chief of both the Sayeret Matkal *and* Aman. What did you expect?"

"We knew what we were getting with Amos, but the prime minister and I are now concerned that he's trying to turn King Saul Boulevard into an outpost of the IDF. We want the Office to retain its original character."

"Insanity?"

"Boldness," countered Shamron. "Audacity. I just wish Amos would think a little less like a battlefield commander and a little more like . . ." His voice trailed off while he searched for the right word. When he found it, he rubbed his first two fingers against his thumb and said, "Like an *artist*. I need someone by his side who thinks more like Caravaggio."

"Caravaggio was a madman."

"Exactly."

Shamron started to light another cigarette, but this time Gabriel managed to stay his hand before he'd struck his lighter. Shamron looked at him, his eyes suddenly serious.

"We need you *now*, Gabriel. Two hours ago the chief of Special Operations handed Amos his letter of resignation."

"Why?"

"London." Shamron looked down at his captured hand. "May I have that back?"

Gabriel let go of the thick wrist. Shamron rolled the unlit cigarette between his thumb and forefinger.

"What happened in London?" Gabriel asked.

"I'm afraid we had a bit of a mishap there last night."

"A mishap? When the Office has a mishap, someone usually ends up dead."

Shamron nodded in agreement. "Well, at least there's something to be said for consistency."

"DOES THE NAME Ali Massoudi mean anything to you?"

"He's professor of something or other at a university in Germany," Gabriel replied. "Likes to play the role of an iconoclast and a reformer. I actually met him once."

Shamron's eyebrows went up in surprise. "Really? Where?"

"He came to Venice a couple of years ago for a big Middle East symposium. As part of their stipend the participants got a guided tour of the city. One of their stops was the Church of San Zaccaria, where I was restoring the Bellini altarpiece."

For several years Gabriel had lived and worked in Venice under the name Mario Delvecchio. Six months earlier he had been forced to flee the city after being discovered there by a Palestinian masterterrorist named Khaled al-Khalifa. The affair had ended at the Gare de Lyon, and in the aftermath Gabriel's name and secret past had been splashed across the French and European press, including an exposé in *The Sunday Times* that referred to him as "Israel's Angel of Death." He was still wanted for questioning by the Paris police, and a Palestinian civil rights group had filed a lawsuit in London alleging war crimes.

"And you actually *met* Massoudi?" Shamron asked incredulously. "You shook his hand?"

"As Mario Delvecchio, of course."

"I suppose you didn't realize that you were shaking hands with a terrorist."

Shamron stuck the end of the cigarette between his lips and struck his Zippo. This time Gabriel didn't intervene.

"Three months ago we got a tip from a friend at the Jordanian GID that Professor Ali Massoudi, that great moderate and reformer, was actually a talent scout for al-Qaeda. According to the Jordanians, he was looking for recruits to attack Israeli and Jewish targets in Europe. Peace conferences and anti-Israel demonstrations were his favorite hunting grounds. We weren't surprised by that part. We've known for some time that the *peace* conferences have become a meeting place for al-Qaeda operatives and European extremists of both the left-wing and right-wing variety. We decided it would be wise to put Professor Massoudi under watch. We got to the telephone in his apartment in Bremen, but the yield was disappointing, to put it mildly. He was very good on the phone. Then about a month ago, London Station chipped in with a timely piece of information. It seems the Cultural section of the London embassy had been asked to provide a warm body for something called the Policy Forum for Peace and Security in Palestine, Iraq, and Beyond. When Cultural asked for a list of the other participants, guess whose name appeared on it?"

"Professor Ali Massoudi."

"Cultural agreed to send a representative to the conference, and Special Ops set its sights on Massoudi."

"What kind of operation was it?"

"Simple," Shamron said. "Catch him in the act. Compromise him. Threaten him. Turn him around. Can you imagine? An agent inside the al-Qaeda personnel department? With Massoudi's help we could have rolled up their European networks."

"So what happened?"

"We put a girl on his plate. She called herself Hamida al-Tatari. Her real name is Aviva and she's from Ramat Gan, but that's neither here nor there. She met Massoudi at a reception. Massoudi was intrigued and agreed to meet her again later that evening for a more lengthy discussion of the current state of the world. We followed Massoudi after the last session of the conference, but Massoudi apparently spotted the watcher and started to run. He looked the wrong way while crossing the Euston Road and stepped in front of a delivery truck."

Gabriel winced.

"Fortunately we didn't come away completely empty-handed," Shamron said. "The watcher made off with Massoudi's briefcase. Among other things it contained a laptop computer. It seems Professor Ali Massoudi was more than just a talent spotter."

Shamron placed the file folder in front of Gabriel and, with a terse nod of his head, instructed Gabriel to open the cover. Inside he found a stack of surveillance photographs: St. Peter's Square from a dozen different angles; the façade and interior of the Basilica; Swiss Guards standing watch at the Arch of Bells. It was clear the photos had not been taken by an ordinary tourist, because the cameraman had been far less interested in the visual aesthetics of the Vatican than the security measures surrounding it. There were several snapshots of the barricades along the western edge of the square and the metal detectors along Bernini's Colonnade—and several more of the Vigilanza and Carabinieri who patrolled the square during large gatherings, including close-ups of their sidearms. The final three photographs showed Pope Paul VII greeting a crowd in St. Peter's Square in his glass-enclosed popemobile. The camera lens had been focused not on the Holy Father but on the plain-clothes Swiss Guards walking at his side.

Gabriel viewed the photos a second time. Based on the quality of the light and the clothing worn by the crowds of pilgrims, it appeared that they had been taken on at least three separate occasions. Repeated photographic surveillance of the same target, he knew, was a hallmark of a serious al-Qaeda operation. He closed the file and held it out to Shamron, but Shamron wouldn't accept it. Gabriel regarded the old man's face with the same intensity he'd studied the photographs. He could tell there was more bad news to come.

"Technical found something else on Massoudi's computer," Shamron said. "Instructions for accessing a numbered bank account in Zurich—an account we've known about for some time, because it's received regular infusions of money from something called the Committee to Liberate al-Quds."

Al-Quds was the Arabic name for Jerusalem.

"Who's behind it?" Gabriel asked.

"Saudi Arabia," said Shamron. "To be more specific, the interior minister of Saudi Arabia, Prince Nabil."

Inside the Office, Nabil was routinely referred to as the Prince of Darkness for his hatred of Israel and the United States and his support of Islamic militancy around the globe.

"Nabil created the committee at the height of the second intifada," Shamron continued. "He raises the money himself and personally oversees the distribution. We believe he has a hundred million dollars at his disposal, and he's funneling it to some of the most violent terror groups in the world, including elements of al-Qaeda."

"Who's giving Nabil the money?"

"Unlike the other Saudi charities, the Committee for the Liberation of al-Quds has a very small donor base. We think Nabil raises the money from a handful of Saudi multimillionaires."

Shamron peered into his coffee for a moment. "Charity," he said, his tone disdainful. "A lovely word, isn't it? But Saudi charity has always been a two-edged sword. The Muslim World League, the International Islamic Relief Organization, the al-Haramayn Islamic Foundation, the Benevolence International Foundation—they are to Saudi Arabia what the Comintern was to the old Soviet Union. A means of propagating the faith. Islam. And not just any form of Islam. Saudi Arabia's puritanical brand of Islam. Wahhabism. The charities build mosques and Islamic centers around the world and madrassas that churn out the Wahhabi militants of tomorrow. And they also give money directly to the terrorists, including our friends in Hamas. The engines of America run on Saudi oil, but the networks of global Islamic terrorism run largely on Saudi money."

"Charity *is* the third pillar of Islam," Gabriel said. *"Zakat."*

"And a noble quality," Shamron said, "except when the *zakat* ends up in the hands of murderers."

"Do you think Ali Massoudi was connected to the Saudis by more than money?"

"We may never know because the great professor is no longer with us. But whomever he was working for clearly has his sights set on the Vatican—and someone needs to tell them."

"I suspect you have someone in mind for the job."

"Consider it your first assignment as chief of Special Ops," Shamron said. "The prime minister wants you to step into the breach. *Immediately."*

"And Amos?"

"Amos has another name in mind, but the prime minister and I have made it clear to him who we want in the job."

"My own record is hardly free of scandal, and unfortunately the world now knows about it."

"The Gare de Lyon affair?" Shamron shrugged. "You were lured into it by a clever opponent. Besides, I've always believed that a career free of controversy is not a proper career at all. The prime minister shares that view."

"Maybe that's because he's been involved in a few scandals of his own." Gabriel exhaled heavily and looked down at the photographs once more. "There are risks to sending me to Rome. If the French find out I'm on Italian soil—"

"There's no need for you to go to Rome," Shamron said, cutting him off. "Rome is coming to you."

"Donati?"

Shamron nodded.

"How much did you tell him?"

"Enough for him to ask Alitalia if he could borrow a plane for a few hours," Shamron said. "He'll be here first thing in the morning. Show him the photographs. Tell him as much as you need to in order to impress upon him that we think the threat is credible."

"And if he asks for help?"

Shamron shrugged. "Give him whatever he needs."

3

JERUSALEM

MONSIGNOR LUIGI DONATI, private secretary to His Holiness Pope Paul VII, was waiting for Gabriel in the lobby of the King David Hotel at eleven the following morning. He was tall and lean and handsome as an Italian movie idol. The cut of his black clerical suit and Roman collar suggested that the monsignor, while chaste, was not without personal vanity—as did the expensive Swiss watch on his wrist and the gold fountain pen lodged in his breast pocket. His dark eyes radiated a fierce and uncompromising intelligence, while the stubborn set of his jaw revealed that he was a dangerous man to cross. The Vatican press corps had described him as a clerical Rasputin, the power behind the papal throne. His enemies within the Roman Curia often referred to Donati as "the Black Pope," an unflattering reference to his Jesuit past.

It had been three years since their first meeting.

Gabriel had been investigating the murder of an Israeli scholar living in Munich, a former Office agent named Benjamin Stern. The trail of clues had led Gabriel to the Vatican and into Donati's capable hands, and together they had destroyed a grave threat to the papacy. A year later Donati had helped Gabriel find evidence in a Church archive that allowed him to identify and capture Erich Radek, a Nazi war criminal living in Vienna. But the bond between Gabriel and Donati extended far beyond the two men. Donati's master, Pope Paul VII, was closer to Israel than any of his predecessors and had taken monumental steps to improve relations between Catholics and Jews. Keeping him alive was one of Shamron's highest priorities.

When Donati spotted Gabriel coming across the lobby, he smiled warmly and extended a long, dark hand. "It's good to see you, my friend. I only wish the circumstances were different."

"Have you checked into your room?"

Donati held up the key.

"Let's go upstairs. There's something you need to see."

They walked to the elevators and entered a waiting carriage. Gabriel knew, even before Donati reached out for the panel of call buttons, that he would press the one for the sixth floor—just as he knew that the key in Donati's hand opened the door to Room 616. The spacious suite overlooking the Old City walls was permanently reserved for Office use. Along with the usual luxury amenities, it contained a built-in audio recording system, which could be engaged by a tiny switch concealed beneath the bathroom sink. Gabriel made certain the system was turned off before showing the photographs to Donati. The priest's face showed no emotion as he regarded each image carefully, but a moment later, as he stood at the window gazing out toward the Dome of the Rock sparkling in the distance, Gabriel noticed the muscles of his jaw alternatively clenching and unclenching with stress.

"We've been through this many times before, Gabriel—the Millennium, the Jubilee, nearly every Christmas and Easter. Sometimes the warnings are delivered to us by the Italian security services, and sometimes they come from our friends in the Central Intelligence Agency. Each time, we respond by clamping down on security, until the threat is deemed to have subsided. Thus far, nothing has materialized. The Basilica is still standing. And so, too, I'm pleased to say, is the Holy Father."

"Just because they haven't succeeded doesn't mean they aren't trying, Luigi. The Wahhabi-inspired terrorists of al-Qaeda and its affiliates regard everyone who doesn't adhere to its brand of Islam as *kafur* and *mushrikun,* worthy only of death. *Kafur* are infidels, and *mushrikun* are polytheists. They regard even Sunni and Shiite Muslims as *mushrikun,* but to their way of thinking, there's no bigger symbol of polytheism than the Vatican and the Holy Father."

"I understand all that, but as you say at your Passover seder, why is this night different from all other nights?"

"You're asking me why you should take *this* threat seriously?"

"Precisely."

"Because of the messenger," Gabriel said. "The man on whose computer we found these photographs."

"Who is he?"

"I'm afraid I can't tell you that."

Donati turned slowly away from the window and regarded Gabriel imperiously. "I've laid bare some of the darkest secrets of the Roman Catholic Church to you. The least you can do in return is tell me where you got the photographs."

Gabriel hesitated. "Are you familiar with the name Ali Massoudi?"

"*Professor* Ali Massoudi?" Donati's expression darkened. "Wasn't he killed in London a couple of nights ago?"

"He wasn't *killed*," Gabriel said. "He died in an accident."

"Dear God, please tell me you didn't push him in front of that truck, Gabriel."

"Save your sorrow for someone worthy of it. We know Massoudi was a terrorist recruiter. And based on what we found on his laptop, he might have been a planner as well."

"Too bad he's dead. We could have put him on the

rack and tortured him until he told us what we wanted to hear." Donati looked down at his hands. "Forgive my sarcastic tone, Gabriel, but I'm not a great supporter of this war on terror we're engaged in. Nor for that matter is the Holy Father."

Donati looked out the window once again, at the walls of the Old City. "Ironic, isn't it? My first visit to this holy city of yours, and this is the reason for it."

"You've really never been?"

Donati slowly shook his head.

"Care to have a look at where it all started?"

Donati smiled. "Actually, I'd like nothing better."

THEY CROSSED the Valley of Hinnom and labored up the slope of the hill to the eastern wall of the Old City. The footpath at the base of the wall was in shadow. They followed it southward, toward the Church of the Dormition, then rounded the corner and slipped through the Zion Gate. On the Jewish Quarter Road, Donati produced a slip of paper from the pocket of his clerical suit. "The Holy Father would like me to leave this in the Western Wall."

They followed a cluster of *haredim* down Tif'eret Yisra'el. Donati, in his black clothing, looked as though he might be part of the group. At the end of the street they descended the wide stone steps that led to the plaza in front of the wall. A long line stretched from the security kiosk. Gabriel, after murmuring something to a female border police officer, led Donati around the metal detectors and into the square.

"Don't you do anything like a normal person?"

"You go ahead," Gabriel said. "I'll wait here."

Donati turned and inadvertently headed toward the women's side of the wall. Gabriel, with a discreet cluck of his tongue, guided him to the portion reserved for men. Donati selected a *kippah* from the public basket and placed it precariously atop his head. He stood before the wall a moment in silent prayer, then slipped the small scroll of paper into a crevice in the tan Herodian stone.

"What did it say?" Gabriel asked, when Donati returned.

"It was a plea for peace."

"You should have left it up there," Gabriel said, pointing in the direction of the Al-Aqsa mosque.

"You've changed," Donati said. "The man I met three years ago would never have said that."

"We've all changed, Luigi. There's not much of a peace camp in this country anymore, only a security camp. Arafat didn't count on that when he unleashed the suicide bombers."

"Arafat is gone now."

"Yes, but the damage he left behind will take at least a generation to repair." He shrugged. "Who knows? Maybe the wounds of the second intifada will never heal."

"And so the killing will go on? Surely you can't contemplate a future like that."

"Of course we can, Luigi. That's the way it's always been in this place."

They left the Jewish Quarter and walked to the Church of the Holy Sepulcher. Gabriel waited in the courtyard while Donati, after fending off a freelance Palestinian tour guide, went inside. He returned ten minutes later. "It's dark," he said. "And a little disappointing, to be honest with you."

"I'm afraid that's what everyone says."

They left the courtyard and walked in the Via Dolorosa. A group of American pilgrims, led by a brown-cassocked monk clutching a red helium balloon, hustled toward them from the opposite direction. Donati watched the spectacle with a bemused expression on his face.

"Do you still believe?" Gabriel asked suddenly.

Donati took a moment before answering. "As I'm sure you've guessed by now, my personal faith is something of a complex matter. But I do believe in the power of the Roman Catholic Church to be a force for good in a world filled with evil. And I believe in this Pope."

"So you're a faithless man at the side of a man of great faith."

"Well put," Donati said. "And what about you? Do you still believe? Did you ever?"

Gabriel stopped walking. "The Canaanites, the Hittites, the Amalekites, the Moabites—they're all gone. But for some reason we're still here. Was it because God made a covenant with Abraham four thousand years ago? Who's to say?"

" 'I will bless you greatly and make your descendants as numerous as the stars of heaven and the sands of the seashore,' " Donati said, quoting the twenty-second chapter of Genesis.

" 'And your descendants shall come to possess the gates of your enemies,' " Gabriel said, finishing the passage for him. "And now my enemy wants those gates back, and he's willing to do anything, including sacrifice his own son, to get them back."

Donati smiled at Gabriel's clever interpretation of Scripture. "We're not so different, you and I. We've both given our lives over to higher powers. For me, it's the Church. For you, it's your people." He paused. "And the land."

They walked farther along the Via Dolorosa, into the Muslim Quarter. When the street was enveloped in shadow, Gabriel pushed his sunglasses onto his forehead. Palestinian shopkeepers eyed him curiously from their crowded stalls.

"Is it all right for you to be here?"

"We'll be fine."

"I take it you're armed."

Gabriel allowed his silence to serve as an answer. As they walked on Donati's gaze was on the cobblestones, and his dark brow was furrowed in concentration.

"If I know Ali Massoudi is dead, is it safe to assume his comrades know he's dead, too?"

"Of course."

"Do they also know his computer contained those photographs? And that it fell into your hands?"

"It's possible."

"Might that encourage them to accelerate their plans?"

"Or it might cause them to postpone the operation until you and the Italians let your guard down again."

They passed through Damascus Gate. Gabriel lowered his sunglasses as they entered the crowded, cacophonous market square beyond the walls.

"There's something you should know about those photos," Donati said. "They were all taken during the Holy Father's general audience, when he greets pilgrims from around the world in St. Peter's Square."

Gabriel stopped walking and gazed at the golden Dome of the Rock, floating above the stone walls. "The general audience takes place on Wednesdays, does it not?"

"That's correct."

Gabriel looked at Donati and said, "Today is Tuesday."

Donati looked at his wristwatch. "Will you give me a ride back to the airport? If we hurry, we can be in Rome in time for supper."

"We?"

"We'll stop at your apartment on the way out of town so you can pack a bag," Donati said. "It's been stormy in Rome. Make sure you pack a raincoat."

He would have to bring more than a raincoat, Gabriel thought as he led Donati through the crowded market. He was going to need a false passport, too.

4

VATICAN CITY

I**T WAS A RATHER** ordinary office for so powerful a man. The Oriental carpet was faded and timeworn, and the curtains were heavy and drab. As Gabriel and Donati entered the room, the small figure in white seated behind the large austere desk was gazing intently at the screen of a television. A scene of violence played there: fire and smoke, bloodstained survivors pulling at their hair and weeping over the tattered bodies of the dead. Pope Paul VII, Bishop of Rome, Pontifex Maximus, successor to St. Peter, pressed the Power button on his remote control, and the image turned to black. "Gabriel," he said. "It's so good to see you again."

The Pope rose slowly to his feet and extended a small hand—not with the fisherman's ring facing upward, the way he did toward most people, but with the palm sideways. The grip was still strong, and the eyes that gazed fondly up at Gabriel were still vibrant and clear. Gabriel

had forgotten how diminutive Pietro Lucchesi really
was. He thought of the afternoon Lucchesi had emerged
from the conclave, an elfin figure, swimming in the hastily
prepared cassock and barely visible over the balustrade of
the Basilica's great loggia. A commentator for Italian television had proclaimed him Pietro the Improbable. Cardinal Marco Brindisi, the reactionary secretary of state
who had assumed *he* would be the one to emerge from
the conclave dressed in white, had acidly referred to Lucchesi as "Pope Accidental I."

For Gabriel, though, it was another image of Pietro
Lucchesi that he would always think of first, the sight of
him standing on the bimah of the Great Synagogue of
Rome, speaking words no pope had ever spoken before.
*"For these sins, and others soon to be revealed, we offer our
confession, and we beg your forgiveness. There are no words
to describe the depth of our grief. In your hour of greatest
need, when the forces of Nazi Germany pulled you from
your houses in the very streets surrounding this synagogue,
you cried out for help, but your pleas were met by silence.
And so today, as I plead for forgiveness, I will do it in the
same manner. In silence . . ."*

The Pope retook his seat and looked at the television
screen, as if the images of distant mayhem could still be
seen there. "I warned him not to do it, but he didn't listen to me. Now he intends to come to Europe to mend
fences with his former allies. I wish him well, but I think
his chances for success are slim."

Gabriel looked to Donati for an explanation.

"The White House informed us last night that the president will be coming here early next year for a tour of European capitals. The president's men are hoping to project a warmer, less confrontational image and repair some of the damage over the decision to go to war in Iraq."

"A war I steadfastly opposed," the Pope said.

"Is he coming to the Vatican?" Gabriel asked.

"He's coming to Rome—that much we know. The White House hasn't told us yet whether the president would like an audience with the Holy Father. We fully expect that a request will be arriving soon."

"He wouldn't dream of coming to Rome without dropping by the Vatican," the Pope said. "Conservative Catholics are an important part of his constituency. He'll want a nice photo opportunity and some kind words from me. He'll get his photo. As for the kind words . . ." The Pope's voice trailed off. "I'm afraid he'll have to look elsewhere for those."

Donati motioned for Gabriel to sit, then settled himself in the chair next to him. "The president is a man who appreciates straight talk, as our American friends like to say. He'll listen to what you have to say, Holiness."

"He should have listened to me the *first* time. I made it very clear to him when he came to the Vatican before the war that I believed he was embarking on a disastrous path. I told him that war was not justified because there was no true imminent threat to America and her allies. I told him that he had not exhausted every last avenue to avert conflict and that the United Nations, not the United States, was the proper authority for dealing with this problem. But I reserved most of my passion for my final argument against the war. I told the president that America would win a quick battlefield victory. 'You are powerful,' I said, 'and your enemy is weak.' But I also predicted that for years after the war America would face a violent insurgency. I warned him that in trying to solve one crisis with violence, he would only create another more dangerous crisis. That war would be seen by the Muslim world as a new Crusade by white Christians. That terrorism could not be defeated by more terrorism but only through social and economic justice."

The Pope, having finished his homily, looked at his small audience for reaction. His eyes moved back and forth several times before settling on Gabriel's face. "Something tells me you wish to take issue with something I've said."

"You are a man of great eloquence, Holiness."

"You are among family, Gabriel. Speak your mind."

"The forces of radical Islam have declared war on us—America, the West, Christianity, Israel. Under God's law and the laws of man, we have the right, indeed the moral duty, to resist."

"Resist the terrorists with justice and opportunity rather than violence and bloodshed. When statesmen resort to violence, it is humanity that suffers."

"You seem to believe that the problem of terrorism and radical Islam can be swept away if they were more like us—that if poverty, illiteracy, and tyranny weren't so prevalent in the Muslim world, there would be no young men willing to sacrifice their lives in order to maim and kill others. But they've seen the way we live, and they want nothing of it. They've seen our democracy, and they reject it. They view democracy as a religion that runs counter to the central tenets of Islam, and therefore they will resist it with a sacred rage. How do we deliver justice and prosperity to these men of Islam who believe only in death?"

"It certainly cannot be imposed on them by the barrel of a white man's gun."

"I agree, Holiness. Only when Islam reforms itself will there be social justice and true prosperity within the Arab world. But in the meantime we cannot sit idly by and do nothing while the jihadists plot our destruction. That, Holiness, is immoral, too."

The Pope rose from his desk and pushed open the large window overlooking St. Peter's Square. Night had fallen. Rome stirred beneath his feet.

"I was right about the war, Gabriel, and I'm right about the future that awaits us all—Muslim, Christian, and Jew—if we do not choose another path. But who's going to listen to me? I'm just an old man in a cassock who lives in a gilded cage. Even my own parishioners don't listen to me anymore. In Europe we are living as if God does not exist. Anti-Americanism is our only religion now." He turned and looked at Gabriel. "And anti-Semitism."

Gabriel was silent. The Pope said, "Luigi tells me you've uncovered evidence of a plot against my life. *Another* plot," he added with a sad smile.

"I'm afraid so, Holiness."

"Isn't it ironic? I'm the one who tried to prevent the war in Iraq. I'm the one who has tried to build a bridge between Christians and Muslims, and yet I'm the one they want to kill." The Pope looked out his window. "Perhaps I was mistaken. Perhaps they don't want a bridge after all."

MOST EVENINGS Pope Paul VII and Monsignor Donati dined alone in the private papal apartments with one or two invited guests for company. Donati tended to keep the mood deliberately light and relaxed, and talk of work was generally restricted to the sort of Curial gossip that the Pope secretly loved. On that evening, however, the atmosphere in the papal dining room was decidedly different. The hastily assembled guest list consisted not of old friends but of men responsible for protecting the pontiff's life: Colonel Karl Brunner, commandant of the Pontifical Swiss Guard, General Carlo Marchese of the Carabinieri, and Martino Bellano, deputy chief of the Italian security service.

Gabriel passed around the photographs and briefed them in his Venetian-accented Italian. His presentation was more sanitized than the one he had given Donati in Jerusalem that morning, and the name Ali Massoudi was not spoken. Still, his tone left little doubt that Israeli intelligence regarded the threat as credible and that steps needed to be taken to safeguard the pontiff and the territory of the Holy See. When he finished speaking, the faces of the security men were somber, but there was no visible sense of panic. They had been through this many times, and together they had put in place automatic procedures for elevating the security around the Vatican and the Holy Father when it was deemed necessary. Gabriel listened while the three men reviewed those procedures now. During a pause in their conversation, he carefully cleared his throat.

"You wish to suggest something?" Donati asked.

"Perhaps it might be wise to move tomorrow's ceremony indoors—to the Papal Audience Chamber."

"The Holy Father is announcing the beatification of a Portuguese nun tomorrow," Donati said. "We're expecting several thousand Portuguese pilgrims, along with the usual crowds. If we move the audience into the chamber, many of those will have to be turned away."

"Better to turn away a few pilgrims than expose the Holy Father unnecessarily."

The Pope looked at Gabriel. "Do you have specific credible evidence that the terrorists intend to strike *tomorrow*?"

"No, Holiness. Operational intelligence of that nature is very difficult to come by."

"If we move the audience into the chamber, and turn away good people, then the terrorists have won, have they not?"

"Sometimes it is better to give an opponent a small victory than suffer a devastating defeat yourself."

"Your people are famous for living their lives normally in the face of terrorist threats."

"We still take sensible precautions," Gabriel said. "For example, one cannot enter most public places in my country without being searched."

"So search the pilgrims and take other sensible precautions," the Pope replied, "but I'll be in St. Peter's Square tomorrow afternoon, where I belong. And it's *your* job to make certain nothing happens."

IT WAS JUST after ten o'clock when Donati escorted Gabriel down the flight of steps that led from the Apostolic Palace to the Via Belvedere. A light mist was falling; Gabriel zipped his jacket and hitched his overnight bag over his shoulder. Donati, coatless, seemed not to notice the weather. His eyes remained on the paving stones as they walked past the Vatican central post office toward St. Anne's Gate.

"Are you sure I can't offer you a lift?"

"Until this morning, I thought I might never be allowed to set foot here again. I think I'll use the opportunity to take a walk."

"If the Italian police arrest you before you reach your

flat, tell them to give me a call. His Holiness will vouch for your fine character." They walked in silence for a moment. "Why don't you come back for good?"

"To Italy? I'm afraid Shamron has other plans for me."

"We miss you," Donati said. "So does Tiepolo."

Francesco Tiepolo, a friend of the Pope and Donati, owned the most successful restoration firm in the Veneto. Gabriel had restored two of Bellini's greatest altarpieces for him. Nearly two, he thought. Tiepolo had had to finish Bellini's San Giovanni Crisostomo altarpiece after Gabriel's flight from Venice.

"Something tells me Tiepolo will survive without me."

"And Chiara?"

Gabriel, with his moody silence, made it clear he had no desire to discuss with the Pope's private secretary the state of his tangled love life. Donati adroitly changed the subject.

"I'm sorry if you felt the Holy Father was putting you on the spot. I'm afraid he's lost much of his old forbearance. It happens to all of them a few years into their papacy. When one is regarded as the Vicar of Christ, it's difficult not to become the slightest bit overbearing."

"He's still the gentle soul I met three years ago, Luigi. Just a bit older."

"He wasn't a young man when he got the job. The cardinals wanted a caretaker Pope, someone to keep the throne of St. Peter warm while the reformers and the reactionaries sorted out their differences. My master never had any intention of being a mere caretaker, as you well know. He has much work to do before he dies—things that aren't necessarily going to make the reactionaries happy. Obviously, I don't want his papacy cut short."

"Nor do I."

"Which is why you're the perfect man to be at his side tomorrow during the general audience."

"The Swiss Guard and their helpers from the Carabinieri are more than capable of looking after your master."

"They're very good, but they've never experienced an actual terrorist attack."

"Few people have," Gabriel said. "And usually they don't live to tell about it."

Donati looked at Gabriel. "*You* have," he said. "You've seen the terrorists up close. And you've seen the look in a man's eyes as he was about to press the button on his detonator."

They stopped a few yards from St. Anne's Gate. On the left was the round, butter-colored Church of St. Anne, parish church of Vatican City; to their right the entrance to the Swiss Guards barracks. One of the guards stood watch just inside the gate, dressed in his simple blue night uniform.

"What do you want me to do, Luigi?"

"I leave that in your capable hands. Make a general nuisance of yourself. If you see a problem, address it."

"On whose authority?"

"Mine," Donati said resolutely. He reached into the pocket of his cassock and produced a laminated card, which he handed to Gabriel. It was a Vatican ID badge with Security Office markings. "It will get you anywhere in the Vatican—except for the Secret Archives, of course. I'm afraid we can't have you rummaging around in there."

"I already have," said Gabriel, then he dropped the badge into his coat pocket and slipped into the street. Donati waited at St. Anne's Gate until Gabriel had disappeared into the darkness, then he turned and headed back to the palace. And though he would not realize it until later, he was murmuring the words of the Hail Mary.

GABRIEL CROSSED the Tiber over the Ponte Umberto. On the opposite embankment he turned left and made his way to the Piazza di Spagna. The square was deserted, and the Spanish Steps shone in the lamplight like polished wood. On the twenty-eighth step sat a girl. Her hair was similar to Chiara's, and for a moment Gabriel thought it might actually be her. But as he climbed higher he saw it was only Nurit, a surly courier from Rome Station. She gave him a key to the safe flat and, in Hebrew, told him that behind the tins of soup in the pantry he would find a loaded Beretta and a spare clip of ammunition.

He hiked up the rest of the steps to the Church of the Trinità dei Monti. The apartment house was not fifty yards from the church, on the Via Gregoriana. It had two bedrooms and a small terrace. Gabriel retrieved the Beretta from the pantry, then went into the larger of the two bedrooms. The telephone, like all safe-flat telephones, had no ringer, only a red light to indicate incoming calls. Gabriel, lying in bed in the clothes he'd donned to meet the prime minister, picked up the receiver and dialed a number in Venice. A woman's voice answered. "What is it?" she asked in Italian. Then, receiving no answer, she muttered a curse and slammed down the phone—hard enough so that Gabriel jerked the receiver away from his ear before replacing it gently in the cradle.

He removed his clothing and pillowed his head, but as he was sliding toward sleep the room was suddenly illuminated by a flash of lightning. Instinctively he began to count to calculate the proximity of the strike. He saw a skinny black-haired boy with eyes as green as emeralds chasing lightning in the hills above Nazareth. The thunderclap exploded before he reached the count of four. It shook the building.

More strikes followed in quick succession, and rain hammered against the bedroom window. Gabriel tried to sleep but could not. He switched on the bedside lamp, opened the file containing the photographs taken from Ali Massoudi's computer, and worked his way through them slowly, committing each image to memory. An hour later he switched off the light and, in his mind, flipped through the images once more. Lightning flashed over the bell towers of the church. Gabriel closed his eyes and counted.

5

VATICAN CITY

B Y SUNRISE THE RAIN was gone. Gabriel left the safe
flat early and headed back to the Vatican through
the empty streets. As he crossed the river, dusty
pink light lay on the umbrella pine atop the Janiculum
Hill, but St. Peter's Square was in shadow and lamps still
burned in the Colonnade. A café was open not far from
the entrance of the Vatican Press Office. Gabriel drank
two cups of cappuccino at a sidewalk table and read the
morning newspapers. None of the major Rome dailies
seemed to know that the Pope's private secretary had
made a brief visit to Jerusalem yesterday—or that last
night the Vatican and Italian security chiefs had gathered
in the papal dining room to discuss a terrorist threat
against the Holy Father's life.

By eight o'clock, preparations were under way in St.
Peter's Square for the general audience. Vatican work
crews were erecting folding chairs and temporary metal

dividers in the esplanade in front of the Basilica, and security personnel were placing magnetometers along the Colonnade. Gabriel left the café and stood along the steel barricade separating the territory of the Holy See from Italian soil. He acted in a deliberately tense and agitated manner, made several glances at his wristwatch, and paid particular attention to the operation of the magnetometers. In short, he engaged in all the behaviors that the Carabinieri and Vigilanza, the Vatican police force, should have been looking for. It took ten minutes for a uniformed carabiniere to approach him and ask for identification. Gabriel, in perfect Italian, informed the officer that he was attached to the Vatican Security Office.

"My apologies," the carabiniere said, and moved off.

"Wait," Gabriel said.

The carabiniere stopped and turned around.

"Aren't you going to ask to see my identification?"

The carabiniere held out his hand. He gave the ID badge a bored glance, then handed it back.

"Don't trust anyone," Gabriel said. "Ask for identification, and if it doesn't look right, call your superior."

Gabriel turned and walked over to St. Anne's Gate, where a flock of nuns in gray habits was being admitted simply by saying "Annona," the name of the Vatican supermarket. He tried the same tactic and, like the nuns, was waved onto Vatican territory. Just inside the gate he withdrew his Vatican ID badge and chastised the Swiss Guard in the Berlin-accented German he had acquired from his mother. Then he went back into the street. A moment later there came an elderly priest with very white hair who informed the Swiss Guard he was going to the Vatican pharmacy. The Guard detained the priest at the gate until he could produce ID from the pocket of his cassock.

Gabriel decided to check security at the other main entrance of the Vatican, the Arch of Bells. He arrived five minutes later, just in time to see a Curial cardinal and his two aides passing through the arch without so much as a glance from the Swiss Guard standing at attention near his weather shelter. Gabriel held his badge in front of the Guard's eyes.

"Why didn't you ask that cardinal for some identification?"

"His red hat and pectoral cross are his identification."

"Not today," Gabriel said. "Check everyone's ID."

He turned and walked along the outer edge of the Colonnade, pondering the scenes he had just witnessed. St. Peter's Square, for all its vastness, was largely secure. But if there was a chink in the Vatican's armor, it was the relatively large number of people who were allowed free movement *behind* the square. He thought of the photographs on Ali Massoudi's computer and wondered whether the terrorists had discovered the very same thing.

HE CROSSED the square to the Bronze Doors. There were no magic words to gain admittance to what was essentially the front door of the Apostolic Palace. Gabriel's badge was examined outside by a Swiss Guard in full dress uniform and a second time inside the foyer by a Guard in plain clothes. His Security Office clearance allowed him to enter the palace without signing in at the Permissions Desk, but he was required to surrender his firearm, which he did with a certain reluctance.

The marble steps of the Scala Regia rose before him, shimmering in the glow of the vast iron lamps. Gabriel climbed them to the Cortile di San Damaso and crossed the courtyard to the other side, where a waiting elevator bore him upward to the third floor. He paused briefly in the loggia to admire the Raphael fresco, then hurried along the wide corridor to the papal apartments. Donati, wearing a cassock with a magenta sash, was seated behind the desk in his small office adjacent to the Pope's. Gabriel slipped inside and closed the door.

"How many people *work* inside the Vatican?" Donati said, repeating Gabriel's question. "About half."

Gabriel frowned.

"Forgive me," Donati said. "It's an old Vatican joke. The answer is about twelve hundred. That includes the priests and prelates who work in the Secretariat of State and the various congregations and councils, along with their lay support staff. Then there are the laypeople who make the place run: the tour guides, the street sweepers, the maintenance people and gardeners, the clerks in places like the post office, the pharmacy, and the supermarket. And then there's the security staff, of course."

Gabriel held up his Vatican ID badge. "And they all get one of these?"

"Not everyone can get into the Apostolic Palace, but they all have credentials that get them beyond the public sections of the Vatican."

"You mean the square and the Basilica?"

"Correct."

"What kind of background check do you perform on them?"

"I take it you're not referring to the cardinals, bishops, *monsignori*, and priests."

"We'll leave them aside." Gabriel frowned, then added, "For now."

"Jobs at the Vatican are highly coveted. The salaries aren't terribly high, but all our employees have shopping privileges at the pharmacy and the supermarket. The prices are subsidized and much lower than those at Italian markets. The same is true for the prices at our gas station. Aside from that, the hours are reasonable, vacations are long, and the fringe benefits are quite good."

"What about a background check for the people who get those jobs?"

"The jobs are so coveted—and there are so few of them—that they almost always go to someone with a family connection, so the background check is fairly cursory."

"I was afraid of that," Gabriel said. "And what about people like me? People with temporary credentials?"

"You're asking how many?" Donati shrugged. "At

any given time, I'd say there are several hundred people with temporary access to the Vatican."

"How does the system work?"

"They're usually assigned to one of the various pontifical councils or commissions as support staff or professional consultants. The prefect or an undersecretary vouch for the character of the individual, and the Vatican Security Office issues the badges."

"Does the Security Office keep all the paperwork?"

"Of course."

Gabriel lifted the receiver of the telephone and held it out to Donati.

TWENTY MINUTES ELAPSED before Donati's phone rang again. He listened in silence, then replaced the receiver and looked at Gabriel, who was standing in the window overlooking the square, watching the crowds streaming into the square.

"They're starting to pull the paperwork now."

"Starting?"

"It required authorization from the chief. He was in a meeting. They'll be ready for you in fifteen minutes."

Gabriel looked at his wristwatch. It was nearly ten-thirty.

"Move it indoors," he said.

"The Holy Father won't hear of it." Donati joined Gabriel at the window. "Besides, it's too late. The guests have started to arrive."

*   *   *

THEY SETTLED HIM in a tiny cell with a sooty window overlooking the Belvedere Courtyard and gave him a boyish-looking ex-carabiniere named Luca Angelli to fetch the files. He limited his search to laypersons only. Even Gabriel, a man of boundless suspicion, could not imagine a scenario under which a Catholic priest could be recruited, knowingly or unwittingly, to the cause of al-Qaeda. He also struck from his list members of the Swiss Guard and Vigilanza. The ranks of the Vigilanza were filled largely by former officers of the Carabinieri and Polizia di Stato. As for the Swiss Guard, they were drawn exclusively from Catholic families in Switzerland and most came from the German- and French-speaking cantons in the mountainous heart of the country, hardly a stronghold of Islamic extremism.

He started with the lay employees of the Vatican city-state itself. To limit the parameters of his search he reviewed only the files of those who had been hired in the previous five years. That alone took him nearly thirty minutes. When he was finished he set aside a half dozen files for further evaluation—a clerk in the Vatican pharmacy, a gardener, two stock boys in the Annona, a janitor in the Vatican museum, and a woman who worked in one of the Vatican gift shops—and gave the rest back to Angelli.

The next files to arrive were for the lay employees attached to various congregations of the Roman Curia.

The congregations were the approximate equivalent of government ministries and dealt with central areas of Church governance, such as doctrine, faith, the clergy, saints, and Catholic education. Each congregation was led by a cardinal, and each cardinal had several bishops and *monsignori* beneath him. Gabriel reviewed the files for the clerical and support staff of each of the nine congregations and, finding nothing of interest, gave them back to Angelli.

"What's left?"

"The pontifical commissions and councils," said Angelli. "And the other offices."

"Other offices?"

"The Administration of the Patrimony of the Holy See, the Prefecture of the Economic Affairs of the Holy See—"

"I get it," Gabriel said. "How many files?"

Angelli held up his hands to indicate that the pile was well over a foot high. Gabriel looked at his watch: *11:20* . . .

"Bring them."

ANGELLI STARTED WITH the pontifical commissions. Gabriel pulled two more files for further review, a consultant to the Commission for Sacred Archaeology, and an Argentine scholar attached to the Pontifical Commission for Latin America. He gave the rest back to Angelli and looked at his watch: *11:45* . . . He'd promised Donati that he would stand guard over the Pope in the square during the general audience at noon. He had time for only a few more files.

"Skip the financial departments," Gabriel said. "Bring me the files for the pontifical councils."

Angelli returned a moment later with a six-inch stack of manila folders. Gabriel reviewed them in the order Angelli handed them over. The Pontifical Council for the Laity . . . The Pontifical Council for Promoting Christian Unity . . . The Pontifical Council for the Family . . . The Pontifical Council for Justice and Peace . . . The Pontifical Council for the Pastoral Care of Migrants and Itinerant People . . . The Pontifical Council for Legislative Texts . . .

The Pontifical Council for Interreligious Dialogue . . .

Gabriel held up his hand. He had found what he was looking for.

HE READ FOR a moment, then looked up sharply. "Does this man really have access to the Vatican?"

Angelli bent his thin body at the waist and peered over Gabriel's shoulder. "Professor Ibrahim el-Banna? He's been here for more than a year now."

"Doing what?"

"He's a member of a special commission searching for ways to improve relations between the Christian and Islamic worlds. There are twelve members in all, an ecumenical team of six Christian scholars and six Muslim scholars representing the various Islamic sects and schools of Islamic law. Ibrahim el-Banna is a professor of Islamic jurisprudence at Al-Azhar University in Cairo. He's also among the most respected scholars of the Hanafi school of Islamic law in the world. Hanafi is predominant among—"

"Sunni Muslims," Gabriel said, pointedly finishing Angelli's sentence for him. "Don't you know that Al-Azhar is a hotbed of Islamic militancy? It's been thoroughly penetrated by the forces of al-Qaeda and the Muslim Brotherhood."

"It is also one of the oldest and most prestigious schools of Islamic theology and law in the world. Professor el-Banna was chosen for the position because of his moderate views. He's met several times with the Holy Father himself. On two occasions they were alone together."

"Where does the commission meet?"

"Professor el-Banna has an office in a building near the Piazza Santa Marta, not far from the Arch of Bells."

Gabriel looked at his watch: *11:55* . . . There was no way to talk to Donati. He would be downstairs with the Pope by now, preparing to enter the square. He thought of the instructions he'd given him the previous night in the Via Belvedere. *Make a general nuisance of yourself. If you see a problem, address it.* He got to his feet and looked at Angelli.

"I'd like to have a word with the imam."

Angelli hesitated. "The initiative is very important to

the Holy Father. If you level an accusation against Professor el-Banna without just cause, he will take great offense and the commission's work will be placed in jeopardy."

"Better an irate imam than a dead Pope. What's the quickest way to the Piazza Santa Marta?"

"We'll take the shortcut," Angelli said. "Through the Basilica."

THEY SLIPPED THROUGH the passage from the Scala Regia into the Chapel of the Blessed Sacrament, then hurried diagonally across the vast nave. Beneath the Monument to Alexander VII was a doorway leading into the Piazza Santa Marta. As they stepped outside into the bright sunlight, a roar of wild applause rose from St. Peter's Square. The Pope had arrived for the General Audience. Angelli led Gabriel across the small piazza and into a gloomy-looking Baroque office building. In the lobby a nun sat motionless behind a reception table. She gave Gabriel and Angelli a disapproving look as they burst inside.

"Ibrahim el-Banna," said Luca Angelli without elaboration.

The nun blinked twice rapidly. "Room four-twelve."

They mounted the stairs, Angelli leading the way, Gabriel at his heels. When another swell of applause rose from the square, Gabriel gave Angelli a jab in the kidneys, and the Vatican security man began taking the steps two at a time. When they arrived at Room 412 they found the door was closed. Gabriel reached for the latch, but Angelli stayed his hand and knocked firmly but politely.

"Professor el-Banna? Professor el-Banna? Are you there?"

Greeted by silence, Gabriel pushed Angelli aside and examined the ancient lock. With the slender metal pick in his wallet he could have coaxed it open in a matter of seconds, but another roar of approval from the square reminded him there wasn't time. He seized hold of the latch with both hands and drove his shoulder into the door. It held fast. He threw his body against the door a second time, then a third. On the fourth attempt, Angelli joined him. The wood of the doorjamb splintered, and they tumbled inside.

The room was empty. Not just empty, thought Gabriel. Abandoned. There were no books or files, no pens or loose papers. Just a single letter-sized envelope, positioned in the precise center of the desk. Angelli reached for the light switch, but Gabriel shouted at him not to touch it, then pushed the Italian back into the corridor. He drew a pen from his coat pocket and used it as a probe to examine the density of the envelope's contents. When he was reasonably certain it contained nothing but paper, he picked it up and carefully lifted the flap. Inside was a single sheet, folded in thirds. Handwritten, Arabic script:

We declare war on you, the Crusaders, with the destruction of your infidel temple to polytheism and the death of your so-called Supreme Pontiff, this man in white who you treat as though he were a god. This is your punishment for the sins of Iraq, Abu Ghraib, and Guantánamo Bay. The attacks will continue until the land of Iraq is no longer in American bondage and Palestine has been liberated from the clutches of the Jews. We are the Brotherhood of Allah. There is no God but Allah, and all praise to him.

Gabriel ran down the stairs, Angelli at his back.

6

VATICAN CITY

*I*N NOMINE *PATRIS ET Filii et Spiritus Sanctus.*"

The Pope's voice, amplified by the Vatican public address system, resounded across St. Peter's Square and down the length of the Via della Conciliazione.

Twenty thousand voices replied: "Amen."

Gabriel and Luca Angelli sprinted across the Piazza Santa Marta, then along the exterior wall of the Basilica. Before reaching the Arch of Bells, Angelli turned to the right and entered the Permissions Office, the main security checkpoint for most visitors to the Vatican. If Ibrahim el-Banna had cleared anyone else into the Vatican, the paperwork would exist there. Gabriel kept going toward the Arch of Bells. The Swiss Guard on duty there, startled by the sight of a man running toward him, lowered his halberd defensively as Gabriel approached. He raised it again when he saw Gabriel waving his Security Office ID badge.

"Give me your sidearm," Gabriel ordered.

"Sir?"

"Give me your gun!" Gabriel shouted at the Guard in German.

The Guard reached inside his multicolored Renaissance tunic and came out with a very modern SIG-Sauer 9mm, just as Luca Angelli emerged through the archway.

"El-Banna cleared a delegation of three German priests into the Vatican at eleven-thirty."

"They're not priests, Luca. They're *shaheed*s. Martyrs." Gabriel looked at the crowd gathered in the square. "And I doubt they're inside the Vatican any longer. They're probably out there now, armed with explosives and only God knows what else."

"Why did they come through the Arch of Bells into the Vatican?"

"To get their bombs, of course." It was the chink in the Vatican's security armor. The terrorists had discovered it through repeated surveillance and had used the Holy Father's initiative of peace to exploit it. "El-Banna probably smuggled the bombs inside over time and stored them in his office. The *shaheed*s collected them after clearing security at the Permissions Office, then made their way into the square by some route without metal detectors."

"The Basilica," said Angelli. "They could have entered the Basilica from the side and come out through one of the front doors. We could have passed them a few moments ago, and we never would have known it."

Gabriel and Angelli vaulted the wooden fencing separating the Arch of Bells entrance area from the rest of the square and mounted the dais. Their sudden movement sent a murmur through the audience. Donati was standing behind the Pope. Gabriel went quietly to his side and handed him the note he'd taken from el-Banna's office.

"They're here."

Donati looked down, saw the Arabic script, then looked up at Gabriel again.

"We found that in Ibrahim el-Banna's office. It says they're going to destroy the Basilica. It says they're going to kill the Holy Father. We have to get him off the dais. *Now*, Luigi."

Donati looked out at the multitude in the square: Catholic pilgrims and dignitaries from around the globe, schoolchildren in white, groups of sick and elderly come to the get the pontiff's blessing. The Pope was seated in a scarlet ceremonial throne. In the tradition he'd inherited from his predecessor, he was greeting the pilgrims in their native languages, moving rapidly from one to the next.

"And what about the pilgrims?" Donati asked. "How do we protect them?"

"It may be too late for them. Some of them, at least. If we try to warn them, there'll be panic. Get the Holy Father out of the square as quickly and quietly as possible. Then we'll start moving the pilgrims out."

Colonel Brunner, the Swiss Guard commandant, joined them on the dais. Like the rest of the Pope's personal security detail, he was dressed in a dark business suit and wore an earpiece. When Donati explained the situation, Brunner's face drained of color.

"We'll take him through the Basilica."

"And if they've concealed bombs in there?" Gabriel asked.

Brunner opened his mouth to reply, but his words were swept away by a searing blast wave. The sound came a millisecond later, a deafening thunderclap made more intense by the vast echo chamber of St. Peter's Square. Gabriel was blown from the dais—a scrap of paper on a gale-force wind. His body took flight and turned over at least once. Then he landed hard on the steps of the Basilica and blacked out.

WHEN HE opened his eyes he saw Christ's Apostles peering down at him from their perch atop the façade. He did not know how long he had been unconscious. A few seconds, perhaps, but not longer. He sat up, ears ringing, and looked around. To his right were the Curial prelates who had been on the dais with the Pope. They appeared shocked and tousled but largely unhurt. To his left lay Donati and next to Donati was Karl Brunner. The commandant's eyes were closed, and he was bleeding heavily from a wound at the back of his head.

Gabriel got to his feet and looked around.

Where was the Pope?

Ibrahim el-Banna had cleared *three* priests into the Vatican.

Gabriel suspected there were two more blasts to come.

He found the SIG-Sauer he'd taken from the Swiss Guard and shouted at the prelates to stay down. Then, as he climbed back onto the dais to look for Lucchesi, the second bomb exploded.

Another wave of searing heat and wind.

Another thunderclap.

Gabriel was hurled backward. This time he came to rest atop Donati.

He got to his feet again. He wasn't able to reach the dais before the third bomb detonated.

When the thunderclap finally died out, he mounted the platform and looked out at the devastation. The *shaheed*s had distributed themselves evenly throughout the crowd near the front of the dais: one near the Bronze Doors, the second in the center of the square, and the third close to the Arch of Bells. All that remained of them were three plumes of black smoke rising toward the cloudless pale-blue sky. On the spots where the bombers had been standing, the paving stones were blackened by fire, drenched in blood, and littered with human limbs and tissue. Farther away from the blast points, it was possible to imagine that the tattered corpses had moments before been human beings. The folding chairs that Gabriel had watched being put into place earlier that morning had been tossed about like playing cards, and everywhere there were shoes. *How many dead?* Hundreds, he thought. But his concern at that moment was not with the dead but with the Holy Father.

We declare war on you, the Crusaders, with the destruction of your infidel temple to polytheism. . . .

The attack, Gabriel knew, was not yet finished.

And then, through the screen of black smoke, he saw the next phase unfolding. A delivery van had stopped just beyond the barricade at the far end of the square. The rear cargo doors were open and three men were scrambling out. Each one had a shoulder-launched missile.

IT WAS THEN that Gabriel saw the throne on which the Pope had been seated. It had been blown sideways by the force of the first blast and had come to rest upside down on the steps of the Basilica. Poking from beneath it was a small hand with a gold ring . . . and the skirt of a white cassock stained in blood.

Gabriel looked at Donati. "They've got missiles, Luigi! Get everyone away from the Basilica!"

Gabriel leaped from the dais and lifted the throne. The Pope's eyes were closed, and he was bleeding from several small cuts. As Gabriel reached down and cradled the Pope in his arms, he heard the distinctive whoosh of an approaching RPG-7. He turned his head, long enough to glimpse the missile streaking over the square toward the Basilica. An instant later the warhead struck

Michelangelo's dome and exploded in a shower of fire, glass, and stone.

Gabriel sheltered the Pope from the falling debris, then lifted him and started running toward the Bronze Doors. Before they could reach the shelter of the Colonnade, the second missile came streaking across the square. It struck the façade of the Basilica, just beneath the balustrade on the Loggia of the Blessings.

Gabriel lost his balance and fell to the paving stones. He lifted his head and saw the third missile on its way. It was coming in lower than the others and heading directly toward the dais. In the instant before it struck, Gabriel glimpsed a nightmarish image: Luigi Donati trying desperately to move the Curial cardinals and prelates to safety. Gabriel stayed on the ground and covered the Pope's body with his own as another shower of wreckage rained down upon them.

"Is it you, Gabriel?" the Pope asked, eyes still closed.

"Yes, Holiness."

"Is it over?"

Three bombs, three missiles—symbolic of the Holy Trinity, Gabriel reckoned. A calculated insult to the *mushrikun*.

"Yes, Holiness. I believe it's over."

"Where's Luigi?"

Gabriel looked toward the burning remains of the dais and saw Donati stagger out of the smoke, the body of a dead cardinal in his arms.

"He's alive, Holiness."

The Pope closed his eyes and whispered, "Thank God."

Gabriel felt a hand grasp his shoulder. He turned around and saw a quartet of men in blue suits, guns drawn. "Let go of him," one of the men shouted. "We'll take him from here."

Gabriel looked at the man for a moment, then slowly shook his head. "I've got him," he said, then he stood up and carried the Pope into the Apostolic Palace, surrounded by Swiss Guards.

THE APARTMENT HOUSE stood in a cobbled *vicolo* near the Church of Santa Maria in Trastevere. Four floors in height, its faded tan exterior was hung with power and telephone lines and contained several large patches of exposed brickwork. On the ground floor was a small motorcycle repair shop that spilled into the street. To the right of the shop was a doorway leading to the flats above. Ibrahim el-Banna had the key in his pocket.

The attack had commenced five minutes after el-Banna's departure from the Vatican. On the Borgo Santo Spirito he had taken advantage of the panic to carefully remove his *kufi* and hang a large wooden cross round his neck. From there he had walked to the Janiculum Park and from the park down the hill to Trastevere. On the Via della Paglia a distraught woman had asked el-Banna for his blessing. He had bestowed it, imitating the words and gestures he'd seen at the Vatican, then immediately asked Allah to forgive his blasphemy.

Now, safely inside the apartment house, he removed the offensive cross from his neck and mounted the dimly lit stairs. He had been ordered to come here by the Saudi who had conceived and planned the attack— the Saudi he knew only as Khalil. It was to be the first stop on a secret journey out of Europe and back to the Muslim world. He had hoped to return to his native Egypt, but Khalil had convinced him that he would never be safe there. *The American lackey Mubarak will hand you over to the infidels in the blink of an eye*, Khalil had said. *There's only one place on earth where the infidels can't get you.*

That place was Saudi Arabia, land of the Prophet, birthplace of Wahhabi Islam. Ibrahim el-Banna had been promised a new identity, a teaching position at the prestigious University of Medina, and a bank account with a half-million dollars. The sanctuary was a reward from Prince Nabil, the Saudi interior minister. The money was a gift from the Saudi billionaire who had financed the operation.

And so the Muslim cleric who climbed the steps of the Roman apartment house was a contented man. He had just helped carry off one of the most important acts of jihad in the long, glorious history of Islam. And now he was setting out for a new life in Saudi Arabia, where his words and beliefs could help inspire the next generation of Islamic warriors. Only Paradise would be sweeter.

He reached the third-floor landing and went to the door of apartment 3A. When he inserted the key into the lock he felt a slight electric shock in his fingers. When he turned it, the door exploded. And then he felt nothing at all.

AT THAT same moment, in the section of Washington known as Foggy Bottom, a woman woke from a nightmare. It was filled with the same imagery she saw every morning at this time. A flight attendant with her throat slashed. A handsome young passenger making one final phone call. An inferno. She rolled over and looked at the clock on her nightstand. It was six-thirty. She picked up the remote control, aimed it at her television, and pressed the Power button. *God no,* she thought when she saw the Basilica in flames. *Not again.*

7

ROME

GABRIEL REMAINED AT THE safe flat near the Church of the Trinità dei Monti for the next week. There were moments when it seemed as though none of it had really happened. But then he would wander out to the balcony and see the dome of the Basilica looming over the rooftops of the city, shattered and blackened by fire, as if God, in a moment of disapproval or carelessness, had reached down and destroyed the handiwork of his children. Gabriel, the restorer, wished it was only a painting—an abraded canvas that he might heal with a bottle of linseed oil and a bit of pigment.

The death toll climbed with each passing day. By the end of Wednesday—Black Wednesday, as Rome's newspapers christened it—the number of dead stood at six hundred. By Thursday it was six hundred fifty, and by the weekend it had exceeded seven hundred. Colonel

Karl Brunner of the Pontifical Swiss Guards was among the dead. So was Luca Angelli, who clung to life for three days in the Gemelli Clinic before being removed from life support. The Pope administered Last Rites and remained at Angelli's side until he died. The Roman Curia suffered terrible losses. Four cardinals were among the dead, along with eight Curial bishops, and three *monsignori*. Their funerals had to be conducted in the Basilica of Saint John Lateran, because two days after the attack an international team of structural engineers concluded the Basilica was unsafe to enter. Rome's largest newspaper, *La Repubblica*, reported the news by printing a full-page photograph of the ruined dome, headlined with a single word: CONDEMNED.

The government of Israel had no official standing in the investigation, but Gabriel, with his proximity to Donati and the Pope, quickly came to know as much about the attack as any intelligence officer in the world. He gathered most of his intelligence at the Pope's dinner table, where he sat each evening with the men leading the investigation: General Marchese of the Carabinieri and Martino Bellano of the Italian security service. For the most part they spoke freely in front of Gabriel, and anything they withheld was dutifully passed along to him by Donati. Gabriel in turn forwarded all his information to King Saul Boulevard, which explained why Shamron was in no hurry to see him leave Rome.

Within forty-eight hours of the attack the Italians had managed to identify all those involved. The missile strike

had been carried out by a four-man team. The driver of
the van was of Tunisian origin. The three men who fired
the RPG-7s were of Jordanian nationality and were veterans of the insurgency in Iraq. All four were killed in a
volley of Carabinieri gunfire seconds after launching
their weapons. As for the three men who had posed as
German priests, only one was actually German, a young
engineering student from Hamburg named Manfred
Zeigler. The second was a Dutchman from Rotterdam,
and the third was a Flemish-speaking Belgian from
Antwerp. All three were Muslim converts, and all had
taken part in anti-American and anti-Israeli demonstrations. Gabriel, though he had no proof of it, suspected
they had been recruited by Professor Ali Massoudi.

Using closed-circuit surveillance video and eyewitness
accounts, the Vatican and Italian authorities were able to
retrace the last moments of the bombers' lives. After
being admitted into the Vatican by an *adetto* at the Permissions Office, the three men had made their way to
Ibrahim el-Banna's office near the Piazza Santa Marta.
Upon leaving each was carrying a large briefcase. As Angelli had suspected, the three men had then slipped into
the Basilica through a side entrance. They made their
way into St. Peter's Square, fittingly enough, through
the Door of Death. The door, like the other four leading
from the Basilica into the square, should have been
locked. By the end of the first week the Vatican police
still had not determined why it wasn't.

The body of Ibrahim el-Banna was identified three

days after it was pulled from the rubble of the apartment house in Trastevere. For the time being his true affiliation remained a matter of speculation. Who were the Brotherhood of Allah? Were they an al-Qaeda offshoot or simply al-Qaeda by another name? And who had planned and financed so elaborate an operation? One thing was immediately clear. The attack on the home of Christendom had reignited the fires of the global jihadist movement. Wild street celebrations erupted in Tehran, Cairo, Beirut, and the Palestinian territories, while intelligence analysts from Washington to London to Tel Aviv immediately detected a sharp spike in activity and recruitment.

On the following Wednesday, the one-week anniversary of the attack, Shamron decided it was time for Gabriel to come home. As he was packing his bag in the safe flat, the red light on the telephone flashed to indicate an incoming call. He raised the receiver and heard Donati's voice.

"The Holy Father would like a word with you in private."

"When?"

"This afternoon before you leave for the airport."

"A word about what?"

"You are a member of a very small club, Gabriel Allon."

"Which club is that?"

"Men who would dare to ask a question such as that."

"Where and when?" Gabriel asked, his tone conciliatory.

Donati gave him the information. Gabriel hung up the phone and finished packing.

GABRIEL CLEARED a Carabinieri checkpoint at the edge of the Colonnade and made his way across St. Peter's Square through the dying twilight. It was still closed to the public. The forensic crews had completed their gruesome task, but the opaque barriers that had been erected around the three blast sites remained in place. An enormous white tarpaulin hung from the façade of the Basilica, concealing the damage beneath the Loggia of the Blessings. It bore the image of a dove and a single word: PEACE.

He passed through the Arch of Bells and made his way along the left flank of the Basilica. The side entrances were closed and barricaded, and Vigilanza officers stood watch at each one. In the Vatican Gardens it was possible to imagine that nothing had happened—possible, thought Gabriel, until one looked at the ruined dome, which was lit now by a dusty sienna sunset. The Pope was waiting near the House of the Gardener. He greeted Gabriel warmly and together they set out toward the distant corner of the Vatican. A dozen Swiss Guards in plain clothes drifted alongside them amid the stone pines, their long shadows thin upon the grass.

"Luigi and I have pleaded with the Swiss Guard to reduce the size of their detail," the Pope said. "For the moment it is nonnegotiable. They're a bit jumpy—for understandable reasons. Not since the Sack of Rome has a Swiss Guard commander died defending the Vatican from enemy attack."

They walked on in silence for a moment. "So this is my fate, Gabriel? To be forever surrounded by men with radios and guns? How can I communicate with my flock? How can I give comfort to the sick and the afflicted if I am cut off from them by a phalanx of bodyguards?"

Gabriel had no good answer.

"It will never be the same, will it, Gabriel?"

"No, Holiness, I'm afraid it will not."

"Did they mean to kill me?"

"Without a doubt."

"Will they try again?"

"Once they set their sights on a target, they usually don't stop until they succeed. But in this case, they managed to kill seven hundred pilgrims and several cardinals and bishops—not to mention the commandant of the Swiss Guard. They also managed to inflict severe physical damage to the Basilica itself. In my opinion, they will regard their historical account as settled."

"They may not have succeeded in killing me, but they have succeeded in making me a prisoner of the Vatican." The Pope stopped and looked at the ruined dome. "My cage isn't so gilded anymore. It took more than a century to build and a few seconds to destroy."

"It's not destroyed, Holiness. The dome can be restored."

"That remains to be seen," the Pope said with uncharacteristic gloominess. "The engineers and architects aren't so sure it can be done. It might have to be brought down and rebuilt entirely. And the *baldacchino* suffered severe damage when the debris rained down upon it. This is not something that can simply be replaced, but then you know that better than most."

Gabriel snuck a glance at his wristwatch. He would have to be leaving for the airport soon, or he would miss his flight. He wondered why the Pope had asked him here. Surely it wasn't to discuss the restoration of the Basilica. The Pope turned and started walking again. They were heading toward St. John's Tower, at the southwest corner of the Vatican.

"There's only one reason why I'm not dead now," the Pope said. "And that's because of you, Gabriel. In all the sorrow and confusion of this terrible week, I haven't had a chance to properly thank you. I'm doing so now. I only wish I could do so in public."

Gabriel's role in the affair had been carefully guarded from the media. So far, against all the odds, it had remained a secret.

"And I only wish I'd discovered Ibrahim el-Banna sooner," Gabriel said. "Seven hundred people might still be alive."

"You did everything that could have been done."

"Perhaps, Holiness, but it still wasn't enough."

They arrived at the Vatican wall. The Pope mounted a stone staircase and climbed upward, Gabriel following silently after him. They stood at the parapet and looked out over Rome. Lights were coming on all over the city. Gabriel glanced over his shoulder and saw the Swiss Guards stirring nervously beneath them. He gave them a reassuring hand gesture and looked at the Pope, who was peering downward at the cars racing along the Viale Vaticano.

"Luigi tells me a promotion awaits you in Tel Aviv." He had to raise his voice over the din of the traffic. "Is this a promotion you sought for yourself, or is this the work of Shamron?"

"Some have greatness thrust upon them, Holiness."

The Pope smiled, the first Gabriel had seen on his face since his arrival in Rome. "May I give you a small piece of advice?"

Gabriel nodded.

"Use your power wisely. Even though you will find yourself in a position to punish your enemies, use your power to pursue peace at every turn. Seek justice rather than vengeance."

Gabriel was tempted to remind the Pope that he was only a secret servant of the State, that decisions of war and peace were in the hands of men far more powerful than he. Instead he assured the Pope that he would take his advice to heart.

"Will you search for the men who attacked the Vatican?"

"It's not our fight—not yet, at least."

"Something tells me it will be soon."

The Pope was watching the traffic below him with a childlike fascination.

"It was my idea to put the dove of peace on the shroud covering the façade of the Basilica. I'm sure you find the sentiment hopelessly naïve. You probably consider me naïve as well."

"I wouldn't want to live in this world without men such as you, Holiness."

Gabriel made no attempt to hide the next glance at his watch.

"Your plane awaits you?" the Pope asked.

"Yes, Holiness."

"Come," he said. "I'll see you out."

Gabriel started toward the steps, but the Pope remained at the parapet. "Francesco Tiepolo called me this morning from Venice. He sends his regards." He turned and looked at Gabriel. "So does Chiara."

Gabriel was silent.

"She says she wants to see you before you go home to Israel. She was wondering whether you might stop in Venice on your way out of the country." The Pope took Gabriel by the elbow and, smiling, led him down the steps. "I realize I have very little experience when it comes to matters of the heart, but will you allow an old man to give you one more piece of advice?"

8

VENICE

IT WAS A SMALL terra-cotta church, built for a poor
parish in the *sestiere* of Cannaregio. The plot of land
had been too cramped for a proper church square,
and so the main entrance opened directly onto the busy
Salizzada San Giovanni Crisostomo. Gabriel had once
carried a key to the church in his pocket. Now he entered like an ordinary tourist and paused for a moment
in the vestibule, waiting for his eyes to adjust to the dim
light while a breath of cool air, scented with candle wax
and incense, brushed against his cheek. He thought of
the last time he had set foot in the church. It was the
night Shamron had come to Venice to tell Gabriel that
he had been discovered by his enemies and that it was
time for him to come home again. *There'll be no trace of
you here*, Shamron had said. *It will be as though you never
existed.*

He crossed the intimate nave to the Chapel of

St. Jerome on the right side of the church. The altarpiece was concealed by heavy shadow. Gabriel dropped a coin into the light meter, and the lamps flickered into life, illuminating the last great work by Giovanni Bellini. He stood for a moment, right hand pressed to his chin, head tilted slightly to one side, examining the painting in raked lighting. Francesco Tiepolo had done a fine job finishing it for him. Indeed it was nearly impossible for Gabriel to tell where his inpainting left off and Tiepolo's began. Hardly surprising, he thought. They had both served their apprenticeships with the master Venetian restorer Umberto Conti.

The meter ran out, and the lights switched off automatically, plunging the painting into darkness again. Gabriel went back into the street and made his way westward across Cannaregio until he came to an iron bridge, the only one in all of Venice. In the Middle Ages there had been a gate in the center of the bridge, and at night a Christian watchman had stood guard so that those imprisoned on the other side could not escape. He crossed the bridge and entered a darkened *sottoportego*. At the end of the passageway, a broad square opened before him, the Campo del Ghetto Nuovo, center of the ancient ghetto of Venice. More than five thousand Jews had once lived in the ghetto. Now it was home to only twenty of the city's four hundred Jews, and most of those were elderly who resided in the Casa di Riposo Israelitica.

He crossed the *campo* and stopped at Number 2899.

A small brass plaque read *COMUNITÀ EBRAICA DI VENEZIA*—Jewish Community of Venice. He pressed the bell and quickly turned his back to the security camera over the doorway. After a long silence a woman's voice, familiar to him, crackled over the intercom. "Turn around," she said. "Let me have a look at your face."

HE WAITED WHERE she had told him to wait, on a wooden bench in a sunlit corner of the *campo*, near a memorial for the Venetian Jews who were rounded up in December 1943 and sent to their deaths at Auschwitz. Ten minutes elapsed, then ten minutes more. When finally she emerged from the office she took her time crossing the square, then stopped several feet away from him, as though she were afraid to come any closer. Gabriel, still seated, pushed his sunglasses onto his forehead and regarded her in the dazzling autumn light. She wore faded blue jeans, snug around her long thighs and flared at the bottom, and a pair of high-heeled suede boots. Her white blouse was tailored in such a way that it left no doubt about the generous figure beneath it. Her riotous auburn hair was held back by a chocolate-colored satin ribbon, and a silk scarf was wound round her neck. Her olive skin was very dark. Gabriel suspected she'd been in the sun recently. Her eyes, wide and Oriental in shape, were the color of caramel and flecked with gold. They tended to change color with her mood. The last time Gabriel had seen Chiara's eyes they were nearly black with anger and streaked with mascara. She folded her arms defensively beneath her breasts and asked what he was doing in Venice.

"Hello, Chiara. Don't you look lovely."

The breeze took her hair and blew a few strands across her face. She brushed it away with her left hand. It was absent the diamond engagement ring Gabriel had given her. There were other rings on her fingers now and a new gold watch on her wrist. Gabriel wondered if they were gifts from someone else.

"I haven't heard from you since I left Jerusalem," Chiara said in the deliberately even tone she used whenever she was trying to keep her emotions in check. "It's been months. Now you show up here without warning and expect me to greet you with my arms open and a smile on my face?"

"Without warning? I came here because you asked me to come."

"Me? What on earth are you talking about?"

Gabriel searched her eyes. He could tell she was not dissembling. "Forgive me," he said. "It seems I was brought here under false pretenses."

She toyed with the ends of her scarf, clearly enjoying his discomfort. "Brought here by whom?"

Donati and Tiepolo, reckoned Gabriel. Maybe even His Holiness himself. He stood abruptly. "It doesn't matter," he said. "I'm sorry, Chiara. It was nice to see you again."

He turned and started to walk away, but she seized his arm.

"Wait," she said. "Stay for a moment."

"Are you going to be civil?"

"Civility is for divorced couples with children."

Gabriel sat down again, but Chiara remained standing. A man in dark glasses and a tan blazer emerged from the *sottoportego*. He looked admiringly at Chiara, then crossed the *campo* and disappeared over the bridge that led to the pair of old Sephardic synagogues at the southern end of the ghetto. Chiara watched the man go, then tilted her head and scrutinized Gabriel's appearance.

"Has anyone ever told you that you bear more than a passing resemblance to the man who saved the Pope?"

"He's an Italian," Gabriel said. "Didn't you read about him in the newspapers?"

She ignored him. "When I saw the footage on television, I thought I was hallucinating. I knew it was you. That night, after things calmed down, I checked in with Rome. Shimon told me you'd been at the Vatican."

A sudden movement in the *campo* caused her to turn her head. She watched as a man with a salt-and-pepper beard and a fedora hurried toward the entrance of the community center. It was her father, the chief rabbi of Venice. She raised the toe of her right boot and balanced her weight on the heel. Gabriel knew the gesture well. It meant something provocative was coming.

"Why are you here, Gabriel Allon?"

"I was told you wanted to see me."

"And so you came? Just like that?"

"Just like that."

The corners of her lips started to curl into a smile.

"What's so funny?" he asked.

"Poor Gabriel. You're still in love with me, aren't you?"

"I always was."

"Just not enough to marry me?"

"Can we do this in private?"

"Not for a while. I need to keep an eye on the office. My *other* job," she said in a tone of mock conspiracy.

"Please give Rabbi Zolli my regards."

"I'm not sure that's such a good idea. Rabbi Zolli is still furious with you."

She dug a key from her pocket and tossed it to him. He looked at it for a long moment. Even after months of separation it was difficult for Gabriel to imagine Chiara leading a life of her own.

"In case you're wondering, I live there alone. It's more than you have a right to know, but it's the truth. Make yourself comfortable. Get some rest. You look like hell."

"Full of compliments today, aren't we?" He slipped the key into his pocket. "What's the address?"

"You know, for a spy, you're a terrible liar."

"What are you talking about?"

"You know my address, Gabriel. You got it from Operations, the same place you got my telephone number."

She leaned down and kissed his cheek. When her hair

fell across his face, he closed his eyes and inhaled the scent of vanilla.

HER BUILDING WAS on the other side of the Grand Canal in Santa Croce, in a small enclosed *corte* with but one passage in and out. Gabriel, as he slipped into her apartment, had the sensation of walking into his own past. The sitting room seemed posed for a magazine photo shoot. Even her old magazines and newspapers appeared to have been arranged by a fanatic in pursuit of visual perfection. He walked over to an end table and browsed the framed photographs: Chiara and her parents; Chiara and an older brother who lived in Padua; Chiara with a friend on the shore of the Sea of Galilee. It was during that trip, when she was just twenty-five, that she'd come to the attention of an Office talent scout. Six months later, after being vetted and trained, she was sent back to Europe as a *bat leveyha*, a female escort officer. There were no photographs of Chiara with Gabriel, for none existed.

He went to the window and looked out. Thirty feet below, the oily green waters of the Rio del Megio flowed sluggishly by. A clothing line stretched to the building opposite. Shirts and trousers hung drunkenly in the sunlight, and at the other end of the line an old woman sat in an open window with her fleshy arm draped over the sill. She seemed surprised to see Gabriel. He held up the key and said he was Chiara's friend from Milan.

He lowered the blinds and went into the kitchen. In the sink was a half-drunk bowl of milky coffee and a crust of buttered toast. Chiara, fastidious in all other things, always left her breakfast dishes in the sink until the end of the day. Gabriel, in an act of domestic pettiness, left them where they stood and went into her bedroom.

He tossed his bag onto the unmade bed and, resisting the temptation to search her closet and drawers, went into the bathroom and turned on the shower. He opened the medicine chest, looking for razors or cologne or any other evidence of a man. There were two things he'd never seen before: a bottle of sleeping tablets and a bottle of antidepressants. He returned them to the precise position in which he'd found them. Chiara, like Gabriel, had been trained to notice even the subtlest of changes.

He stripped off his clothes and tossed them into the hallway, then spent a long time standing beneath the shower. When he was finished he wrapped a towel around his waist and padded into the bedroom. The duvet smelled of Chiara's body. When he placed his head atop her pillow the bells of Santa Croce tolled midday. He closed his eyes and plunged into a dreamless sleep.

HE WOKE IN late afternoon to the sound of a key being pushed into the lock, followed by the clatter of Chiara's boot heels in the entrance hall. She didn't bother calling out that she was home. She knew he came awake at the slightest sound or movement. When she entered the bedroom she was singing softly to herself, a silly Italian pop song she knew he loathed.

She sat on the edge of the bed, close enough so that her hip pressed against his thigh. He opened his eyes and watched her remove her boots and wriggle out of her jeans. She pressed her palm against his chest. When he pulled the ribbon from her hair, auburn curls tumbled about her face and shoulders. She repeated the question she had posed to him in the ghetto: *Why are you here, Gabriel Allon?*

"I was wondering whether we might try this again," Gabriel said.

"I don't need to try it. I tried it once, and I liked it very much."

He unwound the silk scarf from her throat and slowly loosened the buttons of her blouse. Chiara leaned down and kissed his mouth. It was like being kissed by Raphael's Alba Madonna.

"If you hurt me again, I'll hate you forever."

"I won't hurt you."

"I never stopped dreaming of you."

"Good dreams?"

"No," she said. "I dreamed only of your death."

THE ONLY TRACE of Gabriel in the apartment was an old sketchpad. He turned to a fresh page and regarded

Chiara with a professional dispassion. She was seated at
the end of the couch, with her long legs folded beneath
her and her body wrapped in a silk bedsheet. Her face
was turned toward the window and lit by the setting sun.
Gabriel was relieved to see the first lines around Chiara's
eyes. He always feared she was far too young for him and
that one day, when he was old, she would leave him for
another man. He tugged at the bedsheet, exposing her
breast. She held his gaze for a moment, then closed
her eyes.

"You're lucky I was here," she said. "I might have
been away on assignment."

She was a talker. Gabriel had learned long ago it was
pointless to ask her to remain silent while posing for him.

"You haven't worked since that job in Switzerland."

"How do you know about that operation?"

Gabriel gave her an inscrutable glance over the top of
his sketchpad and reminded her not to move.

"So much for the concept of need to know. It seems
you can walk into Operations any time you feel like it
and find out what I'm doing." She started to turn her
head, but Gabriel stilled her with a sharp *tsk-tsk*. "But I
shouldn't be surprised. Have they given you the directorate yet?"

"Which directorate is that?" Gabriel said, being deliberately obtuse.

"Special Operations."

Gabriel confessed that the post had been offered
and accepted.

"So you're my boss now," she pointed out. "I suppose we just violated about a half dozen different Office edicts about fraternization between senior officers and staff."

"At least," said Gabriel. "But my promotion isn't official yet."

"Oh, thank goodness. I wouldn't want the great Gabriel to get into any sort of trouble because of his sex life. How much longer are we allowed to plunder each other's bodies before we run into trouble with Personnel?"

"As long as we like. We'll just have to go on the record with them at some point."

"And what about God, Gabriel? Will you go on the record with God this time?" There was silence, except for the scratching of a charcoal pencil across paper. She changed the subject. "How much do you know about what I was doing in Switzerland?"

"I know that you went to Zermatt to seduce a Swiss arms merchant who was about to make a deal with someone who didn't have our best interests at heart. King Saul Boulevard wanted to know when the shipment was leaving and where it was bound."

After a long silence he asked her whether she had slept with the Swiss.

"It wasn't that kind of operation. I was working with another agent. I just kept the arms dealer entertained in the bar while the other agent broke into his room and stole the contents of his computer. Besides, you know that a *bat leveyha* isn't supposed to be used for sex. We hire professionals for that sort of thing."

"Not always."

"I could never use my body like that. I'm a religious girl." She smiled at him mischievously. "We got it, by the way. The boat had a mysterious accident near the coast of Crete. The weapons are now on the bottom of the sea."

"I know," Gabriel said. "Close your eyes again."

"Make me," she said, then she smiled and did what he wanted. "Aren't you going to ask me whether I was with anyone while we were apart?"

"It's none of my business."

"But you must be curious. I can only imagine what you did to my apartment when you walked through the door."

"If you're suggesting I searched your things, I didn't."

"Oh, please."

"Why can't you sleep?"

"Do you really want me to answer that?"

He made no reply.

"There was no one else, Gabriel, but then you knew that, didn't you? How could there be?" She gave him a bittersweet smile. "They never tell you that when they ask you to join their exclusive club. They never tell you how the lies begin to add up, or that you'll never truly be comfortable around people who aren't members. Is that the only reason why you fell in love with me, Gabriel? Because I was Office?"

"I liked your fettuccini and mushrooms. You make the best fettuccini and mushrooms in all of Venice."

"And what about you? Were you with any other women while I was gone?"

"I spent all my time with a very large canvas."

"Oh, yes, I forgot about your affliction. You can't make love to a woman unless she knows you've killed on behalf of your country. I'm sure you could have found someone suitable at King Saul Boulevard if you'd set your mind to it. Every woman in the Office lusts after you."

"You're talking too much. I'll never finish this if you keep talking."

"I'm hungry. You shouldn't have mentioned food. How's Leah, by the way?"

Gabriel stopped sketching and glared at Chiara over the top of the sketchpad, as if to tell her he did not appreciate the rather cavalier juxtaposition of food and his wife.

"I'm sorry," Chiara said. "How is she?"

Gabriel heard himself say that Leah was doing well, that two or three days a week he drove up to the psychiatric hospital atop Mount Herzl to spend a few minutes with her. But as he told her these things his mind was elsewhere: on a tiny street in Vienna not far from the Judenplatz; on the car bomb that killed his son and the inferno that destroyed Leah's body and stole her memory. For thirteen years she had been silent in his presence. Now, for brief periods, she spoke to him. Recently, in the garden of the hospital, she had posed to him the same question Chiara had a moment earlier: Were there other women while I was gone? He had answered her truthfully.

"*Did you love this girl, Gabriel?*"

"*I loved her, but I gave her up for you.*"

"*Why on earth would you do that, my love? Look at me. There's nothing left of me. Nothing but a memory.*"

Chiara had lapsed into silence. The light on her face was fading slowly from coral red to gray. The plump woman appeared in the window opposite and began reeling in her laundry. Chiara lifted the sheet to her throat.

"What are you doing?"

"I don't want Signora Lorenzetto to see me naked."

Gabriel, in pulling the sheet down to its original position, left a smudge of charcoal on her breast.

"I suppose I have to move back to Jerusalem," she said. "Unless you feel like telling Shamron that you can't take over Special Ops because you're coming back to Venice."

"It's tempting," Gabriel said.

"Tempting, but not possible. You're a loyal soldier, Gabriel. You always do what you're told. You always did." She brushed the charcoal from her breast. "At least I won't have to decorate the apartment."

Gabriel's eyes remained downward toward the sketchpad. Chiara studied his expression, then asked, "Gabriel, what have you done to the apartment?"

"I'm afraid I needed a place to work."

"So you just moved some things around?"

"You know, I'm getting hungry, too."

"Gabriel Allon, is there anything left?"

"It's warm tonight," he said. "Let's take the boat out to Murano and have fish."

9

JERUSALEM

I T WAS EIGHT O'CLOCK the following evening when Gabriel returned to Narkiss Street. Shamron's car was parked at the curb and Rami, his bodyguard, was standing watch in the walkway outside Number 16. Upstairs Gabriel found all the lights on and Shamron drinking coffee at the kitchen table.

"How did you get in?"

"In case you've forgotten, this used to be an Office safe flat. There's a key in Housekeeping."

"Yes, but I changed the locks over the summer."

"Really?"

"I guess I'll have to change them again."

"Don't bother."

Gabriel pushed open the window to vent the smoke from the room. Six cigarette butts lay like spent bullets in one of Gabriel's saucers. Shamron had been here for some time.

"How was Venice?" Shamron asked.

"Venice was lovely, but the next time you break into my flat, please have the courtesy to not smoke." Gabriel picked up the saucer by the edge and poured the cigarette butts into the garbage. "What's so urgent it couldn't wait till the morning?"

"Another Saudi link to the attack on the Vatican."

Gabriel looked up at Shamron. "What is it?"

"Ibrahim el-Banna."

"The Egyptian cleric? Why am I not surprised."

Gabriel sat down at the table.

"Two nights ago our station chief in Cairo held a secret meeting with one of our top sources inside the Egyptian Mukhabarat. It seems Professor Ibrahim el-Banna had a well-established militant pedigree, long before he went to the Vatican. His older brother was a member of the Muslim Brotherhood and was a close associate of Ayman al-Zawahiri, the number-two man in al-Qaeda. A nephew went to Iraq to fight the Americans and was killed in the siege of Fallujah. Apparently tapes of the imam's sermons are required listening among Egyptian Islamic militants."

"Too bad our friend in the Mukhabarat didn't tell the Vatican the truth about el-Banna. Seven hundred people might be alive—and the Dome of the Basilica might not have a hole in it."

"The Egyptians knew something else about Professor el-Banna," Shamron said. "Throughout much of the eighties and nineties, when the problem of Islamic fundamentalism was exploding in Egypt, Professor el-Banna received regular cash payments and instructions from a Saudi who posed as an official of the International Islamic Relief Organization, one of the main Saudi charities. This man called himself Khalil, but Egyptian intelligence knew his real name: Ahmed bin Shafiq. What makes this even more interesting is bin Shafiq's occupation at that time."

"He was GID," said Gabriel.

"Exactly."

The GID, or General Intelligence Department, was the name of the Saudi intelligence service.

"What do we know about him?"

"Until four years ago, bin Shafiq was chief of a clandestine GID unit code-named Group 205, which was responsible for establishing and maintaining links between Saudi Arabia and Islamic militant groups around the Middle East. Egypt was one of Group 205's top priorities, along with Afghanistan, of course."

"What's the significance of the number?"

"It was the extension of bin Shafiq's office in GID Headquarters."

"What happened four years ago?"

"Bin Shafiq and his operatives were funneling matériel and money to the terrorists of Hamas and Islamic Jihad. A Palestinian informant told us about the operation, and we told the Americans. The American president showed our evidence to the king and brought pressure on him to shut down Group 205. That was six months after 9/11, and the king had no choice but to accede to the president's wishes, much to the dismay of bin Shafiq and other hardliners inside the kingdom. Group 205 was terminated, and bin Shafiq was run out of the GID."

"Has he gone over to the other side of the street?"

"Are you asking whether he's a terrorist? The answer is, we don't know. What we *do* know is that Islamic militancy is in his blood. His grandfather was a commander of the Ikhwan, the Islamic movement created by Ibn Saud at the turn of the nineteenth century in the Najd."

Gabriel knew the Ikhwan well. In many respects they were the prototype and spiritual precursor of today's Islamic militant groups.

"Where else did bin Shafiq operate when he was with Group 205?"

"Afghanistan, Pakistan, Jordan, Lebanon, Algeria. We even suspect he's been in the West Bank."

"So it's possible we're dealing with someone who has terrorist contacts ranging from al-Qaeda to Hamas to the Muslim Brotherhood of Egypt. If bin Shafiq *has* gone over to the other side, he's the nightmare scenario. The perfect terrorist mastermind."

"We found another interesting tidbit in our own files," Shamron said. "About two years ago we were receiving reports of a Saudi trolling the camps of southern Lebanon looking for experienced fighters. According to the reports, this Saudi called himself Khalil."

"The same name bin Shafiq used in Cairo."

"Unfortunately, we didn't pursue it. Frankly, if we

chased down every moneyed Saudi who was trying to raise an army to wage jihad, we wouldn't get much else done. Hindsight, as they say, is twenty-twenty."

"How much more do we have on bin Shafiq?"

"Precious little, I'm afraid."

"What about a photograph?"

Shamron shook his head. "As you might expect, he's somewhat camera shy."

"We need to share, Ari. The Italians need to know that there may be a Saudi connection. So do the Americans."

"I know." Shamron's tone was gloomy. The idea of sharing a hard-won piece of intelligence was heresy to him, especially if nothing was to be gained in return. "It used to be blue and white," he said, referencing the national colors of Israel. "That was our motto. Our belief system. We did things ourselves. We didn't ask others for help, and we didn't help others with problems of their own making."

"The world has changed, Ari."

"Perhaps it's a world I'm not cut out for. When we were fighting the PLO or Black September, it was simple Newtonian physics. Hit them here, squeeze them there. Watch them, listen to them, identify the members of their organization, eliminate their leadership. Now we're fighting a *movement*—a cancer that has metastasized to every vital organ of the body. It's like trying to capture fog in a glass. The old rules don't apply. Blue and white isn't enough. I can tell you one thing, though. This isn't going to go down well in Washington. The Saudis have many friends there."

"Money will do that," Gabriel said. "But the Americans need to know the truth about their best friend in the Arab world."

"They *know* the truth. They just don't want to face it. The Americans know that in many ways the Saudis are the wellspring of Islamic terrorism, that the Saudis planted the seeds, watered them with petrodollars, and fertilized them with Wahhabi hatred and propaganda. The Americans seem content to live with this, as if Saudi-inspired terrorism is just a small surcharge on every tank of gasoline. What they don't understand is that terrorism can never be defeated unless they go after the source: Riyadh and the al-Saud."

"All the more reason to share with them intelligence linking the GID and the al-Saud to the attack on the Vatican."

"I'm glad you think so, because you've been nominated to go to Washington to brief them on what we know."

"When do I leave?"

"Tomorrow morning."

Shamron looked absently out the window and for the second time asked Gabriel about his trip to Venice.

"I was lured there under false pretenses," Gabriel said. "But I'm glad I went."

"Who did the luring?"

Gabriel told him. The smile that appeared on Shamron's face made Gabriel wonder whether he was involved in the operation as well.

"Is she coming here?"

"We spent a single day together," Gabriel said. "We weren't able to make any plans."

"I'm not sure I believe that," Shamron said warily. "Surely you're not contemplating a return to Venice. Have you forgotten you've made a commitment to take over Special Ops?"

"No, I haven't forgotten."

"By the way, your appointment will be made official when you return from Washington."

"I'm counting the hours."

Shamron looked around the apartment. "Did you confess to Chiara that you gave away all her furniture?"

"She knows I had to make some *changes* to accommodate my studio."

"She's not going to be happy," Shamron said. "I'd give anything to see Chiara's face when she walks in here for the first time."

SHAMRON STAYED FOR another hour, debriefing Gabriel about the attack on the Vatican. At nine-fifteen Gabriel walked him down to the car, then stood in the street for a moment and watched the taillights disappear around the corner. He went back upstairs and put the kitchen in order, then shut out the lights and went into his bedroom. Just then the apartment block shook with the clap of a thunderous explosion. Like all Israelis, he had become adept at estimating the casualty toll of suicide bombs by counting the sirens. The more sirens, the more ambulances. The more ambulances, the more dead and wounded. He heard a single siren, then another, then a third. Not too large, he thought. He switched on the television and waited for the first bulletin, but fifteen minutes after the explosion there was still no word. In frustration he picked up the phone and dialed Shamron's car. There was no answer.

PART TWO

DR. GACHET'S DAUGHTER

10

EIN KEREM, JERUSALEM

GILAH SHAMRON'S LIFE HAD been a succession of tense vigils. She had endured the secret missions to dangerous lands, the wars and the terror, the crises and the Security Cabinet meetings that never seemed to end before midnight. She had always feared an enemy from Shamron's past would one day rise and take his revenge. She had always known that one day Ari would force her to wait for word of whether he was going to live or die.

Gabriel found her seated calmly in a private waiting room in the intensive care unit of the Hadassah Medical Center. Shamron's famous bomber jacket lay across her lap, and she was absently plucking at the tear in the right breast that Shamron had never seen fit to repair. Gabriel had always seen something of Golda Meir in Gilah's sad gaze and wild gray hair. He could not look at Gilah without thinking of the day Golda pinned a medal on his chest in secret and, with tears in her eyes, thanked him for avenging the eleven Israelis murdered at Munich.

"What happened, Gabriel? How did they get to Ari in the middle of Jerusalem?"

"He's probably been under surveillance for a very long time. When he left my apartment tonight, he told me he was going back to the Prime Minister's Office to do a bit of work." Gabriel sat down and took Gilah's hand. "They hit him at a traffic signal on King George Street."

"A suicide bomber?"

"We think there were two men. They were in a van and disguised as *haredi* Jews. The bomb was abnormally large."

She looked up at the television mounted high on the wall. "I can see that from the pictures. It's remarkable anyone survived."

"A witness saw Ari's car accelerate suddenly an instant before the bomb went off. Rami or the driver must have seen something that made them suspicious. The armor plating withstood the force of the blast, but the car was thrown into the air. Apparently it rolled at least twice."

"Who did this? Was it Hamas? Islamic Jihad? The al-Aqsa Martyrs Brigades?"

"There's been a claim by the Brotherhood of Allah."

"The same people who did the Vatican?"

"Yes, Gilah."

"Do you believe them?"

"It's early," Gabriel said. "What have the doctors told you?"

"He's going to be in surgery for at least another three hours. They say we'll be able to see him when he comes out, but only for a minute or two. They've warned me he won't look good."

Gilah studied him for a moment, then looked up at the television again. "You're worried he's not going to live, aren't you, Gabriel?"

"Of course I am."

"Don't worry," said Gilah. "Shamron is indestructible. Shamron is eternal."

"What did they tell you about his injuries?"

She recited them calmly. The inventory of damaged organs, head trauma, and broken bones made clear to Gabriel that Shamron's survival was by no means assured.

"Ari came through it the best of the three," Gilah said. "Apparently Rami and the driver were hurt much worse. Poor Rami. He's been standing guard over Ari for years. And now this."

"Where's Yonatan?"

"He was on duty in the north tonight. He's on his way."

Shamron's only son was a colonel in the Israel Defense Force. Ronit, his wayward daughter, had moved to New Zealand in order to get away from her domineering father. She was living there on a chicken farm with a gentile. It had been years since she and Shamron had spoken.

"Ronit's coming, too," Gilah said. "Who knows? Maybe something good can come out of all this. Ronit's absence has been very hard on him. He blames himself, as well he should. Ari's very hard on his children. But then you know that, don't you, Gabriel?"

Gilah stared directly into Gabriel's eyes for a moment, then looked suddenly away. For years she had thought him a deskman of some sort who knew much about art and spent a great deal of time in Europe. Like the rest of the country she had learned the true nature of his work by reading the newspapers. Her demeanor toward him had changed since his unmasking. She was quiet around him, careful never to upset him, and incapable of looking him too long in the eye. Gabriel had seen behavior like Gilah's before, as a child, whenever people had entered the Allon home. Death had left its mark on Gabriel's face, just as Birkenau had stained the face of his mother. Gilah couldn't gaze long into his eyes because she feared what she might see there.

"He wasn't well before this. He's been hiding it, of course—even from the prime minister."

Gabriel wasn't surprised. He knew Shamron had been covertly battling various ailments for years. The old man's health, like almost every other aspect of his life, was a closely held secret.

"Is it the kidneys?"

Gilah shook her head. "The cancer is back."

"I thought they got it all."

"So did Ari," she said. "And that's not all. His lungs

are a mess from the cigarettes. Tell him not to smoke so much."

"He never listens to me."

"You're the only one he listens to. He loves you like a son, Gabriel. Sometimes I think he loves you more than Yonatan."

"Don't be silly, Gilah."

"He's never happier than when you're sitting on the terrace together in Tiberias."

"We're usually arguing."

"He likes arguing with you, Gabriel."

"I've gathered that."

On the television cabinet ministers and security chiefs were arriving at the Prime Minister's Office for an emergency session. Under ordinary circumstances Shamron would have been among them. Gabriel looked at Gilah. She was pulling at the torn leather of Shamron's jacket. "It was Ari, wasn't it?" she asked. "It was Ari who dragged you into this life . . . after Munich."

Gabriel looked at the emergency lights flashing on the television screen and nodded absently.

"You were in the army?"

"No, I'd finished with the army. I was studying at the Bezalel Academy of Art by then. Ari came to see me a few days after the hostages had been killed. No one knew it then, but Golda had already given the order to kill everyone involved."

"Why did he select *you*?"

"I spoke languages, and he saw things in my army fitness reports—qualities he thought would make me suitable for the kind of work he had in mind."

"Killing at close range, face-to-face. That's how you did it, isn't it?"

"Yes, Gilah."

"How many?"

"Gilah."

"How many, Gabriel?"

"Six," he said. "I killed six of them."

She touched the gray hair at his temples. "But you were just a boy."

"It's easier when you're a boy. It gets harder as you get older."

"But you did it anyway. You were the one they sent to kill Abu Jihad, weren't you? You walked into his villa in Tunis and killed him in front of his wife and children. And they took their revenge, not on the country but on *you*. They put a bomb beneath your car in Vienna."

She was pulling harder at the tear in Shamron's coat. Gabriel took her hand. "It's all right, Gilah. It was a long time ago."

"I remember when the call came. Ari told me a bomb had gone off beneath a diplomat's car in Vienna. I remember going into the kitchen to make him some coffee and coming back to the bedroom to find him crying. He said, 'It's all my fault. I killed his wife and child.' It's the only time I've ever seen him cry. I didn't see him for a week. When he finally came home, I asked him what had happened. He wouldn't answer, of course. He'd regained his composure by then. But I know it's eaten away at him all these years. He blames himself for what happened."

"He shouldn't," Gabriel said.

"You weren't even allowed to grieve properly, were you? The government told the world that the wife and child of the Israeli diplomat were both dead. You buried your son in secret on the Mount of Olives—just you, Ari, and a rabbi—and you hid your wife away in England under a false name. But Khaled found her. Khaled kidnapped your wife and used her to lure you to the Gare de Lyon." A tear spilled down Gilah's cheek. Gabriel brushed it away and found her wrinkled skin was still as soft as velvet. "All because my husband came to see you one afternoon in September so long ago. You could have had such a different life. You could have been a great artist. Instead we turned you into a killer. Why aren't you bitter, Gabriel? Why don't you hate Ari like his children do?"

"The course of my life was charted the day the Germans chose the little Austrian corporal to be their chancellor. Ari was just the helmsman on the night watch."

"Are you that fatalistic?"

"Believe me, Gilah, I went through a period of time where I couldn't bear to look at Ari. But I've come to realize I'm more like him than I ever knew."

"Maybe that's the quality he saw in your army fitness report."

Gabriel smiled briefly. "Maybe it was."

Gilah fingered the tear in Shamron's jacket. "Do you know the story about how this happened?"

"It's one of the great mysteries inside the Office," Gabriel said. "There are all sorts of wild theories about how it happened, but he always refused to tell us the truth."

"It was the night of the bombing in Vienna. Ari was in a hurry to get to King Saul Boulevard. As he was climbing into his car, the coat got caught on the door, and he tore it." She ran her finger along the wound. "I tried to fix it for him many times, but he would never let me. It was for Leah and Dani, he said. He's been wearing a ripped coat all these years because of what happened to your wife and son."

The telephone rang. Gabriel brought the receiver to his ear and listened in silence for a moment. "I'll be right there, sir," he said a moment later, then rang off.

"That was the prime minister. He wants to see me right away. I'll come back when I'm finished."

"Don't worry, Gabriel. Yonatan will be here soon."

"I'll be back, Gilah."

His tone was too forceful. He kissed her cheek apologetically and stood. Gilah seized his arm as he moved toward the door. "Take this," she said, holding out Shamron's coat. "He would have wanted you to have it."

"Don't talk like he's not going to make it."

"Just take the jacket and go." She gave him a bittersweet smile. "You mustn't keep the prime minister waiting."

Gabriel went into the corridor and hurried to the elevators. *You mustn't keep the prime minister waiting.* It was what Gilah always said to Shamron whenever he left her.

A CAR AND security detail were waiting downstairs in the drive. It took them only five minutes to reach the Prime Minister's Office at 3 Kaplan Street. The guards took Gabriel into the building through an underground entrance and shepherded him upstairs, into the large unexpectedly plain office on the top floor. The room was in semidarkness; the prime minister was seated at his desk in a pool of light, dwarfed by the towering portrait of the Zionist leader Theodore Herzl that hung on the wall at his back. It had been more than a year since Gabriel had been in his presence. In that time his hair had turned from silver to white, and his brown eyes had taken on the rheumy look of an old man. The meeting of the Security Cabinet had just broken up, and the prime minister was alone except for Amos Sharret, the new director-general of the Office, who was seated tensely in a leather armchair. Gabriel shook his hand for the first time. "It's a pleasure to finally meet you," Amos said. "I wish the circumstances were different."

Gabriel sat down.

"You're wearing Shamron's jacket," the prime minister said.

"Gilah insisted I take it."

"It becomes you." He smiled distantly. "You know, you're even beginning to look a little like him."

"Is that supposed to be a compliment?"

"He was very handsome when he was a young man."

"He was never young, Prime Minister."

"None of us were. We were all old before our time. We gave up our youth to build this country. Shamron hasn't taken a day off since 1947. And this is how it ends?" The prime minister shook his head. "No, he'll live. Trust me, Gabriel, I've known him longer than even you."

"Shamron is eternal. That's what Gilah says."

"Maybe not eternal, but he's not going to be killed by a bunch of terrorists."

The prime minister scowled at his wristwatch.

"You had something you wanted to discuss with me, sir?"

"Your promotion to chief of Special Ops."

"I've agreed to take the position, sir."

"I realize that, but perhaps now isn't the best time for you to be running the division."

"May I ask why not?"

"Because all your attention needs to be focused on tracking down and punishing the men who did this to Shamron."

The prime minister lapsed into a sudden silence, as if giving Gabriel an opportunity to mount an objection. Gabriel sat motionless, his gaze downward toward his hands.

"You surprise me," the prime minister said.

"How so?"

"I was afraid you were going to tell me to find someone else."

"One doesn't turn down the prime minister, sir."

"But surely there's more to it than that."

"I was in Rome when the terrorists attacked the Vatican, and I put Shamron in his car tonight. I heard the bomb go off." He paused. "This network, whoever they are and whatever their goals, needs to be put out of business—and soon."

"You sound as though you want vengeance."

Gabriel looked up from his hands. "I do, Prime Minister. Perhaps under those circumstances, I'm the wrong man for the job."

"Actually, under the circumstances, you are exactly the *right* man."

It was Amos who had spoken these words. Gabriel turned and regarded him carefully for the first time. He was a small, broad man, shaped like a square, with a monkish fringe of dark hair and a heavy brow. He still carried the rank of general in the IDF but was dressed now in a pale gray suit. His candor was a refreshing change. Lev had been a dental probe of a man, forever prodding and searching for weakness and decay. Amos was more like a tack hammer. Gabriel would have to watch his step around him, lest the hammer fall on him.

"Just make certain your anger doesn't cloud your judgment," Amos added.

"It never has before," Gabriel said, holding Amos's dark gaze.

Amos gave him a humorless smile, as if to say, *There'll be no shooting up French train stations on my watch, no matter what the circumstances.* The prime minister leaned forward and braced himself on his elbows.

"Do you believe Saudis are behind this?"

"We have some evidence that points to a Saudi connection to the Brotherhood of Allah," Gabriel said judiciously, "but we'll need more intelligence before we start looking for a specific individual."

"Ahmed bin Shafiq, for example."

"Yes, Prime Minister."

"And if it is him?"

"In my opinion, we're dealing with a network, not a movement. A network bought and paid for with Saudi money. If we lop off the head, the network will die. But it won't be easy, Prime Minister. We know very little about him. We don't even know what he really looks like. It will also be complicated politically because of the Americans."

"It's not complicated at all. Ahmed bin Shafiq tried to kill my closest adviser. And so Ahmed bin Shafiq must die."

"And if he's acting at the behest of Prince Nabil or someone in the Royal Family—a family with close historic and economic ties to our most important ally?"

"We'll know soon enough."

The prime minister gave a sideways glance at Amos.

"Adrian Carter of the CIA would like a word with you," Amos said.

"I was supposed to go to Washington tomorrow to brief him on what we've learned about the attack on the Vatican."

"Carter has requested a change of venue."

"Where does he want to meet?"

"London."

"Why London?"

"It was Carter's suggestion," Amos said. "He wanted a convenient neutral location."

"Since when is a CIA safe house in London neutral ground?" Gabriel looked at the prime minister, then Amos. "I don't want to leave Jerusalem—not until we know whether Shamron is going to live."

"Carter says it's urgent," Amos said. "He wants to see you tomorrow night."

"Send someone else then."

"We can't," said the prime minister. "You're the only one invited."

11

LONDON

"How's the old man?" asked Adrian Carter. They were walking side by side in Eaton Place, sheltering from a thin night rain beneath Carter's umbrella. They had met five minutes earlier, as if by chance encounter, in Belgrave Square. Carter had been the one wearing the mackintosh raincoat and holding a copy of *The Independent*. He was orthodox when it came to the conventions of tradecraft. According to the office wits at Langley, Adrian Carter left chalk marks on the bedpost when he wanted to make love to his wife.

"Still unconscious," Gabriel replied, "but he made it through the night, and he's not losing any more blood."

"Is he going to make it?"

"Last night, I would have said no."

"And now?"

"I'm more worried about how he's going to come out of it. If he's left with brain damage or trapped in a body that won't obey his orders . . ." Gabriel's voice trailed off. "Shamron has only one thing in his life, and that's his work. If he can't work, he's going to be miserable—and so will everyone around him."

"So what else is new?" Carter glanced toward the doorway of the Georgian house at Number 24. "The flat is in there. Let's take a walk around the block once, shall we? I like to do things by the book."

"Haven't you heard, Adrian? The Soviet Union collapsed a few years back. The KGB are out of business. You and the Russians are friends now."

"One can never be too careful, Gabriel."

"Didn't your security boys set up a surveillance detection route?"

"There are no boys, Gabriel."

"Is that an Agency safe flat?"

"Not exactly," Carter said. "It belongs to a friend."

"A friend of the Agency?"

"A friend of the president's, actually."

Carter gave a gentle tug on Gabriel's coat sleeve and led him down the darkened street. They made a slow tour of Eaton Square, which was silent except for the grumble of the evening traffic on the King's Road. Carter moved at a ponderous pace, like a man bound for an appointment he would rather not keep. Gabriel was wrestling with a single thought: Why did the deputy director for operations of the Central Intelligence Agency want to talk in a place where his own government wouldn't be listening?

They made their way back to Eaton Place. This time Carter led Gabriel down the steps to the basement entrance. As Carter inserted the key into the lock, Gabriel quietly lifted the lid of the rubbish bin and saw it was empty. Carter opened the door and led them inside, into the sort of kitchen that real estate brochures routinely describe as "gourmet." The countertops were granite and agreeably lit by halogen lamps concealed beneath the custom cabinetry. The floor was covered in the Jerusalem limestone so admired by English and American sophisticates who wish to connect to their Mediterranean roots. Carter walked over to the stainless-steel range and filled the electric teakettle with water. He didn't bother asking Gabriel whether he wanted something stronger. He knew Gabriel drank nothing but the occasional glass of wine and never mixed alcohol with business, except for reasons of cover.

"It's a maisonette," Carter said. "The drawing room's upstairs. Go make yourself comfortable."

"Are you giving me permission to have a look round, Adrian?"

Carter was now opening and closing the cabinet doors with a befuddled expression on his face. Gabriel walked over to the pantry, found a box of Earl Grey tea, and tossed it to Carter before heading upstairs. The drawing room was comfortably furnished but with an air of anonymity common in a pied-à-terre. It seemed to Gabriel that no one had ever loved or quarreled or grieved here. He picked up a framed photograph from a side table and saw a bluff, prosperous American with three well-fed children and a wife who'd had too much cosmetic surgery. Two more photographs showed the American standing stiffly at the side of the president. Both were signed: *To Bill with gratitude.*

Carter came upstairs a moment later, a tea tray balanced between his hands. He had a head of thinning curly hair and the sort of broad mustache once worn by American college professors. Little about Carter's demeanor suggested he was one of the most powerful members of Washington's vast intelligence establishment—or that before his ascension to the rarified atmosphere of Langley's seventh floor, he had been a field man of the highest reputation. Carter's natural inclination to listen rather than speak led most to conclude he was a therapist of some sort. When one thought of Adrian Carter, one pictured a man enduring confessions of affairs and inadequacies, or a Dickensian figure hunched over thick books with long Latin words. People tended to underestimate Carter. It was one of his most potent weapons.

"Who's behind it, Adrian?" Gabriel asked.

"You tell me, Gabriel." Carter placed the tea tray on the center table and removed his raincoat as if weary from too much travel. "It's your neighborhood."

"It's our neighborhood, but something tells me it's your problem. Otherwise you wouldn't be here in London"—Gabriel looked around the room—"in a borrowed safe flat, with no microphones and no backup from the local station."

"You don't miss much, do you? Humor me, Gabriel. Tell me his name."

"He's a former Saudi GID agent named Ahmed bin Shafiq."

"Bravo, Gabriel. Well done." Carter threw his coat over the back of a chair. "Well done, indeed."

CARTER LIFTED the lid of the teapot, savored the aroma, and decided it needed to steep a moment longer.

"How did you know?"

"We didn't *know*," Gabriel said. "It was an educated guess, based on a few threads of evidence."

"Such as?"

Gabriel told Carter everything he knew. The blown operation against Professor Ali Massoudi. The surveillance photos and Zurich bank account information found on Massoudi's computer. The links between Ibrahim el-Banna and the Saudi agent who called himself Khalil. The reports of a Saudi by the same name trolling the refugee camps of southern Lebanon for recruits. All the while Carter was fussing with the tea. He poured the first cup and handed it to Gabriel plain. His own required more elaborate preparation: a careful measure of milk, then the tea, then a lump of sugar. Interrogators referred to such obvious playing for time as displacement activity. Carter was a pipe smoker. Gabriel feared it would make an appearance soon.

"And what about you?" Gabriel asked. "When did you know it was bin Shafiq?"

Carter snared a second lump with the tongs and briefly debated adding it to the cup before plopping it unceremoniously back into the bowl. "Maybe I knew the day we asked His Majesty to shut down Group 205," he said. "Or maybe it was the day bin Shafiq seemed to vanish from the face of the earth. You see, Gabriel, if there's one thing I've learned in this business, it's that for every action we take there's bound to be a negative *re*action. We drove the Russian bear out of Afghanistan and created a Hydra in the process. We smashed the corporate headquarters of al-Qaeda and now the branch offices are running their own affairs. We shut down bin Shafiq's shop inside the GID, and now it seems bin Shafiq has gone into private practice."

"Why?"

"You're asking what drove him over the edge?" Carter shrugged and stirred his tea mournfully. "It didn't take much. Ahmed bin Shafiq is a true Wahhabi believer."

"Grandson of an Ikhwan warrior," said Gabriel, which earned him an admiring nod from Carter.

"One may argue about why the Saudis support terrorism," Carter said. "One may have a learned debate as to whether they truly support the goals of the murderers they arm and finance or whether they are engaged in a clever and cynical policy to control the environment around them and thus ensure their own survival. One may not have such a debate about the man the GID chose to carry out that policy. Ahmed bin Shafiq is a believer. Ahmed bin Shafiq hates the United States, the West, and Christianity, and he would be much happier if your country no longer existed. It was why we insisted that His Majesty shut down his little shop of terror."

"So when you forced the king to shut down Group 205, bin Shafiq snapped? He decided to use all the contacts he'd made over the years and launch a wave of terrorism of his own? Surely there's more to it than that, Adrian."

"I'm afraid we may have given him a little shove," Carter said. "We invaded Iraq against the wishes of the Kingdom and most of its inhabitants. We've captured members of al-Qaeda and locked them away in secret prisons where they belong. This doesn't look good to the Muslim world, and it adds fuel to the fires of jihad. You've had a hand in it as well. The Saudis see your Separation Fence for what it is, a unilateral final border, and they're not pleased with it."

"This might come as a shock to you, Adrian, but we don't care what the Saudis think of our fence. If they hadn't poured millions into the coffers of Hamas and Islamic Jihad, we wouldn't need one."

"Back to my original point," said Carter, pausing for a moment to sip his tea. "The Islamic world is seething with anger, and Ahmed bin Shafiq, true Wahhabi believer, has stepped forward to raise the flag of jihad against the infidel. He's used his contacts from his Group 205 days to construct a new network. He's doing what bin Laden is no longer capable of doing, which is plan and carry out large-scale terror spectaculars like the attack on the Vatican. His network is small, extremely professional, and, as he's proven conclusively, very lethal."

"And it's bought and paid for with Saudi money."

"Most definitely," said Carter.

"How high does it go, Adrian?"

"Very high," said Carter. "Damned near to the top."

"Where's he operating? Who's footing the bill? Where's the money coming from?"

"AAB Holdings of Riyadh, Geneva, and points in between," said Carter unequivocally. "Ahmed bin Shafiq is one of AAB's most successful investments. Can I freshen up your tea?"

THERE WAS ANOTHER break in the proceedings, this time while Carter tried to divine how to light the gas fire. He stood mystified before the grate for a moment, then, with a glance toward Gabriel, appealed for assistance. Gabriel found the key on the mantel, used it to start the flow of gas, then ignited it with an ornamental match.

"How many years do you give them, Gabriel? How long before the House of Saud collapses and the Islamic Republic of Arabia rises in its place? Five years? Ten? Or is it more like twenty? We've never been really good about making predictions like that. We thought the Soviet empire would last forever."

"And we thought Hamas could never win an election."

Carter chuckled mirthlessly. "Our best minds give

them seven years at the most. His Majesty is prepared to spend that seven years playing the game by the old rules: provide cheap oil and pseudofriendship to us while at the same time paying lip service to the forces of Islam and bribing them not to attack *him*. And when it's over, he'll flee to his string of palaces along the Riviera and live out the rest of his days in a luxury that is too grotesque even to contemplate, hopefully with his head still attached to his body."

Carter lifted his palms toward the fire. "It's not hot," he said.

"The logs are made of ceramic. Give it a minute to heat up."

Carter appeared incredulous. Gabriel drifted over to the window and peered into the street as a car rolled slowly past and vanished around the next corner. Carter gave up on the fire and returned to his seat.

"And then there are those in the Royal Family who are willing to play the game by a different set of rules. We'll call them the True Believers. They think the only way the al-Saud can survive is to renew the covenant they formed with Muhammad Abdul Wahhab two centuries ago in the Najd. But this new covenant has to take into account new realities. The monster that the al-Saud created two hundred years ago now holds all the cards, and the True Believers are prepared to give the monster what it wants. Infidel blood. Jihad without end. Some of these True Believers want to go further. The expulsion of all infidels from the Peninsula. An embargo on oil sales to

America and any other country that does business with yours. They believe oil should no longer be treated as simply an unending pool of liquid money that flows from the terminals of Ras Tanura into the Zurich bank accounts of the al-Saud. They want to use it as a weapon—a weapon that could be used to cripple the American economy and make the Wahhabis masters of the planet, just as Allah intended when he placed that sea of oil beneath the sands of the al-Hassa. And some of these True Believers, such as the chairman and CEO of AAB Holdings of Riyadh, Geneva, and points in between, are actually willing to shed a little infidel blood themselves."

"You're referring to Abdul Aziz al-Bakari?"

"I am indeed," said Carter. "Know much about him?"

"At last accounting, he was something like the fifteenth richest man in the world, with a personal fortune in the vicinity of ten billion dollars."

"Give or take a billion or two."

"He's the president, chairman, and lord high emperor of AAB Holdings—*A* for Abdul, *A* for Aziz, and *B* for al-Bakari. AAB owns banks and investment houses. AAB does shipping and steel. AAB is cutting down the forests of the Amazon and strip-mining the Andes of Peru and Bolivia. AAB has a Belgian chemical company and a Dutch pharmaceutical. AAB's real estate and development division is one of the world's largest. Abdul Aziz al-Bakari owns more hotels than anyone else in the world."

Carter picked up where Gabriel left off. "He has a palace in Riyadh he rarely visits and two former wives there he never sees. He owns a mansion on the Île de la Cité in Paris, a princely estate in the English countryside, a townhouse in Mayfair, oceanfront villas in Saint-Tropez, Marbella, and Maui, ski chalets in Zermatt and Aspen, a Park Avenue apartment recently appraised at forty million dollars, and a sprawling compound overlooking the Potomac that I pass every day on the way to work."

Carter seemed to find the mansion on the Potomac the most grievous of al-Bakari's sins. Carter's father had been an Episcopal minister from New Hampshire, and beneath his placid exterior beat the heart of a Puritan.

"Al-Bakari and his entourage travel the world in a gold-plated 747," he continued. "Twice a year, once in February and again in August, AAB's operations go seaborne when al-Bakari and his entourage set up shop aboard *Alexandra*, his three-hundred-foot yacht. Have I forgotten anything?"

"His friends call him Zizi," Gabriel replied. "He has one of the world's largest private collections of French Impressionist art, and we've been telling you for years that he's up to his eyeballs in funding terrorism, especially against us."

"I didn't realize that."

"Realize what?"

"That Zizi's a collector."

"A very aggressive one, actually."

"Ever had the pleasure of meeting him?"

"I'm afraid Zizi and I are at different ends of the trade." Gabriel frowned. "So what's the connection between Zizi al-Bakari and Ahmed bin Shafiq?"

Carter blew thoughtfully on his tea, a sign that he was not yet ready to answer Gabriel's question.

"An interesting fellow, al-Bakari. Did you know that his father was Ibn Saud's personal banker? As you might expect, Papa al-Bakari did quite well—well enough to give his son ten million dollars to start his own company. That was nothing compared to the seed money he got from the al-Saud when things started to take off. A hundred million, if the rumor mill is to be believed. AAB is still a favorite dumping ground for Saudi Royal cash, which is one of the reasons why Zizi is so interested in making sure the House of Saud survives."

Gabriel's heart sank as Carter reached for the tobacco pouch.

"He's among the world's richest men," Carter said, "and one of the world's most charitable. He's built mosques and Islamic centers all across Europe. He's financed development projects in the Nile Delta and famine relief in Sudan. He's given millions to the Palestinian refugees and millions more to development projects in the West Bank and Gaza."

"And more than thirty million dollars to that Saudi telethon to raise money for suicide bombers," Gabriel added. "Zizi was the largest single donor. Now answer my question, Adrian."

"Which question is that?"

"What's the connection between Zizi and bin Shafiq?"

"You're a quick study, Gabriel. You tell *me*."

"Obviously Zizi is bankrolling bin Shafiq's network."

"Obviously," said Carter in agreement.

"But bin Shafiq is a Saudi. He can get money anywhere. Zizi has something more valuable than money. Zizi has a global infrastructure through which bin Shafiq can move men and matériel. And Zizi has a perfect place for a mastermind like bin Shafiq to hide."

"AAB Holdings of Riyadh, Geneva, and points in between."

A SILENCE FELL between them like a curtain while Carter drowsily loaded his pipe. Gabriel was still standing in the window, peering into the street. He was tempted to remain there, for Carter's tobacco, when ignited, smelled like a combination of burning hay and wet dog. He knew, however, that the conversation had passed the point where it might be conducted in front of an insecure window. Reluctantly he lowered himself into the chair opposite Carter and they gazed at each other in silence, Carter puffing contemplatively and Gabriel wearily waving the smoke from his eyes.

"How sure are you?"

"Very."

"How do you know?"

"Sources and methods," said Carter mechanically. "Sources and methods."

"How do you *know*, Adrian?"

"Because we listen to him," Carter said. "The National Security Agency is a wonderful thing. We also have sources inside the moderate wing of the House of Saud and the GID who are willing to tell us things. Ahmed bin Shafiq is living largely in the West under an assumed identity. He is buried somewhere within Zizi's financial empire and the two of them confer on a regular basis. Of this, we are certain."

There was a manila file folder on the center table, next to Carter's tea tray. Inside was a single photograph, which Carter handed to Gabriel. It showed a man in a woolen overcoat and trilby, standing at a wrought-iron gate. The face was in left profile, and the features were somewhat gauzy. Judging from the compression of the image, the photograph had been snapped from some distance.

"Is this him?"

"We think so," Carter replied.

"Where was it taken?"

"Outside Zizi's house on the Île de la Cité in Paris. The cameraman was on the other side of the Seine, on the Quai de l'Hôtel de Ville, which accounts for a certain lack of clarity of the image."

"How long ago?"

"Six months."

Carter rose slowly to his feet and wandered over to

the fireplace. He was about to rap his pipe against the grate when Gabriel reminded him that it was a fake. He sat down again and emptied the pipe into a large cut-glass ashtray.

"How many Americans were killed at the Vatican?" Gabriel asked.

"Twenty-eight, including a Curial bishop."

"How much money has Zizi al-Bakari given to the terrorists over the years?"

"Hundreds of millions."

"Go after him," Gabriel said. "Make a case against him and put him on trial."

"Against Zizi al-Bakari?"

"Section 18 U.S.C. 2339B—have you ever heard of it, Adrian?"

"You're quoting American law to me now?"

"It's a violation of American law to give money to designated terrorist groups, regardless of whether the money was used for specific attacks. You could have probably prosecuted dozens of wealthy Saudis for giving material support to your enemies, including Zizi al-Bakari."

"You disappoint me, Gabriel. I always thought of you as a fairly reasonable fellow—a bit too concerned with questions of right and wrong at times, but reasonable. We can't go after Zizi al-Bakari."

"Why?"

"Money," said Carter, then added, "And oil, of course."

"Of course."

Carter toyed with his lighter. "The Saudi Royal Family has a lot of friends in Washington—the kind of friends only money can buy. Zizi has friends as well. He's endowed academic chairs and filled them with associates and supporters. He's underwritten the creation of Arab studies departments at a half dozen major American universities. He almost single-handedly financed a major renovation of the Kennedy Center. He gives to the pet charitable projects of influential senators and invests in the business ventures of their friends and relatives. He owns a chunk of one of our most prominent banks and bits and pieces of several other prominent American companies. He's also served as a middleman on countless Saudi-American business deals. Is the picture becoming clear to you now?"

It was, but Gabriel wanted to hear more.

"If Zizi's battalion of Washington lawyers even suspected he was the target of a criminal probe, Zizi would call His Majesty, and His Majesty would call Ambassador Bashir, and Ambassador Bashir would pop over to the White House for a little chat with the president. He would remind the president that a twist or two on the oil spigots would send the price of gasoline over five dollars a gallon. He might even point out that a price spike of that magnitude would surely hurt people in the heartland, who tend to drive long distances, and who also tend to vote for the president's party."

"So Zizi gets away with murder—literally."

"I'm afraid so."

"Ask not about things which, if made plain to you, may cause you trouble."

"You know your Quran," Carter said.

"One of the reasons you can't operate against Zizi or prosecute him is because you're afraid of what you might find: business entanglements with prominent Americans, shady dealings with Washington insiders. Imagine the re-action of the American people if they learned that a Saudi billionaire with business ties to prominent figures in Washington is actually financing the activities of your enemies. The relationship barely survived the first 9/11. I doubt it would survive a second."

"No, it wouldn't—at least not in its present form. There's already a movement on Capitol Hill to isolate Saudi Arabia because of its support of the global Islamic extremism. A scandal involving Zizi al-Bakari would only add fuel to the fire. Several foreign policy lights in Con-gress are considering legislation that would put the screws to Saudi Arabia. They have that luxury. They won't take the fall if the American economy goes into the toilet be-cause of higher fuel prices. The president will."

"So what do you want from us, Adrian? What do you wish to say to me, in this room where no one is listen-ing?"

"The president of the United States would like a favor," Carter said, gazing into the fire. "The sort of favor you happen to be very good at. He'd like you to run an agent into the House of Zizi. He'd like you to find out who's coming and going. And if Ahmed bin

Shafiq happens to walk by, he'd like you to take a shot at him. It will be your operation, but we'll give you whatever support you need. We'll be over the horizon—far enough over to make certain that we can maintain plausible deniability in Riyadh."

"You disappoint me, Adrian. I always thought of you as a reasonable fellow."

"What have I done now?"

"I thought you were going to ask me to kill Zizi al-Bakari and be done with it."

"Kill Zizi?" Carter shook his head. "Zizi is untouchable. Zizi is radioactive."

GABRIEL RETURNED TO his outpost by the window and peered into the street as a pair of lovers hurried along the pavement through the swirling rain. "We're not contract killers," he said. "We can't be hired to do dirty jobs you can't do yourself. You want bin Shafiq dead but you're not willing to risk the fallout. You're setting us up to take the fall."

"I could remind you of a few salient facts," said Carter. "I could remind you that this president has remained steadfastly at your side while the rest of the world has treated you as the Jew among nations. I could remind you that he allowed you to build the Separation Fence while the rest of the world accused you of behaving like South Africans. I could remind you that he allowed you to lock Arafat away in the Mukata while the rest of the world accused you of behaving like Nazi storm troopers. I could remind you of the many other times this president has carried your dirty water, but I won't, because that would be impolitic. It would also suggest that this request is a quid pro quo of some sort, which it most certainly is not."

"Then what is it?"

"A recognition," said Carter. "A recognition that we Americans don't have the stomach or the backbone to do the things we have to do to win this fight. Our fingers have been burned. Our image has taken a terrible beating. We've taken a look in the mirror, and we don't like what we see. Our politicians would like us to make reservations on the first flight out of Iraq so they can start spending money on the sorts of things that win votes. Our people want to go back to their fat, happy lives. They want to bury their heads in the sand and pretend that there really isn't an organized force in their world that is actively plotting and planning their destruction. We've paid a terrible price for climbing into the gutter with the terrorists and fighting them on their level, but I'm sure you always knew we would. No one's paid a higher price than you."

"So you want us to do it for you. I suppose that's what they call outsourcing. How American of you, Adrian."

"Under the current circumstances, the United States cannot target a former high-ranking Saudi intelligence officer for assassination because to do so would shatter our relationship with Riyadh. Nor can we arrest and prosecute Zizi al-Bakari, for the reasons I've given you."

"So you want the problem to go away?"

"Precisely."

"Sweep it under the rug? Postpone the reckoning until a more convenient date?"

"In so many words."

"You think this is the way to defeat your Hydra? Chop off a head and hope for the best? You have to burn out the roots, the way Hercules did. You have to attack the beast with arrows dipped in gall."

"You want to take on the House of Saud?"

"Not just the House of Saud," Gabriel said. "The Wahhabi fanatics with whom they made a covenant of blood two hundred years ago on the barren plateau of Najd. They're your real enemy, Adrian. They're the ones who created Hydra in the first place."

"A wise prince chooses the time and place of the battle, and this is not the time to tear down the House of Saud."

Gabriel lapsed into a moody silence. Carter was peering into the bowl of his pipe and making minor adjustments in the disposition of his tobacco, like a don waiting for an answer from a dull student.

"Do I need to remind you that they targeted Shamron?"

Gabriel gave Carter a dark look that said he most certainly did not.

"Then why the hesitation? I would have thought you'd be straining at the leash to get bin Shafiq after what he did to the old man."

"I want him more than anyone, Adrian, but I never strain at the leash. This is a dangerous operation—too dangerous for *you* even to attempt. If something goes wrong, or if we're caught in the act, it will end badly— for all three of us."

"Three?"

"You, me, and the president."

"So obey Shamron's Eleventh Commandment, and you'll be fine. *Thou shalt not get caught.*"

"Bin Shafiq is a ghost. We don't even have a picture."

"That's not entirely true." Carter reached into his manila file folder again and came out with another photograph, which he dropped onto the coffee table for Gabriel to see. It showed a man with narrow black eyes, his face partially concealed by a kaffiyeh. "That's bin Shafiq, almost twenty years ago, in Afghanistan. He was our friend then. We were on the same side. We supplied the weapons. Bin Shafiq and his masters in Riyadh supplied the money."

"And the Wahhabi ideology that helped give birth to the Taliban," Gabriel said.

"No good deed goes unpunished," said Carter contritely. "But we have something more valuable than a twenty-year-old photograph. We have his voice."

Carter picked up a small black remote, aimed it at a Bose Wave radio, and pressed the Play button. A moment later two men began to converse in English: one with the accent of an American, the other of an Arab.

"I take it the Saudi is bin Shafiq?"

Carter nodded.

"When was it recorded?"

"In 1988," Carter said. "In a safe house in Peshawar."

"Who's the American?" Gabriel asked, though he knew the answer already. Carter hit the Stop button and looked into the fire. "Me," he said distantly. "The American at the CIA safe house in Peshawar was me."

"Would you recognize bin Shafiq if you saw him again?"

"I might, but our sources tell us he had several rounds of plastic surgery before going operational. I *would* recognize the scar on his right forearm, though. He got hit by a piece of shrapnel during a trip to Afghanistan in 1985. The scar runs from just above the wrist to just below the elbow. No plastic surgeon could have done anything about that."

"Inside the arm or outside?"

"Inside," Carter said. "The injury left him with a bit of a withered hand. He had several operations to try to repair it, but nothing ever worked. He tends to keep it in his pocket. He doesn't like to shake hands. He's a proud Bedouin, bin Shafiq. He doesn't respect physical infirmity."

"I don't suppose your sources in Riyadh can tell us where he's hiding within Zizi's empire?"

"Unfortunately they can't. But we know he's there. Put an agent into the House of Zizi, and eventually bin Shafiq will walk through the back door."

"Put an agent close to Zizi al-Bakari? How do you

propose we do that, Adrian? Zizi has more security than most heads of state."

"I wouldn't dream of interfering in matters operational," Carter said. "But rest assured that we're willing to be patient and that we intend to see it through to the end."

"Patience and follow-through aren't typical American virtues. You like to make a mess and move on to the next problem."

There was another long silence, broken this time by the clatter of Carter's pipe against the rim of the ashtray.

"What do you want, Gabriel?"

"Guarantees."

"There are no guarantees in our business. You know that."

"I want everything you have on bin Shafiq and al-Bakari."

"Within reason," Carter said. "I'm not going to give you a truckload of dirt on prominent figures in Washington."

"I want protection," Gabriel said. "When this thing goes down, we'll be the number-one suspect. We always are, even when we're not responsible. We're going to need your help weathering the storm."

"I can speak only for the DO," said Carter. "And I can assure you that we'll be there for you."

"We take out bin Shafiq at the time and place of our choosing, with no interference from Langley."

"The president would be grateful if you could avoid doing it on American soil."

"There are no guarantees in our business, Adrian."

"Touché."

"You might find this hard to believe, but I can't make this decision on my own. I need to speak to Amos and the prime minister."

"Amos and the prime minister will do what you tell them."

"Within reason."

"So what are you going to tell them?"

"That the American president needs a favor," Gabriel said. "And I want to help him."

12

TEL MEGIDDO, ISRAEL

THE PRIME MINISTER GRANTED Gabriel his operational charter at two-thirty the following afternoon. Gabriel headed straight for Armageddon. He reckoned it was a fine place to start.

The weather seemed perversely glorious for such an occasion: cool temperatures, a pale blue sky, a soft Judean breeze that plucked at his shirtsleeves as he sped along the Jaffa Road. He switched on the radio. The mournful music that had saturated the airwaves in the hours after the attempt on Shamron's life was now gone. A news bulletin came suddenly on the air. The prime minister had promised to do everything in his power to track down and punish those responsible for the attempt on Shamron's life. He made no mention of the fact that he already knew who was responsible, or that he had granted Gabriel the authority to kill him.

Gabriel plunged down the Bab al-Wad toward the sea,

weaving impatiently through the slower traffic, then raced the setting sun northward along the Coastal Plain. There was a security alert near Hadera—according to the radio, a suspected suicide bomber had managed to slip through a crossing in the Separation Fence near Tulkarm—and Gabriel was forced to wait by the side of the road for twenty minutes before heading into the Valley of Jezreel. Five miles from Afula a rounded hillock appeared on his left. In Hebrew it was known as Tel Megiddo, or the Mound of Megiddo. The rest of the world knew it as Armageddon, forecast in the Book of Revelation to be the site of the final earthly confrontation between the forces of good and evil. The battle had not yet begun, and the parking lot was empty except for a trio of dusty pickup trucks, a sign that the archaeological team was still at work.

Gabriel climbed out of his car and headed up the steep footpath to the summit. Tel Megiddo had been under periodic archaeological excavation for more than a century, and the top of the hill was cut by a maze of long, narrow trenches. Evidence of more than twenty cities had been discovered beneath the soil atop the *tel*, including one believed to have been built by King Solomon.

He stopped at the edge of a trench and peered down. Crouched on all fours was a small figure in a tan bush jacket, picking at the soil with a hand trowel. Gabriel thought of the last time he had stood over a man in an excavation pit and felt as though a lump of ice had been placed suddenly at the back of his neck. The archaeologist looked up and regarded him with a pair of clever brown eyes, then looked down again and resumed his work. "I've been waiting for you," said Eli Lavon. "What took you so long?"

Gabriel sat in the dirt at the edge of the pit and watched Lavon work. They had known each other since the Black September operation. Eli Lavon had been an *ayin*, a tracker. His job was to follow the terrorists and learn their habits. In many respects his assignment had been more dangerous even than Gabriel's, for Lavon had sometimes been exposed to the terrorists for days and weeks on end with no backup. After the unit disbanded, he'd settled in Vienna and opened a small investigative bureau called Wartime Claims and Inquiries. Operating on a shoestring budget, he had managed to track down millions of dollars' worth of looted Jewish assets and had played a significant role in prying a multibillion-dollar settlement from the banks of Switzerland. These days Lavon was working the dig at Megiddo and teaching archaeology part-time at Hebrew University.

"What have you got there, Eli?"

"A piece of pottery, I suspect." A gust of wind took his wispy, unkempt hair and blew it across his forehead. "What about you?"

"A Saudi billionaire who's trying to destroy the civilized world."

"Haven't they already done that?"

Gabriel smiled. "I need you, Eli. You know how to read balance sheets. You know how to follow the trail of money without anyone else knowing it."

"Who's the Saudi?"

"The chairman and CEO of Jihad Incorporated."

"Does the chairman have a name?"

"Abdul Aziz al-Bakari."

"*Zizi* al-Bakari?"

"One and the same."

"I suppose this has something to do with Shamron?"

"And the Vatican."

"What's Zizi's connection?"

Gabriel told him.

"I guess I don't need to ask what you intend to do with bin Shafiq," Lavon said. "Zizi's business empire is enormous. Bin Shafiq could be operating from anywhere in the world. How are we going to find him?"

"We're going to put an agent into Zizi's inner circle and wait for bin Shafiq to walk into it."

"An agent in Zizi's camp?" Lavon shook his head. "Can't be done."

"Yes, it can."

"How?"

"I'm going to find something Zizi wants," Gabriel said. "And then I'm going to give it to him."

"I'm listening."

Gabriel sat down at the edge of the excavation trench with his legs dangling over the side and explained how he planned to penetrate Jihad Incorporated. From the

bottom of the trench came sound of Lavon's work—
pick, pick, brush, brush, blow . . .

"Who's the agent?" he asked when Gabriel had finished.

"I don't have one yet."

Lavon was silent for a moment—*pick, pick, brush, brush, blow* . . .

"What do you want from me?"

"Turn Zizi al-Bakari and AAB Holdings inside out. I want a complete breakdown of every company he owns or controls. Profiles of all his top executives and the members of his personal entourage. I want to know how each person got there and how they've stayed. I want to know more about Zizi than Zizi knows about himself."

"And what happens when we go operational?"

"You'll go, too."

"I'm too old and tired for any rough stuff."

"You're the greatest surveillance artist in the history of the Office, Eli. I can't do this without you."

Lavon sat up and brushed his hands on his trousers. "Run an agent into Zizi al-Bakari's inner circle? Madness." He tossed Gabriel a hand trowel. "Get down here and help me. We're losing the light."

Gabriel climbed down into the pit and knelt beside his old friend. Together they scratched at the ancient soil, until night fell like a curtain over the valley.

IT WAS AFTER nine o'clock by the time they arrived at King Saul Boulevard. Lavon was long retired from the

Office but still gave the odd lecture at the Academy and still had credentials to enter the building whenever he pleased. Gabriel cleared him into the file rooms of the Research division, then headed down to a gloomy corridor two levels belowground. At the end of the hall was Room 456C. Affixed to the door was a paper sign, written in Gabriel's own stylish Hebrew hand: TEMPORARY COMMITTEE FOR THE STUDY OF TERROR THREATS IN WESTERN EUROPE. He decided to leave it for now.

He opened the combination lock, switched on the lights, and went inside. The room seemed frozen in time. They'd had several names for it: the Pod, the Quad, the Tank. Yaakov, a pockmarked tough from the Arab Affairs Department of Shabak, had christened it the Hellhole. Yossi from Research had called it the Village of the Damned, but then Yossi had read classics at Oxford and always brought an air of erudition to his work, even when the subjects weren't worthy of it.

Gabriel paused at the trestle table that Dina and Rimona had shared. Their constant squabbling over territory had driven him to near madness. The separation line he had drawn down the center of the table was still there, along with the warning Rimona had written on her side of the border: *Cross at your own risk*. Rimona was a captain in the IDF and worked for Aman, military intelligence. She was also Gilah Shamron's niece. She believed in defensible borders and had responded with retaliatory raids each time Dina had strayed over the line. At Dina's place now was the short note she had left there on the final day of the operation: *May we never have to return here again.* How naïve, thought Gabriel. Dina, of all people, should have known better.

He continued his slow tour of the room. In the corner stood the same pile of outmoded computer equipment that no one had ever bothered to remove. Before becoming the headquarters of Group Khaled, Room 456C had been nothing more than a dumping ground for old furniture and obsolete electronics, often used by the members of the night staff as a spot for romantic trysts. Gabriel's chalkboard was still there, too. He could scarcely decipher the last words he had written. He gazed up at the walls, which were covered with photographs of young Palestinian men. One photograph seized his attention, a boy with a beret on his head and a kaffiyeh draped over his shoulders, seated on the lap of Yasir Arafat: Khaled al-Khalifa at the funeral of his father, Sabri. Gabriel had killed Sabri, and he had killed Khaled as well.

He cleared the walls of the old photographs and put two new ones in their place. One showed a man in a kaffiyeh in the mountains of Afghanistan. The other showed the same man in a cashmere overcoat and trilby hat standing before a billionaire's home in Paris.

Group Khaled was now Group bin Shafiq.

FOR THE FIRST forty-eight hours Gabriel and Lavon worked alone. On the third day they were joined by

Yossi, a tall balding man with the bearing of an English intellectual. Rimona came on the fourth day, as did Yaakov, who arrived from Shabak headquarters carrying a box filled with material on the terrorists who had attacked Shamron's car. Dina was the last to arrive. Small and dark-haired, she had been standing in Tel Aviv's Dizengoff Street on October 19, 1994, when a Hamas suicide bomber had turned the Number 5 bus into a coffin for twenty-one people. Her mother and two of her sisters were among those killed; Dina had been seriously wounded and now walked with a slight limp. She had dealt with the loss by becoming an expert in terrorism. Indeed, Dina Sarid could recite the time, place, and butcher's bill of every act of terror ever committed against the State of Israel. She had once told Gabriel she knew more about the terrorists than they knew about themselves. Gabriel had believed her.

They divided into two areas of responsibility. Ahmed bin Shafiq and the Brotherhood of Allah became the province of Dina, Yaakov, and Rimona, while Yossi joined Lavon's excavation of AAB Holdings. Gabriel, at least for the moment, worked largely alone, for he had given himself the unenviable task of attempting to identify every painting ever acquired or sold by Zizi al-Bakari.

As the days wore on, the walls of Room 456C began to reflect the operation's unique nature. Upon one wall slowly appeared the murky outlines of a lethal new terrorist network led by a man who was largely a ghost. To the best of their ability they retraced bin Shafiq's long journey through the bloodstream of Islamic extremism. Wherever there had been trouble, it seemed, there had been bin Shafiq, handing out Saudi oil money and Wahhabi propaganda by the fistful: Afghanistan, Lebanon, Egypt, Algeria, Jordan, Pakistan, Chechnya, Bosnia, and, of course, the Palestinian Authority. They were not without significant leads, however, because in carrying out two major attacks, bin Shafiq and the Brotherhood had surrendered more than a dozen names that could be investigated for connections and associations. And then there was Ibrahim el-Banna, the Egyptian imam of death, and Professor Ali Massoudi, the recruiter and talent spotter.

On the opposite wall there appeared another network: AAB Holdings. Using open sources and some that were not so open, Lavon painstakingly sifted through the layers of Zizi's financial empire and assembled the disparate pieces like bits of an ancient artifact. At the top of the structure was AAB itself. Beneath it was an intricate financial web of subholding companies and corporate shells that allowed Zizi to extend his influence to nearly every corner of the globe under conditions of near-perfect corporate secrecy. With most of his companies registered in Switzerland and the Cayman Islands, Lavon likened Zizi to a financial stealth fighter, capable of striking at will while avoiding detection by enemy radar. Despite the opaque nature of Zizi's empire, Lavon came to the conclusion the numbers didn't add up. "Zizi couldn't possibly have earned enough from his early investments to justify the size of his later acquisitions," he explained to Gabriel. "AAB Holdings is a front for the House of Saud." As for trying to find Ahmed bin Shafiq anywhere within Zizi's financial octopus, Lavon likened it to finding a needle in the Arabian Desert. "Not impossible," he said, "but you're likely to die of thirst trying."

Yossi saw to Zizi's personnel. He focused on the relatively small team that worked inside Zizi's Geneva headquarters, along with companies wholly owned or controlled by AAB. Most of his time, though, was devoted to Zizi's large personal entourage. Their photographs soon covered the wall above Yossi's workspace and stood in stark contrast to those of bin Shafiq's terror network. New photographs arrived each day as Yossi monitored Zizi's frenetic movements around the globe. Zizi arriving for a meeting in London. Zizi consulting with German automakers in Stuttgart. Zizi enjoying the view of the Red Sea from his new hotel in Sharm el-Sheik. Zizi conferring with the king of Jordan about a possible construction deal. Zizi opening a desalination plant in Yemen. Zizi collecting a humanitarian award from an Islamic group in Montreal whose Web site, Yossi pointed out, contained an open call for the destruction of the State of Israel.

As for Gabriel's corner of the room, it was a sanctuary from the realms of terror and finance. His wall was covered not with the faces of terrorists or business executives but with dozens of photographs of French Impressionist prints. And while Lavon and Yossi spent their days digging through dreary ledger sheets and computer printouts, Gabriel could often be seen leafing through old catalogs, Impressionist monographs, and press clippings describing Zizi's exploits on the world art scene.

By the end of the tenth day, Gabriel had decided how he was going to slip an agent into Jihad Incorporated. He walked over to Yossi's collage of photographs and gazed at a single image. It showed a gaunt, gray-haired Englishman, seated next to Zizi six months earlier at the Impressionist and Modern Art auction at Christie's in New York. Gabriel removed the photograph and held it up for the others to see. "This man," he said. "He has to go." Then he called Adrian Carter on a private secure number at Langley and told him how he planned to penetrate the House of Zizi. "All you need now is a painting and a girl," Carter said. "You find the painting. I'll get you the girl."

GABRIEL LEFT King Saul Boulevard a little earlier than usual and drove to Ein Kerem. There were still security guards posted outside the intensive care unit of the Hadassah Medical Center, but Shamron was alone when Gabriel entered his room. "The prodigal son has decided to pay me a visit," he said bitterly. "It's a good thing we're a desert people. Otherwise you would put me on an ice floe and cast me out to sea."

Gabriel sat down next to the bed. "I've been here at least a half dozen times."

"When?"

"Late at night when you're asleep."

"You hover over me? Like Gilah and the doctors? Why can't you come during the day like a normal person?"

"I've been busy."

"The prime minister isn't too busy to come see me at a reasonable hour." Shamron, his injured neck immobilized by a heavy plastic brace, gave Gabriel a vindictive sideways glance. "He told me he's allowing Amos to find his own man for Special Ops so that you can run this fool's errand for Adrian Carter and the Americans."

"I take it you disapprove."

"Vehemently." Shamron closed his eyes for a long moment—long enough for Gabriel to cast a nervous glance at the bank of monitors next to his bed. "Blue and white," he said finally. "We do things for ourselves. We don't ask others for help, and we don't help others with problems of their own making. And we certainly don't volunteer to serve as a patsy for Adrian Carter."

"You're in this hospital bed instead of at your desk in the Prime Minister's Office. That makes Zizi al-Bakari and Ahmed bin Shafiq my problem, too. Besides, the world has changed, Ari. We need to work together to survive. The old rules don't apply."

Shamron lifted his heavily veined hand and pointed toward the plastic water cup on his bedside table. Gabriel held it to Shamron's lips while he sipped water through the straw.

"At whose request are you undertaking this errand?" Shamron asked. "Is it Adrian Carter, or higher up the chain of command?" Greeted by Gabriel's silence, Shamron angrily pushed the water cup away. "Is it your intention to treat me as some sort of invalid? I'm still the prime minister's special adviser on all matters dealing with security and intelligence. I'm still the . . ." His voice trailed off with a sudden fatigue.

"You're still the *memuneh*," Gabriel said, finishing the sentence for him. In Hebrew, *memuneh* meant the one in charge. For many years the title had been reserved for Shamron.

"You're not going after some kid from Nablus, Gabriel. You have Ahmed bin Shafiq and Zizi al-Bakari in your sights. If something goes wrong, the world will fall on you from a very great height. And your friend Adrian Carter won't be there to help scrape you up. You might want to consider taking me into your confidence. I've done this sort of thing a time or two."

Gabriel poked his head into the corridor and asked the protective agents posted there to make certain any audio or visual surveillance of Shamron was switched off. Then he sat down again in the bedside chair and, with his mouth close to Shamron's ear, told him everything. Shamron's gaze, for a moment at least, seemed a little more focused. When he posed his first question it was almost possible for Gabriel to conjure an image of the iron bar of a man who had walked into his life one September afternoon in 1972.

"You've made up your mind about using a woman?"

Gabriel nodded.

"You're going to need someone whose story will withstand the scrutiny of Zizi's well-paid security staff. You can't use one of our girls, and you can't use a non-Israeli Jew. If Zizi even suspects he's looking at a Jewish girl, he'll steer clear of her. You need a gentile."

"What I need," said Gabriel, "is an American girl."

"Where are you going to get one?"

Gabriel's one-word answer caused Shamron to frown. "I don't like the idea of us being responsible for one of their agents. What if something goes wrong?"

"What could go wrong?"

"Everything," Shamron said. "You know that better than anyone."

Shamron seemed suddenly weary. Gabriel lowered the dimmer on the bedside lamp.

"What are you going to do?" Shamron asked. "Read me a bedtime story?"

"I'm going to sit with you until you fall asleep."

"Gilah can do that. Go home and get some rest. You're going to need it."

"I'll stay for a while."

"Go home," Shamron insisted. "There's someone waiting there who's anxious to see you."

*   *   *

TWENTY MINUTES LATER, when Gabriel turned into Narkiss Street, he saw lights burning in his apartment. He parked his Skoda around the corner and stole quietly up the darkened walkway into the building. As he slipped inside the apartment the air was heavy with the scent of vanilla. Chiara was seated cross-legged atop his examination table in the harsh light of his halogen work lamps. She scrutinized Gabriel as he came inside, then turned her gaze once more to what had once been a meticulously decorated living room.

"I like what you've done with the place, Gabriel. Please tell me you didn't give away our bed, too."

Gabriel shook his head, then kissed her.

"How long are you in town?" she asked.

"I leave tomorrow morning."

"As usual, my timing is perfect. How long will you be gone?"

"Hard to say."

"Can you take me with you?"

"Not this time."

"Where are you going?"

Gabriel eased her off the examination table and switched off the lights.

13

LONDON

I NEED A VAN Gogh, Julian."

"Don't we all, petal."

Isherwood pushed back his coat sleeve and glanced at his wristwatch. It was ten in the morning. He was usually in his gallery by now, not strolling along the lakeshore in St. James's Park. He paused for a moment to watch a flotilla of ducks slicing through the calm water toward the island. Gabriel used the opportunity to cast his eyes around the park to see if they were being followed. Then he hooked Isherwood by the inside of the elbow and towed him toward the Horse Guards Road.

They were a mismatched pair, figures from different paintings. Gabriel wore dark jeans and suede brogues that made no sound as he walked. His hands were thrust into the pockets of his leather jacket, his shoulders were slouched forward, and his green eyes were flickering restlessly about the park. Isherwood, fifteen years older than

Gabriel and several inches taller, wore a chalk-striped suit and woolen overcoat. His gray locks hung over the back of his coat collar and floated up and down with each lanky, loose-limbed stride. There was something precarious about Julian Isherwood. Gabriel, as always, had to resist an urge to reach out and steady him.

They had known each other for thirty years. Isherwood's backbone-of-England surname and English scale concealed the fact that he was not, at least technically, English at all. British by nationality and passport, yes, but German by birth, French by upbringing, and Jewish by religion. Only a handful of trusted friends knew that Isherwood had staggered into London as a child refugee in 1942 after being carried across the snowbound Pyrenees by a pair of Basque shepherds. Or that his father, the renowned Paris art dealer Samuel Isakowitz, had been murdered at the Sobibor death camp along with Isherwood's mother. There was something else Isherwood kept secret from his competitors in the London art world—and from nearly everyone else, for that matter. In the lexicon of the Office, Julian Isherwood was a *sayan*, a volunteer Jewish helper. He had been recruited by Ari Shamron for a single purpose: to help build and maintain the cover of a single very special agent.

"How's my friend Mario Delvecchio?" Isherwood asked.

"Vanished without a trace," said Gabriel. "I hope my unveiling didn't cause you any problems."

"None whatsoever."

"No rumors on the street? No awkward questions at the auctions? No visits from the men of MI5?"

"Are you asking me whether people in London regard me as a poisonous Israeli spy?"

"That's exactly what I'm asking you."

"All quiet on this front, but then we were never very flashy about our relationship, were we? That's not your way. You're not flashy about anything. One of the two or three best art restorers in the world, and no one really knows who you are. It's a shame, that."

They came to the corner of Great George Street. Gabriel led them to the right, into Birdcage Walk.

"Who knows about us in London, Julian? Who knows that you had a professional relationship with Mario?"

Isherwood looked up at the dripping trees along the pavement. "Very few people, really. There's Jeremy Crabbe over at Bonhams, of course. He's still miffed at you for stealing that Rubens from under his nose." Isherwood placed a long, bony hand on Gabriel's shoulder. "I have a buyer for it. All I need now is the painting."

"I put the varnish on yesterday before I left Jerusalem," Gabriel said. "I'll use one of our front shippers to get it here as quickly as possible. You could have it by the end of the week. By the way, you owe me a hundred and fifty thousand pounds."

"Check's in the mail, petal."

"Who else?" Gabriel asked. "Who else knows about us?"

Isherwood made a show of thought. "The wretched

Oliver Dimbleby," he said. "You remember Oliver. I introduced you to him at Green's one afternoon when we were having lunch. Tubby little dealer from King Street. Tried to buy my gallery out from under me one time."

Gabriel remembered. Somewhere he still had the showy gold-plated business card Oliver had pressed upon him. Oliver had barely looked in Gabriel's direction. Oliver was that way.

"I've done many a favor for Crabbe over the years," Isherwood said. "The sorts of favors we don't like to talk about in our line of work. As for Oliver Dimbleby, I helped him clean up a terrible mess he made with a girl who worked in his gallery. I took the poor waif in. Gave her a job. She left me for another dealer. Always do, my girls. What is it about me that drives women away? I'm an easy mark, that's it. Women see that. So did your little outfit. Herr Heller certainly did."

Herr Rudolf Heller, venture capitalist from Zurich, was one of Shamron's favorite aliases. It was the one he had used when recruiting Isherwood.

"How is he, by the way?"

"He sends his best."

Gabriel lowered his eyes to the damp pavement of Birdcage Walk. A breath of cold wind rose from the park. Dead leaves rattled across their path.

"I need a van Gogh," Gabriel said again.

"Yes, I heard you the first time. The problem is, I don't *have* a van Gogh. In case you've forgotten, Isherwood Fine Arts specializes in Old Masters. If you want Impressionists, you'll have to look elsewhere."

"But you know where I can get one."

"Unless you're planning on stealing one, there's nothing on the market right now—at least not that I'm aware of."

"But that's not true, is it, Julian? You *do* know about a van Gogh. You told me about it once a hundred years ago—a story about a previously unknown painting your father had seen in Paris between the wars."

"Not just my father," Isherwood said. "I've seen it, too. Vincent painted it in Auvers, during the final days of his life. There's a rumor it might have been his undoing. The problem is, the painting isn't for sale, and it probably never will be. The family has made it clear to me they'll never part with it. They're also bound and determined to keep its very existence a secret."

"Tell me the story again."

"I don't have time now, Gabriel. I have a ten-thirty appointment at the gallery."

"Cancel your appointment, Julian. Tell me about that painting."

ISHERWOOD CROSSED the footbridge over the lake and headed toward his gallery in St. James's. Gabriel shoved his hands a little deeper into his coat pockets and followed after him.

"Ever cleaned him?" Isherwood asked.

"Vincent? Never."

"How much do you know about his final days?"

"About what everyone knows, I suppose."

"Bollocks, Gabriel. Don't try to play the fool with me. Your brain is like the *Grove Dictionary of Art*."

"It was the summer of 1890, wasn't it?"

Isherwood gave a professorial nod of his head. "Please continue."

"After Vincent left the asylum in Saint-Rémy, he came to Paris to see Theo and Johanna. He visited several galleries and exhibits, and stopped at Père Tanguy's artists' supply store to check on some canvases he had in storage there. After three days he began to get restless, so he boarded a train for Auvers-sur-Oise, about twenty miles outside Paris. He thought Auvers would be ideal, a quiet country setting for his work but still close to Theo, his financial and emotional lifeline. He took a room above Café Ravoux and placed himself in the care of Dr. Paul Gachet."

Gabriel took Isherwood's arm and together they darted through an opening in the traffic on the Mall and entered the Marlborough Road.

"He started painting immediately. His style, like his mood, was calmer and more subdued. The agitation and violence that characterized much of his work at Saint-Rémy and Arles was gone. He was also incredibly prolific. In the two months Vincent stayed in Auvers he produced more than eighty paintings. A painting a day. Some days *two*."

They turned into King Street. Gabriel stopped suddenly. Ahead of them, waddling along the pavement toward the entrance of Christie's auction house, was Oliver Dimbleby. Isherwood turned suddenly into Bury Street and picked up where Gabriel had left off.

"When Vincent wasn't at his easel, he could usually be found in his room above Café Ravoux or at the home of Gachet. Gachet was a widower with two children, a boy of fifteen and a daughter who turned twenty-one during Vincent's stay in Auvers."

"Marguerite."

Isherwood nodded. "She was a pretty girl and she was also deeply infatuated with Vincent. She agreed to pose for him—unfortunately with*out* her father's permission. He painted her in the garden of the family home, dressed in a white gown."

"*Marguerite Gachet in the Garden*," Gabriel said.

"And when her father found out, he was furious."

"But she posed for him again."

"Correct," Isherwood said. "The second painting is *Marguerite Gachet at the Piano*. She also appears in *Undergrowth with Two Figures*, a deeply symbolic work that some art historians saw as a prophecy of Vincent's own death. But I believe it's Vincent and Marguerite walking down the aisle—Vincent's premonition of marriage."

"But there was a fourth painting of Marguerite?"

"*Marguerite Gachet at Her Dressing Table*," said Isherwood. "It's the best of the lot by far. Only a handful of people have ever seen it or even know it exists. Vincent painted it a few days before his death. And then it disappeared."

THEY WALKED TO Duke Street, then slipped through a narrow passageway, into a brick quadrangle called Mason's Yard. Isherwood's gallery occupied an old Victorian warehouse in the far corner, wedged between the offices of a minor Greek shipping company and a pub that was inevitably filled with pretty office girls who rode motor scooters. Isherwood started across the yard toward the gallery, but Gabriel snared his lapel and pulled him in the opposite direction. As they strolled the perimeter through the cold shadows, Isherwood talked of Vincent's death.

"On the evening of July 27, Vincent returned to Café Ravoux in obvious pain and struggled up the stairs to his room. Madame Ravoux followed after him and discovered he'd been shot. She sent for a doctor. The doctor, of course, was Gachet himself. He decided to leave the bullet in Vincent's abdomen and summoned Theo to Auvers. When Theo arrived the following morning, he found Vincent sitting up in bed smoking his pipe. He died later that day."

They came into a patch of brilliant sunshine. Isherwood shaded his eyes with his long hand.

"There are many unanswered questions about Vincent's suicide. It's not clear where he got the gun or the precise place where he shot himself. There are questions, too, about his motivation. Was his suicide the culmination of his long struggle with madness? Was he distraught over a letter he'd just received from Theo suggesting that Theo could no longer afford to support Vincent along with his own wife and child? Did Vincent take his own life as part of a plan to make his work relevant and commercially viable? I've never been satisfied with any of those theories. I believe it has to do with Gachet. More to the point, with Dr. Gachet's daughter."

They slipped into the shadows of the yard once more. Isherwood lowered his hand.

"The day before Vincent shot himself, he came to Gachet's house. The two quarreled violently, and Vincent threatened Gachet with a gun. What was the reason for the argument? Gachet later claimed that it had something to do with a picture frame, of all things. I believe it was over Marguerite. I think it's possible it had something to do with *Marguerite Gachet at Her Dressing Table*. It's an exquisite work, one of Vincent's better portraits. The pose and the setting are clearly representative of a bride on her wedding night. Its significance would not have been lost on a man like Paul Gachet. If he'd seen the painting— and there's no reason to believe he didn't—he would have been incensed. Perhaps Gachet told Vincent that marriage to his daughter was out of the question. Perhaps he forbade Vincent ever to paint Marguerite again. Perhaps he forbade Vincent ever to *see* Marguerite again. What we do know is that Marguerite Gachet wasn't present at Vincent's funeral, though she was spotted the next day tearfully placing sunflowers on his grave. She never married, and lived as something of a recluse in Auvers until her death in 1949."

They passed the entrance to Isherwood's gallery and kept walking.

"After Vincent's death his paintings became the property of Theo. He arranged for a shipment of the works Vincent had produced at Auvers and stored them at Père Tanguy's in Paris. Theo, of course, died not long after Vincent, and the paintings became the property of Johanna. None of Vincent's other relatives wanted any of his work. Johanna's brother thought them worthless and suggested they be burned." Isherwood stopped walking. "Can you imagine?" He propelled himself forward again with a long stride. "Johanna catalogued the inventory and worked tirelessly to establish Vincent's reputation. It's because of Johanna that Vincent van Gogh is regarded as a great artist. But there's a glaring omission in her list of Vincent's known works."

Marguerite Gachet at Her Dressing Table.

"Precisely," said Isherwood. "Was it an accident or intentional? We'll never know, of course, but I have a theory. I believe Johanna knew that the painting may have contributed to Vincent's death. Whatever the case, it was sold for a song from the storeroom at Père Tanguy's within a year or so of Vincent's death and never seen again. Which is where my father enters the story."

*   *   *

THEY COMPLETED THEIR first circuit of the yard and started a second. Isherwood's pace slowed as he began to talk of his father.

"He was always a Berliner at heart. He would have stayed there forever. That wasn't possible, of course. My father saw the storm clouds coming and didn't waste any time getting out of town. By the end of 1936, we'd left Berlin and moved to Paris." He looked at Gabriel. "Too bad your grandfather didn't do the same thing. He was a great painter, your grandfather. You come from a good bloodline, my boy."

Gabriel quickly changed the subject. "Your father's gallery was on the rue de la Boétie, wasn't it?"

"Of course," Isherwood replied. "The rue de la Boétie was the center of the art world at that time. Paul Rosenberg had his gallery at Number Twenty-one. Picasso and Olga lived on the other side of the courtyard at Number Twenty-three. Georges Wildenstein, Paul Guillaume, Josse Hessel, Étienne Bignou—*everyone* was there. Isakowitz Fine Arts was next door to Paul Rosenberg's. We lived in an apartment above the exposition rooms. Picasso was my 'Uncle Pablo.' He used to let me watch him paint, and Olga would give me chocolates until I was sick."

Isherwood permitted himself a brief smile, which faded quickly as he resumed the story of his father in Paris.

"The Germans came in May 1940 and started looting the place. My father rented a chateau in Bordeaux on the

Vichy side of the line and moved most of his important pieces there. We followed him soon after. The Germans crossed over into the Unoccupied Zone in 1942, and the roundups and deportations began. We were trapped. My father paid a pair of Basque shepherds to take me over the mountains to Spain. He gave me some documents to carry with me, a professional inventory and a couple of diaries. It was the last time I ever saw him."

A horn sounded loudly in Duke Street; a squadron of pigeons burst into flight over the shadowed yard.

"It was years before I got around to reading the diaries. In one of them I found an entry about a painting my father had seen in Paris one night at the home of man named Isaac Weinberg."

"Marguerite Gachet at Her Dressing Table."

"Weinberg told my father he'd bought the painting from Johanna not long after Vincent's death and had given it to his wife as a birthday gift. Apparently Mrs. Weinberg bore a resemblance to Marguerite. My father asked Isaac whether he would be willing to sell, and Isaac said he wasn't. He asked my father not to mention the painting to anyone, and my father was all too happy to oblige him."

Isherwood's mobile phone chirped. He ignored it.

"In the early seventies, right before I met you, I was in Paris on business. I had a few hours to kill between appointments and decided to look up Isaac Weinberg. I went to the address in the Marais that was listed in my father's notebooks, but Weinberg wasn't there. He hadn't survived the war. But I met his son, Marc, and told him about the entry in my father's notes. He denied the story at first, but finally relented and allowed me to see the painting after swearing me to eternal secrecy. It was hanging in his daughter's bedroom. I asked whether he might be interested in parting with it. He refused, of course."

"You're certain it's Vincent?"

"Without a doubt."

"And you haven't been back since?"

"Monsieur Weinberg made it quite clear the painting would never be for sale. I didn't see the point." Isherwood stopped walking and turned to face Gabriel. "All right, petal. I've told you the story. Now suppose you tell me what this is all about."

"I need that van Gogh, Julian."

"Whatever for?"

Gabriel took Isherwood's sleeve and led him toward the door of the gallery.

THERE WAS an intercom panel next to the glass door, with four buttons and four corresponding nameplates. One read: ISHER OO FINE AR S: BY APPOINTMENT ONLY. Isherwood opened the door with a key and led Gabriel up a flight of stairs covered in a threadbare brown carpet. On the landing were two more doors. To the left was a melancholy little travel agency. The owner, a spinster named Miss Archer, was seated at her desk beneath a poster of a happy couple splashing in azure water. Isherwood's door was on the right. His latest secretary, an apologetic-looking creature named Tanya, glanced up furtively as Isherwood and Gabriel came inside. "This is Mr. Klein," said Isherwood. "He'd like to have a look at something upstairs. No interruptions, please. That's a good girl, Tanya darling."

They entered a lift the size of a phone booth and rode it upward, standing so close to one another that Gabriel could smell last night's claret on Isherwood's breath. A few seconds later the lift shuddered to a stop and the door opened with a groan. Isherwood's exposition room was in semidarkness, illuminated only by the mid-morning sun filtering through the skylight. Isherwood settled himself on the velvet-covered divan in the center of the room while Gabriel led himself on a slow tour. The paintings were nearly invisible in the deep shadows, but he knew them well: a Venus by Luini, a nativity by Perino del Vaga, a baptism of Christ by Bordone, a luminous landscape by Claude.

Isherwood opened his mouth to speak, but Gabriel raised a finger to his lips and from his coat pocket removed what appeared to be an ordinary Nokia cellular telephone. It was indeed a Nokia, but it contained several additional features not available to ordinary customers, such as a GPS beacon and a device that could detect the presence of hidden transmitters. Gabriel toured the room again, this time with his eyes on the display panel of the phone. Then he sat down next to Isherwood and, in a low voice, told him why he needed the van Gogh.

"*Zizi* al-Bakari?" asked Isherwood incredulously. "A bloody terrorist? Are you sure?"

"He's not planting the bombs, Julian. He's not even *making* the bombs. But he's footing the bill, and he's using his business empire to facilitate the movement of the men and matériel around the globe. In today's world that's just as bad. *Worse.*"

"I met him once, but not so he'd remember. Went to a party at his estate out in Gloucestershire. *Huge* party. Sea of people. Zizi was nowhere to be found. Came down at the end like bloody Gatsby. Surrounded by bodyguards, even inside his own home. Strange chap. Voracious collector, though, isn't he? Art. Women. Anything money can buy. Predatory, from what I hear. Never had any dealings with him, of course. Zizi's tastes don't run to the Old Masters. Zizi goes for the Impressionists and a bit of other Modern stuff. All the Saudis are like that. They don't hold with the Christian imagery of the Old Masters."

Gabriel sat down next to Isherwood. "He doesn't have a van Gogh, Julian. He's dropped hints from time to time that he's looking for one. And not just any van Gogh. He wants something special."

"From what I hear, he buys very carefully. He spends buckets of money, but he does it wisely. He's got a museum-quality collection, but I didn't realize it was sans van Gogh."

"His art adviser is an Englishman named Andrew Malone. Know him?"

"Unfortunately, Andrew and I are well acquainted. He's burrowed his way deeply into Zizi's pockets. Spends holidays on Zizi's yacht. Big as the bloody *Titanic*, from what I hear. Andrew is as slippery as they come. Dirty, too."

"In what way?"

"He's taking it on both ends, petal."

"What do you mean, Julian?"

"Andrew has an exclusive agreement with Zizi, which means he's not supposed to take money from any other dealer or collector. It's the way big boys like Zizi ensure that the advice they're being given is untainted by any conflicts of interest."

"What's Malone up to?"

"Shakedowns, double commissions, you name it."

"You're sure?"

"Positive, petal. Everyone in town knows that in order to do business with Zizi, you have to pay a toll to Andrew Malone."

Isherwood was suddenly off the divan and pacing the length of the exposition room.

"So what's your plan then? Lure Zizi out of his hole with a van Gogh? Dangle it in front of him and hope he takes it hook, line, and sinker? But there'll be something at the other end of the line, won't there? One of your agents?"

"Something like that."

"And where are you planning to stage this extravaganza? Here, I take it?"

Gabriel looked around the room approvingly. "Yes," he said. "I think this will do quite nicely."

"I was afraid of that."

"I need a dealer," Gabriel said. "Someone well known in the trade. Someone I can trust."

"I'm Old Masters, not Impressionists."

"It won't matter for a quiet deal like this."

Isherwood didn't argue the point. He knew Gabriel was right. "Have you considered the consequences for *moi* if your little gambit proves successful? I'll be a marked man. I can deal with the likes of Oliver Dimbleby, but al-bloody-fucking-Qaeda is another thing altogether."

"Obviously, we'll have to make some postoperational provisions for your security."

"I love your euphemisms, Gabriel. You and Shamron always resort to euphemisms when the truth is too awful to say aloud. They'll put a fatwa on my head. I'll have to close up shop. Go into bloody hiding."

Gabriel appeared unmoved by Isherwood's protests. "You're not getting any younger, Julian. You're nearing the end of the road. You have no children. No heirs. Who's going to take over the gallery? Besides, have you taken a moment to calculate your commission on the private sale of a previously unknown van Gogh? Add to that your earnings on a fire sale of your existing stock. Things could be a lot worse, Julian."

"I'm picturing a nice villa in the south of France. A new name. A team of Office security boys to look after me in my dotage."

"Make sure you have a spare room for me."

Isherwood sat down again. "Your plan has one serious flaw, petal. It will be easier for you to snare your terrorist than it will be to land that van Gogh. Assuming it's still in the possession of the Weinberg family, what makes you think they're going to give it up?"

"Who said anything about giving it up?"

Isherwood smiled. "I'll get you the address."

14

The Marais, Paris

"YOU SHOULD EAT SOMETHING," said Uzi Navot. Gabriel shook his head. He'd eaten lunch on the train from London.

"Have the borscht," Navot said. "You can't come to Jo Goldenberg and not have the borscht."

"Yes, I can," Gabriel said. "Purple food makes me nervous."

Navot caught the waiter's eye and ordered an extra-large bowl of borscht and a glass of kosher red wine. Gabriel frowned and looked out the window. A steady rain was drumming against the paving stones of the rue des Rosiers, and it was nearly dark. He had wanted to meet Navot someplace other than the most famous delicatessen in the most visible Jewish district of Paris, but Navot had insisted on Jo Goldenberg, based on his long-held belief that the best place to hide a pine tree was in a forest.

"This place is making me nervous," Gabriel murmured. "Let's take a walk."

"In this weather? Forget it. Besides, no one is going to recognize you in that getup. Even I nearly didn't notice you when you came through the door."

Gabriel looked at the ghostly face reflected in the glass. He wore a dark corduroy flat cap, contact lenses that turned his green eyes to brown, and a false goatee that accentuated his already narrow features. He had traveled to Paris on a German passport bearing the name Heinrich Kiever. After arriving at the Gare du Nord he'd spent two hours walking the Seine embankments, checking his tail for surveillance. In his shoulder bag was a worn volume of Voltaire he'd purchased from a *bouquiniste* on the Quai Montebello.

He turned his head and looked at Navot. He was a heavy-shouldered man, several years younger than Gabriel, with short strawberry-blond hair and pale blue eyes. In the lexicon of the Office, he was a *katsa*, an undercover field operative and case officer. Armed with an array of languages, a roguish charm, and a fatalistic arrogance, he had penetrated Palestinian terrorist cells and recruited agents in Arab embassies scattered across western Europe. He had sources in nearly all the European security and intelligence services and oversaw a vast network of *sayanim*. He could always count on getting the best table in the grill room at the Ritz in Paris because the maître d'hôtel was a paid informant, as was the chief of the maid staff. He was dressed now in a gray tweed jacket and black roll-neck sweater, for his identity in Paris was one Vincent Laffont, a freelance travel writer of Breton descent who spent most of his time living out of a suitcase. In London he was known as Clyde Bridges, European marketing director of an obscure Canadian business-software firm. In Madrid he was a German of independent means who idled away the hours in cafés and bars and traveled to relieve the burdens of a restless and complex soul.

Navot reached into his briefcase and produced a manila file folder, which he placed on the table in front of Gabriel. "There's the owner of your van Gogh," he said. "Have a look."

Gabriel discreetly lifted the cover. The photograph inside showed an attractive middle-aged woman with dark wavy hair, olive skin, and a long aquiline nose. She was holding an umbrella above her head and descending a flight of stone steps in Montmartre.

"Hannah Weinberg," Navot said. "Forty-four, unmarried, childless. Jewish demographics in microcosm. An only child with no children. At this rate, we won't *need* a state." Navot looked down and picked morosely at a bowl of potted chicken and vegetables. He was prone to fits of despondency, especially when it came to the future of the Jewish people. "She owns a small boutique up in Montmartre on the rue Lepic. Boutique Lepic is the name of it. I snapped that photo of her earlier this afternoon as she was walking to lunch. One is left with the impression the boutique is more of a hobby than a vocation. I've seen her bank accounts. Marc Weinberg left his daughter very well off."

The waiter approached and placed a bowl of purple dreck in front of Gabriel. He immediately pushed it toward the center of the table. He couldn't bear the smell of borscht. Navot dropped a lump of bread into his broth and prodded it with his spoon.

"Weinberg was an interesting fellow. He was a prominent lawyer here in Paris. He was also something of a memory militant. He brought a great deal of pressure on the government to come clean about the role of the French in the Holocaust. As a result he wasn't terribly popular in some circles here in Paris."

"And the daughter? What are her politics?"

"Moderate Eurosocialist, but that's no crime in France. She also inherited a bit of militancy from her father. She's involved with a group that's trying to combat the anti-Semitism here. She actually met with the French president once. Look underneath that photograph."

Gabriel found a clipping from a French magazine about the current wave of anti-Semitism in France. The accompanying photograph showed Jewish protesters marching across one of the Seine bridges. At the head of the column, carrying a sign that read STOP THE HATRED NOW, was Hannah Weinberg.

"Has she ever been to Israel?"

"At least four times. Shabak is working that end of things to make certain she wasn't sitting up in Ramallah plotting with the terrorists. I'm sure they'll turn up nothing on her. She's golden, Gabriel. She's a gift from the intelligence gods."

"Sexual preferences?"

"Men, as far as we can tell. She's involved with a civil servant."

"Jewish?"

"Thank God."

"Have you been inside her flat."

"I went in with the *neviot* team myself."

Neviot teams specialized in gathering intelligence from hard targets such as apartments, offices, and hotel rooms. The unit employed some of the best break-in artists and thieves in the world. Gabriel had other plans for them later in the operation—provided, of course, Hannah Weinberg agreed to part with her van Gogh.

"Did you see the painting?"

Navot nodded. "She keeps it in her childhood bedroom."

"How did it look?"

"You want my assessment of a van Gogh?" Navot shrugged his heavy shoulders. "It's a very nice painting of a girl sitting at a dressing table. I'm not artistic like you. I'm potted chicken and a nice love story at the movies. You're not eating your soup."

"I don't like it, Uzi. I told you I don't like it."

Navot took Gabriel's spoon and swirled the dab of sour cream, lightening the hue of the purple mixture.

"We had a peek at her papers," Navot said. "We rummaged through her closets and drawers. We left a little something on her phone and computer as well. One can never be too careful in a situation like this."

"Room coverage?"

Navot appeared hurt by the question. "Of course," he said.

"What are you using for a listening post?"

"A van for the moment. If she agrees to help us, we're going to need something more permanent. One of the *neviot* boys is already scouting the neighborhood for a suitable flat."

Navot pushed the remnants of his potted chicken to one side and started in on Gabriel's borscht. For all his European sophistication, he was at heart still a peasant from the shtetl.

"I can see where this is going," he said between spoonfuls. "You get to track down the bad guy, and I get to spend the next year watching a girl. But that's the way it's always been with us, hasn't it? You get all the glory while the field hands like me do all the spade work. My God, you saved the Pope himself. How's a mere mortal like me supposed to compete with that?"

"Shut up and eat your soup, Uzi."

Being Shamron's chosen one had not come without a price. Gabriel was used to the professional jealousy of his colleagues.

"I have to leave Paris tomorrow," Navot said. "I'll be gone only a day."

"Where are you going?"

"Amos wants a word with me." He paused, then

added, "I think it's about the Special Ops job. The job *you* turned down."

It made sense, Gabriel thought. Navot was an extremely capable field agent who'd taken part in several major operations, including a few with Gabriel.

"Is that what you want, Uzi? A job at King Saul Boulevard?"

Navot shrugged. "I've been out here in the field a long time. Bella wants to get married. It's hard to have a stable home life when you live like this. Sometimes when I wake up in the morning, I never know where I'm going to wind up at the end of the day. I can have breakfast in Berlin, lunch in Amsterdam, and be sitting in King Saul Boulevard at midnight briefing the director." Navot gave Gabriel a conspiratorial smile. "That's what the Americans don't understand about us. They put their case officers into little boxes and slap their wrists when they step outside the lines. The Office isn't that way. It never was. That's what makes it the greatest job in the world—and that's why our service is so much better than theirs. They wouldn't know what to do with a man like you."

Navot had lost interest in the borscht. He pushed it across the table, so that it looked as though Gabriel had eaten it. Gabriel reached for the glass of wine but thought better of it. He had a headache from the train ride and the rainy Paris weather, and the kosher wine smelled about as appealing as paint thinner.

"But it takes its toll on marriages and relationships, doesn't it, Gabriel? How many of us are divorced? How many of us have had affairs with girls out there in the field? At least if I'm working in Tel Aviv, I'll be around more often. There's still a lot of travel with the job but less than this. Bella has a place near the beach in Caesarea. It will be a nice life." He shrugged again. "Listen to me. I'm acting as though Amos has offered me the job. Amos hasn't offered me anything. For all I know, he's bringing me to King Saul Boulevard to fire me."

"Don't be ridiculous. You're the most qualified man for the job. You'll be my boss, Uzi."

"Your boss? *Please*. No one is your boss, Gabriel. Only the old man." Navot's expression turned suddenly grave. "How is he? I hear it's not good."

"He's going to be fine," Gabriel assured him.

They lapsed into silence as the waiter came to the table and cleared away the dishes. When he was gone again, Gabriel gave the file folder to Navot, who slipped it back into his briefcase.

"So how are you going to play it with Hannah Weinberg?"

"I'm going to ask her to give up a painting that's worth eighty million dollars. I have to tell her the truth—or at least some version of the truth. And then we'll have to deal with the security consequences."

"What about the approach? Are you going to dance for a while or go straight in for the kill?"

"I don't dance, Uzi. I've never had time for dancing."

"At least you won't have any trouble convincing her

who you are. Thanks to the French security service, everyone in Paris knows your name and your face. When do you want to start?"

"Tonight."

"You're in luck then."

Navot looked toward the window. Gabriel followed his gaze and saw a woman with dark hair walking down the rue des Rosiers beneath the shelter of an umbrella. He stood without a word and headed toward the door. "Don't worry, Gabriel," Navot muttered to himself. "I'll take care of the check."

AT THE END of the street she turned left and disappeared. Gabriel paused on the corner and watched black-coated Orthodox men filing into a large synagogue for evening prayers. Then he looked down the rue Pavée and saw the silhouette of Hannah Weinberg receding gently into the shadows. She stopped at the doorway of an apartment building and reached into her handbag for the key. Gabriel set out down the pavement and stopped a few feet from her, as her hand was outstretched toward the lock.

"Mademoiselle Weinberg?"

She turned and regarded him calmly in the darkness. Her eyes radiated a calm and sophisticated intelligence. If she was startled by his approach, she gave no sign of it.

"You *are* Hannah Weinberg, are you not?"

"What can I do for you, Monsieur?"

"I need your help," Gabriel said. "I was wondering whether we might have a word in private."

"Are we acquainted, Monsieur?"

"No," said Gabriel.

"Then how can I possibly help you?"

"It would be better if we discussed this in private, Mademoiselle."

"I don't make a habit of going to private places with strange men, Monsieur. Now if you'll excuse me."

She turned away and raised the key toward the lock again.

"It's about your painting, Mademoiselle Weinberg. I need to talk to you about your van Gogh."

She froze and looked at him again. Her gaze was still placid.

"I'm sorry to disappoint you, Monsieur, but I don't have a van Gogh. If you'd like to see some paintings by Vincent, I suggest you visit the Musée d'Orsay."

She looked away again.

"Marguerite Gachet at Her Dressing Table," said Gabriel calmly. "It was purchased by your grandfather from Theo van Gogh's widow, Johanna, and given to your grandmother as a birthday present. Your grandmother bore a vague resemblance to Mademoiselle Gachet. When you were a child, the painting hung in your bedroom. Shall I go on?"

Her composure disappeared. Her voice, when she spoke again after a moment of stunned silence, was unexpectedly vehement. "How do you know about the painting?"

"I'm not at liberty to say."

"Of course not." She said this as an insult. "My father always warned me that one day a greedy French art dealer would try to get the painting away from me. It is not for sale, and if it ever turns up missing, I'll make certain to give the police *your* description."

"I'm not an art dealer—and I'm not French."

"Then who are you?" she asked. "And what do you want with my painting?"

15

THE MARAIS, PARIS

THE COURTYARD WAS EMPTY and dark, lit only by the lights burning in the windows of the apartments above. They crossed it in silence and entered the foyer, where an old-fashioned cage lift stood ready to receive them. She mounted a flight of wide stairs instead and led him up to the fourth floor. On the landing were two stately mahogany doors. The door on the right was absent a nameplate. She opened it and led him inside. Gabriel took note of the fact that she punched the code into the keypad before switching on the lights. Hannah Weinberg, he decided, was good at keeping secrets.

It was a large apartment, with a formal entrance hall and a library adjoining the sitting room. Antique furniture covered in faded brocade stood sedately about, thick velvet curtains hung in the windows, and an ormolu clock set to the wrong time ticked quietly on the mantel. Gabriel's professional eye went immediately to the six decent oil paintings that hung on the walls. The effect of the decor was to create the impression of a bygone era. Indeed Gabriel would scarcely have been surprised to see Paul Gachet reading the evening newspapers by gaslight.

Hannah Weinberg removed her coat, then disappeared into the kitchen. Gabriel used the opportunity to look inside the library. Leather-bound legal volumes lined formal wooden bookcases with glass doors. There were more paintings here—prosaic landscapes, a man on horseback, the obligatory sea battle—but nothing that suggested the owner might also be in possession of a lost van Gogh.

He returned to the sitting room as Hannah Weinberg emerged from the kitchen with a bottle of Sancerre and two glasses. She handed him the bottle and a corkscrew and watched his hands carefully as he removed the cork. She was not as attractive as she had appeared in Uzi Navot's photograph. Perhaps it had been a trick of the nickeled Parisian light, or perhaps almost any woman looked attractive descending a flight of steps in Montmartre. Her pleated wool skirt and heavy sweater concealed what Gabriel suspected was a somewhat chunky figure. Her eyebrows were very wide and lent a profound seriousness to her face. Seated as she was now, surrounded by the dated furnishings of the room, she looked much older than her forty-four years.

"I'm surprised to see you in Paris, Monsieur Allon.

The last time I read your name in the newspaper you were still wanted for questioning by the French police."

"I'm afraid that's still the case."

"But you still came—just to see me? It must be very important."

"It is, Mademoiselle Weinberg."

Gabriel filled two glasses with wine, handed one to her, and raised his own in a silent toast. She did the same, then lifted the glass to her lips.

"Are you aware of what happened here in the Marais after the bombing?" She answered her own question. "Things were very tense. Rumors were flying that it had been carried out by Israel. Everyone believed it was true, and unfortunately the French government was very slow to do anything about the situation, even after they knew it was all a lie. Our children were beaten in the streets. Rocks were thrown through the windows of our homes and shops. Terrible things were spray-painted on the walls of the Marais and other Jewish neighborhoods. We suffered because of what happened inside that train station." She gave him a scrutinizing look, as though trying to determine whether he was really the man she had seen in the newspapers and on television. "But you suffered, too, didn't you? Is it true your wife was involved in it?"

The directness of her question surprised Gabriel. His first instinct was to lie, to conceal, to guide the conversation back onto ground of his choosing. But this was a recruitment—and a perfect recruitment, Shamron always said, is at its heart a perfect seduction. And when one was seducing, Gabriel reminded himself, one had to reveal something of oneself.

"They lured me to Gare de Lyon by kidnapping my wife," he said. "Their intention was to kill us both, but they also wanted to discredit Israel and make things unbearable for the Jews of France."

"They succeeded . . . for a little while, at least. Don't misunderstand me, Monsieur Allon, things are still bad for us here. Just not as bad as they were during those days after the bombing." She drank some more of the wine, then crossed her legs and smoothed the pleats of her skirt. "This might sound like a silly question, considering who you work for, but how did you find out about my van Gogh?"

Gabriel was silent for a moment, then he answered her truthfully. The mention of Isherwood's visit to this very apartment more than thirty years earlier caused her lips to curl into a vague smile of remembrance.

"I think I remember him," she said. "A tall man, quite handsome, full of charm and grace but at the same time somehow vulnerable." She paused, then added, "Like you."

"Charm and grace are words that are not often applied to me."

"And vulnerability?" She gave him another slight smile. It served to soften the serious edges of her face. "All of us are vulnerable to some degree, are we not? Even someone like you? The terrorists found where you were vulnerable, and they exploited that. That's what they do best. They exploit our decency. Our respect for life. They go after the things we hold dear."

Navot was right, Gabriel thought. She *was* a gift from the intelligence gods. He placed his glass on the coffee table. Hannah's eyes followed his every movement.

"What happened to this man Samuel Isakowitz?" she asked. "Did he make it out?"

Gabriel shook his head. "He and his wife were captured in Bordeaux when the Germans moved south."

"Where did they send them?"

"Sobibor."

She knew what that meant. Gabriel needn't say anything more.

"And your grandfather?" he said.

She peered into her Sancerre for a moment before answering. "Jeudi Noir," she said. "Do you know this term?"

Gabriel nodded solemnly. Jeudi Noir. Black Thursday.

"On the morning of July 16, 1942, four thousand French police officers descended on the Marais and other Jewish districts in Paris with orders to seize twenty-seven thousand Jewish immigrants from Germany, Austria, Poland, the Soviet Union, and Czechoslovakia. My father and grandparents were on the list. You see, my grandparents were originally from the Lublin district of Poland. The two policemen who knocked on the door of this very apartment took pity on my father and told him to run. A Catholic family who lived a floor below took him in, and he stayed there until liberation. My grandparents weren't so lucky. They were sent to the detention camp at Drancy. Five days after that, a sealed railcar to Auschwitz. Of course, that was the end for them."

"And the van Gogh?"

"There wasn't any time to make arrangements for it, and there was no one in Paris that my grandfather felt he could trust. It was war, you know. People were betraying each other for stockings and cigarettes. When he heard the roundups were coming, he removed the painting from the stretcher and hid it beneath a floorboard in the library. After the war it took my father years to get the apartment back. A French family had moved in after my grandparents were arrested, and they were reluctant to give up a nice apartment on the rue Pavée. Who could blame them?"

"What year did your father regain possession of the apartment?"

"It was 1952."

"Ten years," Gabriel said. "And the van Gogh was still there?"

"Just as my grandfather had left it, hidden under the floorboards of the library."

"Amazing."

"Yes," she said. "The painting has remained in the Weinberg family for more than a century, through war and Holocaust. And now you're asking me to give it up."

"Not give it up," said Gabriel.

"Then what?"

"I just need to—" He paused, searching for the appropriate word. "I need to *rent* it."

"Rent it? For how long?"

"I can't say. Perhaps a month. Perhaps six months. Maybe a year or longer."

"For what purpose?"

Gabriel was not ready to answer her. He picked up the cork and used his thumbnail to scratch away a torn edge.

"Do you know how much that painting is worth?" she asked. "If you're asking me to give it up, even for a brief period, I believe I'm entitled to know the reason why."

"You are," Gabriel said, "but you should also know that if I tell you the truth, your life will never be the same."

She poured more wine for herself and held the glass for a moment against her body without drinking from it. "Two years ago, there was a particularly vicious attack here in the Marais. A young Orthodox boy was set upon by a gang of North Africans as he was walking home from school. They set his hair on fire and carved a swastika into his forehead. He still bears the scar. We organized a demonstration to bring pressure on the French government to do something about the anti-Semitism. As we were marching in the place de la République, there was an anti-Israeli counterdemonstration. Do you know what they were shouting at us?"

"Death to the Jews."

"And do you know what the French president said?"

"There is no anti-Semitism in France."

"My life has never been the same since that day. Besides, as you might have surmised, I'm very good at keeping secrets. Tell me why you want my van Gogh, Monsieur Allon. Perhaps we can come to some accommodation."

THE *NEVIOT* SURVEILLANCE van was parked at the edge of the Parc Royal. Uzi Navot rapped his knuckles twice on the one-way rear window and was immediately admitted. One *neviot* man was seated behind the wheel. The other was in the back, hunched over an electronic console with a pair of headphones over his ears.

"What's going on?" Navot asked.

"Gabriel has her in his sights," the *neviot* man said. "And now he's going in for the kill."

Navot slipped on a pair of headsets and listened while Gabriel told Hannah Weinberg how he was going to use her van Gogh to track down the most dangerous man in the world.

THE KEY WAS hidden in the top drawer of the writing desk in the library. She used it to unlock the door at the end of the unlit corridor. The room behind it was a child's room. Hannah's room, thought Gabriel, frozen in time. A four-poster bed with a lace canopy. Shelves stacked with stuffed animals and toys. A poster of an American heartthrob actor. And hanging above a French provincial dresser, shrouded in heavy shadow, a lost painting by Vincent van Gogh.

GABRIEL MOVED SLOWLY forward and stood motionless before it, right hand on his chin, head tilted slightly to one side. Then he reached out and gently fingered the lavish brushstrokes. They were Vincent's—Gabriel was sure of it. Vincent on fire. Vincent in love. The restorer calmly assessed his target. The painting appeared as though it had never been cleaned. It was covered with a fine layer of surface grime, and there were three horizontal cracks—a result, Gabriel suspected, of having been rolled too tightly by Isaac Weinberg the night before Jeudi Noir.

"I suppose we should talk about the money," Hannah said. "How much does Julian think it will fetch?"

"In the neighborhood of eighty million. I've agreed to let him keep a ten percent commission as compensation for his role in the operation. The remainder of the money will be immediately transferred to you."

"Seventy-two million dollars?"

"Give or take a few million, of course."

"And when your operation is over?"

"I'm going to get the painting back."

"How do you intend to do that?"

"Leave that to me, Mademoiselle Weinberg."

"And when you return the painting to me, what happens to the seventy-two million? Give or take a few million, of course."

"You may keep any interest accrued. In addition, I will pay you a rental fee. How does five million dollars sound?"

She smiled. "It sounds fine, but I have no intention of keeping the money for myself. I don't want their money."

"Then what do you intend to do with it?"

She told him.

"I like the sound of that," he said. "Do we have a deal, Mademoiselle Weinberg?"

"Yes," she said. "I believe we have a deal."

AFTER LEAVING Hannah Weinberg's apartment Gabriel went to an Office safe flat near the Bois de Boulogne. They watched her for three days. Gabriel saw her only in surveillance photographs and heard her voice only in the recordings. Each evening he scoured the tapes for signs of betrayal or indiscretion but found only fidelity. On the night before she was to surrender the painting, he heard her sobbing softly and realized she was saying good-bye to Marguerite.

Navot brought the painting the next morning, wrapped in an old quilt he had taken from Hannah's apartment. Gabriel considered sending it back to Tel Aviv by courier, but in the end decided to carry it out of

France himself. He removed it from the frame, then pried the canvas off the stretcher. As he rolled it carefully he thought of Isaac Weinberg the night before Jeudi Noir. This time, instead of being hidden beneath a floorboard, it was tucked securely into the false lining of Gabriel's suitcase. Navot drove him to the Gare du Nord.

"An agent from London Station will be waiting for you at Waterloo," Navot said. "He'll run you out to Heathrow. El Al is expecting you. They'll make sure you have no problems with your baggage."

"Thanks, Uzi. You won't be making my travel arrangements much longer."

"I'm not so sure about that."

"Things didn't go well with Amos?"

"He's hard to read."

"What did he say?"

"He said he needs a few days to think it over."

"You didn't expect him to offer it to you on the spot, did you?"

"I don't know what I expected."

"Don't worry, Uzi. You'll get the job."

Navot pulled over to the side of the street a block from the station.

"You'll put in a good word for me at King Saul Boulevard, won't you, Gabriel? Amos likes you."

"What gave you that impression?"

"I could just tell," he said. "Everyone likes you."

Gabriel climbed out, took his suitcase from the backseat, and disappeared into the station. Navot waited at the curb until five minutes after Gabriel's scheduled departure, then pulled out into the traffic and drove away.

THE APARTMENT WAS in darkness when Gabriel arrived. He switched on a halogen lamp and was relieved to see his studio was still intact. Chiara was sitting up in bed as he entered their room. Her hair was newly washed and drawn back from her face by a velvet elastic band. Gabriel removed it and loosened the buttons of her nightgown. The painting lay next to them as they made love. "You know," she said, "most men just come home from Paris with an Hermès scarf and some perfume."

The telephone rang at midnight. Gabriel answered it before it could ring a second time. "I'll be there tomorrow," he said a moment later, then hung up the phone.

"Who was that?" Chiara asked.

"Adrian Carter."

"What did he want?"

"He wants me to come to Washington right away."

"What's in Washington?"

"A girl," said Gabriel. "Carter's found the girl."

16

MCLEAN, VIRGINIA

H OW WAS THE FLIGHT?"

"Eternal."

"It's the autumn jet-stream patterns," Carter said pedantically. "It adds at least two hours to flights from Europe to America."

"Israel isn't in Europe, Adrian. Israel is in the Middle East."

"Really?"

"You can ask your director of intelligence. He'll clear up the confusion for you."

Carter gave Gabriel a contemptuous look, then returned his eyes to the road. They were driving toward Washington along the Dulles Access Road in Carter's battered Volvo. Carter was wearing a corduroy sport jacket with patches on the elbows. It reinforced his professorial image. All that was missing was the canvas book bag and the NPR coffee mug. He was driving well below the posted speed limit and making repeated glances into his rearview mirror.

"Are we being followed?" Gabriel asked.

"Traffic cops," said Carter. "They're fanatical on this road. Any problems at passport control?"

"None," Gabriel said. "In fact, they seemed very happy to see me."

It was something Gabriel had never understood about America—the geniality of its border policemen. He'd always found something reassuring in the bored surliness of the Israelis who stamped passports at Ben-Gurion Airport. American customs agents were far too cordial.

He looked out the window. They had left the Dulles Access Road and were driving now through McLean. He'd been to Virginia just once before, a brief visit to a CIA safe house deep in the horse country near Middleburg. He found McLean to be an archetypal American suburb, neat and prosperous but somehow lifeless. They skirted the downtown commercial district, then entered a residential section with large tract homes. The developments had names like Merrywood and Colonial Estates. A road sign floated toward them: GEORGE BUSH CENTER FOR INTELLIGENCE.

"You're not actually thinking about taking me into Headquarters, are you?"

"Of course not," Carter said. "We're going into the District."

The District, Gabriel knew, was the way Washingtonians referred to their little village on the Potomac. They crossed a highway overpass and entered an area of rolling hills and dense woods. Gabriel, through the trees, glimpsed great houses overlooking the river.

"What's her name?"

"Sarah Bancroft," Carter replied. "Her father was a senior executive in the international division of Citibank. For the most part Sarah was raised in Europe. She's comfortable abroad in a way that most Americans aren't. She speaks languages. She knows which fork to use when."

"Education?"

"She came back here for college. Did a bachelor's in art history at Dartmouth, then a stretch at the Courtauld Institute of Art in London. I take it you're familiar with the Courtauld?"

Gabriel nodded. It was one of the world's most prestigious schools of art. Its graduates included an art dealer from St. James's named Julian Isherwood.

"After the Courtauld she did her doctorate at Harvard," Carter said. "Now she's a curator at the Phillips Collection in Washington. It's a small museum near—"

"I know the Phillips Collection, Adrian."

"Sorry," Carter said earnestly.

A large whitetail deer darted from the trees and crossed their path. Carter let his foot off the gas and watched the animal bound silently away through the darkening woods.

"Who brought her to your attention?" Gabriel asked, but Carter made no response. He was hunched over the wheel now and scanning the trees along the edge of the road for more deer. "Where there's one," he said, "there's usually another."

"Just like the terrorists," Gabriel said. He repeated his question.

"She applied to join us a few months after 9/11," Carter said. "She'd just finished her PhD She looked interesting on paper, so we brought her in and gave her to the psychiatrists in Personnel. They put her through the wringer and didn't like what they saw. Too independent-minded, they said. Maybe even a bit *too* smart for her own good. When we turned her down, she landed at the Phillips."

"So you're offering me one of your rejects?"

"The word hardly applies to Sarah Bancroft." Carter reached into the pocket of his corduroy blazer and handed Gabriel a photograph. Sarah Bancroft was a strikingly beautiful woman, with shoulder-length blond hair, wide cheekbones, and large eyes the color of a cloudless summer sky.

"How old?"

"Thirty-one."

"Why isn't she married?"

Carter hesitated a moment.

"Why isn't she married, Adrian?"

"She had a boyfriend while she was at Harvard, a young lawyer named Ben Callahan. It ended badly."

"What happened to Ben?"

"He boarded a flight to Los Angeles at Logan Airport on the morning of September 11, 2001."

Gabriel held out the photograph toward Carter. "Zizi's not going to be interested in hiring someone touched by 9/11. You brought me here for nothing, Adrian."

Carter kept his hands on the wheel. "Ben Callahan was a college boyfriend, not a husband. Besides, Sarah *never* talks about him to anyone. We practically had to beat it out of her. She was afraid Ben's death would follow her around for the rest of her life, that people would treat her like a widow at age twenty-six. She keeps it very much inside. We did some sniffing around for you this week. No one knows."

"Zizi's security hounds are going to do more than sniff around, Adrian. And if they catch one whiff of 9/11, he's going to run from her as fast as he can."

"Speaking of Zizi, his house is just ahead."

Carter slowed to negotiate a bend. A large brick-and-iron security gate appeared on their left. Beyond the gate a long paved drive rose to an enormous faux-chateau mansion overlooking the river. Gabriel looked away as they sped past.

"Zizi will never find out about Ben," Carter said.

"Are you willing to bet Sarah's life on that?"

"Meet her, Gabriel. See what you think."

"I already know what I think. She's perfect."

"So what's the problem?"

"If we make one mistake, Zizi's going to drop her down a very deep hole. That's the problem, Adrian."

*   *   *

THE SUDDENNESS with which they reached the center of Washington took Gabriel by surprise. One moment they were on a two-lane rural road at the edge of the Potomac gorge, the next they were crawling along Q Street through the Georgetown evening rush. Carter, playing the role of tour guide, pointed out the homes of the neighborhood's most celebrated residents. Gabriel, head against the window, couldn't summon the energy even to feign interest. They crossed a short bridge, guarded at each end by a pair of enormous tarnished buffalos, and entered the city's diplomatic quarter. Just beyond Massachusetts Avenue, Carter pointed to a turreted redbrick structure on the left side of the street. "That's the Phillips," he said helpfully. Gabriel looked to his right and saw a bronze version of Mohandas Gandhi hiking across a tiny triangular park. *Why Gandhi?* he wondered. What did the ideals of the Mahatma have to do with this patch of American global power?

Carter drove another block and parked in a restricted diplomatic zone outside a tired-looking Latin American embassy. He left the engine running and made no movement to indicate he intended to get out of the car. "This part of town is called Dupont Circle," he said, still in tour guide mode. "It's what passes for avant-garde in Washington."

An officer of the Secret Service Uniformed Division rapped his knuckle on Carter's window and gestured for him to move along. Carter, eyes straight ahead, held his ID against the glass, and the officer walked back to his squad car. A moment later something caught Carter's attention in the rearview mirror. "Here she comes," he said.

Gabriel looked out his window as Sarah Bancroft floated virtuously past, dressed in a long dark overcoat with a narrow waist. She held a leather briefcase in one hand and a cell phone in the other. Gabriel heard her voice briefly as she passed. Low, sophisticated, a trace of an English accent—a remnant, no doubt, of her time at the Courtauld and a childhood spent in international schools abroad.

"What do you think?" asked Carter.

"I'll let you know in a minute."

She came to the corner of Q Street and 20th Street. On the opposite corner was an esplanade filled with sidewalk vendors and a pair of escalators leading to the Dupont Circle Metro station. The traffic light in Sarah's direction was red. Without stopping she stepped from the curb and started across. When a taxi driver sounded his car horn in protest, she shot him a look that could melt ice and carried on with her conversation. Then she continued slowly across the intersection and stepped onto the down escalator. Gabriel watched with admiration as she sank slowly from view.

"Do you have two more just like her?"

Carter fished a mobile phone from his pocket and dialed. "We're on," he said. A moment later a large black Suburban rounded the corner and parked illegally on Q Street adjacent to the escalators. Five minutes after that

Gabriel saw her again, this time rising slowly out of the depths of the Metro station. She was no longer speaking into her telephone, nor was she alone. Two of Carter's agents were with her, a man and a woman, one on each arm, in case she had a sudden change of heart. The back door of the Suburban swung open, and Sarah Bancroft vanished from sight. Carter started the engine and headed back to Georgetown.

17

GEORGETOWN

THE BLACK SUBURBAN CAME to a stop fifteen minutes later outside a large Federal-style town house on N Street. As Sarah mounted the curved redbrick steps, the door opened suddenly and a figure appeared in the shadows of the portico. He wore creaseless khaki trousers and a corduroy blazer with patches on the elbows. His gaze had a curious clinical detachment that reminded Sarah of the grief counselor she'd seen after Ben's death. "I'm Carter," he said, as if the thought had occurred to him suddenly. He didn't say whether it was his first name or his last, only that it was genuine. "I don't do funny names anymore," he said. "I'm Headquarters now."

He smiled. It was an ersatz smile, like his brief ersatz handshake. He suggested she come inside and once again managed to leave the impression of sudden inspiration. "And you're Sarah," he informed her, as he conveyed her down the wide center hall. "Sarah Bancroft, a curator at the well-regarded Phillips Collection. Sarah Bancroft who courageously offered us her services after 9/11 but was turned away and told she wasn't needed. How's your father?"

She was taken aback by the sudden change in course. "Do you know my father?"

"Never met him actually. Works for Citicorp, doesn't he?"

"You know exactly who he works for. Why are you asking about my father?"

"Where is he these days? London? Brussels? Hong Kong?"

"Paris," she said. "It's his last post. He's retiring next year."

"And then he's coming home?"

She shook her head. "He's staying in Paris. With his new wife. My parents divorced two years ago. My father remarried right away. He's a time-is-money sort of man."

"And your mother? Where is she?"

"Manhattan."

"See your father much?"

"Holidays. Weddings. The occasional awkward lunch when he's in town. My parents divorced badly. Everyone took sides, the children included. Why are you asking me these questions? What do you want from—"

"You believe in that?" he asked, cutting her off.

"Believe in what?"

"Taking sides."

"Depends on the circumstances, I suppose. Is this part of the test? I thought I failed your tests."

"You did," said Carter. "With flying colors."

They entered the sitting room. It was furnished with the formal but anonymous elegance usually reserved for hotel hospitality suites. Carter helped her off with her coat and invited her to sit.

"So why am I back?"

"It's a fluid world, Sarah. Things change. So tell me something. Under what circumstances do you think it's right to take sides?"

"I haven't given it much thought."

"Sure you have," Carter said, and Sarah, for the second time, saw her grief counselor, sitting in his floral wingchair with his ceramic mug balanced on his knee, dully prodding her to visit places she'd rather not go. "Come on, Sarah," Carter was saying. "Give me just one example of when you believe it's all right to take sides."

"I believe in right and wrong," she said, lifting her chin a little. "Which probably explains why I flunked your little tests. Your world is shades of gray. I tend to be a bit too black and white."

"Is that what your father told you?"

No, she thought, it was Ben who accused her of that failing.

"What's this all about?" she asked. "Why am I here?"

But Carter was still turning over the implications of her last response. "And what about the terrorists?" he asked, and once again it seemed to Sarah as if the thought had just popped into his head. "That's what I'm wondering about. How do they fit into Sarah Bancroft's world of right and wrong? Are they evil, or is their cause legitimate? Are we the innocent victims, or have we brought this calamity upon ourselves? Must we sit back and take it, or do we have the right to resist them with all the force and anger we can muster?"

"I'm an assistant curator at the Phillips Collection," she said. "Do you really want me to wax lyrical on the morals of counterterrorism?"

"Let's narrow the focus of our question then. I always find that helpful. Let's take for an example the man who drove Ben's plane into the World Trade Center." Carter paused. "Remind me, Sarah, which plane was Ben on?"

"You know which plane he was on," she said. "He was on United Flight 175."

"Which was piloted by . . ."

"Marwan al-Shehhi."

"Suppose for a moment that Marwan al-Shehhi had managed somehow to survive. I know it's crazy, Sarah, but play along with me for argument's sake. Suppose he managed to make his way back to Afghanistan or Pakistan or some other terrorist sanctuary. Suppose we knew where he was. Should we send the FBI with a warrant for his arrest, or should we deal with him in a more efficient manner? Men in black? Special forces? A Hellfire missile fired from a plane without a pilot?"

"I think you know what I would do to him."

"Suppose I'm interested in hearing it from your own lips before we go further."

"The terrorists have declared war on us," she said. "They've attacked our cities, killed our citizens, and tried to disrupt the continuity of our government."

"So what should be done to them?"

"They should be dealt with harshly."

"And what does that mean?"

"Men in black. Special forces. A Hellfire missile fired from a plane without a pilot."

"And what about a man who gives them money? Is he guilty, too? And if so, to what degree?"

"I suppose it depends on whether he knew what the money would be used for."

"And if he knew damned well what it would be used for?"

"Then he's as guilty as the man who flew the plane into the building."

"Would you feel comfortable—indeed justified—in operating against such an individual?"

"I offered to help you five years ago," she said contentiously. "You told me I wasn't qualified. You told me I wasn't *suited* for this sort of work. And now you want my help?"

Carter appeared unmoved by her protest. Sarah felt a sudden empathy for his wife.

"You offered to help us, and we treated you shabbily. I'm afraid that's what we do best. I suppose I could go on about how we were wrong. Perhaps I might try to soothe your feelings with an insincere apology. But frankly, Miss Bancroft, there isn't time." His voice contained an edge that had been absent before. "So I suppose what I need now is a straight answer. Do you still feel like helping us? Do you want to fight the terrorists, or would you prefer to go on with your life and hope it never happens again?"

"Fight?" she asked. "I'm sure you can find people better suited for that than me."

"There are different ways to fight them, Sarah."

She hesitated. Carter filled the sudden silence by engaging in a prolonged study of his own hands. He wasn't the kind of man who asked things twice. In that regard he was very much like her father. "Yes," she said finally. "I'd be willing."

"And what if it involved working with an intelligence service other than the Central Intelligence Agency?" he asked, as though discussing an abstract theory. "An intelligence service that is closely allied with us in this fight against the Islamic terrorists?"

"And who might that be?"

Carter was good at evading questions. He proved it again now.

"There's someone I'd like you to meet. He's a serious chap. A little rough around the edges. He's going to ask you a few questions. Actually, he's going to put you under the lights for the next few hours. It's going to get rather personal at times. If he likes what he sees, he's going to ask you to help us in a very important endeavor.

This endeavor is not without risk, but it is critical to the security of the United States, and it has the Agency's full support. If you're interested, remain where you are. If not, walk out the door, and we'll pretend you stumbled in here by mistake."

SARAH WOULD NEVER be sure how Carter had summoned him or from where he came. He was small and spare, with short-cropped hair and gray temples. His eyes were the greenest Sarah had ever seen. His handshake, like Carter's, was fleeting but probing as a doctor's touch. His English was fluent but heavily accented. If he had a name, it wasn't yet relevant.

They settled at the long table in the formal dining room, Carter and his nameless collaborator on one side and Sarah on the other like a suspect in an interrogation room. The collaborator was now in possession of her CIA file. He was leafing slowly through the pages as if seeing them for the first time, which she doubted was the case. His first question was put to her as a mild accusation.

"You wrote your doctoral dissertation at Harvard on the German Expressionists."

It seemed a peculiar place to begin. She was tempted to ask why he was interested in the topic of her dissertation, but instead she simply nodded her head and said, "Yes, that's correct."

"In your research did you ever come across a man named Viktor Frankel?"

"He was a disciple of Max Beckmann," she said. "Frankel is little known today, but at the time he was considered extremely influential and was highly regarded by his contemporaries. In 1936 the Nazis declared his work degenerate, and he was forbidden to continue painting. Unfortunately, he decided to remain in Germany. By the time he decided to leave, it was too late. He was deported to Auschwitz in 1942, along with his wife and teenaged daughter, Irene. Only Irene survived. She went to Israel after the war and was one of the country's most influential artists in the fifties and sixties. I believe she died several years ago."

"That's correct," said Carter's collaborator, his eyes still on Sarah's file.

"Why are you interested in whether I knew about Viktor Frankel?"

"Because he was my grandfather."

"You're Irene's son?"

"Yes," he said. "Irene was my mother."

She looked at Carter, who was gazing at his own hands. "I guess I know who's running this *endeavor* of yours." She looked back at the man with gray temples and green eyes. "You're Israeli."

"Guilty as charged. Shall we continue, Sarah, or would you like me to leave now?"

She hesitated a moment, then nodded. "Do I get a name, or are names forbidden?"

He gave her one. It was vaguely familiar. And then she remembered where she had seen it before. *The Israeli*

216   DANIEL SILVA

agent who was involved in the bombing of the Gare de Lyon in Paris . . .

"You're the one who—"

"Yes," he said. "I'm the one."

He looked down at the open file again and turned to a new page. "But let's get back to you, shall we? We have a lot of ground to cover and very little time."

HE STARTED SLOWLY, a climber plodding his way through the foothills, conserving his strength for the unseen perils that lay ahead. His questions were short and efficient and methodically posed, as though he were reading them from a prepared list, which he wasn't. He devoted the first hour to her family. Her father, the high-flying Citicorp executive who'd had no time for his children but plenty of time for other women. Her mother, whose life had crumbled after the divorce and who was now living like a hermit in her classic-eight Manhattan apartment on Fifth Avenue. Her older sister, whom Sarah described as "the one who got all the brains and beauty." Her little brother, who had checked out of life early and, much to her father's disappointment, was now working for pennies in a ski-rental shop somewhere in Colorado.

After family came another hour devoted solely to her expensive European schooling. The American in St. John's Wood, where she'd done her elementary years. The international middle school in Paris, where she'd learned how to speak French and get into trouble. The all-girls boarding school outside Geneva, where she'd been incarcerated by her father for the purpose of "sorting herself out." It was in Switzerland, she volunteered, where she discovered her passion for art. Each of her answers was greeted by the scratching of his pen. He wrote in red ink on a legal pad the color of sunflowers. At first she thought he was scribbling in shorthand or some form of hieroglyphics. Then she realized he was making notes in Hebrew. The fact that it was written right to left—and that he could write with equal speed with either hand—served to reinforce her impression that she had passed through the looking glass.

At times he seemed to have all the time in the world; at others he would glare at his wristwatch and frown, as though calculating how much farther they could push on before making camp for the night. From time to time he slipped into other languages. His French was quite good. His Italian faultless but tinged with a vague accent that betrayed the fact he was not a native speaker. When he addressed her in German a change came over him. A straightening of his back. A hardening of his severe features. She answered him in the language of his question, though invariably her words were recorded in Hebrew on his yellow legal pad. For the most part he did not challenge her, though any inconsistencies, real or imagined, were pursued with a prosecutorial zeal.

"This passion for art," he said. "Where do you think it came from? Why art? Why not literature or music? Why not film or drama?"

"Paintings became a refuge for me. A sanctuary."

"From what?"

"Real life."

"You were a rich girl going to the finest schools in Europe. What was wrong with your life?" He switched from English into German in midaccusation. "What were you running from?"

"You judge me," she responded in the same language.

"Of course."

"May we speak in English?"

"If you must."

"Paintings are other places. Other lives. An instant in time that exists on the canvas and nowhere else."

"You like to inhabit these places."

It was an observation, not a question. She nodded in response.

"You like to lead other lives? Become other people? You like to walk through Vincent's wheat fields and Monet's flower gardens?"

"And even through Frankel's nightmares."

He laid down his pen for the first time. "Is that why you applied to join the Agency? Because you wanted to lead another life? Because you wanted to become another person?"

"No, I did it because I wanted to serve my country."

He gave her a disapproving frown, as if he found her response naïve, and then shot another glance at his wristwatch. Time was his enemy.

"Did you meet Arabs when you were growing up in Europe?"

"Of course."

"Boys? Girls?"

"Both."

"What sort of Arabs?"

"Arabs who walk on two legs. Arabs from Arab countries."

"You're more sophisticated than that, Sarah."

"Lebanese. Palestinians. Jordanians. Egyptians."

"What about Saudis? Did you ever go to school with Saudis?"

"There were a couple of Saudi girls at my school in Switzerland."

"They were rich, these Saudi girls?"

"We were all rich."

"Were you friends with them?"

"They were hard to get to know. They were standoffish. They kept to themselves."

"And what about Arab boys?"

"What about them?"

"Were you ever friends with any of them?"

"I suppose."

"Ever date any of them? Ever sleep with any of them?"

"No."

"Why not?"

"I guess my taste didn't run to Arab men."

"You had French boyfriends?"

"A couple."

"British?"

"Sure."

"But no Arabs?"

"No Arabs."

"Are you prejudiced against Arabs?"

"Don't be ridiculous."

"So it's conceivable you *could* have dated an Arab. You just *didn't*."

"I hope you're not going to ask me to serve as bait in a honey trap because—"

"Don't be ridiculous."

"Then why are you asking me these questions?"

"Because I want to know whether you'd be comfortable in a social and professional setting with Arab men."

"The answer is yes."

"You don't automatically see a terrorist when you see an Arab man?"

"No."

"Are you sure about that, Sarah?"

"I suppose it depends on the sort of Arab you have in mind."

He looked at his watch. "It's getting late," he said to no one in particular. "I'm sure poor Sarah is famished." He drew a heavy red line across his page of hieroglyphics. "Let's order some food, shall we? Sarah will feel better after she has something to eat."

*   *   *

THEY ORDERED KEBABS from a carryout in the heart of Georgetown. The food came twenty minutes later, delivered by the same black Suburban that had brought Sarah to the town house three hours earlier. Gabriel treated its arrival as a signal to begin the night session. For the next ninety minutes he focused on her education and her knowledge of art history. His questions came at such a rapid-fire pace she scarcely had time for her food. As for his own, it sat untouched next to his yellow legal pad. *He's an ascetic,* she thought. *He can't be bothered with food. He lives in a bare room and subsists on coarse bread and a few drops of water a day.* Shortly after midnight he carried his plate into the kitchen and deposited it on the counter. When he returned to the dining room he stood for a moment behind his chair, with one hand pressed to his chin and his head tilted slightly to one side. The light from the chandelier had turned his eyes to emerald, and they were flashing restlessly over her like searchlights. *He can see the summit,* she thought. *He's preparing himself for the final assault.*

"I SEE FROM YOUR file that you're unmarried."

"Correct."

"Are you involved with anyone at the moment?"

"No."

"Sleeping with anyone?"

She looked at Carter, who gazed sadly back at her, as if to say, *I told you things might get personal.*

"No, I'm not sleeping with anyone."

"Why not?"

"Have you ever lost someone close to you?"

The dark look that came suddenly over his face, combined with Carter's restless shifting in his chair, alerted her that she had strayed into some forbidden zone.

"I'm sorry," she said. "I didn't—"

"It's Ben, I take it? Ben is the reason you're not involved with anyone?"

"Yes, it's Ben. Of course it's *Ben*."

"Tell me about him."

She shook her head. "No," she said softly. "You don't get to know about Ben. Ben is mine. Ben isn't part of the deal."

"How long did you date?"

"I told you—"

"How long did you see him, Sarah? It's important, or I wouldn't be asking."

"About nine months."

"And then it ended?"

"Yes, it *ended*."

"You ended it, didn't you?"

"Yes."

"Ben was in love with you. Ben wanted to marry you."

"Yes."

"But you didn't feel the same way. You weren't interested in marriage. Maybe you weren't interested in Ben."

"I cared about him very much. . . ."

"But?"

"But I wasn't in love with him."

"Tell me about his death."

"You can't be serious."

"I'm quite serious."

"I don't talk about his death. I *never* talk about Ben's death. Besides, you know how Ben died. He died at nine-oh-three A.M. Eastern Daylight Time, live on television. Everyone in the world watched Ben die. Did you?"

"Some of the passengers from Flight 175 managed to make phone calls."

"That's correct."

"Was Ben one of them?"

"Yes."

"Did he call his father?"

"No."

"Did he call his mother?"

"No."

"His brother? His sister?"

"No."

"Who did he call, Sarah?"

Her eyes welled with tears.

"He called *me*, you son of a bitch."

"What did he say to you?"

"He told me the plane had been hijacked. He told me they'd killed the flight attendants. He told me the plane was making wild movements. He told me he loved me and that he was sorry. He was about to die, and he told me he was sorry. And then we lost the connection."

"What did you do?"

"I turned on the television and saw the smoke pouring from the North Tower of the World Trade Center. It was a few minutes after Flight 11 struck. No one was really sure then what had happened. I called the FAA and told them about Ben's call. I called the FBI. I called the Boston police. I felt so utterly fucking helpless."

"And then?"

"I watched television. I waited for the phone to ring again. It never did. At nine-oh-three A.M. Eastern Daylight Time, the second plane hit the World Trade Center. The South Tower was burning. Ben was burning."

A single tear spilled onto her cheek. She punched it away and glared at him.

"Are you satisfied?"

He was silent.

"Now it's my turn to ask a question, and you'd better answer it truthfully, or I'm leaving."

"Ask me anything you like, Sarah."

"What do you want from me?"

"We want you to quit your job at the Phillips Collection and go to work for Jihad Incorporated. Are you still interested?"

IT WAS LEFT to Carter to place the contract in front of her. Carter with his Puritan righteousness and corduroy blazer. Carter with his therapeutic demeanor and American-accented English. Gabriel slipped out like a night thief and crossed the street to Carter's battered Volvo. He knew what Sarah's answer would be. She had given it to him already. *The South Tower was burning*, she had said. *Ben was burning.* And so Gabriel was not concerned by the gallows expression on her face, twenty minutes later, when she emerged stoically from the town house and descended the steps to the waiting Suburban. Nor was he disturbed by the sight of Carter, five minutes after that, ambling morosely across the street like a pall-bearer making for the casket. He climbed behind the wheel and started the engine. "We have a plane at Andrews waiting to take you back to Israel," he said. "We need to make one stop along the way. There's someone who'd like a word with you before you leave."

IT WAS AFTER midnight; K Street had been abandoned to the overnight delivery trucks and the taxicabs. Carter was driving at a faster pace than usual and making repeated glances at his wristwatch. "She doesn't come for free, you know. There'll be costs to using her. She'll have to be re-settled when this is over and protected for a long time."

"But you'll handle that, won't you, Adrian? You're the one with all the money. The budget for the American intelligence community alone is far more than the budget of our entire country."

"Have you forgotten that this operation does not exist? Besides, you're going to walk away with a great deal of Zizi's money."

"Fine," said Gabriel. "You can be the one to tell Sarah Bancroft that she's going to spend the next ten years living on a kibbutz in the Galilee hiding from the forces of global jihad."

"All right, we'll pay for her resettlement."

Carter made a series of turns. For a moment Gabriel lost track of what street they were on. They passed the façade of a large neoclassical building, then turned into an official-looking driveway. On the left was a fortified guardhouse with bulletproof glass. Carter lowered his window and handed over his badge to the guard.

"We're expected."

The guard consulted a clipboard, then handed back Carter's ID.

"Pull through, then stop in front of the barricade on the left. The dogs will give the car the once-over, then you can head on in."

Carter nodded and raised his window. Gabriel said, "Where are we?"

Carter wound his way through the barricades and stopped where he'd been told. "The back door of the White House," he said.

"Who are we seeing?" Gabriel asked, but Carter was now speaking to another officer, this one struggling to control a large German shepherd straining at a thick leather leash. Gabriel, whose fear of dogs was legendary within the Office, sat motionless while the animal prowled the perimeter of the Volvo, searching for concealed explosives. A moment later they were directed through another security gate. Carter pulled into an empty parking space on East Executive Drive and shut down the engine.

"This is as far as I go."

"Who am I seeing, Adrian?"

"Go through that gate over there and walk up the drive toward the house. He'll be out in a minute."

THE DOGS came first, two coal-black terriers that shot from the Diplomatic Entrance like bullets from a gun barrel and launched a preemptive strike on Gabriel's trousers. The president emerged a few seconds later. He advanced on Gabriel with one hand out while the other was gesturing for the terriers to break off their onslaught. The two men shook hands briefly, then set off along the footpath that ran around the periphery of the South Lawn. The terriers launched one more sortie against Gabriel's ankles. Carter watched as Gabriel turned and murmured something in Hebrew that sent the dogs scurrying toward the protection of a Secret Service agent.

Their conversation lasted just five minutes, and to Carter it seemed the president did most of the talking. They moved at a brisk pace, stopping only once in order to settle what appeared to be a minor disagreement. Gabriel removed his hands from his coat pockets and used them to illustrate whatever point he was trying to make. The president appeared unconvinced at first, then he nodded and clapped Gabriel hard on the shoulders.

They completed their circuit and parted at the Diplomatic Entrance. As Gabriel started back toward East Executive Drive the dogs trotted after him, then turned and darted into the White House after their master. Gabriel slipped through the open gate and climbed into Carter's car.

"How was he?" Carter asked as they turned into 15th Street.

"Resolute."

"It looked like you had a bit of an argument."

"I'd characterize it as a polite disagreement."

"About what?"

"Our conversation was private, Adrian, and it will remain so."

"Good man," said Carter.

18

LONDON

THE ANNOUNCEMENT THAT Isherwood Fine Arts had sold *Daniel in the Lions' Den* by Peter Paul Rubens for the sum of ten million pounds came on the first Wednesday of the new year. By Friday the clamor had been eclipsed by a rumor that Isherwood was bringing aboard a partner.

It was Oliver Dimbleby, Isherwood's tubby nemesis from King Street, who heard it first, though later even Dimbleby would be hard pressed to pin down its precise origin. To the best of his recollection the seeds were planted by Penelope, the luscious hostess from the little wine bar in Jermyn Street where Isherwood could often be seen whiling away slow afternoons. "She's blond," Penelope had said. "*Natural* blond, Oliver. Not like your girls. Pretty. American with a bit of an English accent." At first Penelope suspected Isherwood was once again making a fool of himself with a younger woman, but she soon realized that she was witnessing a job interview. "And not just any job, Oliver. Sounded like something big."

Dimbleby would have thought nothing of it had he not received a report of a second sighting, this one from Percy, a notorious gossip who waited tables in the breakfast room at the Dorchester Hotel. "They definitely weren't lovers," he told Dimbleby with the assurance of a man who knew his material. "It was all salary and benefits. There was a fair amount of haggling. She was playing hard to get." Dimbleby slipped Percy ten quid and asked whether he'd caught the woman's name. "Bancroft," said Percy. "*Sarah* Bancroft. Stayed two nights. Bill paid in its entirety by Isherwood Fine Arts, Mason's Yard, St. James's."

A third sighting, a cozy dinner at Mirabelle, confirmed to Dimbleby that something was definitely afoot. The next evening he bumped into Jeremy Crabbe, director of the Bonhams Old Masters department, at the bar in Green's restaurant. Crabbe was drinking a very large whiskey and still licking his wounds over Isherwood's monumental coup. "I had that Rubens, Oliver, but Julie outfoxed me. He's ten million richer, and I'm facing a firing squad at dawn. And now he's expanding operations. Getting himself a flashy new front man, from what I hear. But don't quote me, Oliver. It's nothing but malicious talk." When Dimbleby asked whether Isherwood's flashy front man might in fact be an American woman named Sarah Bancroft, Crabbe gave him a sideways smile. "Anything's possible, love. Remember, we are talking about Juicy Julie Isherwood."

For the next forty-eight hours Oliver Dimbleby devoted his copious spare time to researching the provenance of one Sarah Bancroft. A drinking companion on the faculty of the Courtauld described her as "a meteor." The same companion learned from an acquaintance at Harvard that her dissertation was considered required reading for anyone serious about the German Expressionists. Dimbleby then dialed up an old chum who cleaned paintings at the National Gallery of Art in Washington and asked him to poke around the Phillips for clues about her departure. It was a squabble over money, reported the chum. Two days later he called Dimbleby back and said it had something to do with an office love affair gone bad. A third call brought the news that Sarah Bancroft had parted company with the Phillips Collection on good terms and that the motive for her departure was nothing more than a desire to spread her wings. As for her personal life, meaning her marital status, she was described as single and unavailable.

Which left but one unanswered question: Why was Isherwood suddenly taking on a partner? Jeremy Crabbe heard he was ill. Roddy Hutchinson heard he had a tumor in his abdomen the size of a honeydew melon. Penelope, the girl from Isherwood's wine bar, heard he was in love with a wealthy Greek divorcee and was planning to spend his remaining days in blessed fornication on a beach in Mykonos. Dimbleby, though he found the lavish rumors entertaining, suspected that the truth was far more prosaic. Julian was getting on. Julian was tired. Julian had just pulled off a coup. Why not bring someone on board to help lighten the load?

His suspicions were confirmed, three days later, when a small item appeared at the bottom of the *Times* arts page, announcing that Sarah Bancroft, formerly of the Phillips Collection in Washington, would be joining Isherwood Fine Arts as its first associate director. "I've been at this for forty years," Isherwood told the *Times*. "I needed someone to help shoulder the burden, and the angels sent me Sarah."

SHE ARRIVED the following week, on the Monday. By coincidence Oliver Dimbleby was waddling along Duke Street at the precise moment she turned through the passageway into Mason's Yard, wearing a Burberry trench coat, her blond hair swept back so that it hung between her shoulder blades like a satin cape. Dimbleby did not realize then who she was, but Oliver being Oliver, he poked his head through the passageway for a look-see at her backside. To his surprise she was making a beeline toward Isherwood's gallery in the far corner of the quadrangle. She rang the bell that first day and had to wait two very long minutes for Tanya, Isherwood's lethargic secretary, to buzz her up. It was Tanya's initiation of the new girl, thought Dimbleby. Tanya, he suspected, would be gone by Friday.

Her impact was instantaneous. Sarah was a whirlwind. Sarah was a much-needed breath of fresh air. Sarah was all things Isherwood was not: prompt, regimented, disciplined, and, of course, very American. She started arriving at the gallery at eight each morning. Isherwood, who was used to strolling into work at the Italianate hour of ten, was forced to trim his sails accordingly. She put his disgraceful books in order and spruced up the large common office they shared. She replaced the missing letters on the intercom and the soiled brown carpeting on the stairs. She began the painful process of liquidating Isherwood's vast pile of dead stock and entered into quiet negotiations to take over the adjacent office space currently occupied by Miss Archer's dreary little travel agency. "She's an American," said Dimbleby. "She's expansionist by nature. She'll conquer your country and afterwards tell you it's for your own good."

Tanya, as it turned out, did not survive till Friday and was last seen leaving the gallery on the Wednesday evening. Her departure was handled by Sarah and was therefore accomplished with a smoothness not usually seen at Isherwood Fine Arts. The generous severance package—"Very generous from what I hear," said Dimbleby—permitted her to take a long, well-deserved winter holiday in Morocco. By the next Monday there was a new girl on duty in Isherwood's anteroom, a tall olive-skinned Italian woman named Elena Farnese with riotous dark hair and eyes the color of caramel. An informal straw poll, conducted by Roddy Hutchinson,

found that among the men of St. James's she was regarded as even more beautiful than the fetching Sarah.
The name "Isherwood Fine Arts" suddenly took on new
meaning among the denizens of Duke Street, and the
gallery was hit by a rash of drop-bys and pop-ins. Even
Jeremy Crabbe from Bonhams started dropping by
unannounced just to have a glimpse at Isherwood's collection.

After shoring up the gallery Sarah began venturing
out to meet her compatriots. She did formal meetings
with the leading lights at the various London auction
houses. She lunched expensively with the collectors and
had quiet drinks in the late afternoon with their advisers,
their consultants, and their assorted hangers-on. She
popped into the galleries of Isherwood's competitors
and said hello. She stopped at the bar at Green's once or
twice and bought a round for the boys. Oliver Dimbleby
finally screwed up the courage to invite her to lunch, but
wisely she made it a coffee instead. Next afternoon they
had a latte in a paper cup at an American chain on Piccadilly. Oliver fondled her hand and invited her to dinner. "I'm afraid I don't do dinner," she said. *Why ever
not?* wondered Oliver as he waddled back to his gallery
in King Street. *Why ever not indeed?*

UZI NAVOT had had his eye on it for some time. It was
a perfect port in a storm, he'd always thought. The sort
of place to stick in your back pocket for the inevitable

rainy day. It was located just ten miles beyond the M25 ring road in Surrey—or, as he explained to Gabriel, an hour by Tube and car from Isherwood's gallery in St. James's. The house was a rambling Tudor pile with high gables and tiny leaded windows, reached by a long rutted beech drive and shielded by a forbidding brick-and-iron gate. There was a tumbledown barn and a pair of shattered greenhouses. There was a tangled garden for thinking deep thoughts, eight private acres for wrestling with one's demons, and a stock pond that hadn't been fished for fifteen years. The rental agent, when handing Navot the keys, had referred to it as Winslow Haven. To a field hand like Navot it was Nirvana.

Dina, Rimona, and Yaakov worked in the dusty library; Lavon and Yossi set up shop in a rambling rumpus room hung with the heads of many dead animals. As for Gabriel, he made a shakedown studio for himself in a light-filled second-floor drawing room overlooking the garden. Because he could not show his face round the art world of London, he dispatched others to procure his supplies. Their missions were special operations unto themselves. Dina and Yossi made separate trips to L. Cornelissen & Sons in Russell Street, carefully dividing the order between them so that the girls who worked there would not realize they were filling the order of a professional restorer. Yaakov went to a lighting shop in Earl's Court to purchase Gabriel's halogen lamps and then to a master carpenter in Camden Town to collect a custom easel. Eli Lavon saw to the frame. A newly minted expert in all things al-Bakari, he took issue with Gabriel's decision to go antique Italian. "Zizi's taste is haute French," he said. "The Italian will clash with Zizi's sense of style." But Gabriel always found that the more muscular carving of the Italian frames best suited Vincent's impasto style, and so it was an Italian frame that Lavon ordered from the enchanted Bury Street premises of Arnold Wiggins & Sons.

Sarah came to them early each evening, always by a different route, and always with Lavon handling the countersurveillance. She was a quick study and, as Gabriel had anticipated, was blessed with a flawless memory. Still, he was careful not to smother her beneath an avalanche of information. They started usually by seven, broke at nine for a family dinner in the formal dining room, then carried on until nearly midnight, when she was shuttled back to her apartment in Chelsea by Yossi, who was staying in a flat across the street.

They spent a week on Zizi al-Bakari himself before branching off into his associates and the other members of his entourage and inner circle. Special attention was paid to Wazir bin Talal, the omnipresent chief of AAB security. Bin Talal was an intelligence service unto himself, with a staff of security agents inside AAB and a network of paid informants scattered around the world that fed him reports about potential threats to AAB properties or Zizi himself. "If Zizi likes the merchandise, it's bin Talal who does the due diligence," explained Lavon. "No one gets near the chief without first passing muster with bin

Talal. And if anyone steps out of line, it's bin Talal who lowers the boom." Yossi's research uncovered no fewer than a half dozen former al-Bakari associates who had died under mysterious circumstances, a fact that was withheld from Sarah at Gabriel's request.

In the days that followed, the Surrey safe house was visited by what were known in the Office as "experts with handles." The first was a woman from Hebrew University who spent two nights lecturing Sarah on Saudi social customs. Next came a psychiatrist who spent two more nights counseling her on ways to combat fear and anxiety while working undercover. A specialist in communications gave her a primer on elementary forms of secret writing. A martial arts trainer taught her the basics of Israeli-style hand-to-hand combat. Gabriel chose Lavon, the greatest watcher in the history of the Office, to give her a crash course in the art of human and electronic surveillance. "You will be entering a hostile camp," he told her in summation. "Assume they're watching your every move and listening to your every word. If you do that, nothing can go wrong."

Gabriel, for the most part, remained a spectator to her training. He greeted her when she arrived at the house each evening, joined the team for dinner, then saw her off again at midnight when she set out for London with Yossi. As the days wore on, they began to detect a restlessness in him. Lavon, who had worked with him more than the others, diagnosed Gabriel's mood as impatience. "He wants to put her into play," Lavon said, "but he knows she's not ready." He began spending extended periods before the canvas, painstakingly repairing the damage done to Marguerite. The intensity of the work only increased his restiveness. Lavon advised him to take breaks now and again, and Gabriel reluctantly agreed. He found a pair of Wellington boots in the mudroom and ventured out on solitary marches over the footpaths surrounding the village. He dug a rod and reel from a storage room in the cellar and used it to haul an enormous brown trout from the stock pond. In the barn, concealed beneath a tarpaulin, he found an ancient MG motorcar that looked as though it hadn't been driven in twenty years. Three days later the others heard a sputtering sound emanating from the barn, followed by an explosion that reverberated over the countryside. Yaakov came running down from the house, fearful Gabriel had blown himself to bits, but instead found him standing over the open hood of the MG, covered in engine grease up to his elbows and smiling for the first time since they'd come to Surrey. "It works," he shouted over the thunderous rattle of the motor. "The damned thing still runs."

That evening he joined in Sarah's training session for the first time. Lavon and Yaakov were not surprised, for the topic of discussion was none other that Ahmed bin Shafiq, the man who had become Gabriel's personal bête noire. He chose Dina, with her pleasant voice and patina of early widowhood, to deliver the briefings. On the first night she lectured on Group 205, bin Shafiq's secret unit within the GID, and showed how the combination of Wahhabi ideology and Saudi money had wreaked havoc across the Middle East and South Asia. On the second night she recounted bin Shafiq's journey from loyal servant of the Saudi state to mastermind of the Brotherhood of Allah. Then she described in detail the operation against the Vatican, though she made no mention of the fact that Gabriel had been present at the scene of the crime. Gabriel realized that much of the information was superfluous, but he wanted Sarah to have no doubt in her mind that Ahmed bin Shafiq had earned the fate that awaited him.

On the final night they showed her a series of computer-generated photo illustrations of how bin Shafiq might look now. Bin Shafiq with a beard. Bin Shafiq with a balding pate. Bin Shafiq with a gray wig. With a black wig. With curly hair. With no hair at all. With his sharp Bedouin features softened by a plastic surgeon. But it was the wounded arm that would be her most valuable clue to his identity, Gabriel told her. The scar on the inside of his forearm he would never show. The slightly withered hand that he would never offer and keep safely tucked away, hidden from infidel eyes.

"We know he's concealed somewhere within Zizi's empire," Gabriel said. "He might come as an investment banker or a portfolio manager. He might come as a real estate developer or a pharmaceutical executive. He might come in a month. He might come in a year. He might *never* come. But if he does come, you can be certain he'll be well mannered and worldly and seem like anything but a professional terrorist. Don't look for a terrorist or someone who acts like a terrorist. Just look for a man."

He gathered up the photo illustrations. "We want to know about everyone who moves in and out of Zizi's orbit. We want you to gather as many names as you can. But this is the man we're looking for." Gabriel placed a photograph on the table in front of her. "This is the man we want." Another photograph. "This is the man we're after." *Another.* "He's the reason we're all here instead of being home with our families and our children." *Another.* "He's the reason we asked you to give up your life and join us." *Another.* "If you see him, you're to get us the name he's using and the company he's working for. Get the country of his passport if you can." Another photograph. "If you're not sure it's him, it doesn't matter. Tell us. If it doesn't turn out to be him, it doesn't matter. Tell us. Nothing happens based on your word alone. No one gets hurt because of you, Sarah. You're only the messenger."

"And if I give you a name?" she asked. "What happens then?"

Gabriel looked at his watch. "I think it's time Sarah and I had a word in private. Would you all excuse us?"

HE LED HER upstairs to his studio and switched on the halogen lamps. Marguerite Gachet glowed seductively under the intense white light. Sarah sat down in an ancient wingchair; Gabriel slipped on his magnifying visor and prepared his palette.

"How much longer?" she asked.

It was the same question Shamron had posed to him that windswept afternoon in October, when he had come to Narkiss Street to haul Gabriel out of exile. *A year*, he should have said to Shamron that day. And then he wouldn't be here, in a safe house in Surrey, about to send a beautiful American girl into the heart of Jihad Incorporated.

"I've removed the surface dirt and pressed the creases back into place with a warm, damp spatula," Gabriel said. "Now I have to finish the inpainting and apply a light coat of varnish—just enough to bring out the warmth of Vincent's original colors."

"I wasn't talking about the painting."

He looked up from his palette. "I suppose that depends entirely on you."

"I'm ready when you are," she said.

"Not quite."

"What happens if Zizi doesn't bite? What happens if he doesn't like the painting—or me?"

"No serious collector with money like Zizi is going to turn down a newly discovered van Gogh. And as for you, he won't have much choice in the matter. We're going to make you irresistible."

"How?"

"There are some things it's better you not know."

"Like what happens to Ahmed bin Shafiq if I see him?"

He added pigment to a puddle of medium and mixed it with a brush. "You know what happens to Ahmed bin Shafiq. I made that very clear to you in Washington the night we met."

"Tell me everything," she said. "I need to know."

Gabriel lowered his visor and lifted his brush to the canvas. When he spoke again, he spoke not to Sarah but to Marguerite. "We'll watch him. We'll listen to him if we can. We'll take his photograph and get his voice on tape and send it to our experts for analysis."

"And if your experts determine it's him?"

"At a time and place of our choosing, we'll put him down."

"Put him down?"

"Assassinate him. Kill him. Liquidate him. You choose the word that makes you most comfortable, Sarah. I've never found one."

"How many times have you done this?"

He put his face close to the painting and murmured, "Many times, Sarah."

"How many have you killed? Ten? Twenty? Has it solved the problem of terrorism? Or has it just made things worse? If you find Ahmed bin Shafiq and kill him, what will it accomplish? Will it end, or will another man step forward and take his place?"

"Eventually another murderer will take his place. In the meantime, lives will be saved. And justice will be done."

"Is it really justice? Can justice really be done with a silenced pistol or a booby-trapped car?"

He lifted the visor and turned around, his green eyes flashing in the glare of the lamps. "Are you enjoying this little debate about the moral relevancy of counterterrorism? Is it making you feel better? You can rest assured Ahmed bin Shafiq never wastes time wrestling with these questions of morality. You can be certain that if he ever manages to acquire a nuclear device, the only debate he'll have is whether to use it against New York or Tel Aviv."

"Is it justice, Gabriel? Or only vengeance?"

Again he saw himself and Shamron. This time the setting was not Gabriel's flat in Narkiss Street but a warm afternoon in September 1972—the day Shamron first came for him. Gabriel had posed the same question.

"It's not too late, Sarah. You can get out if you want. We can find someone else to take your place."

"There is no one else like me. Besides, I don't want out."

"Then what do you want?"

"Permission to sleep at night."

"Sleep, Sarah. Sleep very well."

"And you?"

"I have a painting to finish."

He turned around and lowered his visor again. Sarah was not done with him.

"Was it true?" she asked. "All the things written about you in the newspapers after the Gare de Lyon attack?"

"Most of it."

"You killed the Palestinians from Black September who carried out the Munich Massacre?"

"Some of them."

"Would you do it again, knowing everything you know now?"

He hesitated a moment. "Yes, Sarah, I would do it again. And I'll tell you why. It wasn't about vengeance. Black September was the most lethal terror group the world had ever seen, and it needed to be put out of business."

"But look at what it cost you. You lost your family."

"Everyone who engages in this fight loses something. Take your country, for example. You were innocent, a shining beacon of freedom and decency. Now you have blood on your hands and men in secret prisons. We don't do this sort of work because we enjoy it. We do it because we *have* to. We do it because we have no choice. You think I have a choice? You think Dina Sarid has a *choice*? We don't. And neither do you." He looked at her for a moment. "Unless you'd like me to find someone else to go in your place."

"There is no one else like me," she repeated. "When will I be ready?"

Gabriel turned and lifted his brush to the painting. *Soon*, he thought. One or two days more of inpainting. Then a coat of varnish. Then she would be ready.

*　　*　　*

ALL THAT REMAINED was her field training. Lavon and Uzi
Navot put her through her paces. For three days and
nights they took her into the streets of London and drilled
her on the basic tenets of tradecraft. They taught her how
to make a clandestine meeting and how to determine if
a site was compromised. They taught her how to spot
physical surveillance and simple techniques for shaking
it. They taught her how to make a dead drop and how
to hand material to a live courier. They taught her how
to dial the Office emergency lines on ordinary pay telephones and how to signal them with her body if she were
blown and required extraction. Lavon would later describe her as the finest natural amateur field agent he had
ever trained. He could have completed the course in two
days, but Gabriel, if only for his own peace of mind, insisted on a third. When Lavon finally returned to Surrey
that afternoon he found Gabriel standing morosely at
the edge of the stock pond, with a rod in one hand and
his eyes trained on the surface of the water as though
willing a fish to rise. "She's ready," Lavon said. "The
question is, are you?" Gabriel slowly reeled in his line
and followed Lavon back to the house.

LATER THAT SAME evening the lights went dark in the
melancholy little travel agency in Mason's Yard. Miss
Archer, clutching a batch of old files, paused for a moment
on the landing and peered through the sparkling glass entrance of Isherwood Fine Arts. Seated behind the recep-

tionist desk was Elena, Mr. Isherwood's scandalously pretty Italian secretary. She glanced up from her computer screen and blew Miss Archer an elaborate farewell kiss, then looked down again and resumed her work.

Miss Archer smiled sadly and headed down the stairway. There were no tears in her eyes. She'd done her crying in private, the way she did most things. Nor was there hesitation in her step. For twenty-seven years she'd been coming to this office five mornings a week. Saturdays, too, if there was housekeeping to be done. She was looking forward to retirement, even if it had come a bit earlier than expected. Maybe she'd take a long holiday. Or maybe she'd take a cottage in the countryside. She'd had her eye on a little place in the Chilterns for some time. She was certain of only one thing: She wasn't sorry to be leaving. Mason's Yard would never be the same again, not with the flashy Miss Bancroft in residence. It wasn't that Miss Archer had anything against Americans personally. She just wasn't terribly interested in living next door to one.

As she neared the bottom of the stairs a buzzer groaned, and the automatic locks on the outer door snapped open. *Thank you, Elena,* she thought as she stepped outside into the chill evening air. *Can't get off your shapely little backside to give a proper good-bye, and now you're practically shoving me out the door.* She was tempted to violate Mr. Isherwood's long-standing edict about waiting for the door to lock again, but, professional to the end, she stayed ten more seconds, until the dull thump of the dead bolts sent her shuffling slowly toward the passageway.

She did not know that her departure was being monitored by a three-man *neviot* team waiting in a van parked on the opposite side of Duke Street. The team remained in their van for another hour, just to make certain she hadn't forgotten anything. Then, shortly before eight, they slipped through the passageway and made their way slowly across the bricks of the old yard toward the gallery. To Julian Isherwood, who watched their unhurried approach from the window of his office, they seemed like gravediggers with a long night ahead.

19

LONDON

THE OPERATION BEGAN IN earnest late the following morning, when Julian Isherwood, London
art dealer of some repute, placed a discreet telephone call to the Knightsbridge residence of Andrew
Malone, exclusive art adviser to Zizi al-Bakari. It was answered by a drowsy woman who informed Isherwood
that Malone was out of the country.

"A fugitive from justice?" he asked, trying to make
light of an awkward situation.

"Try his mobile," the woman said before slamming
down the phone.

Fortunately, Isherwood had the number. He immediately dialed it and, as instructed, left a brief message. The
better part of the day elapsed before Malone bothered to
call him back.

"I'm in Rome," he said sotto voce. "Something big.
Very big."

"Hardly surprising, Andrew. You only do big."

Malone batted away Isherwood's attempt at flattery. "I'm afraid I only have a moment," he said. "What can I do for you, Julie?"

"I think I might have something for you. Something for your client, actually."

"My client doesn't do the Old Masters."

"The something I have for your client isn't Old Master. It's Impressionist. And not just any Impressionist, if you're getting my drift. It's special, Andrew. It's the sort of thing that only a handful of collectors in the world can even dream about owning, and your man happens to be one of them. I'm offering you a first look, Andrew—an *exclusive* first look. Any interest, or shall I take my business elsewhere?"

"Do tell more, Julie."

"Sorry, darling, but it's not the sort of thing one discusses over the telephone. How about lunch tomorrow? I'm buying."

"I'm going to Tokyo tomorrow. There's a collector there who has a Monet my man wants."

"How about the day after tomorrow then?"

"That's my jet-lag day. Let's make it Thursday, shall we?"

"You won't regret this, Andrew."

"Regrets are what sustain us. Ciao, Julie."

Isherwood hung up the telephone and looked at the heavy-shouldered man with strawberry-blond hair seated on the opposite side of the desk. "Nicely done," said Uzi Navot. "But next time let Zizi buy lunch."

*   *   *

IT CAME as no surprise to Gabriel that Andrew Malone
was in Rome, because he had been under electronic and
physical surveillance for nearly a week. He had gone to
the Eternal City to acquire a certain Degas sculpture that
Zizi had had his eye on for quite some time but left
empty-handed on Monday night and proceeded to
Tokyo. The anonymous collector whom Malone hoped
to relieve of a Monet was none other than the famed in-
dustrialist Morito Watanabe. Based on the defeatist expression on Malone's face as he was leaving Watanabe's
apartment, Gabriel concluded the negotiations had not
gone well. That evening Malone phoned Isherwood to
say he was staying in Tokyo a day longer than expected.
"I'm afraid we're going to have to postpone our little
get-together," he said. "Can we do it next week?"
Gabriel, who was anxious to get under way, instructed
Isherwood to hold fast, and the meeting was pushed
back just one day, from the Thursday to the Friday,
though Isherwood did agree to make it a late lunch so
that Malone could catch a few hours of sleep in his own
bed. Malone did in fact remain in Tokyo for an additional day, but Tokyo Station detected no further contact
between him and Watanabe or any of Watanabe's agents.
He returned to London late Thursday evening, looking,
according to Eli Lavon, like a cadaver in a Savile Row
suit. At three-thirty the next afternoon, the cadaver crept
through the doorway of Green's restaurant in Duke

Street and made his way to the quiet corner table, where Isherwood was already waiting. Isherwood poured him a very large glass of white burgundy. "All right, Julie," said Malone. "Let's cut the bullshit, shall we? What have you got up your sleeve? And who the fuck put it there? Cheers."

CHIARA WAS WAITING at the top of the landing ninety minutes later when Isherwood, fortified by two bottles of excellent white burgundy at Gabriel's expense, came teetering up the newly carpeted stairs. She directed him to the left, into the former premises of Archer Travel, where he was met by one of Gabriel's *neviot* listeners. He removed his coat and unbuttoned his shirt, revealing the small digital recording device secured to his chest by an elastic cummerbund.

"I don't usually do this sort of thing on the first date," he said.

The *neviot* man removed the recorder and smiled. "How was the lobster?"

"Bit chewy but otherwise fine."

"You did well, Mr. Isherwood. Very well."

"It's my last deal, I suspect. Now let's hope I don't go out with a bang."

THE RECORDING could have been sent by secure transmission, but Gabriel, like Adrian Carter, was still old-fashioned about some things, and he insisted that it be downloaded onto a disk and hand-carried to the Surrey safe house. As a result it was after eight by the time it finally arrived. He loaded the disk into a computer in the drawing room and clicked the Play icon. Dina was sprawled on the couch. Yaakov was seated in an armchair with his chin in his hands and elbows on his knees, hunched forward as though he were awaiting word from the front. It was Rimona's night to cook. As Andrew Malone began to speak, she shouted at Gabriel from the kitchen to turn up the volume so she could hear it, too.

"DO YOU take me for a fool, Julian?"

"It's the real thing, Andrew. I've seen it with my own eyes."

"Do you have a photograph?"

"I wasn't allowed."

"Who's the owner?"

"The owner wishes to remain anonymous."

"Yes, of course, but who the hell is it, Julian?"

"I cannot divulge the name of the owner. Period. End of discussion. She's entrusted me as her representative in this matter, and that's as far as it goes."

"She? So the owner is a woman?"

"The painting has been in the same family for three generations. Currently, it is in the hands of a woman."

"What sort of family, Julian? Give me a tickle."

"A French family, Andrew. And that's all you're getting from me."

"I'm afraid that's not going to work, Julian. You have to give me something I can hang my hat on. I can't go to Zizi empty-handed. Zizi gets annoyed when that happens. If you want Zizi in the game, you'll have to play by Zizi's rules."

"I won't be bullied, Andrew. I came to you as a favor. Frankly I don't give a shit about Zizi's rules. Frankly, I don't need Zizi at all. If I put the word on the street that I'm sitting on an undiscovered van Gogh, every major collector and museum in the world will be beating down my door and throwing money at me. Do please try to keep that in mind."

"Forgive me, Julie. It's been a long week. Let's start over, shall we?"

"Yes, let's."

"May I pose a few harmless questions?"

"Depends on how harmless."

"Let's start with an easy one. Where's the painting now? France or England?"

"It's here in London."

"In your gallery?"

"Not yet."

"What sort of painting are we talking about? Landscape? Still life? Portrait?"

"Portrait."

"Self?"

"No."

"Male or female?"

"Female."

"Dreamy. Early or late?"

"Very late."

"Saint-Rémy? Auvers?"

"The latter, Andrew. It was painted during the final days of his life in Auvers."

"You're not sitting on an undiscovered portrait of Marguerite Gachet, are you, Julian?"

"Maybe we should have a glance at the menu."

"Fuck the menu, Julian. Answer the question: Are you sitting on an undiscovered portrait of Marguerite?"

"I've gone as far as I can in terms of the content, Andrew. And that's final. If you want to know what it is, you'll have to take a look at it for yourself."

"You're offering me a look?"

"I'm offering your man a look, not you."

"Easier said than done. Running the world keeps my man busy."

"I'm prepared to offer you and Zizi exclusivity for seventy-two hours. After that, I'll have to open it up to other collectors."

"Bad form, Julian. My man doesn't like ultimatums."

"It's not an ultimatum. It's just business. He understands that."

"What kind of price tag are we talking about?"

"Eighty-five million."

"Eighty-five million? Then you do indeed need Zizi. You see, money's a bit tight at the moment, isn't it? Can't remember the last time someone's laid down eighty-five million for something. Can you, Julie?"

"This painting is worth every penny."

"If it's what you say it is, and if it's in perfect condition, I'll get you your eighty-five million in very short order. You see, my man has been looking for something splashy like this for a very long time. But then you knew that, didn't you, Julie? That's why you brought it to me first. You knew we could get the deal done in an afternoon. No auctions. No press. No nagging questions about your quiet little French woman who wants to remain anonymous. I'm the goose that lays the golden egg as far as you're concerned, and you're going to have to give the goose his due."

"What on earth are you talking about, Andrew?"

"You know precisely what I'm talking about."

"Maybe I'm a bit slow today. Mind spelling it out?"

"I'm talking about money, Julian. I'm talking about a very small slice of a very large pie."

"You want a cut? A piece of the action, as the Americans like to say."

"Let's leave the Americans out of this, shall we? My man's not terribly fond of the Americans at the moment."

"What sort of slice are we talking about, Andrew?"

"Let's say, just for argument's sake, that your commission on the sale is ten percent. That means you'll clear eight and a half million dollars for an afternoon's work. I'm asking for ten percent of your ten percent. Actually, I'm not asking, I'm demanding it. And you'll pay it, because that's the way the game is played."

"To the best of my faded recollection, you are Zizi al-Bakari's exclusive art consultant. Zizi pays you an outrageous salary. You practically live on Zizi's expense account. And you spend most of your free time relaxing at Zizi's properties. He does this so that the advice you bring him remains untainted by other dealings on your part. But you've been playing both sides of the street, haven't you, Andrew? How long has it been going on? How much have you been skimming? How much of Zizi's money have you got salted away?"

"It's not Zizi's money. It's my money. And what Zizi doesn't know won't hurt him."

"And if he finds out? He'll drop you in the Empty Quarter and let the vultures pick over your bones."

"Precisely, love. Which is why you're never going to mention a word of this to Zizi. I'm offering you seven and a half million dollars for an afternoon's work. Not bad, Julie. Take the deal. Let's get rich together, shall we?"

"All right, Andrew. You'll get your ten percent. But I want Zizi al-Bakari in my gallery in all his glory in seventy-two hours or the deal's off."

GABRIEL STOPPED THE RECORDING, reset it, and played the final bit again.

"But you've been playing both sides of the street, haven't you, Andrew? How long has it been going on? How much have you been skimming? How much of Zizi's money have you got salted away?"

"It's not Zizi's money. It's my money. And what Zizi doesn't know won't hurt him."

"And if he finds out? He'll drop you in the Empty Quarter and let the vultures pick over your bones."

"Precisely, love. Which is why you're never going to mention a word of this to Zizi."

Gabriel closed the file and removed the disk from the computer.

"Mr. Malone has been a very bad boy," said Yaakov.

"Yes, he has," said Gabriel, but then Gabriel had known that for some time.

"Don't you think that someone should tell Zizi about it?" asked Dina. "It's only right."

"Yes," said Gabriel, slipping the disk into his pocket. "Someone should. But not yet."

IT WAS among the longest seventy-two hours any of them had ever endured. There were false starts and false promises, commitments made and broken within the span of an afternoon. Malone played the role of the intimidator one minute and the supplicant the next. "Zizi's in a bit of a bind," he said late Saturday. "Zizi's in the middle of a major deal. Zizi's doing Delhi today and Singapore tomorrow. He can't possibly make time for London until midweek." Isherwood held firm. Zizi's exclusive window closed Monday at 5:00 P.M., he said. After that Zizi would find himself in scrum fighting it out with all comers.

Late on Sunday evening Malone phoned with the disappointing news that Zizi was taking a pass. Gabriel was not the least bit concerned, because that very afternoon the *neviot* team stationed in Archer Travel had seen a well-dressed Arab in his mid-thirties making an obvious reconnaissance run of Mason's Yard. Lavon, after viewing the surveillance photographs, identified the man as Jafar Sharuki, a former Saudi national guardsman who served as one of Zizi's advance security men. "He's coming," Lavon said. "Zizi always likes to play hard to get."

The call they were all expecting came at precisely 10:22 the following morning. It was Andrew Malone, and even though they could not see him, they knew the cadaver was all smiles. Zizi was on his way to London, he said. Zizi would be at Isherwood's gallery at 4:30. "Zizi has a few rules," Malone said before ringing off. "No alcohol or cigarettes. And make sure those two girls of yours are properly dressed. Zizi likes pretty girls, but he likes them modestly attired. He's a religious man, our Zizi. He's easily offended."

20

LONDON

MARGUERITE GACHET WAS THE first to arrive. She came in the back of an unmarked van, driven by a *bodel* from London Station, and was secreted into the premises of Isherwood Fine Arts through the secure loading bay. The delivery was monitored by two men from Wazir bin Talal's security unit, who were seated in a parked car in Duke Street, and by Jafar Sharuki, the advance man, who was picking at a plate of fish and chips in the pub next door to Isherwood's gallery. Confirmation of the painting's safe transfer arrived at the Surrey safe house at 3:18 P.M. in the form of a secure e-mail from the *neviot* team. It was taken in by Dina, then read aloud to Gabriel, who was at that moment slowly pacing the threadbare carpet in the drawing room. He paused for a moment and tipped his head, as though listening to distant music, then resumed his restless journey.

He felt as helpless as a playwright on opening night.

He had created the characters, given them their lines, and could see them now on a stage of his making. He could see Isherwood in his chalk-stripe suit and lucky red tie, craving a drink and nibbling on the nail of his left forefinger to relieve the tension. And Chiara seated behind her glossy new receptionist's desk, with her hair drawn sensibly back and her long legs crossed primly at the ankle. And Sarah, in the black Chanel suit she'd bought at Harrods two weeks earlier, propped serenely on the divan in the upstairs exhibition room, with her eyes on Marguerite Gachet and her thoughts on the monster who would be coming up the lift in two hours' time. If he could have rewritten anyone's role, it would have been Sarah's. It was too late for that now. The curtain was about to rise.

And so all the playwright could do now was pace the drawing room of his safe house and wait for the updates. At 3:04 Mr. Baker's 747 was seen on low approach to Heathrow Airport, Mr. Baker being their code name for Zizi al-Bakari. At 3:32 came word that Mr. Baker and his entourage had cleared VIP customs. At 3:45 they were seen boarding their limousines, and at 3:52 those same limousines were seen trying to set a land-speed record on the A4. At 4:09 Mr. Baker's artistic adviser, whom they code-named Marlowe, telephoned Isherwood from the motorcade to say they were running a few minutes behind schedule. That turned out not to be the case, however, because at 4:27 the same motorcade was spotted turning into Duke Street from Piccadilly.

There then followed the first stumble of the afternoon. Thankfully it was Zizi's and not theirs. It came as the first limousine was attempting to negotiate the narrow passageway from Duke Street into Mason's Yard. A moment into the exercise the driver determined that the cars were too large to fit through the breach. Sharuki, the advance man, had neglected to take a proper measurement. And so the final message that Gabriel received from the *neviot* team stated that Mr. Baker, chairman and CEO of Jihad Inc., was getting out of his car and walking to the gallery.

BUT SARAH was not waiting in the upstairs exhibition room. She was at that moment one floor below, in the office she shared with Julian, gazing out at the rather farcical scene taking place in the passageway. It was her first act of rebellion. Gabriel had wanted her to remain upstairs, hidden from view until the final moment, so that she could be unveiled along with Marguerite. She would obey his order eventually, but not until she saw Zizi once with her own eyes. She had studied his face in Yossi's magazine clippings and had memorized the sound of his voice in the videos. But clippings and videos were no substitute for a glimpse of the real thing. And so she stood there, in blatant contravention of Gabriel's instructions, and watched as Zizi and his entourage came filing through the passage into the darkened quadrangle.

Rafiq al-Kamal, chief of Zizi's personal security detail,

came first. He was bigger than he had appeared in the photographs, but moved with the agility of a man half his size. He had no overcoat, because an overcoat would interfere with his draw. He had no conscience either, Eli Lavon had told her. He made one quick survey of the yard, like a scout looking for signs of the enemy, then turned and with an old-fashioned hand signal beckoned the others forward.

Next came two very pretty girls with long black hair and long coats, looking peeved for having to walk the one hundred feet from the stranded cars to the gallery. The one on the right was Nadia al-Bakari, Zizi's spoiled daughter. The one on the left was Rahimah Hamza, daughter of Daoud Hamza, the Stanford-educated Lebanese reputed to be the true financial genius behind AAB Holdings. Hamza himself was trailing a few paces behind the girls with a mobile phone pressed to his ear.

After Hamza came Herr Manfred Wehrli, the Swiss banker who handled Zizi's money. Next to Wehrli was a child with no apparent owner, and behind the child two more beautiful women, one blond, the other with short hair the color of sandstone. When the child bolted suddenly across the yard in the wrong direction, he was snared in a pantherlike movement by Jean-Michel, the French kickboxer who now served as Zizi's personal trainer and auxiliary bodyguard.

Abdul-Jalil and Abdul-Hakim, the American-trained lawyers, came next. Yossi had broken up one of the briefings by contemptuously pointing out that Zizi had chosen lawyers whose names meant Servant of the Great and Servant of the Wise One. After the lawyers came Mansur, chief of Zizi's travel department, then Hassan, chief of communications, then Andrew Malone, Zizi's soon-to-be-former exclusive art consultant. And finally, sandwiched between Wazir bin Talal and Jafar Sharuki, was Zizi himself.

Sarah turned away from the window. Under Chiara's watchful gaze, she entered the tiny lift and pressed the button for the top floor. A moment later she was deposited into the upper exhibition room. In the center of the room, propped on a stately easel and veiled like a Muslim woman, was the van Gogh. From below she could hear Rafiq the bodyguard tramping heavily up the stairs.

You're not to think of him as a terrorist, Gabriel had said. *You're not to wonder whether any of his money ended up in the pocket of Marwan al-Shehhi or any of the other terrorists who murdered Ben. You're to think of him as an extraordinarily wealthy and important man. Don't flirt with him. Don't try to seduce him. Think of it as a job interview. You're not going to bed with him. You're going to work for him. And whatever you do, don't try to give Zizi any advice. You'll ruin the sale. Both of them.*

She turned and examined her appearance in the reflection of the elevator door. She was vaguely out of focus, which she found fitting. She was still Sarah Bancroft, just a different version. A reworking of the same painting. She smoothed the front of her Chanel suit—

not for Zizi, she told herself, but for Gabriel—and from below she heard the voice of the monster for the first time. "Good afternoon, Mr. Isherwood," said the chairman and CEO of Jihad Incorporated. "I'm Abdul Aziz al-Bakari. Andrew tells me you have a picture for me."

THE FIRST ELEVATOR dispensed only security men. Rafiq plunged into the room and groped her unabashedly with his eyes, while Sharuki peered beneath the divan for hidden weapons and Jean-Michel, the kickboxer, roamed the perimeter on the balls of his feet like a lethal ballet dancer. The next elevator brought Malone and Isherwood, who were wedged happily between Nadia and Rahimah. Zizi came on the third, with only the trusted bin Talal for company. His dark handmade suit hung gracefully over what was an otherwise paunchy physique. His beard was carefully trimmed, as was his deeply receded head of graying hair. His eyes were alert and active. They settled immediately on the one person in the room whose name he did not know.

Don't attempt to introduce yourself, Sarah. Don't look him directly in the eye. If there's a move to be made, let it be Zizi who makes it.

She looked down at her shoes. The elevator doors opened again, this time disgorging Abdul & Abdul, Servants of the Great Wise One, and Herr Wehrli the Swiss moneyman. Sarah watched them enter, then cast a glance at Zizi, who was still staring at her.

"Forgive me, Mr. al-Bakari," Isherwood said. "My manners are atrocious today. This is Sarah Bancroft, our assistant director. It's because of Sarah we're all here this afternoon."

Don't try to shake his hand. If he offers his, take it briefly and let go.

She stood very straight, with her hands behind her back and her eyes downward at a slight angle. Zizi's eyes were roving over her. Finally he stepped forward and extended his hand. "It's a pleasure to meet you." She took it and heard herself say: "The pleasure is mine, Mr. al-Bakari. It's an honor to meet you, sir."

He smiled and held on to her hand a moment more than was comfortable. Then he released it suddenly and made for the painting. Sarah turned and this time was treated to a view of his back, which was soft through the shoulders and wide in the hips. "I'd like to see the painting, please," he said to no one in particular, but Sarah was once more listening only to the voice of Gabriel. *Do the presentation on Zizi's timetable,* he had said. *If you force him to sit through a story, you'll only make him angry. Remember, Zizi is the star of the show, not Marguerite.*

Sarah slipped past him, careful not to brush his shoulder, then reached up and slowly removed the baize covering. She remained in front of the canvas for a moment longer, gathering up the fabric and blocking Zizi's view, before finally stepping to one side. "May I present *Marguerite Gachet at Her Dressing Table* by Vincent van

Gogh," she said formally. "Oil on canvas, of course, painted in Auvers in July 1890."

A collective gasp rose from Zizi's entourage, followed by an excited murmur. Only Zizi remained silent. His dark eyes were casting about the surface of the painting, his expression inscrutable. After a moment he lifted his gaze from the canvas and looked at Isherwood.

"Where did you find it?"

"I wish I could take credit for it, Mr. al-Bakari, but it was Sarah who discovered Marguerite."

Zizi's gaze moved to Sarah. "You?" he asked with admiration.

"Yes, Mr. al-Bakari."

"Then I'll ask you the same question I asked of Mr. Isherwood. Where did you find her?"

"As Julian explained to Mr. Malone, the owner wishes to remain anonymous."

"I'm not asking for the identity of the owner, Miss Bancroft. I'd just like to know how you discovered it."

You'll have to give him something, Sarah. He's entitled to it. But do it reluctantly and be discreet. A man like Zizi appreciates discretion.

"It was the result of several years of investigation on my part, Mr. al-Bakari."

"How interesting. Tell me more, please, Miss Bancroft."

"I'm afraid I can't without violating my agreement with the owners, Mr. al-Bakari."

"Owner," said Zizi, correcting her. "According to Andrew, the painting is the property of a French woman."

"Yes, that's correct, sir, but I'm afraid I can't be any more specific."

"But I'm just curious about how you found it." He folded his arms across his chest. "I love a good detective story."

"I would love to indulge you, Mr. al-Bakari, but I'm afraid I can't. All I can tell you is that it took me two years of searching in Paris and Auvers to find the painting and another year to convince the owner to give it up."

"Perhaps someday, when sufficient time has elapsed, you'll be gracious enough to share more of this fascinating story with me."

"Perhaps, sir," she said. "As for the authentication, we have determined the work is unquestionably Vincent's and, of course, we are prepared to stand behind that authentication."

"I'd be happy to examine the reports of your authenticators, Miss Bancroft, but quite frankly I don't need to see them. You see, it's quite obvious to me that this painting is truly the work of van Gogh." He placed his hand on her shoulder. "Come here," he said paternally. "Let me show you something."

Sarah took a step closer to the canvas. Zizi pointed to the upper right corner.

"Do you see that slight mark on the surface? If I'm not mistaken, that's Vincent's thumbprint. You see, Vincent was notoriously cavalier in the way he handled his work. When he finished this one, he probably picked it up by the corner and carried it through the streets of Auvers to his room above Café Ravoux. At any given time there were dozens of paintings in his room there. He used to lean them against the wall, one atop the next. He was working so quickly that the previous paintings were never quite dry when he laid the new ones on top. If you look carefully at this one, you can see the crosshatched impression of canvas on the surface of the paint."

His hand was still resting on her shoulder. "Very impressive, Mr. al-Bakari. But I'm not surprised, sir. Your reputation precedes you."

"I learned a long time ago that a man in my position cannot rely on the promises of others. He must be constantly on guard against deceptive schemes and clever forgeries. I'm quite confident no one could ever slip a forgery past me, in business or in art."

"One would be foolish even to try, Mr. al-Bakari."

Zizi looked at Isherwood. "You have quite a knack for finding undiscovered work. Didn't I read something the other day about a Rubens of yours?"

"You did, sir."

"And now a van Gogh." Zizi's gaze moved back to the painting. "Andrew tells me you have a price in mind."

"We do, Mr. al-Bakari. We think it's quite reasonable."

"So do I." He looked over his shoulder at Herr Wehrli, the banker. "Do you think you can find eighty-five million somewhere in the accounts, Manfred?"

"I think it's quite possible, Zizi."

"Then we have a deal, Mr. Isherwood." He looked at Sarah and said, "I'll take her."

AT 4:53 the *neviot* team sent word to Gabriel that the proceedings had moved to the lower offices and that Isherwood was now in discussions with Herr Wehrli and Abdul & Abdul over matters of payment and transfer of custody. Said discussions lasted slightly more than an hour, and at 6:05 came the flash that Mr. Baker and his party were traipsing across the darkened yard toward the motorcade parked in Duke Street. Eli Lavon handled the pursuit. For a few minutes it seemed the mansion in Mayfair was their destination, but by 6:15 it was clear that Mr. Baker and party were headed back to Heathrow and destinations unknown. Gabriel ordered Lavon to break off the chase. He didn't care where Mr. Baker was going now. He knew they would all meet again soon.

The video recording arrived at 7:45. It had been shot by the security camera mounted in the far corner of the exhibition room above the Claude landscape. Gabriel, as he watched it, felt as though he were seated in a box high above the stage.

"*. . . This is Sarah Bancroft, our assistant director. It's because of Sarah we're all here tonight. . . .*"

"*. . . Then, we have a deal, Mr. Isherwood. I'll take her. . . .*"

Gabriel stopped the recording and looked at Dina.

"You've sold him one girl," she said. "Now you just have to sell him the other."

Gabriel opened the audio file of Isherwood's meeting with Andrew Malone and clicked Play.

"It's not Zizi's money. It's my money. And what Zizi doesn't know won't hurt him."

"And if he finds out? He'll drop you in the Empty Quarter and let the vultures pick over your bones."

21

LONDON

THE DENUNCIATION of Andrew Malone arrived at the headquarters of AAB Holdings in Geneva at 10:22 A.M. the following Thursday. It was addressed to "Mr. Abdul Aziz al-Bakari, Esq." and hand-delivered by a motorcycle courier wearing the uniform of a local Geneva messenger service. The sender's name was a Miss Rebecca Goodheart, Earl's Court, London, but inspection by an AAB security underling determined that Miss Goodheart was merely a pseudonym for an anonymous snitch. After finding no evidence of radiological, biological, or explosive material, the underling forwarded the parcel to the office of Wazir bin Talal. There it remained until late Friday afternoon, when bin Talal returned to Geneva after a one-day trip to Riyadh.

He had other more pressing matters to attend to, and so it was nearly eight o'clock before he got around to opening the envelope. He immediately regretted the delay, for the allegations were quite serious in nature. On no fewer than nine occasions, according to Miss Goodheart, Andrew Malone had taken cash payments in violation of his personal services contract with Abdul Aziz al-Bakari. The allegations were supported by a packet of corroborating evidence, including bank deposit receipts, faxes, and personal e-mails taken from Malone's home computer. Bin Talal immediately placed a call to his superior's lakeside Geneva mansion and by nine that evening he was placing the documents on the desk of an irate Zizi al-Bakari.

That same evening, at eleven London time, bin Talal placed a call to Malone's Knightsbridge residence and ordered him to come to Geneva on the first available flight. When Malone protested that he had a prior commitment—and that it was a weekend, for heaven's sake—bin Talal made it clear that the summons was mandatory and failure to appear would be regarded as a grave offense. The call was recorded by a *neviot* team and forwarded immediately to Gabriel at the Surrey safe house, along with the rather shaky call Malone placed to British Airways ten minutes later, reserving a seat on the 8:30 A.M. flight to Geneva.

Eli Lavon booked a seat on the flight as well. Upon arrival in Geneva the two men were met by a pair of incongruous cars, Malone by a black S-Class Mercedes driven by one of Zizi's chauffeurs, and Lavon by a mudspattered Opel piloted by a courier from Geneva Station. Lavon ordered the *bodel* to give the Mercedes wide berth. As a result they arrived at Zizi's mansion several minutes after Malone. They found a secluded parking space farther down the street but did not have to wait long, because twenty minutes later Malone emerged from the house, looking more ashen than usual.

He proceeded directly back to the airport and booked a seat on the earliest flight back to London, which was at five o'clock. Lavon did the same. At Heathrow the two men went their separate ways, Lavon to Surrey and Malone to Knightsbridge, where he informed his wife that unless he could come up with four million pounds in extremely short order, Zizi al-Bakari was going to personally throw him off an extremely high bridge.

That was Saturday night. By the following Wednesday it was clear to Gabriel and the rest of his team that Zizi was in the market for a new exclusive art consultant. It was also clear he had his eye on someone in particular, because Sarah Bancroft, assistant director of Isherwood Fine Arts of Mason's Yard, St. James's, was under surveillance.

SHE BEGAN to think of them as friends. They rode with her in the Tube. They strolled in Mason's Yard and loitered in Duke Street. They followed her to lunch and there was always one waiting in Green's each evening when she stopped at the bar for a quick one with Oliver and the boys. They went with her to an auction at Sotheby's and watched her pick over the dreary contents of a saleroom in Hull. They even made a long trip with her down to Devon, where she sweet-talked a dusty minor aristocrat into parting with a lovely Venetian *Madonna and Child* that Isherwood had coveted for years. "Zizi's coming for you," Gabriel told her in a brief telephone call on the Monday afternoon. "It's only a matter of time. And don't be alarmed if your things seem a bit out of place when you go home tonight. Sharuki broke into your flat and searched it this morning."

The next day the first gift arrived, a Harry Winston diamond watch. Attached to the gift-wrapped box was a handwritten note: *Thank you for finding Marguerite. Eternally grateful, Zizi.* The earrings from Bulgari came the following day. The double strand of Mikimoto pearls the day after that. The gold mesh bangle from Tiffany on Thursday evening, just as she was preparing to leave work. She stuck it on her right wrist and walked over to Green's, where Oliver made a clumsy pass at her. "In another lifetime," she said, kissing his cheek, "but not tonight. Be a love, Oliver, and walk me to the Tube."

Evenings were the hardest on her. There were no more trips to the Surrey safe house. As far as Sarah was concerned the Surrey safe house did not exist. She found she missed them all terribly. They were a family, a loud, quarrelsome, cacophonous, loving family—the sort of family Sarah had never had. All that remained of them now was the occasional cryptic phone call from Gabriel and the light in the flat on the opposite side of the street. Yossi's light, but soon even Yossi would be lost to her. At night, when she was alone and afraid, she sometimes wished she had told them to find someone else. And sometimes she would think of poor Julian and wonder how on earth he was going to get along without her.

THE FINAL PACKAGE arrived at three o'clock the next afternoon. It was hand-delivered by a messenger dressed in a suit and tie. Inside was a handwritten note and a single airline ticket. Sarah opened the ticket jacket and looked at the destination. Ten seconds later the telephone on her desk rang.

"Isherwood Fine Arts. This is Sarah."

"Good afternoon, Sarah."

It was Zizi.

"Hello, Mr. al-Bakari. How are you, sir?"

"I'll know in a moment. Did you receive the invitation and the airline tickets?"

"I did, sir. And the earrings. *And* the watch. *And* the pearls. *And* the bangle."

"The bangle is my favorite."

"Mine, too, sir, but the gifts were completely unnecessary. As is this invitation. I'm afraid I can't accept."

"You insult me, Sarah."

"It's not my intention, sir. As much as I would love to spend a few days in the sun, I'm afraid I can't go jetting off at a moment's notice."

"It's not a moment's notice. If you look carefully at

the tickets, you see that you have three days until your departure."

"I can't go jetting off three days from now either. I have business to attend to here at the gallery."

"I'm sure Julian can spare you for a few days. You just made him a great deal of money."

"This is true."

"So how about it, Sarah? Will you come?"

"I'm afraid the answer is no, sir."

"You should know one thing about me, Sarah, and that is I never take no for an answer."

"I just don't think it would be appropriate, sir."

"Appropriate? I think you've misinterpreted my motives."

"What are your motives, sir?"

"I'd like you to come to work for me."

"As what, sir?"

"I never discuss such matters over the phone, Sarah. Will you come?"

She allowed ten seconds to elapse before she gave him her answer.

"Brilliant," he said. "One of my men will accompany you. He'll collect you at your flat at eight A.M. Monday morning."

"I'm perfectly capable of traveling alone, Mr. al-Bakari."

"I'm sure you are, but it will be easier if one of my security men comes with you. I'll see you Monday evening."

And then he rang off. As Sarah replaced the receiver, she realized he hadn't asked for her address.

*   *   *

GABRIEL WAS breaking down his studio at the Surrey safe house when Lavon came pounding up the stairs, holding a printout of the message that had just arrived from the *neviot* team in Mason's Yard. "Zizi's made his move," he said, handing the printout to Gabriel. "He wants to see her right away."

Gabriel read the message, then looked up at Lavon. "Shit," he murmured. "We're going to need a boat."

THEY HAD a champagne supper to celebrate, complete with a place setting for Sarah, the one member of the team who could not join them. The next morning Lavon drove Gabriel to Heathrow Airport, and by four-thirty that afternoon he was enjoying the view of the sunset from a CIA safe flat on Collins Avenue in Miami Beach. Adrian Carter was wearing chinos, a cotton pullover, and penny loafers with no socks. He handed Gabriel a glass of lemonade and a photograph of a very large boat.

"She's called *Sun Dancer*," Carter said. "She's a seventy-four-foot oceangoing luxury motor yacht. I'm sure you and your team will find her more than comfortable."

"Where did you get it?"

"We seized it a few years ago from a Panamanian drug runner named Carlos Castillo. Mr. Castillo now resides in a federal prison in Oklahoma, and we've been using his boat to do the Lord's work down here in the Caribbean."

"How many times has it been used?"

"Five or six times by the DEA, and we've used it twice."

Gabriel handed the photograph back to Carter. "It's dirty," he said. "Can't you get me something with a clean provenance?"

"We've changed her name and registry several times. There's no way Zizi or any of his security goons can trace it back to us."

Gabriel sighed. "Where is it now?"

"A marina on Fisher Island," Carter said, pointing to the south. "It's being provisioned right now. We have a CIA crew leaving Langley tonight."

"Nice try," Gabriel said, "but I'll use my own crew."

"You?"

"We have a navy, Adrian. A very good one, in fact. I have a crew on standby in Haifa. And tell your boys to take out the listening devices. Otherwise, we'll do it for them, and *Sun Dancer* won't look very good when we give it back to you."

"It's already been taken care of," Carter said. "How are you planning to get your team over here?"

"I was hoping a friend of mine from American intelligence would extend a helping hand."

"What do you need?"

"Airlift and landing rights."

"How quickly can your crew get from Haifa to London?"

"They can leave first thing in the morning."

"I'll send one of our planes to London tonight. It will collect your team and bring them back here. We'll set it down at Homestead and dispense with passports and customs. You can put out to sea on Sunday night and rendezvous with Zizi Monday afternoon."

"Sounds like we have ourselves a deal," Gabriel said. "All we need now is Ahmed bin Shafiq."

"He'll come," Carter said with certainty. "The only question is will your girl be there when he does?"

"She's *our* girl, Adrian. Sarah belongs to all of us."

PART THREE

THE NIGHT JOURNEY

22

HARBOR ISLAND, BAHAMAS

"THERE SHE IS," Wazir bin Talal shouted above the roar of the Sikorsky's rotor blades. He pointed out the right side of the aircraft. *Alexandra*, Zizi's vast private yacht, was slicing through the waters west of the island. "Isn't she beautiful?"

"She's very large," Sarah shouted back at him.

"Two hundred seventy-five feet," said bin Talal, as though he had built it himself.

Two hundred eighty-two, Sarah thought. *But who's counting?* Yossi had described it as a floating emirate. She permitted them to enter her thoughts. Her last contact had been Sunday afternoon. Eli Lavon had bumped into her in Oxford Street while she was picking up a few odds and ends for the trip. *We'll be with you the entire time*, he had told her. *Don't look for us. Don't try to make contact unless it's a force-ten calamity. We'll come to you. Have a nice trip.*

She leaned back in her seat. She was still wearing the jeans and woolen sweater she put on that morning. Only ten hours removed from the chilly damp of London, her body was unprepared for the onslaught of tropical heat. The jeans felt as though they were glued to her thighs, and the sweater seemed to be sawing at the side of her neck. She glanced at bin Talal, who seemed to be having no difficulty adjusting to the abrupt change of climate. He had a wide face, two small dark eyes, and a goatee beard. Dressed as he was now, in his tailored gray suit and tie, he might have been mistaken for a financier. His hands, however, betrayed the true nature of his work. They looked like mallets.

The roar of the rotor blade made further conversation impossible, and for this she was eternally grateful. Her loathing of him was now limitless. Since just after dawn he had been a constant presence at her side, menacing in his politeness. At the airport he had insisted on coming with her to the duty-free shops and had intervened with a company credit card when she bought a flask of aloe lotion. During the flight he had shown an endless interest in all aspects of her life. *Please, Miss Sarah, tell me about your childhood . . . Please, Miss Sarah, tell me about your interest in art . . . Please, Miss Sarah, tell me why you decided to leave Washington and come to London . . .* To escape him she had feigned sleep. Two hours later, when she feigned waking, he probed at her some more. *You say your father worked for Citicorp? You know, it's quite possible he and Mr. al-Bakari have actually met. Mr. al-*

Bakari has had many dealings with Citicorp . . . With that she had slipped on her headphones to watch an in-flight film. Bin Talal had selected the same one.

When she looked out the window again, *Alexandra* seemed to fill the horizon. She could see Nadia and Rahimah catching the last of the day's sunlight on the foredeck, their black hair twisting in the wind. And Abdul & Abdul huddled with Herr Wehrli on the after-deck, plotting their next conquest. And floating above it all, dressed in white with one arm raised in greeting, was Zizi. *Turn back,* she thought. *Drop me on solid ground. You stay here, Mr. bin Talal. I'll see myself back to London, thank you.* But she knew there was no turning back now. Gabriel had given her one last chance in Surrey, and she had agreed to see it through.

The Sikorsky settled over *Alexandra*'s stern and sank slowly toward the helipad. Sarah saw something else: Zizi in the exhibition room of Julian's gallery, warning her that no one could slip a forgery past him, in business or in art. *I'm not a forgery,* she told herself as she climbed out of the helicopter. *I'm Sarah Bancroft. I used to be a curator at the Phillips Collection in Washington. Now I work for Isher-wood Fine Arts in London. I've forgotten more about art than you'll ever know. I don't want your job or your money. In fact, I don't want anything to do with you.*

BIN TALAL showed her to her quarters. They were larger than her flat in Chelsea: a sprawling bedroom with separate seating area, a marble bathroom with sunken tub and Jacuzzi, a sweeping private deck which at that moment was lit by the setting sun. The Saudi laid her bag on the king-sized bed like a hotel bellman and started to pull at the zipper. Sarah tried to stop him.

"That's not necessary. I can see to my own bag, thank you."

"I'm afraid it *is* necessary, Miss Sarah."

He lifted the top and started removing her things.

"What are you doing?"

"We have rules, Miss Sarah." The profound courtesy was now absent from his voice. "It's my job to make certain the guests adhere to those rules. No alcohol, no tobacco, and no pornography of any kind." He held up an American fashion magazine she'd picked up at the airport in Miami. "I'm afraid I have to confiscate this. Do you have any alcohol?"

She shook her head. "And no cigarettes either."

"You don't smoke?"

"Occasionally, but I don't make a habit of it."

"I'll need your mobile phone until you leave *Alexandra*."

"Why?"

"Because guests aren't allowed to use cellular telephones aboard this craft. Besides, they won't function because of the ship's electronics."

"If it won't function, then what's the use of confiscating it?"

"I assume your cell phone has the ability to take photographs as well as record and store video and audio clips?"

"That's what the little man said who sold it to me, but I never use it that way."

He held out his enormous hand. "Your telephone, please. I can assure you it will be well cared for."

"I have work to do. I can't be cut off from the world."

"You're more than welcome to use our shipboard satellite phone system."

And you'll be listening in, won't you?

She dug her phone from her handbag, switched off the power, and surrendered it to him.

"Now your camera, please. Mr. al-Bakari does not like cameras around when he is trying to relax. It is against the rules to photograph him, his employees, or any of his guests."

"Are there other guests besides me?"

He ignored her question. "Did you bring a Black-Berry or any other kind of PDA?"

She showed it to him. He held out his hand.

"If you read my e-mail, so help me—"

"We have no desire to read your e-mail. Please, Miss Sarah, the sooner we get this over with, the sooner you can settle in and relax."

She handed him the BlackBerry.

"Did you bring an iPod or any other type of personal stereo?"

"You've got to be kidding."

"Mr. al-Bakari believes personal stereos are rude and

inconsiderate. Your room contains a state-of-the-art audio and visual entertainment system. You won't need your own."

She gave him the iPod.

"Any other electronics?"

"A hair dryer."

He held out his hand.

"You can't take a girl's hair dryer."

"You have one in your bathroom that's compatible with the ship's electrical system. In the meantime, let me have yours, just so there's no confusion."

"I promise not to use it."

"Your hair dryer, please, Miss Sarah."

She pulled the hair dryer from her suitcase and gave it to him.

"Mr. al-Bakari has left a gift for you in the closet. I'm sure he would be flattered if you wore it to dinner. It's scheduled for nine o'clock this evening. I suggest you try to sleep until then. You've had a long day—and then there's the time difference, of course."

"Of course."

"Would you like to be awakened at eight o'clock?"

"I can manage on my own. I brought a travel alarm clock."

He smiled humorlessly. "I'll need that, too."

MUCH TO HER surprise she did sleep. She dreamt nothing and woke in darkness, unsure of where she was. Then a puff of warm sea wind caressed her breast, like the breath of a lover, and she realized she was aboard *Alexandra* and that she was utterly alone. She lay very still for a moment, wondering if they were looking at her. *Assume they're watching your every move and listening to your every word,* Eli had told her. She pictured another scene taking place somewhere aboard the ship. Wazir bin Talal downloading every e-mail from her BlackBerry. Wazir bin Talal running a check on every number dialed from her mobile telephone. Wazir bin Talal tearing apart her hair dryer and her iPod and her travel alarm clock, looking for bugs and tracking devices. But there were no bugs or tracking devices, for Gabriel had known they would ransack her possessions the moment she entered their camp. *In a situation like this, Sarah, simple is best. We'll do it the old-fashioned way. Telephone codes. Physical recognition signals.*

She raised her wristwatch to her face and saw it was five minutes to eight. She closed her eyes again and allowed the breeze to flow over her body. Five minutes later the bedside telephone purred softly. She reached out in the darkness and brought the receiver to her ear.

"I'm awake, Mr. bin Talal."

"I'm so glad to hear that."

The voice wasn't bin Talal's. It was Zizi's.

"I'm sorry, Mr. al-Bakari. I thought you were someone else."

"Obviously," he said pleasantly. "Did you manage to get a little rest?"

"I think so."

"And your flight?"

"It was fine, sir."

"Can we make a deal?"

"That depends entirely on the deal, Mr. al-Bakari."

"I would prefer it if you called me Zizi. It's what my friends call me."

"I'll try." Then she added playfully: *"Sir."*

"I look forward to seeing you at dinner, Sarah."

The connection went dead. She hung up the phone and went onto the sundeck. It was very dark now. A fingernail moon hung low on the horizon, and the sky was a blanket of wet shimmering stars. She looked toward the stern and saw a pair of winking emerald navigation lights hovering several miles in the distance. There were more lights off the prow. She remembered what Eli had said during her street training. *Sometimes the easiest way to tail a man is to walk in front of him.* She supposed the same applied to watching at sea.

She went back into her room, shed her clothing, and padded into the bathroom. *Avert your eyes, Wazir,* she thought. *No pornography.* She bathed in Zizi's hedonistic Jacuzzi tub and listened to Keith Jarrett on Zizi's state-of-the-art audio system. She wrapped herself in Zizi's terry-cloth robe and dried her hair with Zizi's hair dryer. She applied makeup to her face, just enough to erase the effects of the transatlantic journey, and as she arranged her hair loosely about her shoulders she thought briefly of Gabriel.

"How do you like to wear your hair, Sarah?"

"Down, mostly."

"You have very nice cheekbones. A very graceful neck. You should think about wearing your hair up from time to time. Like Marguerite."

But not tonight. When she was satisfied with her appearance she went into the bedroom and opened the closet door. Lying on one of the shelves was a gift-wrapped box. She removed the paper and lifted the lid. Inside was an ivory-colored crushed-silk pantsuit and silk camisole. It fit her perfectly, just like everything else. She added the Harry Winston watch, the Bulgari earrings, the Mikimoto pearls, and the Tiffany bracelet. At five minutes to nine she left the room and made her way to the afterdeck. *Try to forget we even exist. Be Sarah Bancroft, and nothing can go wrong.*

ZIZI GREETED her lavishly.

"Sarah! So lovely to see you again. Everyone, this is Sarah. Sarah, this is everyone. There are too many names for you to remember at once, unless you're one of those people who's extremely good with names. I suggest we do it slowly. Please sit down, Sarah. You've had a very long day. You must be famished."

He settled her near the end of the long table and went to his own place at the opposite end. An Abdul was seated to her right and Herr Wehrli the banker to her left. Across from her was Mansur, the chief of the travel department, and Herr Wehrli's skittish wife, who seemed to find the entire spectacle appalling. Next to Frau Wehrli sat Jean-Michel, the personal trainer. His long blond hair was pulled back into a ponytail, and he was gazing at Sarah with unabashed interest, much to the distress of his wife, Monique. Farther along the table sat Rahimah and her beautiful boyfriend, Hamid, who was an Egyptian film star of some sort. Nadia sat proprietarily next to her father. Several times during the long meal, Sarah cast her eyes in Zizi's direction only to find Nadia glaring back at her. Nadia, she suspected, was going to be as much of a problem as bin Talal.

Zizi, after reliably establishing that Sarah did not speak Arabic, decreed that the languages of the night were French and English. Their conversation was frighteningly banal. They talked of clothing and films, restaurants that Zizi liked to commandeer and a hotel in Nice that he was thinking about buying. The war, terrorism, the plight of the Palestinians, the American president— none of these seemed to exist. Indeed, nothing seemed to exist beyond the rails of *Alexandra* or the boundaries of Zizi's empire. Zizi, sensing that Sarah was being left out, asked her once again to explain how she had found the van Gogh. When she refused to rise to his baiting, he smiled wolfishly and said, "One day I'll get it out of you." And Sarah, for the first time, felt a sickening rush of complete terror.

During the dessert course he rose from his place and pulled a chair alongside hers. He was dressed in a cream-colored linen suit, and the tops of his pudgy cheeks were colored red from the sun.

"I trust you found the food to your liking."

"It was delicious. You must have been cooking all afternoon."

"Not me," he said modestly. "My chefs."

"You have more than one?"

"Three, actually. We have a crew and staff of forty. They work exclusively for me, regardless of whether *Alexandra* is at sea or waiting in port. You'll get to know them during our trip. If you need something, don't hesitate to ask. I take it your accommodations are satisfactory?"

"More than satisfactory, Mr. al-Bakari."

"Zizi," he reminded her. He toyed with a strand of ebony prayer beads. "Mr. bin Talal told me you were upset by some of our rules and security procedures."

"Perhaps taken by surprise would be a better description. I wish you would have told me in advance. I would have packed lighter."

"Mr. bin Talal can be somewhat fanatical in his devotion to my security. I apologize for his behavior. That said, Sarah, when one enters the world of AAB Holdings, one has to adhere to certain rules—for the safety of everyone." He flicked his wrist, and wrapped his prayer beads around the first two fingers of his right hand. "Did you have a chance to think about my offer?"

"I still don't know what it is."

"But you *are* interested. Otherwise you wouldn't be here."

"Let's just say I'm intrigued, and I'm willing to discuss the matter further."

"You are a shrewd businesswoman, Sarah. I admire that. Enjoy the sun and the sea. We'll talk in a few days when you've had a chance to relax."

"A few days? I have to get back to London."

"Julian Isherwood got along without you for many years, Sarah. Something tells me he'll survive while you take a much deserved vacation with us."

And with that he went back to his own end of the table and sat down next to Nadia. "Welcome to the family," said Herr Wehrli. "He likes you very much. When you negotiate your salary, be unreasonable. He'll pay whatever you want."

DINNER THAT EVENING aboard *Sun Dancer* had been far less extravagant and the conversation far more animated. They did not avoid topics such as war and terrorism. Indeed they embraced them wholeheartedly and argued about them long past midnight. At the end of the evening there was another quarrel, this one about whose night it was to do the dishes. Dina and Rimona claimed exemption on the grounds that they had performed the task the last night in Surrey. Gabriel, in one of his few command decisions of the day, inflicted the task on the new boys: Oded and Mordecai, two experienced all-purpose field hands, and Mikhail, a gunman on loan to the Office from the Sayeret Matkal. He was a Russian-born Jew with bloodless skin and eyes the color of glacial ice. "A younger version of you," Yaakov had said. "Good with a gun, but no conscience. He practically took down the command structure of Hamas by himself."

Their accommodations lacked the grandeur of *Alexandra*'s, and no one was granted the privilege of private quarters. Gabriel and Lavon, veterans of manhunts past, bunked together in the prow. Lavon was used to Gabriel's erratic operational sleeping habits and was not surprised the following morning when he woke before dawn to find Gabriel's bed unoccupied. He climbed out of his bunk and went up to the deck. Gabriel was standing at the prow, coffee in hand, his gaze fixed on the smudge of light on the distant horizon. Lavon went back to his bunk and slept two more hours. When he returned to the deck, Gabriel was standing in the exact same spot, staring out at the empty sea.

23

OFF THE BAHAMAS

HER DAYS QUICKLY ACQUIRED SHAPE.

She would rise early each morning and linger in a drowsy half-sleep in the enormous bed, listening to *Alexandra* slowly stirring to life around her. Then, usually around seven-thirty, she would ring the steward and order her morning coffee and brioche, which would come on a tray, always with a fresh flower, five minutes later. If there was no rain she would take her breakfast in the shade of her starboard-facing private sundeck. *Alexandra* was on a southeasterly heading, steaming without haste toward an unnamed destination, and usually Sarah could just make out the low, flat islands of the Bahamian chain in the distance. Zizi's suite was one level above her. Some mornings she could hear him on the telephone, closing the day's first deals.

After breakfast she would place two calls to London on the shipboard system. First she would dial her apartment in Chelsea and, invariably, would find two or three ersatz voice messages left by the Office. Then she would call the gallery and speak to Chiara. Her soft, Italian-accented English was like a lifeline. Sarah would pose questions about pending deals; Chiara would then read Sarah's telephone messages. Contained in the seemingly benign patter was vital information: Sarah telling Chiara that she was safe and that there was no sign of Ahmed bin Shafiq; Chiara telling Sarah that Gabriel and the others were close by and that she was not alone. Hanging up on Chiara was the hardest part of Sarah's day.

By then it was usually ten o'clock, which meant that Zizi and Jean-Michel were finished working out and the gym was now free to other staff and guests. The rest of them were a sedentary lot; Sarah's only company each morning was Herr Wehrli, who would torment himself on the elliptical machine for a few minutes before retiring to the sauna for a proper Swiss sweat. Sarah would run thirty minutes on the treadmill, then row for thirty more. She had been on the Dartmouth crew, and within a few days began to see definition in her shoulders and back that hadn't been there since Ben's death.

After her workout Sarah would join the other women on the foredeck for a bit of sun before lunch. Nadia and Rahimah remained distant, but the wives gradually warmed to her, especially Frau Wehrli and Jihan, the fair-haired young Jordanian wife of Hassan, Zizi's communications specialist. Monique, Jean-Michel's wife, spoke rarely to her. Twice Sarah peered over the top of her paperback novel and saw Monique glaring at her, as though she were plotting to shove Sarah over the rail when no one else was looking.

Lunch was always a slow, lengthy affair. Afterward the ship's crew would bring *Alexandra* to a stop for what Zizi referred to as the afternoon jet-ski derby. For the first two days Sarah remained safely on the deck, watching while Zizi and his executives leaped and plunged through the swells. On the third day he convinced her to take part and personally gave her a lesson in how to operate her craft. She sped away from *Alexandra*'s stern, then killed the engine and gazed for a long time at the pinprick of white on the horizon behind them. She must have strayed too far, because a few moments later Jean-Michel came alongside her and gestured for her to return to the mother ship. "One hundred meters is the boundary," he said. "Zizi's rules."

His day was rigorously scheduled. A light breakfast in his room. Phone calls. Exercise with Jean-Michel in the gym. A late-morning meeting with staff. Lunch. The jet-ski derby. Another meeting with staff that usually lasted until dinner. Then, after dinner, phone calls late into the night. On the second day the helicopter departed *Alexandra* at ten in the morning and returned an hour later with a delegation of six men. Sarah examined their faces as they filed into Zizi's conference room and concluded that none of them was Ahmed bin Shafiq. Later, an Abdul volunteered three of their names, which Sarah stored in her memory for later retrieval. That afternoon she encountered Zizi alone in one of the lounges and asked him whether they could discuss his job offer.

"What's the rush, Sarah? Relax. Enjoy yourself. We'll talk when the time is right."

"I have to be getting back to London, Zizi."

"To Julian Isherwood? How can you go back to Julian after this?"

"I can't stay forever."

"Of course you can."

"Can you at least tell me where we're headed?"

"It's a surprise," he said. "One of our little traditions. As honorary captain, I get to pick our destination. I keep it secret from the others. We're planning to make a call tomorrow at Grand Turk. You can go ashore if you like and do a bit of shopping."

Just then Hassan appeared, handed Zizi a phone, and murmured something in Arabic into his ear that Sarah couldn't understand. "Will you excuse me, Sarah? I have to take this." And with that he disappeared into his conference room and closed the door.

She woke the following morning to the sensation of utter stillness. Instead of lingering in bed, she rose immediately and went out onto the sundeck and saw that they had anchored off Cockburn Town, the capital of Turks and Caicos. She had breakfast in her room, checked in with Chiara in London, then made arrangements with the crew for a shore craft to take her into town. At eleven-thirty she went astern and found Jean-

Michel waiting for her, dressed in a black pullover and white Bermuda shorts.

"I volunteered to be your escort," he said.

"I don't need an escort."

"No one goes ashore without security, especially the girls. Zizi's rules."

"Is your wife coming?"

"Unfortunately, Monique is not well this morning. It seems dinner didn't agree with her."

They rode into the harbor in silence. Jean-Michel docked the boat expertly, then followed her along a waterfront shopping street while she ran her errands. In one boutique she selected two sundresses and a new bikini. In another she bought a pair of sandals, a beach bag, and a pair of sunglasses to replace the pair she'd lost in the previous day's jet-ski derby. Then it was over to the pharmacy for shampoo and body lotion and a loofah to remove the peeling skin from her sunburned shoulders. Jean-Michel insisted on paying for everything with one of Zizi's credit cards. On the way back to the boat, Rimona walked past, hidden behind a pair of large sunglasses and a floppy straw hat. And in a tiny bar overlooking the harbor, she noticed a familiar-looking man with a white bucket hat and sunglasses, peering mournfully into a drink with a festive umbrella. Only when she was back aboard *Alexandra* did she realize it had been Gabriel.

When she telephoned London the next day, Julian came briefly on the line and asked when she was planning to return. Two days later he did so again, but this time his voice contained an audible note of agitation. Late that afternoon Zizi rang Sarah's room. "Would you come up to my office? I think it's time we talked." He hung up the phone without waiting for an answer.

SHE DRESSED as professionally as possible: white Capri pants, a yellow blouse that covered her arms, a pair of flat-soled sandals. She considered putting on a bit of makeup but decided she could make no improvements to what a week in the Caribbean sun had already accomplished. Ten minutes after receiving the summons, she left her suite and headed upstairs to Zizi's office. He was seated at the conference table along with Daoud Hamza, Abdul & Abdul, and Herr Wehrli. They rose in unison as Sarah was shown into the room, then gathered up their papers and filed wordlessly out. Zizi gestured for Sarah to sit. At the opposite end of the room, Al Jazeera flickered silently on a large flat-panel television: Israeli troops destroying the home of a Hamas suicide bomber while his mother and father wept for the cameras. Zizi's gaze lingered on the screen a moment before turning toward Sarah.

"I've invested tens of millions of dollars in the Palestinian territories, and I've given them millions more in charitable donations. And now the Israelis are tearing it to shreds while the world stands by and does nothing."

Where was the world's condemnation yesterday, Sarah

thought, *when twenty-two charred and broken bodies lay scattered along a Tel Aviv street?* She looked down at her hands, at Zizi's gold bangle and Zizi's Harry Winston watch, and said nothing.

"But let's talk about something more pleasant," Zizi said.

"Please, let's." She looked up and smiled. "You'd like to make me an extravagant offer to come work for you."

"I would?"

"Yes, you would."

Zizi returned her smile. "We have an opening in our art department." His smile faded. "An unexpected opening, but an opening nonetheless. I'd like you to fill it."

"Your art *department?*"

"I'm sorry," he said. "It's how we refer to the various divisions of the operation. Hassan is chief of the communications department. Mansur's department is travel. Herr Wehrli is banking. Mr. bin Talal is—"

"Security."

"Exactly," Zizi said.

"Who's the chief of your art department?"

"At the moment, it's me. But I'd like you to take over that job."

"What about Andrew Malone?"

"Andrew Malone is no longer working for me." Zizi fussed for a moment with his prayer beads. His eyes went again to the television screen and remained there while he spoke. "My arrangement with Andrew was supposed to be exclusive. I paid him a generous retainer. In return he was to give me advice with no possible conflict of interest on his part. As it turned out, Andrew repeatedly betrayed me. For the last several years he's been taking money from me *and* from the people I've been buying from, a flagrant violation of our agreement. Among the dealers and collectors who made payments to Andrew in violation of his contract was Julian Isherwood." He looked at her. "Were you aware of any cash payment by Julian Isherwood to Andrew Malone?"

"I wasn't," she said. "And if it happened, I'm sorry."

"I believe you," he said. "Andrew would have sworn Julian to secrecy. He was careful to cover his tracks in his double dealings. Unfortunately he could not hide the evidence of his betrayal inside his bank accounts. That's how we found out about it."

He made another glance at the television and frowned. "The job I have in mind for you is much larger than Andrew's. Not only will you assist me in the acquisition of works, but you will also be responsible for the care and conservation of the collection. It's my intention to begin lending some of my pieces to European and American museums as a means of fostering better cultural relations between my country and the West. As a former curator, you are more than suited to manage those transactions." He scrutinized her for a moment. "Would you be interested in such a position?"

"I would, but—"

"—but you would like to discuss money and benefits before giving me an answer, which I understand completely. If you don't mind my asking, how much is Julian paying you now?"

"Actually, I think I would mind."

He sighed heavily and gave his prayer beads a twirl. "Is it your intention to make this as difficult as possible?"

"I try not to make a habit of negotiating against myself."

"I'm prepared to pay you a salary of five hundred thousand dollars a year, plus housing, plus an unlimited expense account. The job would require a great deal of travel—and, of course, you would be spending a great deal of time with me and my extended family. That was the reason I invited you on this cruise. I wanted you to get to know us. I trust you've enjoyed yourself and our hospitality."

"Very much," she said.

He held up his hands. "Well?"

"I'll need a guaranteed contract of three years."

"Done."

"Five hundred the first year, six hundred the second, and seven fifty the third."

"Done."

"And then there's the signing bonus."

"Name your figure."

"Two hundred and fifty thousand."

"I was prepared to give you another five hundred. Do we have a deal?"

"I believe we do." Her smile quickly faded. "I'm not looking forward to telling Julian about it."

"It's just business, Sarah. Julian will understand."

"He's going to feel very hurt."

"Perhaps it would be easier if I spoke to him."

"No," she said, shaking her head. "I'll do it myself. I owe it to him."

"You're obviously a woman of integrity." He stood suddenly. "I'll instruct the lawyers to draw up your contract. Herr Wehrli will issue you a check for your signing bonus, along with an AAB credit card for your expenses." He extended his hand. "Welcome to the family, Sarah."

She shook it, then moved toward the door.

"Sarah?"

She turned around.

"Please don't make the same mistake Andrew did. As you can see I'm very generous to the people who work for me, but I get very angry when they betray me."

JULIAN ISHERWOOD, upon hearing the news, was predictably appalled. He railed against Zizi, then against Sarah. "Don't bother coming back to the gallery for your things!" he shouted. "You're not welcome here— you *or* your bloody Saudi sheikh!" After slamming down the phone he made his way over to Green's, where he found Oliver Dimbleby and Jeremy Crabbe huddled conspiratorially at the end of the bar.

"Why the long face, Julie?" Dimbleby asked a touch too gleefully.

"I've lost her."

"Who?"

"*Sarah,*" said Isherwood. "She's left me for Zizi al-Bakari."

"Don't tell me she's actually taken Andrew Malone's old job."

Isherwood nodded solemnly.

"Tell her to stay out of Zizi's cookie jar," said Crabbe. "He'll chop off her hand. Legal there, you know."

"How did he get her?" Dimbleby asked.

"Money, of course. That's how they get everything."

"True, indeed," said Dimbleby. "At least we still have the lovely Elena."

We do, thought Isherwood. *But for how long?*

FOUR THOUSAND MILES away, aboard *Sun Dancer,* Gabriel shared in Isherwood's gloomy mood, though for very different reasons. After hearing news of Sarah's hiring he retreated to his outpost at the prow, refusing to acknowledge the congratulations offered him by the rest of his team.

"What's his problem?" Yaakov asked Lavon. "He actually did it! He's put an agent inside Jihad Incorporated!"

"Yes," said Lavon. "And one day he'll have to get her out again."

24

GUSTAVIA,
SAINT-BARTHÉLEMY

ZIZI'S SECRET DESTINATION TURNED out to be the French island of Saint-Barthélemy. They arrived the following morning and dropped anchor off Gustavia, the island's picturesque port and administrative capital. Sarah was finishing her workout when Nadia came into the gym, dressed in a flattering white bikini and sheer white beach dress.

"Why aren't you ready?" she asked.

"What are you talking about?"

"I'm taking you to Saline Beach—the greatest beach in the world."

When Sarah hesitated, Nadia touched her arm affectionately. "Listen, Sarah, I know I haven't been terribly friendly since you arrived, but we're going to be spending a lot of time together now that you're working for my father. We might as well be friends."

Sarah made a show of thought. "I need ten minutes."

"Five." Nadia smiled warmly. "What do you expect? I'm my father's daughter."

Sarah went up to her cabin, showered quickly, and changed into a bathing suit and a sundress. She dropped a few things into her new beach bag, then went astern. Nadia was already aboard the launch, along with Rafiq al-Kamal and Jafar Sharuki. Jean-Michel was behind the wheel, checking the instrument panel.

"Just us?" Sarah asked as she climbed aboard and settled next to Nadia in the forward compartment.

"Rahimah might join us later," Nadia said. "But to tell you the truth, I hope she doesn't. I could use a break from her."

Jean-Michel eased the boat away from *Alexandra*'s stern, then increased the throttle and sped away. They raced along the southern side of the island, past the outskirts of Gustavia, then around the Grande Pointe. Two minutes later they entered a small bay guarded at either end by rugged outcroppings of gray-brown volcanic rock. Between the rocks, and beneath a sky of intense luminous blue, lay a sweeping crescent beach. "Welcome to Saline," Nadia said.

Jean-Michel guided the craft carefully through the gentle breakers and came to a stop a few yards from the shoreline. Rafiq and Sharuki leaped overboard into the shallow water and made their way to the prow. Nadia stood and slipped overboard into Rafiq's powerful arms. "It's the best part about having bodyguards," she said. "You never have to get wet on the way to the beach."

Sarah reluctantly climbed into the arms of Sharuki. A few seconds later she was deposited gently in the hard sand at the water's edge. As Jean-Michel turned the launch around and headed back to *Alexandra,* Nadia stood at the tide line and looked for a suitable place to make camp. "Down there," she said, then she took Sarah's arm and led her toward the distant end of the beach, which was empty of other people. Rafiq and Sharuki trailed after them with the chairs and the bags. Fifty yards removed from the nearest beachgoer, Nadia stopped and murmured something in rapid Arabic to Rafiq, who responded by spreading a pair of towels on the sand and opening the chairs.

The two bodyguards made an outpost for themselves about twenty yards away. Nadia removed her beach dress and sat on her towel. Her long dark hair was combed straight back and shimmering with gel. She wore silver-tinted sunglasses, through which it was possible to see her wide liquid eyes. She glanced over her shoulder toward the bodyguards, then removed her top. Her breasts were heavy and beautifully formed. Her skin, after two weeks in the sun, was deeply tanned. Sarah sat down in one of the chairs and buried her feet in the sand.

"Do you like having them?" Sarah asked.

"The bodyguards?" Nadia shrugged. "When you're the daughter of Zizi al-Bakari, bodyguards are a fact of life. Do you know how much I'm worth to a kidnapper or a terrorist?"

"Billions."

"Exactly." She reached into her beach bag and pulled out a pack of Virginia Slims. She lit one for herself and offered one to Sarah, who shook her head. "I don't smoke on *Alexandra* in deference to my father's wishes. But when I'm away from him . . ." Her voice trailed off. "You won't tell him, will you?"

"Cross my heart." Sarah inclined her head toward the bodyguards. "What about them?"

"They wouldn't *dare* tell my father."

Nadia returned the cigarettes to her bag and exhaled smoke toward the cloudless blue sky. Sarah closed her eyes and turned her face to the sun. "You wouldn't happen to have a bottle of very cold rosé in there, would you?"

"I wish," Nadia said. "Jean-Michel always manages to smuggle a little wine on board. I'm sure he'd give you a bottle or two if you asked nicely."

"I'm afraid Jean-Michel wants to give me more than just wine."

"Yes, he's very attracted to you." Nadia pushed her sunglasses onto her forehead and closed her eyes. "There's a restaurant just behind the dunes. We can have a drink at the bar later if you like."

"I didn't realize you drank."

"Not much, but I do love banana daiquiris on a day like today."

"I thought your religion forbade it."

Nadia waved her hand dismissively.

"You're not religious?" Sarah asked.

"I love my faith, but I'm also a modern Saudi woman.

We have two faces. When we are at home, we are obligated to keep it hidden behind a black veil. But in the West . . ."

"You can drink the occasional daiquiri and lie topless on the beach."

"Exactly."

"Does your father know?"

She nodded. "He wants me to be a true woman of the West but remain faithful to the tenets of Islam. I've told him that's not possible, at least not in the strictest sense, and he respects that. I'm not a child, Sarah. I'm twenty-seven years old." She rolled onto her side and propped her head on her hand. "And how old are you?"

"Thirty-one," Sarah said.

"Have you ever been married?"

Sarah shook her head. Her face was still turned to the sun, and her skin felt as though it was burning. *Nadia knows,* she thought. *They all know.*

"You're a beautiful girl," Nadia said. "Why aren't you married yet?"

Because of a telephone call I received at 8:53 the morning of September 11, 2001 . . .

"All the usual excuses," she said. "First there was college, then my doctorate, then work. I suppose I've never had time for love."

"No time for love? How sad."

"It's an American disease."

Nadia lowered her sunglasses over her eyes and rolled onto her back.

"The sun is strong," Sarah said. "You should cover up."

"I never burn. It's one of the good things about being a Saudi." She reached out and lazily buried the end of her cigarette in the sand. "It must be very strange for you."

"What's that?"

"An all-American girl like you, working for Zizi al-Bakari."

"Sorry to disappoint you, Nadia, but I'm hardly an all-American girl. I spent most of my childhood in Europe. When I went back to America to go to college, I felt terribly out of place. It took me a long time to adjust."

"It doesn't bother you working for a Saudi?"

"Why should it?"

"Because many people in your country blame us for the attacks on 9/11."

"I don't happen to be one of them," Sarah said, then she recited the lines that Gabriel had given her in Surrey. "Osama chose Saudis to carry out the attacks so he could drive a wedge between your country and ours. He's declared war on the House of Saud as well as America. We're allies in the fight against al-Qaeda, not adversaries."

"The Saudi intelligence services have warned my father repeatedly that he is a target of the terrorists because of his close relationship with the Royal Family. That's why we have such stringent security." She gestured toward the bodyguards. "That's why we have to bring gorillas to the beach instead of two nice-looking boys."

She rolled over onto her stomach, exposing her back to the warm sun. Sarah closed her eyes and drifted into a hazy dream-filled sleep. She woke an hour later to find their once-secluded spot surrounded by other people. Rafiq and Sharuki were now seated directly behind them. Nadia appeared to be sleeping. "I'm hot," she murmured to the bodyguards. "I'm going for a swim." When Rafiq started to get to his feet, Sarah motioned for him to stay. "I'll be fine," she said.

She walked slowly into the water, until the waves began breaking over her waist, then plunged beneath the surface and kicked hard several times until she was past the rough surf. When she broke through the surface again, Yaakov was floating next to her.

"How long are you planning to stay in Saint Bart's?"

"I don't know. They never tell me anything."

"Are you safe?"

"As far as I can tell."

"Have you seen anyone who could be bin Shafiq?"

She shook her head.

"We're here with you, Sarah. All of us. Now swim away from me and don't look back. If they ask about me, tell them I was flirting with you."

And with that he disappeared beneath the surface and was gone. Sarah went back to the beach and laid down on a towel next to Nadia.

"Who was that man you were talking to?" she asked.

Sarah felt her heart give a sideways lurch. She managed to answer calmly. "I don't know," she said, "but he was hitting on me right in front of his girlfriend."

"What do you expect? He's a Jew."

"How can you tell?"

"Trust me, I can tell. Never talk to strangers, Sarah. Especially Jews."

SARAH WAS in her cabin dressing for dinner when she heard the whine of the Sikorsky's engine. She fastened the pearls around her neck and hurried up to the afterdeck, where she found Zizi seated on a couch in the cool evening air, dressed in a pair of fashionably cut faded blue jeans and a white pullover. "We're going to the island for dinner tonight," he said. "Nadia and I are taking the last helicopter. You'll come with us."

They boarded the Sikorsky twenty minutes later. As they floated over the harbor, the lights of Gustavia glowed softly against the gathering darkness. They passed over the ridge of steep hills behind the port and descended toward the airfield, where the others were waiting at the end of the tarmac, clustered around a convoy of gleaming black Toyota Land Cruisers.

With Zizi safely in place, the convoy set out toward the airport exit. On the opposite side of the road, in the parking lot of the island's main shopping center, Sarah briefly glimpsed Yossi and Rimona sitting astride a motor scooter. She leaned forward and looked over at Zizi, who was seated next to his daughter.

"Where are we going?"

"We've commandeered a restaurant in Gustavia for dinner. But first we're going to a villa on the other side of the island for drinks."

"Have you commandeered the villa, too?"

Zizi laughed. "Actually it's being rented by a business associate of ours."

A cell phone shrieked. It was answered on the first ring by Hassan, who handed it to Zizi after ascertaining the identity of the caller. Sarah looked out her window. They were speeding now along the Baie de Saint-Jean. She glanced over her shoulder and saw the headlights of the last Land Cruiser trailing close behind them. An image formed in her mind: Yossi at the helm of his scooter, with Rimona clinging to his waist. She dropped the image into an imaginary shredder and made it go away.

The convoy slowed suddenly as they entered the busy little beach town of Saint-Jean. There were shops and restaurants on both sides of the narrow road and sun-burned pedestrians weaving haphazardly through the sluggish traffic. Jean-Michel swore softly as a man and a woman on a motorbike squirted past through a narrow opening in the traffic jam.

On the other side of the village the traffic thinned suddenly, and the road climbed the cliffs along the edge of the bay. They rounded a hairpin turn and for an instant the sea lay below them, mercury-colored in the light of the newly risen moon. The next town was Lorient, less glamorous than Saint-Jean and far less crowded: a tidy shopping center, a shuttered gas station, a beauty salon that served local women, a burger stand that catered to shirtless boys who rode motorcycles. Seated alone at a chrome-topped table, dressed in khaki shorts and sandals, was Gabriel.

Zizi closed his cell phone with a loud snap and handed it over his shoulder without looking to Hassan. Nadia was holding a strand of her own hair and inspecting the ends for damage. "There's a decent nightclub in Gustavia," she said absently. "Maybe we can go dancing after dinner." Sarah made no reply and looked out the window again. They passed a cemetery with aboveground grave sites and started up a steep hill. Jean-Michel downshifted and pressed the accelerator to the floor. Halfway up the grade the road bent sharply to the left. As the Land Cruiser swerved, Sarah was thrust against Nadia's body. Her bare skin felt feverish from the sun.

A moment later they were heading onto a narrow windswept point. Near the end of the point the convoy slowed suddenly and turned through a security gate, into the forecourt of a large white villa ablaze with light. Sarah glanced over her shoulder as the iron gate began to close automatically. A motor scooter sped past, ridden by a man with khaki shorts and sandals, then disappeared. The door of the Land Cruiser opened. Sarah climbed out.

HE STOOD in the entranceway, next to a fair-haired woman of early middle age, and greeted each member of Zizi's large entourage as they came filing up the flagstone steps. He was tall, with the broad square shoulders of a swimmer and narrow hips. His hair was dark and tightly curled. He wore a pale blue Lacoste sweater and white trousers. The sleeves of the sweater were pulled down to his wrists, and his right hand was thrust into his pocket. Zizi took Sarah by the arm and made the introduction.

"This is Sarah Bancroft, the new chief of my art department. Sarah, this is Alain al-Nasser. Alain runs a venture capital firm for us in Montreal."

"It's very nice to meet you, Sarah."

Fluent English, lightly accented. Hand firmly in the pocket. He nodded at the woman.

"My wife, Sophie."

"*Bonsoir*, Sarah."

The woman extended her hand. Sarah shook it, then held out her own hand to Alain al-Nasser, but he looked quickly away and threw his arms elaborately around Wazir bin Talal. Sarah went inside the villa. It was large and airy with one side open to a large outdoor terrace.

There was a turquoise swimming pool, and beyond the pool only the darkening sea. A table had been laid with drinks and snacks. Sarah searched in vain for a bottle of wine and settled for papaya juice instead.

She carried her drink onto the terrace and sat down. The gas lanterns were twisting in the night wind. So was Sarah's hair. She tucked the rebellious strands behind her ears and looked back into the villa. Alain al-Nasser had abandoned Sophie to Jean-Michel and was now in close consultation with Zizi, Daoud Hamza, and bin Talal. Sarah sipped her juice. Her mouth was sandpaper. Her heart was banging against her breastbone.

"Do you think he's handsome?"

She looked up, startled, and saw Nadia standing over her.

"Who?"

"Alain."

"What are you talking about?"

"I saw the way you were looking at him, Sarah."

Think of something, she thought.

"I was looking at Jean-Michel."

"Don't tell me you're actually considering it?"

"It's never a good idea to mix romance and work."

"He *is* beautiful, though."

"Very," said Sarah. "But trouble."

"They all are."

"How well do you know Alain?"

"Not very," she said. "He's been working for my father for about three years."

"I take it he's not Saudi?"

"We don't do names like Alain. He's Lebanese. Raised in France, I think."

"And now he lives in Montreal?"

"I suppose." Nadia's expression darkened. "It's best not to ask too many questions about my father's business—or the people who work for him. My father doesn't like it."

Nadia walked away and sat down next to Rahimah. Sarah looked out to sea, at the lights of a passing vessel.

We know he's concealed somewhere within Zizi's empire. He might come as an investment banker or a portfolio manager. He might come as a real estate developer or a pharmaceutical executive. . . .

Or a venture capitalist named Alain al-Nasser. Alain who is Lebanese but was raised in France, I think. Alain with a rounded face that does not quite match his body but looks vaguely like one she had seen in a country house in Surrey that does not exist. Alain who was at that very moment being led into a back room for a private meeting with the chairman and CEO of Jihad Incorporated. Alain who would not shake Sarah's hand. Is it merely because he fears contamination by an infidel female? Or is it because the hand is slightly withered, the result of a shrapnel wound he received in Afghanistan?

"In a situation like this, Sarah, simple is best. We'll do it the old-fashioned way. Telephone codes. Physical recognition signals."

"Physical recognition signals?"

"*Wristwatch on the left hand, wristwatch on the right. Coat collar up, coat collar down. Handbag in the left, handbag in the right.*"

"*Newspapers folded under the arm?*"

"*You'd be surprised. I've always been partial to hair myself.*"

"*Hair?*"

"*How do you like to wear your hair, Sarah?*"

"*Down, mostly.*"

"*You have very nice cheekbones. A very graceful neck. You should think about wearing your hair up from time to time. Like Marguerite.*"

"*Too old-fashioned.*"

"*Some things never go out of fashion. Put your hair up for me now.*"

She reached into her handbag, for the clasp Chiara had given her on her last day at the gallery, and did as Gabriel asked.

"*You look very beautiful with your hair up. This will be our signal if you see a man you think is bin Shafiq.*"

"*And what happens then?*"

"*Leave that to us, Sarah.*"

25

GUSTAVIA,
SAINT-BARTHÉLEMY

THAT NIGHT, for the first time since boarding *Alexandra*, Sarah did not sleep. She lay in the large bed, forcing herself to remain motionless so that bin Talal, if he was watching her through concealed cameras, would not suspect her of a restless conscience. Shortly before six the sky began to grow light, and a red stain appeared above the horizon. She waited another half-hour before ordering coffee. When it came she had a pounding headache.

She went onto the sundeck and stood at the rail, her gaze on the light slowly coming up in the harbor, her thoughts on Alain al-Nasser of Montreal. They had remained at his villa a little more than an hour, then had driven to Gustavia for dinner. Zizi had taken over a restaurant called La Vela on the edge of the harbor. Alain al-Nasser had not come with them. Indeed his name had not been mentioned at dinner, at least not within earshot of Sarah. A man who might have been Eli Lavon had strolled past the restaurant during dessert. Sarah had looked down to dab her lips on her napkin, and when she had looked up again the man had vanished.

She felt a sudden craving for physical movement and decided to go to the gym before it was commandeered by Zizi. She pulled on a pair of spandex shorts, a tank top, and her running shoes, then went into the bathroom and pinned up her hair in front of the mirror. The gym, when she arrived, was in silence. She had expected to find it empty but instead saw Jean-Michel hunched over an apparatus, working on his biceps. She greeted him coolly and mounted the treadmill.

"I'm going to the island for a real run. Care to join me?"

"What about Zizi's workout?"

"He says his back is sore."

"It sounds as though you don't believe him."

"His back is always sore whenever he wants a day off." He finished his set and wiped his glistening arms with a towel. "Let's go before the traffic gets too heavy."

They boarded a launch and set out toward the inner harbor. There was no wind yet, and the waters were still calm. Jean-Michel tied up at a public dock, near an empty café that was just opening for breakfast. They stretched for a few moments on the quay, then set out through the quiet streets of the old town. Jean-Michel moved effortlessly beside her. As they started the twisting ascent up the hillside behind the port, Sarah fell a few paces behind. A motor scooter overtook her, ridden by a helmeted girl in blue jeans with shapely hips. She pushed herself harder and closed the gap. At the top of the hill she stopped to catch her breath while Jean-Michel jogged lightly in place.

"What's wrong?"

"I've gained nearly ten pounds on this trip."

"It's nearly over."

"How much longer are we staying?"

"Two more days in Saint Bart's." He pulled his lips down in typical Gallic expression. "Maybe three. Zizi's getting anxious to leave. I can tell."

Just then the first flight of the day swept low over their heads and plunged down the opposite side of the hill toward the runway below. Without warning Jean-Michel started down the road after it. They ran past the airport and the island's main shopping center, then rounded a bend in the road and started toward Saint-Jean village. The first traffic began to appear; twice they had to leap onto the sandy shoulder of the road to avoid approaching trucks. Jean-Michel led her through an opening in the stone wall at the edge of the road and down a sandy pathway to the beach. "It's better if we run here," he said. "I'm going to do a couple of fast intervals. Do you think you can stay out of trouble?"

"What makes you think I can't keep up with you?"

He lengthened his stride. Sarah struggled to keep pace with him.

"The interval is about to begin," he said. "Are you ready?"

"I thought this *was* the interval."

Jean-Michel sprinted away. Sarah, exhausted from her sleepless night, slowed to a walk, reveling in the fact that for the first time since entering Zizi's camp she was alone. It did not last long. Two minutes later Jean-Michel came sprinting back toward her, arms pumping like pistons. Sarah turned and started running again. Jean-Michel overtook her and slowed his pace.

"I'm famished," she said. "How about some breakfast?"

"First we finish the run. We'll have something at that café next to the boat."

It took them twenty minutes to cover the distance back to the harbor. The café was beginning to fill by the time they arrived, but Jean-Michel found an empty table outside in the shade and sat down. Sarah looked over the menu for a few moments, then lifted her gaze toward the men's clothing boutique opposite the café. The window display was filled with handmade French dress shirts of expensive-looking cotton. Sarah closed the menu and looked at Jean-Michel.

"I should buy Zizi a thank-you present."

"The last thing Zizi needs is a gift. He truly is the man who has everything."

"I should get him *something*. He was very generous to me."

"I'm sure he was."

She touched Jean-Michel's arm and pointed to the boutique.

"The last thing Zizi needs is another shirt," he said.

"They're very nice-looking, though."

Jean-Michel nodded. "They're French," he said. "We still can do a few things well."

"Give me your credit card."

"It's an AAB company card."

"I'll reimburse you."

He produced a card from the pocket of his running shorts and handed it over. "Don't bother paying me back," he said. "Trust me, Sarah, you won't be the first person to buy Zizi a present with his own money."

"What size shirt does he wear?"

"Sixteen-and-a-half-inch neck, thirty-three sleeve."

"Very impressive."

"I'm his personal trainer."

She gave Jean-Michel her breakfast order—*tartin*, scrambled eggs, and café au lait—then walked over to the boutique. She stood outside for a moment, gazing at the shirts in the window, then slipped through the entrance. An attractive young woman with short blond hair greeted her in French. Sarah selected two shirts, one dark blue, the other pale yellow, and gave the woman Zizi's measurements. The woman disappeared into a back room and returned a moment later with the shirts.

"Do you have a gift box?"

"Of course, Madame."

She produced one from beneath the counter, then

carefully wrapped the shirts in tissue paper and placed them inside.

"Do you have a gift card of some sort?" Sarah asked. "Something with an envelope?"

Again the woman reached beneath the counter. She placed the card before Sarah and handed her a pen.

"How will you be paying, Madame?"

Sarah gave her the credit card. While the saleswoman rang up the purchases, Sarah leaned over the gift card and wrote: *Alain al-Nasser—Montreal.* Then she inserted the card into the envelope, licked the adhesive flap, and sealed it tightly. The saleswoman then placed the credit card receipt in front of Sarah. She signed it, then handed the woman the pen, along with the sealed envelope.

"I don't understand, Madame."

"Sometime this morning a friend of mine is going to come here to see whether I forgot something," Sarah said. "Please give my friend this envelope. If you do, you'll be paid handsomely. Discretion is important. Do you understand me, Madame?"

"Of course." She smiled at Sarah mischievously, then looked at Jean-Michel sitting in the café. "Your secret is safe with me."

The woman placed the gift box in a paper bag and handed it to Sarah. Sarah winked at her, then went out and returned to the café. Her breakfast was waiting for her when she sat down.

"Any problems?" Jean-Michel asked.

Sarah shook her head and handed him the credit card. "No," she said. "No problems at all."

THIRTY MINUTES LATER Sarah and Jean-Michel boarded the launch and returned to *Alexandra*. Gabriel waited another fifteen minutes before entering the boutique. He collected the gift card from the saleswoman and gave her one hundred euros for her trouble. Five minutes after that he was seated at the tiller of a Zodiac, heading out of the inner harbor toward the anchorage.

Alexandra lay directly before him, by far the largest private vessel in port, second in scale only to the cruise ship that had come in overnight. Gabriel turned a few degrees to port and headed toward *Sun Dancer,* which was anchored several hundred yards away, near the twin rocks that stood guard over the entrance of the harbor. He tied off the Zodiac at the stern and went into the main salon, which had been converted into a mobile command and operations center. There was a secure satellite telephone and a computer with a link to King Saul Boulevard. Two dozen cellular phones and several handheld radios stood in formation in their chargers, and a video camera with telephoto lens was trained on *Alexandra*.

Gabriel stood before the monitor and watched Sarah step out onto her private sundeck. Then he looked at Yaakov, who was on the phone to Tel Aviv. When Yaakov hung up a moment later, Gabriel held up the gift card. *Alain al-Nasser—Montreal.*

"That's our girl," Yaakov said. "Have a seat, Gabriel. King Saul Boulevard has had a busy morning."

GABRIEL POURED HIMSELF a cup of coffee from a thermos and sat down.

"Technical hacked into the reservation system of the villa rental firm early this morning," Yaakov said. "The villa where Sarah went last night was rented by a company called Meridian Construction of Montreal."

"Meridian Construction is controlled entirely by AAB Holdings," Lavon said.

"Did the reservation say who would be staying there?" Gabriel asked.

Yaakov shook his head. "The booking was handled by a woman named Katrine Devereaux at Meridian headquarters. She paid for everything in advance and instructed the rental company to have the house open and ready for his arrival."

"When did he get here?"

"Three days ago, according to the records."

"How much longer is he staying?"

"The reservation is for four more nights."

"What about his car?"

"There's a Cabriolet parked at the house now. The sticker on the back says Island Rental Cars. No computerized reservation system. Everything's on paper. If we want the particulars we'll have to break in the old-fashioned way."

Gabriel looked at Mordecai, a *neviot* man by training. "Their office is at the airport," Mordecai said. "It's nothing more than a booth with a sliding aluminum shutter over the window and one door for the staff to come in and out. We could be inside in a matter of seconds. The problem is that the airport itself is under guard at night. We could lose the entire operation just to find out the name and credit card number he used to rent his car."

"Too risky," Gabriel said. "Any activity on the telephone?"

Mordecai had placed a transmitter in the junction box overnight. "One call this morning," he said. "A woman. She phoned a hair salon in Saint-Jean and made an appointment for this afternoon."

"What did she call herself?"

"Madame al-Nasser," Mordecai said. "There's one small problem with the tap. As it stands now, we're at the outside edge of its range. The signal is weak and full of interference. If bin Shafiq picked up the phone right now we might not be able to make a voice ID on him because of static on the line. We need a listening post."

Gabriel looked at Yaakov. "What about moving the boat?"

"The waters off that point are too rough to be used as an anchorage. If we dropped anchor out there to watch the villa, we'd stick out like a sore thumb. We might as well just walk up to al-Nasser's front door and introduce ourselves."

"That's not a bad idea," said Mikhail as he entered the salon. "I volunteer."

"We need a static post," Yaakov said.

"So we'll get one." Gabriel held up the gift card again. "What about this name? Do you recognize it?"

"It's not an alias that we know about," Yaakov said. "I'll have King Saul Boulevard run it through the computers and see what they come up with."

"What now?" asked Mikhail.

"We'll spend the day watching him," Gabriel said. "We'll try to get his photograph and his voice. If we can, we'll send them to King Saul Boulevard for analysis."

"It's a small island," Lavon said, his tone cautionary. "And we have limited personnel."

"That can work to our advantage. In a place like this, it's not uncommon to see the same people every day."

"True," Lavon said, "but bin Talal's goons will get nervous if they see too many familiar faces."

"And what if King Saul Boulevard tells us that Alain al-Nasser of Montreal is really a Saudi GID officer named Ahmed bin Shafiq?" Mikhail asked. "What do we do then?"

Gabriel glanced up at the monitor and looked at Sarah. "I'm going back to Gustavia," he said, still gazing at the screen. "We need a listening post."

THE WELL-BRED ENGLISHWOMAN who greeted him fifteen minutes later at the Sibarth villa rental agency had sun-streaked brown hair and pale blue eyes. Gabriel played the role of Heinrich Kiever, a German of means who had stumbled upon paradise and now wished to stay on a bit longer. The Englishwoman smiled—she had heard many such tales before—then printed out a listing of available properties. Gabriel scanned it and frowned. "I was hoping for something here," he said, tapping the map that lay spread over her desk. "On this point on the north side of the Island."

"Pointe Milou? Yes, it's lovely, but I'm afraid we have nothing available there at the moment. We do have something here, though." She tapped the map. "The next point over. Pointe Mangin."

"Can you see Pointe Milou from the house?"

"Yes, quite clearly. Would you like to see some photographs?"

"Please."

The woman produced a brochure and opened it to the appropriate page. "It's four bedrooms, Herr Kiever. Did you need something that large?"

"Actually, we might be having some company."

"Then I suspect this will do brilliantly. It's a bit pricey, twelve thousand a week, and I'm afraid there's a two-week minimum."

Gabriel shrugged, as if to say money was no object.

"No children and absolutely no pets. You don't have a dog, do you?"

"Heavens no."

"There's a two-thousand-dollar security deposit as

well, bringing the grand total to twenty-six thousand, payable in advance, of course."

"When can we have it?"

She looked at her watch. "It's ten-fifteen now. If we rush things along, we should be able to have you and your wife in by eleven-thirty at the latest."

Gabriel smiled and handed her a credit card.

THOUGH THE ENGLISHWOMAN did not know it, the first guests arrived at the villa fifteen minutes after Gabriel and Dina had settled in. Their possessions were quite unlike those of ordinary visitors to the island. Mordecai brought a voice-activated receiver and a Nikon camera with a long lens, while Mikhail arrived with a nylon rucksack containing cellular phones, radios, and four handguns. An hour later they glimpsed their quarry for the first time when he strode onto the terrace, dressed in white shorts and a long-sleeved white shirt. Mordecai snapped several photos of him. Five minutes later, when al-Nasser emerged shirtless from the pool after a vigorous swim, he snapped several more. Gabriel examined the images on the computer but deemed them unworthy of sending to King Saul Boulevard for analysis.

At one in the afternoon the light on the voice-activated recorder turned from red to green. A burst of tone came over the line, followed by the sound of someone inside the house dialing a local number. After two rings the call was answered by a woman at La Gloriette restaurant. Gabriel closed his eyes in disappointment when the next voice on the line was that of Madame al-Nasser, requesting a lunch reservation for two o'clock. He briefly considered putting a team inside the restaurant but ruled it out after obtaining a description of the cramped beachside dining room. Mordecai, however, managed to take two more photographs of al-Nasser, one as he was climbing out of his car in the parking lot and a second as he was sipping a drink at his table. In both he was wearing dark sports sunglasses and a long-sleeved shirt. Gabriel dispatched them to King Saul Boulevard for analysis. One hour later, as al-Nasser and his wife were leaving the restaurant, King Saul Boulevard sent a flash over the secure link that the results were inconclusive.

At 3:30 they departed La Gloriette and drove to Saint-Jean village, where al-Nasser dropped his wife at the hair salon. From there he went to Gustavia, where, at 3:50, he boarded a launch and headed to *Alexandra*. Yossi recorded his arrival from the bridge of *Sun Dancer*, along with the warm embrace he received from Zizi al-Bakari as they entered the upstairs office suite for a private meeting. Sarah was not on board to see al-Nasser's arrival, for at that moment she and most of Zizi's entourage were snorkeling in Île Fourche, a small deserted island about a mile northeast of Saint-Bart's.

The meeting lasted a little over an hour. Yossi recorded al-Nasser's departure from Zizi's office and the altogether determined expression on his face as he boarded the launch and headed back to Gustavia. Mikhail followed him back to Saint-Jean village, where he collected his newly coiffed wife from the salon shortly after six o'clock. By 6:30 al-Nasser was once again swimming laps in his pool, and Mikhail was seated glumly next to Gabriel in the villa on the other side of the inlet.

"We've been chasing him all day," Mikhail said, "and what have we got to show for it? A few useless pictures. Alain al-Nasser is obviously bin Shafiq. Let's take him now and be done with it."

Gabriel gave him a disdainful look. "Someday, when you're a little older and wiser, I'll tell you a story about the night an Office hit team thought they had the prize in their sights and killed an innocent waiter by mistake."

"I know the story, Gabriel. It happened in Lillehammer. Inside the Office you still refer to it as *Leyl-ha-Mar*: the Night of Bitterness. But it was a long time ago."

"It is still the greatest operational blunder in the history of the Office. They killed the wrong man, *and* they got caught doing it. They broke all the rules. They acted hastily, and they let their emotions get the better of them. We've come too far to have another *Leyl-ha-Mar*. First we get proof—airtight, unassailable *proof*—that Alain al-Nasser is Ahmed bin Shafiq. Only then do we start talking about killing him. And we pull the trigger only if we can get Sarah and the entire team off this island without getting caught."

"How are we going to get proof?"

"The photographs aren't good enough," Gabriel said. "We need his voice."

"He doesn't speak."

"Everyone speaks. We just have to make him speak while we're listening."

"And how are you going to do that?"

Just then the green light shone on the telephone recorder and a burst of dial tone came blaring over the speakers. Madame al-Nasser's call lasted less than thirty seconds. When it was over, Gabriel listened to it again, just to make certain he'd got the details right.

"Le Poivre."

"We'd like a table for two at nine o'clock."

"We're booked then, Madame. I can do eight or nine-thirty."

"Eight is too early. We'll take the nine-thirty, please."

"You're name?"

"Al-Nasser."

Gabriel pressed the Stop button and looked at Mikhail—*Patience, my boy. Good things come to those who wait.*

THE RESTAURANT known as Le Poivre is one of the island's undiscovered gems. It stands at the far end of a pleasant little shopping center in Saint-Jean, at the intersection of the main coast road and a narrow track that climbs the heights overlooking the beach. It has no view, other than the traffic and the parking lot, and little in the way of ambience. The dining room is the size of an average suburban patio. The service is sometimes listless, but the food, when it finally arrives, is always among the best on the island. Still, because of its unremarkable location, those who come to Saint Bart's to be seen are rarely seen at Le Poivre, and nothing much out of the ordinary ever happens there. It is why, to this day, they still talk about the incident that occurred there involving Monsieur and Madame al-Nasser.

The staff know the story well, as do the locals who drink at the tiny bar. Afternoons, during the docile period between lunch and the evening rush, they often recount it over a glass of rosé or an espresso and a cigarette. The reservation had been for 9:30, but they had come on the early side. Odette, the hostess on duty that night, remembers it as 9:15, but Étienne, the bartender, will tell you with great certainty that it was 9:20. There were no tables yet available, and so they had a seat at the bar to wait. Étienne saw to the drinks, of course. A glass of champagne for Madame al-Nasser. A pineapple juice for the gentleman. "Nothing else?" Étienne had asked, but the gentleman had smiled without charm and in a voice barely above a whisper had replied: "Just the juice, please."

A table opened sometime after 9:30. Again there is mild dispute over the time. Denise, the waitress, recalls it as 9:40, but Odette, keeper of the reservation sheet and watcher of the clock, swears it was no later than 9:35. Regardless of the time, Monsieur and Madame al-

Nasser were not happy with the table. Madame com-
plained that it was too close to the entrance of the toilet,
but one had the impression that Monsieur al-Nasser dis-
liked the table for a different reason, though he never
voiced an opinion.

It was nearly ten before the next table opened. This
one was against the rail overlooking the street. Monsieur
al-Nasser sat in the chair facing the bar, but Étienne remembers that his gaze was fixed permanently on the traffic flowing along the coast road. Denise apprised them of
the evening's menu and took their drink orders.
Madame ordered a bottle of wine. Côtes du Rhône, says
Denise. Bordeaux, according to Étienne. Of the wine's
color, however, there is no dispute. It was red, and much
of it would soon be splashed across Madame's white
tropical pantsuit.

The catalyst for the incident arrived at Le Poivre at
10:15. He was small of stature and unimpressive of build.
Étienne made him at five-eight, a hundred fifty pounds at
the most. He wore a pair of baggy khaki shorts that hadn't
been washed in some time, an oversized gray T-shirt with
a tear in the left sleeve, a pair of sandals with Velcro straps,
and a golf cap that had seen better days. Strangely, no one
can summon a compelling portrait of his face. Étienne remembers a pair of outdated eyeglasses. Odette recalls an
untrimmed mustache that really didn't suit his features.
Denise only remembers the walk. His legs had a slight
outward bend to them, she will tell you. Like a man who
can run very fast or is good at football.

He had no name that night but later would come to be known simply as "Claude." He had come to Saint-Jean by motorbike from the direction of Gustavia and had spent the better part of the evening drinking Heineken at the bar a few doors down. When he arrived at ten-fifteen looking for a table, his breath stank of cigarettes and hops, and his body didn't smell much better. When Odette explained that there were no tables— *"And that I wouldn't seat him if we had one"*—he mumbled something unintelligible and asked for the key to the toilet. To which Odette replied that the toilet was for paying customers only. He then looked at Étienne and said, "Heineken." Étienne put a bottle on the bar, shrugged at Odette, and handed him the key.

How long he remained inside is also a matter of some dispute. Estimates range from two minutes to five, and wild theories have been spun as to exactly what he was doing in there. The poor couple seated at the table rejected by Monsieur and Madame al-Nasser later described his piss as one for the ages and said it was followed by much flushing and running of water into the basin. When finally he emerged he was pulling at the fly of his khaki shorts and smiling like a man relieved of a great burden. He started back toward the bar, with his gaze targeted squarely upon the waiting Heineken. And then the trouble began.

Denise had just finished refilling Madame al-Nasser's glass of wine. Madame was raising it for a drink but lowered it in disgust as Claude came out of the toilet tugging at his crotch. Unfortunately, she placed the glass on the table and released it in order to lean forward and tell Monsieur al-Nasser about the spectacle. As Claude teetered past, his hand knocked against the glass, spilling its contents into the lap of Madame al-Nasser.

Accounts of what transpired next vary according to who is telling the story. All agree Claude made what appeared to be a good-faith attempt to apologize, and all agree that it was Monsieur al-Nasser who chose the path of escalation. Harsh words were exchanged, as were threats of violence. The incident might have been resolved peacefully had not Claude offered to pay the dry-cleaning bill. When the offer was hotly refused, he reached into the pocket of his soiled khaki shorts and hurled a few wrinkled euro notes into Monsieur al-Nasser's face. Denise managed to get out of the way just before Monsieur al-Nasser seized Claude by the throat and pushed him toward the exit. He held him there for a moment, shouting more insults into his face, then pushed him down the steps into the street.

There was a smattering of applause from the other patrons and much concern about the wretched state of Madame al-Nasser's garments. Only Étienne bothered to tend to the figure sprawled on the pavement. He helped the man to his feet and, with serious reservations, watched as he mounted his motorbike and wobbled down the coast road. To this day Étienne harbors doubts about the authenticity of that evening's events. A black belt in karate, he saw something in the drunkard's carriage that told him he was a fellow student of the arts. Had the little man in the glasses and golf hat chosen to fight back, Étienne says with the conviction of one who knows, he could have torn Monsieur al-Nasser's arm from the socket and served it to him for dinner with his Bordeaux.

"It wasn't Bordeaux," Denise will tell you. "It was Côtes du Rhône."

"Côtes du Rhône, Bordeaux—it doesn't matter. And I'll tell you something else. When that little bastard drove away, he was grinning from ear to ear. Like he just won the lotto."

ELI LAVON had watched Gabriel's performance from the parking lot, and so it was Lavon who described it for the rest of the team that evening at the villa. Gabriel was slowly pacing the tiled floor, nursing a club soda for his hangover and holding a bag of ice to a swollen left elbow. His thoughts were on the scene now taking place half a world away in Tel Aviv, where a team of specialists in the science of voice identification was deciding whether the man known as Alain al-Nasser would live or die. Gabriel knew what the answer would be. He had known it the instant his quarry had risen from his table in a killing rage. And he had seen proof of it a few seconds later, when he'd managed to lift the right sleeve of his quarry's shirt and sneak a glance at the ugly shrapnel scar on his forearm. At 11:30 the lights came on in the villa across the inlet. Gabriel went out onto the terrace, and on the opposite point Ahmed bin Shafiq did the same. To Mikhail it seemed that the two men were staring at each other over the darkened divide. At 11:35 the satellite phone purred softly. Yaakov answered it, listened a moment in silence, then rang off and called Gabriel inside.

26

POINTE MANGIN,
SAINT-BARTHÉLEMY

THEY GATHERED IN THE open-air living room of the villa and sprawled on the sailcloth couches and wicker chairs. Dina made the first pot of coffee, while Lavon taped a large-scale map of the island onto the wall. Gabriel stared at it gloomily for a long time in silence. When finally he spoke, he uttered a single word: "Zwaiter." Then he looked at Lavon. "Do you remember Zwaiter, Eli?"

Lavon raised an eyebrow but said nothing. Of course Lavon remembered Zwaiter. Chief of Black September in Italy. First to die for Munich. Gabriel could almost see him now, a skinny intellectual in a plaid jacket, crossing the Piazza Annibaliano in Rome with a bottle of fig wine in one hand and a copy of *A Thousand and One Nights* in the other.

"How long did you watch him, Eli? Two weeks?"

"Nearly three."

"Tell them what you learned about Wadal Zwaiter before we even thought about killing him."

"That he stopped each evening in the same small market. That he always went to the Trieste Bar to make a few phone calls, and that he always went into his apartment building through Entrance C. That the lights in the foyer operated on a timer, and that he always stood in the dark for a moment, searching his pockets for a ten-lira coin to operate the lift. That's where you did it, wasn't it, Gabriel? In front of the lift?"

"*Excuse me, but are you Wadal Zwaiter?*"

"*No! Please, no!*"

"And then you vanished," Lavon continued. "Two escape cars. A team to cover the route. By morning you were in Switzerland. Shamron said it was like blowing out a match."

"We controlled every detail. We chose the time and the place of the execution and planned it down to the smallest detail. We did everything right that night. But we can't do any of those things on this island." Gabriel looked at the map. "We operate best in cities, not places like this."

"That might be true," said Dina, "but you can't let him leave here alive."

"Why not?"

"Because he has the resources of a billionaire at his fingertips. Because he can fly off to the Najd at a moment's notice and be lost to us forever."

"There are right ways to do these things, and there are wrong ways. This is definitely the wrong way."

"Don't be afraid to pull the trigger because of what happened at the Gare de Lyon, Gabriel."

"This has nothing to do with Paris. We have a professional target. A small battlefield. A hazardous escape route. And an unpredictable variable named Sarah Bancroft. Shall I go on?"

"But Dina is right," Yossi said. "We have to do it now. We might never get another shot at him."

"The Eleventh Commandment. *Thou shalt not get caught.* That's our first responsibility. Everything else is secondary."

"Did you see him aboard Zizi's yacht today?" Rimona asked. "Shall we watch the tape again? Did you see his face when he came out? What do you think they were talking about, Gabriel? Investments? He tried to kill my uncle. He has to die."

"What would we do about the woman?" Yossi asked.

"She's an accomplice," Lavon said. "She's obviously part of his network. Why is her voice the only one we hear? Doesn't she find it a bit odd that her husband never picks up the phone?"

"So do we *kill* her?"

"If we don't, we'll never make it off this island."

Dina suggested they put the entire operation to a vote. Yaakov shook his head. "In case you haven't noticed," he said, "this is not a democracy."

Gabriel looked at Lavon. The two held each other's gaze for a moment, then Lavon closed his eyes and nodded once.

*   *   *

THEY DID NOT sleep that night. In the morning Yossi rented a second Suzuki Vitara four-wheel-drive, while Yaakov and Rimona each rented Piaggio motorbikes. Oded and Mordecai went to a marine supply outlet in Gustavia and purchased two Zodiacs with outboard engines. Dina spent much of that day calling the island's most exclusive restaurants trying to book a table for thirty. At 1:30 she learned that Le Tetou, a trendy beachside restaurant in Saint-Jean, had already been booked that evening for a private party and would not be open to the public.

Gabriel rode into Saint-Jean to have a look for himself. The restaurant was an open-air structure, with swatches of colorful cloth hanging from the ceiling and ear-shattering dance music blaring from the speakers. A dozen tables stood beneath a peaked wooden shelter and several more were scattered along the beach. There was a small bar and, like many restaurants on the island, a boutique that sold atrociously expensive women's beachwear. Lunch service had reached fever pitch, and barefoot girls clad only in bikini tops and ankle-length beach dresses rushed from table to table, dispensing food and drink. A feline-looking bathing-suit model emerged from the boutique and posed for him. When Gabriel gave no sign of approval, the girl frowned and moved on to a table of well-lubricated Americans, who bayed in approval.

He walked over to the bar and ordered a glass of rosé,

then carried it over to the boutique. The changing rooms and toilets were down a narrow passage, at the end of which was the parking lot. He stood there for a moment, visualizing movement, calculating time. Then he swallowed half of the rosé and went out.

It was perfect, he thought. But there was one problem. Snatching Sarah from a table was out of the question. Zizi's bodyguards were heavily armed and to a man were all former officers of the Saudi National Guard. To get Sarah cleanly, they had to move her into the changing rooms at a prearranged time. And to do that they would have to get her a message. As Gabriel rode off on his motorbike, he called Lavon at the villa and asked whether she was on the island.

THE RESTAURANT at Saline has no view of the sea, only of the sand dunes and a broad salt marsh framed by scrub-covered green hills. Sarah sat on the shaded veranda, her fingers wrapped around the stem of a wineglass filled with icy rosé. Next to her sat Nadia, the modern Muslim woman, who was working on her third daiquiri and improving in mood with each passing minute. On the opposite side of the table Monique and Jean-Michel were silently quarreling. The Frenchman's eyes were concealed behind a pair of dark wraparound sunglasses, but Sarah could see he was scrutinizing the young couple who had just arrived on a motorbike and were now tramping up the stairs to the veranda.

The man was tall and lanky, clad in knee-length swimming trunks, flip-flops, and a cotton pullover. His English accent betrayed an Oxbridge education, as did the imperious manner in which he inquired about the availability of a table. The girl's accent was indeterminate middle European. Her bikini top was still wet from her swim and clung suggestively to a pair of generous suntanned breasts. She asked the hostess about the location of the toilet, loudly enough for Sarah and everyone else in the restaurant to hear, then calmly held Jean-Michel's gaze as she walked past the table, her emerald beach wrap flowing from a pair of childbearing hips.

Nadia sucked at her daiquiri, while Monique scowled at Jean-Michel, as if she suspected his interest in the girl extended beyond the professional. Two minutes later, when the girl emerged, she was fussing with her hair and swaying playfully to the reggae music issuing from the stereo behind the bar. *Office Doctrine,* thought Sarah. *When operating in public places like bars and restaurants, don't sit quietly or read a magazine. That only makes you look like a spy. Call attention to yourself. Flirt. Be loud. Drink too much. A quarrel is always nice.* But there was something else Sarah noticed that she was sure Jean-Michel had not. Rimona was wearing no earrings, which meant she had left a message for Sarah inside the toilet.

Sarah watched as Rimona sat down next to Yossi and snapped at him for not having a drink waiting for her. A line of clouds was coming over the dunes, and a sudden wind was chasing in the marsh grass. "Looks like a big storm," said Jean-Michel, and he ordered a third bottle of rosé to help ride it out. Nadia lit a Virginia Slims, then gave the pack to Monique, who did the same. Sarah turned to watch the approaching storm. All the while she was thinking of the clock and wondering how many minutes she should let pass before she went to the bathroom. And what she might find when she went there.

Five minutes later the clouds opened, and a gust of wind hurled rain against Sarah's back. Jean-Michel signaled the waitress and asked her to lower the awning. Sarah stood, seized her beach bag, and started toward the back of the restaurant.

"Where are you going?" asked Jean-Michel.

"We're working on our third bottle of wine. Where do you think I'm going?"

He stood suddenly and followed after her.

"This is very thoughtful of you, but I really don't need your help. I've been doing this sort of thing alone since I was a little girl."

He took her by the arm and led her to the restroom. The door was ajar. He pushed it all the way open, looked quickly around, then stepped aside and allowed her to enter. Sarah closed the door and bolted it, then dropped the toilet seat, loudly enough so that it could be heard beyond the door.

We have several places we like to hide things, Gabriel had told her. *Taped to the inside of the toilet tank or hidden inside the seat-cover dispenser. Rubbish bins are always good, especially if they have a lid. We like to hide messages inside tampon boxes, because we've found that Arab men, even professionals, are loath to touch them.*

She looked beneath the sink, saw an aluminum canister, and put her foot on the pedal. When the lid rose she saw the box, partially concealed by crumpled paper towels. She reached down and plucked it out. *Read the message quickly,* Gabriel had said. *Trust yourself to remember the details. Never, I mean never, take the message with you. We like to use flash paper, so if you have a lighter or matches, set it on fire in the sink and it will disappear. If not, flush it down the toilet. Worst case, put it back in the box and leave it in the trash. We'll clean it out after you leave.*

Sarah looked in her beach bag and saw she had a book of matches. She started to take them out but decided she didn't have the nerve for it, so she tore the message to bits and flushed them down the toilet. She stood before the mirror a moment and examined her face while she ran water into the basin. *You're Sarah Bancroft,* she told herself. *You don't know the woman who left the tampon box in the trash. You've never seen her before.*

She shut off the taps and returned to the veranda. Rainwater was now spilling over the gutters in torrents. Yossi was in the process of noisily sending back a bottle of Sancerre; Rimona was examining the menu as though she found it of little interest. And Jean-Michel was watching her coming across the room as though seeing her for the first time. She sat down and watched the storm rolling across the marsh, knowing it would soon be over. *You're having dinner at Le Tetou tonight,* the message had said. *When you see us, pretend to be ill and go to the bathroom. Don't worry if they send a bodyguard. We'll take care of him.*

ALL THEY NEEDED now was the guest of honor. For much of that day they did not see him. Gabriel grew concerned that bin Shafiq had somehow managed to slip away undetected and briefly considered placing a phone call to the villa to make certain it was still occupied. But at 11:30 they saw him emerge onto the terrace, where, after his customary vigorous swim, he sunned himself for an hour.

At 12:30 he went inside again, and a few minutes later the white Cabriolet came rolling down the drive with the top down and the woman behind the wheel. She drove to a charcuterie in Lorient village, spent ten minutes inside, then returned to the villa on Pointe Milou for an alfresco lunch.

At three o'clock, as the storm was breaking over the coast, the Cabriolet again came down the drive, but this time it was bin Shafiq behind the wheel. Lavon set off after him on one of the newly acquired scooters, with Mordecai and Oded following in support. It quickly became apparent the Saudi was checking for surveillance, because he forsook the crowded roads along the northern coast of the island and headed instead toward the sparsely developed eastern shore. He sped along the rocky coastline of Toiny, then turned inland and raced through a string of scruffy hamlets in the grassy hills of the Grand Fond. He paused for a few seconds at the turnoff for Lorient, long enough so that Mordecai had to come around him. Two minutes later, at the intersection of the road to Saint-Jean, he engaged in the same time-tested routine. This time it was Oded who had to abandon the chase.

Lavon was convinced that bin Shafiq's ultimate destination was Gustavia. He hurried into town by a different route and was waiting near the Carl Gustav Hotel when the Cabriolet came down the hill from Lurin. The Saudi parked along the edge of the harbor. Ten minutes later, after making another careful check of his tail, this one on foot, he joined Wazir bin Talal at a quayside café. Lavon had sushi at a restaurant up the street and waited them out. An hour later he was back at the villa, telling Gabriel they had a problem.

"WHY IS he meeting with bin Talal? Bin Talal is security—*Zizi's* security. We have to consider the possibility that Sarah's blown. We've been operating in close proximity for several days now. It's a small island. We're all professionals but . . ." Lavon's voice trailed off.

"But what?"

"Zizi's boys are professionals, too. And so is bin Shafiq. He was driving this afternoon like a man who knew he was being followed."

"It's standard procedure," said Gabriel, playing devil's advocate without much enthusiasm.

"You can always tell the difference between someone who's going through the motions and someone who thinks he's got a watcher on his tail. It feels to me like bin Shafiq knows he's being watched."

"So what are you suggesting, Eli? Call it off?"

"No," Lavon said. "But if we can only get one target tonight, make sure it's Sarah."

TEN MINUTES LATER. The green light. The burst of dial tone. The sound of a number being dialed.

"La Terrazza."

"I'd like to make a reservation for this evening, please."

"How many in your party?"

"Two."

"What time?"

"Nine o'clock."

"Can you hold a moment while I check the book?"

"Sure."

"Would nine-fifteen be all right?"

"Yes, of course."

"All right, we have a reservation for two at nine-fifteen. Your name, please?"

"Al-Nasser."

"Merci, Madame. Au revoir."

Click.

*   *   *

GABRIEL WALKED over to the map.

"La Terrazza is here," he said, tapping his finger against the hills above Saint-Jean. "They won't have to leave the villa until nine at the earliest."

"Unless they go somewhere first," said Lavon.

"Zizi's dinner begins at eight. That gives us almost an hour before we would have to move Sarah into place for the extraction."

"Unless Zizi arrives late," said Lavon.

Gabriel walked over to the window and looked across the inlet. The weather had broken, and it was now dusk. The sea was beginning to grow dark, and lights were coming on in the hills.

"We'll kill them at the villa—inside the house or behind the walls in the drive."

"Them?" asked Lavon.

"It's the only way we'll get off the island," Gabriel said. "The woman has to die, too."

27

GUSTAVIA HARBOR, SAINT-BARTHÉLEMY

IN THE TWO HOURS that followed Gabriel's declaration, there took place a quiet movement of personnel and matériel that went largely unnoticed by the island's docile population. Sarah was witness to only one element of the preparations, for she was seated on her private deck, wrapped in a white terry robe, as *Sun Dancer* got under way and receded silently into the gathering darkness. The gusty winds of the afternoon had died away, and there was only a gentle warm breeze chasing around the yachts anchored at the mouth of the harbor. Sarah closed her eyes. She had a headache from the sun, and her mouth tasted of nickel from too much rosé. She latched on to her discomfort. It gave her something to dwell upon besides what lay ahead. She glanced at her wristwatch, the Harry Winston wristwatch that had been given to her by the chairman and CEO of Jihad Incorporated. It read 7:20. She was almost home.

She looked toward *Alexandra*'s stern and saw that the Sikorsky was darkened and motionless. They were going ashore by launch tonight, departure scheduled for 7:45, arrangements having been made by Hassan, ever-efficient chief of Zizi's travel department. *And please don't be late, Miss Sarah,* Hassan had told her. Zizi had advised her to wear something special. *Le Tetou is my favorite restaurant on the island,* he had said. *It promises to be a memorable evening.*

The breeze rose and from somewhere in the harbor came the clanging of a buoy. She gave another glance at her watch and saw it was 7:25. She allowed herself to picture a reunion. Perhaps they would have a family meal, like the meals they had shared together in the manor house in Surrey that did not exist. Or perhaps the circumstances would be such that food was not appropriate. Whatever the mood, she craved their embrace. She loved them. She loved all of them. She loved them because everyone else hated them. She loved them because they were an island of sanity surrounded by a sea of zealots and because she feared that the tide of history might one day sweep them away and she wanted to be a part of them, if only for a moment. She loved their hidden pain and their capacity for joy, their lust for life and their contempt for those who murdered innocents. To each of their lives was attached a purpose, and to Sarah each seemed a small miracle. She thought of Dina— scarred, beautiful Dina, the last of six children, one child for each million murdered. Her father, she had told

Sarah, had been the only member of his family to survive the Holocaust. After coming to Israel he had chosen the name Sarid, which in Hebrew means remnant, and he had named his last child Dina, which means avenged. *I'm Dina Sarid,* she had said. *I'm the avenged remnant.*

And tonight, thought Sarah, *we stand together.*

Seven-thirty and still she did not move from her chair on the deck. Her procrastination had purpose. She wanted to give herself only a few minutes to dress—less time to send an inadvertent signal that she had no intention of coming back. *Bring nothing with you,* Rimona's message had said. *Leave your room in a mess.*

And so she remained on the deck another five minutes before rising and entering her cabin. She let the robe slide from her shoulders and fall to the floor, then quickly pulled on underpants and a bra. Her clothing, a loose-fitting saffron-colored pantsuit that Nadia had bought for her the previous afternoon in Gustavia, was laid out on the unmade bed. She pulled it on quickly and went to the vanity in the bathroom. She slipped on the gold bangle but left the rest of the jewelry Zizi had given her on the counter. When deciding how to wear her hair, she hesitated for the first time. Up or down? Down, she decided. The first step back toward her old life. A life that Gabriel had warned would never be the same.

She went back into the room and took one last look around. *Leave your room in a mess.* Mission accomplished. *Bring nothing with you.* No handbag or wallet, no credit cards or money, but then who needs credit cards and money when one is attached to the entourage of Zizi al-Bakari? She went out into the corridor and closed the door, making certain it was unlocked. Then she headed to the stern, where the launches were waiting. Rafiq handed her aboard to Jean-Michel, and she squeezed between the Abduls in the aft seating compartment. Zizi was opposite her, next to Nadia. As the boat started toward shore, they were eyeing her intently in the darkness.

"You should have worn your pearls, Sarah. They would have gone nicely with your pantsuit. But I'm pleased to see your hair is down again. It looks much nicer that way. I never liked you with your hair up." He looked at Nadia. "Don't you think she looks better with her hair down?"

But before Nadia could answer, Hassan pressed an open cell phone into Zizi's palm and murmured something in Arabic that sounded frightfully urgent. Sarah looked toward the inner harbor, where four black Toyota Land Cruisers waited at the edge of the quay. A small cluster of onlookers had gathered, hoping to catch a glimpse of the celebrity who could command such an impressive motorcade on so small an island. The dark-haired girl seated beneath the shelter of a gazebo fifty yards away couldn't be bothered by the spectacle of celebrity. The avenged remnant was gazing off into space, her mind obviously wrestling with more weighty matters.

*　　*　　*

THE BEACH at Saline, one of the few on the island to have no hotels or villas, was dark except for the phosphorous glow of the breakers in the bright moonlight. Mordecai brought the first Zodiac ashore at 8:05. Oded came two minutes later, piloting his own Zodiac and towing a third by a nylon line. At 8:10 they signaled Gabriel. Team Saline was in place. The escape hatch was now open.

As USUAL the beach at Saint-Jean had been slow to empty that evening, and there were still a few steadfast souls sitting in the sand in the gathering darkness. At the end of the airport runway, near a weather-beaten sign that warned of low-flying aircraft, a small party was under way. They were four in number, three men and a dark-haired girl who had arrived by motor scooter from Gustavia a few moments earlier. One of them had brought some Heineken beer; another a small portable CD player, which was now playing a bit of Bob Marley. The three men were laying about in various states of relaxation. Two of them, a tough-looking man with pockmarked skin and a gentle soul with quick brown eyes and flyaway hair, were chain-smoking for their nerves. The girl was dancing to the music, her white blouse glowing softly in the moonlight.

Though it was not evident in their demeanor, they had taken great care in choosing the location for their party. From their position they could monitor traffic on the road from Gustavia, along with the large private dinner party now beginning about a hundred yards down the beach at Le Tetou restaurant. At 8:30, one of the men, the tough one with a pockmarked face, appeared to receive a call on his mobile phone. It was not an ordinary phone but a two-way radio capable of sending and receiving secure transmissions. A moment after hanging up, he and the other two men got to their feet and made their way noisily back to the road, where they climbed into a Suzuki Vitara.

The girl dressed in white remained behind on the beach, listening to Bob Marley as she watched a private turboprop plane descending low over the waters of the bay toward the runway. She looked at the weather-beaten sign: BEWARE OF LOW-FLYING AIRCRAFT. The girl was dissident by nature and paid it no heed. She turned up the volume of the music and danced as the plane roared over her head.

THE BEACH at Marigot Bay is small and rocky and rarely used except by locals as a place to store their boats. There is a small turnout just off the coast road with room for two or three cars and a flight of rickety wood stairs leading down to the beach. On that night the turnout was occupied by a pair of Piaggio motorbikes. Their owners were on the darkened beach, perched on the belly of an overturned rowboat. Both had nylon rucksacks at their feet and both rucksacks contained two silenced handguns. The younger man carried .45-caliber

Barak SP-21s. The older man preferred smaller weapons and had always been partial to Italian guns. The weapons in his bag were 9mm Berettas.

Unlike their compatriots at Saint-Jean, the two men were not drinking or listening to music or engaging in false gaiety of any kind. Both were silent and both were taking slow and steady breaths to calm their racing hearts. The older man was watching the traffic along the road, the younger man was contemplating the gentle surf. Both, however, were picturing the scene that would take place in a few minutes in the villa at the end of the point. At 8:30 the older one raised his radio to his lips and uttered two words: "Go, Dina."

IT WAS MONIQUE, Jean-Michel's wife, who spotted the girl first.

Drinks had just been served; Zizi had just finished ordering everyone to enjoy the meal, because it was to be their last on Saint-Bart's. Sarah was seated at the opposite end of the table, next to Herr Wehrli. The Swiss banker was discussing his admiration for the work of Ernst Ludwig Kirchner when Sarah, from the corner of her eye, noticed the swift turn of Monique's angular head and the supple movement of her dark hair.

"There's that girl," Monique said to no one in particular. "The one with the terrible scar on her leg. Remember her, Sarah? We saw her on the beach at Saline yesterday. Thank God she's wearing pants tonight."

Sarah politely disengaged herself from the Swiss banker and followed Monique's gaze. The girl was walking along the water's edge, dressed in a white blouse and blue jeans rolled up to her calves. As she approached the restaurant one of the bodyguards came forward and tried to block her path. Sarah, though she could not hear their conversation, could see the girl exerting her right to walk along a public stretch of beach, regardless of the high-security private party taking place at Le Tetou. *Office Doctrine,* she thought. *Don't try to appear inconspicuous. Make a spectacle of yourself.*

The bodyguard finally relented, and the girl limped slowly past and vanished into the darkness. Sarah allowed another moment to elapse, then leaned across the table in front of Monique and spoke quietly into Jean-Michel's ear.

"I think I'm about to be sick."

"What's wrong?"

"Too much wine at lunch. I nearly threw up in the launch."

"You want to go to the restroom?"

"Can you take me, Jean-Michel?"

Jean-Michel nodded and stood up.

"Wait," Monique said. "I'll come with you."

Jean-Michel shook his head, but Monique stood abruptly and helped Sarah to her feet. "The poor girl's sick," she hissed at him in French. "She needs a woman to look after her."

*   *   *

AT THAT same moment a Suzuki Vitara pulled into the parking lot of Le Tetou. Yossi was behind the wheel; Yaakov and Lavon were seated in back. Yaakov chambered the first round in his 9mm Beretta, then peered down the passage and waited for Sarah to appear.

SARAH GLANCED over her shoulder as they left the beach and saw Zizi and Nadia staring at her. She turned and looked straight ahead. Jean-Michel was on her left, Monique on her right. Each held an arm. They led her quickly through the interior portion of the restaurant and past the boutique. The passageway was in heavy shadow. Jean-Michel opened the door of the ladies' room and switched on the light, then looked quickly around and gestured for Sarah to enter. The door slammed shut. *Too hard,* she thought. She locked it securely and looked in the mirror. The face staring back at her was no longer hers. It might have been painted by Max Beckmann or Edvard Munch. Or perhaps Gabriel's grandfather, Viktor Frankel. A portrait of a terrified woman. Through the closed door she heard the voice of Monique asking if she was all right. Sarah made no reply. She braced herself on the sink, then closed her eyes and waited.

"SHIT," murmured Yaakov. "Why did she have to bring the fucking kickboxer?"

"Can you take him?" asked Lavon.

"I think so, but if things start to go badly out there make sure you shoot him in the head."

"I've never shot anyone in my life."

"It's easy," Yaakov said. "Put your finger on the trigger and pull."

It was precisely 8:32 p.m. when Gabriel mounted the wooden stairs on the beach at Marigot Bay. He wore a motorcycle helmet with a dark visor and, beneath the helmet, a lip microphone and miniature earpiece. The black nylon rucksack containing the Berettas was secured to his back by the shoulder straps. Mikhail, one step behind him, was identically attired. They climbed aboard the motorbikes and fired the engines simultaneously. Gabriel nodded his head once, and together they accelerated into the empty road.

They plunged down a steep hill, Gabriel leading the way, Mikhail a few yards behind. The road was narrow and bordered on both sides by a stone wall. Ahead of them, at the top of another hill, was the turnoff for Pointe Milou. Parked along the edge of the stone wall was a motorcycle, and sitting astride the saddle, wearing blue jeans and a tight-fitting shirt, was Rimona, her face concealed by a helmet and visor.

She flashed her headlamp twice, the signal that the road was clear. Gabriel and Mikhail took the corner at speed, leaning hard through the turn, and sped out onto the point. The sea opened before them, luminous in the moonlight. To their left rose the slope of a barren hillside; on their right stood a row of small cottages. A black dog emerged from the last cottage and barked savagely as they swept past.

At the next intersection was a kiosk of postboxes and a small unoccupied bus shelter. An approaching car rounded the corner too fast and strayed into Gabriel's side of the road. He slowed and waited for it to pass, then opened the throttle again.

It was then he heard the voice of Rimona in his ear.

"We have a problem," she said calmly.

Gabriel, as he made the turn, glanced over his shoulder and saw what it was. They were being followed by a battered blue Range Rover with Gendarmerie markings.

IN THE parking lot of Le Tetou, Yaakov was reaching for the door latch when he heard Rimona in his earpiece. He looked at Lavon and asked, "What the fuck is going on?"

It was Gabriel who told him.

THERE WERE two gendarmes in the Rover, one behind the wheel and a second, more senior-looking man in the passenger seat with a radio handset pressed to his lips. Gabriel resisted the temptation to turn around for a second look and kept his eyes straight ahead.

Just beyond the bus shelter, the road forked. Bin

Shafiq's villa lay to the right. Gabriel and Mikhail went left. A few seconds later they slowed and looked behind them.

The gendarmes had gone the other way.

Gabriel braked to a halt and debated what to do next. Were the gendarmes on a routine patrol, or were they responding to a call of some sort? Was it merely bad luck or something more? He was certain of only one thing. Ahmed bin Shafiq was within his grasp, and Gabriel wanted him dead.

He turned around, rode back to the fork, and looked toward the end of the point. The road was clear, and the gendarmes were nowhere in sight. He twisted the throttle and plunged forward through the darkness. When he arrived at the villa he found the security gate open and the Gendarmerie Range Rover parked in the drive. Ahmed bin Shafiq, the most dangerous terrorist in the world, was loading his suitcases into the back of his Subaru.

And the two French policemen were helping him!

Gabriel rode back to the spot where Mikhail was waiting and broke the news to the entire team simultaneously.

"Our friend is about to leave the island. And Zizi's arranged a police escort."

"Are we blown?" Mikhail asked.

"We have to assume that's the case. Take Sarah and get over to Saline."

"I'm afraid that's no longer possible," Lavon replied.

"What's not possible?"

"We can't get Sarah," he said. "We're losing her."

A FIST crashed against the door three times. A tense voice shouted at her to come out. Sarah turned the latch and opened the door. Jean-Michel was standing outside in the passage, along with four of Zizi's bodyguards. They seized her arms and pulled her back to the beach.

THE WHITE CABRIOLET came through the security gate and turned onto the road, followed by the police Rover. Fifteen seconds later the little convoy sped past Gabriel and Mikhail. The top of the convertible was still down. Bin Shafiq had both hands on the wheel, and his eyes were straight ahead.

Gabriel looked at Mikhail and spoke to the entire team simultaneously over the radio. "Evacuate to Saline now. *Everyone.* Leave me a boat, but get off the island."

Then he set off after bin Shafiq and the gendarmes.

"YOU'RE HURTING ME."

"I'm sorry, Miss Sarah, but we have to hurry."

"For what? The main course?"

"There's been a bomb threat. We're leaving the island."

"A bomb threat? Against who? Against *what*?"

"Please don't say another word, Miss Sarah. Just walk quickly."

"I will, but let go of my arms. You're *hurting* me!"

GABRIEL STAYED two hundred yards behind the Range Rover and rode with his headlamp doused. They sped through the village of Lorient, then Saint-Jean. As they raced along the edge of the bay he saw the sign for Le Tetou. He throttled down and peered into the parking lot, just as Zizi and the rest of his entourage were climbing into the Land Cruisers under the gaze of two more gendarmes. Sarah was sandwiched between Rafiq and Jean-Michel. There was nothing Gabriel could do now. Reluctantly he accelerated and set off after bin Shafiq.

The airport was now directly ahead of them. Without warning the two vehicles swerved into the service road and headed through an open security gate onto the tarmac. A turboprop was waiting at the end on the tarmac, engines running. Gabriel stopped on the shoulder of the road and watched as bin Shafiq, the woman, and the two gendarmes emerged from their vehicles.

The Saudi terrorist and the woman immediately boarded the plane, while the gendarmes loaded the bags into the storage compartment in the belly. Fifteen seconds after the cabin door closed, the plane lurched forward and swept down the runway. As it rose over the Baie de Saint-Jean, Zizi's motorcade came roaring past in a black blur and started up the hill toward Gustavia.

*   *   *

IT WAS 8:40 when Mordecai and Oded spotted Mikhail and Rimona clambering down the dunes toward Saline beach. Two minutes later four more figures appeared. By 8:43 everyone was aboard the boats but Lavon.

"You heard him, Eli," Yaakov shouted. "He wants everyone off the island."

"I know," Lavon said, "but I'm not leaving without him."

Yaakov could see there was no point in arguing. A moment later the Zodiacs were bounding through the surf toward *Sun Dancer*. Lavon watched them melt into the darkness; then he turned and began pacing the water's edge.

THE MOTORCADE snaked its way at high speed down the hill into Gustavia. Gabriel, following after them, could see *Alexandra* ablaze with light at the edge of the harbor. Two minutes later the Land Cruisers turned into the parking lot of the marina. Zizi's bodyguards handled the disembarkation and loading process with the speed and precision of professionally trained men. Rescue was not an option. Gabriel saw Sarah only once—a flash of saffron wedged between two large dark figures—and a moment later they were seaborne once more, bound for the sanctuary of *Alexandra*. He had no choice but to turn and head to Saline, where Lavon was waiting for him. Gabriel sat morosely in the prow as they headed into the bay.

"Do you remember what I told you this afternoon, Gabriel?"

"I remember, Eli."

"If you can only get one target tonight, make sure it's Sarah. That's what I told you."

"I know, Eli."

"Who made the mistake? Was it us? Or was it Sarah?"

"It doesn't matter now."

"No, it doesn't. He's going to kill her unless we can somehow get her back."

"He won't do it here. Not after involving the French police."

"He'll find a way. No one betrays Zizi and gets away with it. Zizi's rules."

"He'll have to move her," Gabriel said. "And, of course, he'll want to know who she's working for."

"Which means we *might* have a very small window, depending on the methods Zizi is willing to use to get answers."

Gabriel was silent. Lavon could read his thoughts.

We'll get her, Gabriel was thinking. *Let's just hope there's something left of her when we do.*

28

CIA HEADQUARTERS

WORD OF THE DISASTER in Saint-Barthélemy arrived in the Operations Room at King Saul Boulevard within ten minutes of Gabriel's return to *Sun Dancer*. Amos Sharrett, the director-general, was upstairs in his office at the time and was informed of the developments by the duty officer. Despite the lateness of the hour, he immediately woke the prime minister and told him the news. Five minutes later there was a second secure call from *Sun Dancer,* this one to Langley, Virginia. It went not to the Ops Center but to the private line of Adrian Carter's seventh-floor office. Carter took the news calmly, as he did most things, and toyed with a stray paper clip as Gabriel made his request. "We have a plane in Miami at the moment," Carter said. "It can be on the ground in Saint Maarten by dawn."

Carter hung up the phone and gazed toward the bank

of television monitors on the opposite side of the room. The president was in Europe on his fence-mending tour. He had spent the day meeting with the new German chancellor while outside the police had waged running street battles across Berlin with anti-American demonstrators. More of the same was expected at the president's final two stops: Paris and Rome. The French were bracing for a wave of Muslim rioting, and the Carabinieri were anticipating demonstrations on a scale not seen in the Italian capital in a generation—hardly the scenes of transatlantic harmony the White House imagemakers had been hoping for.

Carter switched off the television and locked his papers in his wall safe, then took his overcoat from the hook on the back of his door and slipped out. The secretaries had gone for the night, and the vestibule was in shadow except for a trapezoid of light that shone from a half-open door on the opposite side. The door led to the office of Shepard Cantwell, the deputy director of intelligence, Carter's counterpart on the analytical side of the Agency. From inside the room came the clattering of a computer keyboard. Cantwell was still there. According to the Agency wits, Cantwell never left. He simply locked himself into his wall safe some time around midnight and let himself out again at dawn, so he could be at his desk when the director arrived.

"That you, Adrian?" Cantwell inquired in his lazy Back Bay drawl. When Carter poked his head into Cantwell's lair, the DDI stopped typing and looked up over a batch of files. He was prim as a prior and twice as crafty. "Christ, Adrian, you look like death warmed over. What's bothering you?"

When Carter mumbled something vague about the chaos surrounding the president's goodwill trip to Europe, Cantwell launched into a dissertation about the false dangers of anti-Americanism. Cantwell was analysis. He couldn't help it.

"It's always fascinated me, Adrian, this ludicrous need of ours to be powerful and loved at the same time. The American president reached halfway around the world and toppled the ruler of Mesopotamia in an afternoon. Not even Caesar could manage that. And now he wants to be adored by those who oppose him. The sooner we stop worrying about being liked, the better off we'll be."

"You've been reading Machiavelli again, Shep?"

"Never stopped." He interlaced his fingers behind his neck and splayed his elbows, treating Carter to an unwanted view of his armpits. "There's a nasty rumor going round the village, Adrian."

"Really?" Carter gave his wristwatch a glance that Cantwell seemed not to notice.

"According to the rumor you're involved in some sort of special operation against a well-to-do friend of the al-Saud. And your partners in this endeavor—again, I'm just telling you what I've heard, Adrian—are the Israelites."

"You shouldn't listen to rumors," Carter said. "How far has it traveled?"

"Beyond Langley," replied Cantwell, which was another way of saying it had reached some of the brother agencies that had been steadily encroaching on CIA turf ever since the dreaded reorganization of the American intelligence community.

"How far beyond?"

"Far enough so that some people in town are starting to get nervous. You know how the game is played, Adrian. There's a pipeline between Riyadh and Washington, and it flows green with cash. This town is awash with Saudi money. It pours into the think tanks and the law firms. Hell, the lobbyists dine out on the stuff. The Saudis have even managed to devise a system for bribing us while we're still in office. Everyone knows that if they look out for the al-Saud while they're working for Club Fed, the al-Saud will look out for them when they return to the private sector. Maybe it will be in the form of a lucrative consulting contract or some legal work. Maybe a chair at some insipid institute that spouts the Saudi party line. And so when rumors start flying around town that some cowboy at Langley is going after one of the most generous benefactors of this unholy system, people get nervous."

"Are you one of them, Shepard?"

"Me?" Cantwell shook his head. "I'm heading back to Boston the minute my parole comes through. But there are other people in the building planning to hang around town and cash in."

"And what if the generous benefactors of this unholy

system are also filling the coffers of the people who fly airplanes into our buildings? What if these friends of ours are up to their necks in terror? What if they're willing to make any deal with the devil necessary to ensure their survival, even if it leads to dead Americans?"

"You shake their hands and smile," said Cantwell. "And you think of the terrorism as an inconvenient surcharge on your next tank of gas. You still driving that old Volvo of yours?"

Cantwell knew exactly what Carter drove. Their assigned spaces were next to each other in the west parking lot. "I can't afford a new car," Carter said. "Not with three kids in college."

"Maybe you should sign up for the Saudi retirement plan. I see a lucrative consulting contract in your future."

"Not my style, Shep."

"So what about those rumors? Any truth to them?"

"None at all."

"Glad to hear it," Cantwell said. "I'll be sure to set everyone straight. Night, Adrian."

"Night, Shep."

Carter went downstairs. The executive parking lot was nearly empty of other cars. He climbed into his Volvo and headed toward Northwest Washington, following the route he and Gabriel had taken eight weeks earlier. As he passed Zizi al-Bakari's estate, he slowed and peered through the bars of the gate, toward the hideous faux-chateau mansion perched on the cliff overlooking the river. *Don't touch her,* Carter thought savagely. *Harm one hair on her head, and I'll kill you myself.* As he headed over Chain Bridge, he glanced down at his dash. A warning light was glowing red. *How appropriate,* he thought. His gas tank was nearly empty.

AT THAT same moment, *Sun Dancer* was rounding Grande Pointe and returning to the anchorage off Gustavia. Gabriel stood alone in the prow, field glasses pressed to his eyes, gazing at the afterdeck of *Alexandra,* where the ship's crew were serving a hastily prepared dinner for thirty. Gabriel saw them as figures in a painting. *The Boating Party,* he thought. Or was it *The Last Supper?*

There was Zizi, seated regally at the head of the table, as though the events of the evening had been a welcome diversion from the monotony of an otherwise ordinary journey. At his left hand sat his beautiful daughter, Nadia. At his right hand, stabbing at his food without appetite, was his trusted second in command, Daoud Hamza. Farther down the table were the lawyers, Abdul & Abdul, and Herr Wehrli, minder of Zizi's money. There was Mansur, maker of travel arrangements, and Hassan, chief of communications, secure and otherwise. There was Jean-Michel, tender of Zizi's fitness and supplementary security man, and his sullen wife, Monique. There was Rahimah Hamza and her lover, Hamid, the beautiful Egyptian film star. There was a quartet of anxious-looking bodyguards and several attractive women with guiltless faces. And then, seated at the far end of the table, as far from Zizi as possible, there was a beautiful woman in saffron silk. She provided the balance to the composition. She was innocence to Zizi's evil. And Gabriel could see that she was frightened to death. Gabriel knew he was witnessing a performance. But for whose benefit was it being staged? His or Sarah's?

At midnight the figures in his painting stood and bade each other goodnight. Sarah disappeared through a passageway and was lost to him once more. Zizi, Daoud Hamza, and Wazir bin Talal entered Zizi's office. Gabriel saw it as a new painting: *Meeting of Three Evil Men*, artist unknown.

Five minutes later Hassan rushed into the office and handed Zizi a mobile telephone. Who was calling? Was it one of Zizi's brokers asking for instructions on what position to take at the opening of trading in London? Or was it Ahmed bin Shafiq, murderer of innocents, telling Zizi what to do with Gabriel's girl?

Zizi accepted the phone and with a wave of his hand banished Hassan from the office. Wazir bin Talal, chief of security, walked over to the windows and drew the blinds.

SHE LOCKED the door and switched on every light in the room. She turned on the satellite television system and changed the channel to CNN. German police battling protesters in the streets. More proof, said a breathless reporter, of America's failure in Iraq.

She went out onto the deck and sat down. The yacht she had watched leaving the harbor that afternoon had now returned. Was it Gabriel's yacht? Was bin Shafiq alive or dead? Was Gabriel alive or dead? She knew only that something had gone wrong. *These things happen from time to time,* Zizi had said. *It's why we take matters of security so seriously.*

She gazed at the yacht, looking for signs of movement on the deck, but it was too far off to see anything. *We're here with you, Sarah. All of us.* The wind rose. She wrapped her arms around her legs and drew her knees to her chin.

I hope you're all still there, she thought. *And please get me off this boat before they kill me.*

AT SOME POINT, she did not remember when, the cold had driven her inside to her bed. She woke to a gray dawn and the patter of a gentle rain on her sundeck. The television was still on; the president had arrived in Paris, and the place de la Concorde was a sea of protesters. She picked up the telephone and ordered coffee. It was delivered five minutes later. Everything was the same except for the handwritten note, which was folded in half and leaning against her basket of brioche. The note was from Zizi. *I have a job for you, Sarah. Pack your bags and be ready to leave by nine. We'll talk before you leave.* She poured herself a cup of coffee and carried it to the door of the sundeck. It was then she noticed that *Alexandra* was under way and that they had left Saint Bart's. She looked again at Zizi's note. It didn't say where she was going.

29

OFF SAINT MAARTEN

SARAH PRESENTED HERSELF ON the aft deck promptly at nine o'clock. It was raining heavily now; the clouds were low and dark, and a strong wind was playing havoc with the sea. Zizi was wearing a pale marine raincoat and dark sunglasses despite the gray weather. Bin Talal stood next to him, dressed in a tropical-weight blazer to conceal his sidearm.

"Never a dull moment," Sarah said as amiably as possible. "First a bomb threat, then a note with my breakfast telling me to pack my bags." She looked toward the helipad and saw Zizi's pilot climbing behind the controls of the Sikorsky. "Where am I going?"

"I'll tell you on the way," Zizi said, taking her by the arm.

"You're coming with me?"

"Only as far as Saint Maarten." He pulled her toward the stairs that led to the helipad. "There's a private jet for you there."

"Where's the private jet going?"

"It's taking you to see a painting. I'll tell you about it on the way."

"Where's it going, Zizi?"

He stopped halfway down the stairs and looked at her, his eyes concealed behind the dark glass.

"Is something bothering you, Sarah? You seem tense."

"I just don't like getting on airplanes when I don't know where they're going."

Zizi smiled and started to tell her, but his words were drowned out by the engine of the Sikorsky.

GABRIEL WAS STANDING in the prow of *Sun Dancer* when the helicopter lifted off. He watched for a moment, then rushed up to the bridge, where a navy lieutenant was at the helm.

"They're moving her to Saint Maarten. How far are we from shore?"

"About five miles."

"How long will it take us to get there?"

"Given the weather, I'd say thirty minutes. Maybe a bit less."

"And the Zodiacs?"

"You don't want to try it in a Zodiac—not in these conditions."

"Get us close—as quickly as possible."

The lieutenant nodded, and started making preparations to change heading. Gabriel went to the command center and dialed Carter.

"She's headed toward the airport on Saint Maarten as we speak."

"Is she alone?"

"Zizi and his chief of security are with her."

"How long before you can get there?"

"Forty-five minutes to shore. Another fifteen to the airport."

"I'll put the crew on standby. The plane will be ready when you arrive."

"Now we just need to know where Zizi's sending her."

"Thanks to al-Qaeda, we're now tapped into every traffic control tower in the hemisphere. When Zizi's pilot files a flight plan, we'll know where she's going."

"How long will it take?"

"Usually it takes us only a few minutes."

"I don't suppose I need to remind you that sooner is better."

"Just get to shore," Carter said. "I'll take care of the rest."

"IT'S A MANET," Zizi said as they swept toward the coastline, just beneath the deck of low dark clouds. "I've had my eye on it for several years now. The owner has been reluctant to part with it, but last night he telephoned my office in Geneva and said he was interested in making a deal."

"What do you want me to do?"

"Inspect the painting and make certain it's in reasonable condition. Then review the provenance carefully. As I'm sure you're aware, thousands of French Impressionist paintings entered Switzerland during the war under illicit circumstances. The last thing I need is some Jewish family beating down my door demanding their painting back."

Sarah felt a stab of fear in the center of her chest. She turned away and looked out the window.

"And if the provenance is in order?"

"Work out a suitable price. I'm willing to go to thirty million, but for God's sake, don't tell him that." He handed her a business card with a handwritten number on the back. "Once you've got a final number, call me before you accept."

"What time do I see him?"

"Ten o'clock tomorrow morning. One of my drivers will meet you at the airport tonight and take you to your hotel. You can get a good night's sleep before you see the painting."

"Do I get to know the owner's name?"

"Hermann Klarsfeld. He's one of the richest men in Switzerland, which is saying something. I've warned him about how beautiful you are. He's looking forward to meeting you."

"Lovely," she said, still looking out the window at the approaching coastline.

"Herr Klarsfeld is an octogenarian, Sarah. You needn't worry about any inappropriate behavior."

Zizi looked at bin Talal. The security chief reached under his seat and produced a new Gucci bag. "Your things, Miss Sarah," he said, his tone apologetic. Sarah accepted the bag and opened it. Inside were the electronic items taken from her the afternoon of her arrival: the mobile phone and the PDA; the iPod and the hair dryer; even the travel alarm clock. Nothing remained of her aboard *Alexandra*, no evidence she'd ever been there.

The helicopter started to lose altitude. Sarah looked out the window again and saw that they were descending toward the airport. At the end of the airfield were a handful of private jets. One was being fueled for takeoff. Zizi was once more extolling the wealth of Herr Klarsfeld, but Sarah heard none of it. She was now thinking only of escape. *There is no Herr Klarsfeld*, she told herself. *And there is no Manet*. She was being put on an airplane to oblivion. She remembered Zizi's benediction the afternoon she accepted his job offer. *As you can see I'm very generous to the people who work for me, but I get very angry when they betray me*. She *had* betrayed him. She had betrayed him for Gabriel. And now she would pay with her life. *Zizi's rules*.

She looked down at the airfield, wondering if Zizi had somehow left a crack through which she might escape. Surely there would be a customs officer to check her passport. Maybe an airport official or a policeman or two. She rehearsed the lines she would say to them. *My name is Sarah Bancroft. I am an American citizen, and*

*these men are trying to transport me to Switzerland
against my will.* Then she looked at Zizi and his chief of
security. *You've taken that scenario into account, haven't
you? You've paid off the customs officials and bribed the
local police.* Zizi didn't countenance delays, especially not
for a hysterical infidel woman.

The Sikorsky's skids bumped down on the tarmac.
Bin Talal opened the cabin door and climbed out, then
reached back inside and offered Sarah his hand. She took
it and climbed down the staircase, into a vortex of
swirling wind. Fifty yards from the helicopter stood a
waiting Falcon 2000, engines screaming in preparation
for takeoff. She looked around: no customs officials, no
policeman. Zizi had closed her only window. She looked
back into the cabin of the Sikorsky and saw him for the
last time. He gave her a genial wave, then looked at his
gold Rolex, like an attending physician marking the time
of death.

Bin Talal seized her bags, reminded her to duck her
head, then took her by the arm and led her toward the
Falcon. On the staircase she tried to pull away from him,
but he squeezed her upper arm in a painful viselike grip
and conveyed her up the steps. She screamed for help,
but the sound was drowned out by the whining of the jet
engines and the thumping of the Sikorsky's rotor blade.

She staged one more rebellion at the top of the staircase, which bin Talal suppressed with a single shove between her shoulder blades. She stumbled inside, into a
small cabin luxuriously appointed in polished wood and

soft tan leather. It reminded her of a coffin. At least her journey to oblivion was going to be comfortable. She gathered herself for one more revolt and flew at the Saudi in a rage. Now, shielded from view by the outside world, there was no discretion in his response. He gave her a single open-handed blow that landed hard on her right cheekbone and sent her whirling to the cabin floor. The Saudis knew how to treat mutinous women.

She heard ringing in her ears and for a moment was blinded by exploding stars. When her vision cleared she saw Jean-Michel standing over her, drying his hands on a linen towel. The Frenchman sat on her legs and waited until bin Talal had pinned her arms to the floor before producing the hypodermic needle. She felt a single stab, then molten metal flowing into her veins. The skin of Jean-Michel's face slid from his skull, and Sarah slipped beneath the surface of cold black water.

30

SAINT MAARTEN

THE ZODIAC ENTERED THE waters of Great Bay one hour later. The four men on board were dressed in sport jackets and trousers, and each carried a small overnight bag for the benefit of local authorities. After docking at Bobby's Marina, the men climbed into a waiting taxi and proceeded to the airport at considerable speed. There, after clearing passport control, all on false travel documents, they boarded a waiting Gulfstream V private jet. The crew had already filed a flight plan and requested a takeoff slot. One hour later, at 11:37 A.M. local time, the plane departed. Its destination was Kloten Airport. Zurich, Switzerland.

AS THE GULFSTREAM rose over the waters of Simpson Bay, Adrian Carter made three telephone calls: one to the director of the CIA, the second to the arm of the

Agency that specialized in clandestine travel, and a third to an Agency physician who specialized in treating wounded agents under less than optimum conditions. He then opened his wall safe and removed one of three billfolds. Inside was a false passport, along with corresponding identification, credit cards, a bit of cash, and photographs of a family that did not exist. Ten minutes later he was walking across the west parking lot toward his Volvo sedan. The headquarters man was a field man once more. And the field man was going to Zug.

IN DOWNTOWN MUNICH, Uzi Navot was enjoying a late lunch with a paid informant from the German BND when he received an urgent call from Tel Aviv. It came not from the Operations Desk but directly from Amos Sharrett. Their conversation was brief and one-sided. Navot listened in silence, grunting occasionally to convey to Amos that he understood what he was to do, then rang off.

Navot was unwilling to let the German security man know the Office was in the midst of a full-blown crisis, so he remained at the restaurant for another thirty minutes, picking his thumbnail to shreds beneath the table while the German had strudel and coffee. At 3:15 he was behind the wheel of his E-Class Mercedes, and by 3:30 he was speeding westward along the E54 motorway.

Think of it as an audition, Amos had said. *Pull this off cleanly and Special Ops is yours.* But as Uzi Navot raced toward Zurich through the fading afternoon light, personal promotion was the last thing on his mind. It was Sarah he wanted—and he wanted her in one piece.

BUT SARAH, lost in a fog of narcotics, was unaware of the events swirling around her. Indeed she had no conception of even the state of her own body. She did not know she was reclining in an aft-facing chair of an eastbound Falcon 2000, operated by Meridian Executive Air Services of Caracas, wholly owned by AAB Holdings of Riyadh, Geneva, and points in between. She did not know that her hands were cuffed and her ankles shackled. Or that a crimson welt had arisen on her right cheek, compliments of Wazir bin Talal. Or that seated opposite her, separated by a small polished table, Jean-Michel was leafing through a bit of Dutch pornography and sipping a single-malt scotch he'd picked up duty-free at the Saint Maarten airport.

Sarah was aware only of her dreams. She had a vague sense the images playing out for her were not real, yet she was powerless to seize control of them. She heard a telephone ring and when she picked up the receiver she heard the voice of Ben, but instead of hurtling toward the South Tower of the World Trade Center he had landed safely in Los Angeles and was bound for his meeting. She entered a stately town house in Georgetown and was greeted not by Adrian Carter but by Zizi al-Bakari. Next she was in a shabby English country house, occupied not by Gabriel and his team but by a cell of Saudi terrorists plotting their next strike. More images followed, one upon the next. A beautiful yacht slicing through a sea of blood. A gallery in London hung with portraits of the dead. And finally an art restorer with ashen temples and emerald eyes, standing before a portrait of a woman handcuffed to a dressing table. The restorer was Gabriel, and the woman in the portrait was Sarah. The image burst into flames, and when the flames receded, she saw only the face of Jean-Michel.

"Where are we going?"

"First we're going to find out who you're working for," he said. "And then we're going to kill you."

Sarah closed her eyes in pain as a needle plunged into her thigh.

Molten metal. *Black water . . .*

31

KLOTEN, SWITZERLAND

THE HOTEL FLYAWAY AT 19 Marktgasse is a house of convenience rather than luxury. Its façade is flat and drab, its lobby plain and antiseptic. Indeed its only notable attribute is its proximity to Kloten Airport, which is only five minutes away. On that snowy February evening the hotel was the site of a secret gathering, of which management and the local police still know nothing. Two men came from Brussels, another from Rome, and a fourth from London. All four were specialists in physical surveillance. All four checked in under assumed names and with false passports. A fifth man arrived from Paris. He checked in under his own name, which was Moshe. He was not a surveillance specialist but a low-level field courier known as a *bodel*. His car, an Audi A8, was parked outside in the street. In the trunk was a suitcase filled with guns, radios, night-vision goggles, and balaclava helmets.

The last man to arrive was known to the girls at the check-in counter, for he was a frequent traveler through Kloten Airport and had spent more nights at the Hotel Flyaway than he cared to remember. "Good evening, Mr. Bridges," one of the girls said to him as he strode into the lobby. Five minutes later he was upstairs in his room. Within two minutes the rest had joined him. "A plane is about to land at Kloten," he told them. "There's going to be a girl on board. And we're going to make sure she doesn't die tonight."

SARAH WOKE a second time. She opened her eyes just long enough to take a mental snapshot of her surroundings, then closed them before Jean-Michel could stab her in the leg again with another loaded syringe. They were descending now and being buffeted by heavy turbulence. Her head had fallen sideways, and with each lurch of the aircraft her throbbing temple banged against the cabin wall. Her fingers were numb from the pressure of the handcuffs, and the soles of her feet felt as though they were being jabbed by a thousand needles. Jean-Michel was still reclining in the seat across from her. His eyes were closed, and his fingers interlaced over his genitals.

She opened her eyes a second time. Her vision was hazy and unclear, as if she were enveloped in a black fog. She lifted her hands to her face and felt fabric. *A hood*, she thought. Then she looked down at her own body and saw it was enveloped in a black veil. Jean-Michel had shrouded her in an *abaya*. She wept softly. Jean-Michel opened one eye and gazed at her malevolently.

"What's the problem, Sarah?"

"You're taking me to Saudi Arabia, aren't you?"

"We're going to Switzerland, just like Zizi told you."

"Why the *abaya*?"

"It will make your entry into the country go more smoothly. When the Swiss customs men see a Saudi woman in a veil, they tend to be highly respectful." He gave her another grotesque smile. "I think it's a shame covering a girl like you in black, but I did enjoy putting it on you."

"You're a pig, Jean-Michel."

Sarah never saw the blow coming—a well-aimed backhand that landed precisely on her swollen right cheek. By the time her vision cleared Jean-Michel was once more reclining in his seat. The plane heaved in a sudden burst of turbulence. Sarah felt bile rising into her throat.

"I think I'm going to be sick."

"Just like at Le Tetou?"

Think quickly, Sarah.

"I *was* sick at Le Tetou, you idiot."

"You made a very quick recovery. In fact, you looked fine to me after we returned to *Alexandra*."

"Those drugs you're shooting into me are making me nauseated. Take me into the bathroom."

"You want to check for messages?"

Fast, Sarah. Fast.

"What are you talking about? Take me to the toilet so I can throw up."

"You're not going anywhere."

"At least lift the *abaya* for me."

He looked at her disbelievingly, then leaned across the divide and lifted the veil, exposing her face to the cool air of the cabin. To Sarah it seemed appallingly like a bridegroom lifting the veil of his new wife. A wave of anger broke within her, and she lashed out at his face with her cuffed hands. Jean-Michel easily swatted away her blow, then landed one of his own against the left side of her head. It knocked her from the leather seat and sent her to the floor. Without rising he kicked her in the abdomen, knocking the breath from her lungs. As she fought to regain it, the contents of her stomach emptied onto the carpet.

"Fucking bitch," the Frenchman said savagely. "I should make you clean that up."

He grabbed hold of the chain linking her wrists and pulled her back into her seat, then rose and went into the toilet. Sarah heard the sound of water splashing into the basin. When Jean-Michel emerged he was holding a damp linen towel, which he used to punitively scrub the vomit from her lips. Then, from a small leather case, he produced another syringe and a vial of clear liquid. He loaded the syringe without much care for the dosage, then seized hold of her arm. Sarah tried to pull away, but he hit her twice in the mouth. As the drug entered her bloodstream, she remained conscious but felt as though a great weight was pressing down on her body. Her eyelids closed, but she remained trapped in the present.

"I'm still awake," she said. "Your drugs aren't working anymore."

"They're working just fine."

"Then why am I still conscious?"

"It's easier to get answers that way."

"Answers to what?"

"Better fasten your seat belt," he said mockingly. "We'll be landing in a few minutes."

Sarah, the model prisoner, tried to do as she was told, but her arms lay limply in her lap, unable to obey her commands.

SHE LEANED her face against the cold glass of the window and looked out. The darkness was absolute. A few moments later they entered the clouds, and the plane pitched in wave after wave of turbulence. Jean-Michel poured himself another glass of whiskey and drank it in a single swallow.

They emerged from the clouds into a snowstorm. Sarah looked down and studied the pattern of the ground lights. There was a mass of brilliant illumination wrapped around the northern end of a large body of water and strands of lesser light laying along the shoreline like jewels. She tried to remember where Zizi had said she'd be going. *Zurich,* she thought. *Yes, that was it. Zurich . . . Herr Klarsfeld . . . The Manet for which Zizi would pay thirty million and not a million more . . .*

The plane passed north of central Zurich and banked toward the airport. Sarah prayed for a crash landing. It was obscenely smooth, though—so smooth she was unaware of the moment of touchdown. They taxied for several minutes. Jean-Michel was gazing calmly out the window, while Sarah was sliding further into oblivion. The fuselage seemed as long as an Alpine tunnel, and when she tried to speak, words would not form in her mouth.

"The drug I just gave you is shorter in duration," Jean-Michel said, his tone maddeningly reassuring. "You'll be able to talk soon. At least I hope so—for your sake."

The plane began to slow. Jean-Michel lowered the black veil over her face, then unlocked the handcuffs and the shackles. When they finally came to a stop he opened the rear cabin door and poked his head out to make certain things were in order. Then he seized Sarah beneath the arms and pulled her upright. Blood returned painfully to her feet, and her knees buckled. Jean-Michel caught her before she could fall. "One foot in front of the other," he said. "Just walk, Sarah. You remember how to walk."

She did, but barely. The door was just ten feet away, but to Sarah it seemed a mile at least. A few paces into her journey she stepped on the hem of the *abaya* and pitched forward, but once again Jean-Michel prevented her from falling. When finally she reached the door she was met by a blast of freezing air. It was snowing heavily and bitterly cold, the night made darker by the black fabric of the veil. Once again there were no customs officers or security men in evidence, only a black Mercedes sedan with diplomatic plates. Its rear door hung ajar, and through the opening Sarah could see a man in a gray overcoat and fedora. Even with the drugs clouding her thoughts, she could comprehend what was happening. AAB Holdings and the Saudi consulate in Zurich had requested VIP diplomatic treatment for a passenger arriving from Saint Maarten. It was just like the departure: no customs, no security, no avenue of escape.

Jean-Michel helped her down the stairs, then across the tarmac and into the back of the waiting Mercedes. He closed the door and headed immediately back toward the jet. As the car lurched forward, Sarah looked at the man seated next to her. Her vision blurred by the veil, she saw him only in the abstract. Enormous hands. A round face. A tight mouth surrounded by a bristly goatee. Another version of bin Talal, she thought. A well-groomed gorilla.

"Who are you?" she asked.

"I'm unimportant. I'm no one."

"Where are we going?"

He drove his fist into her ear and told her not to speak again.

*   *   *

THIRTY SECONDS LATER the Mercedes sedan with diplomatic plates sped past a snow-covered figure peering forlornly beneath the open hood of a stalled car. The man seemed to pay the Mercedes no heed as it swept by, though he did look up briefly as it headed up the ramp to the motorway. He forced himself to count slowly to five. Then he slammed the hood and climbed behind the wheel. When he turned the key, the engine started instantly. He slipped the car into gear and pulled onto the road.

SHE DID NOT know how long they drove—an hour, perhaps longer—but she knew the purpose of their journey. The stops, the starts, the sudden double-backs and nauseating accelerations: Eli Lavon had referred to such maneuvers as countersurveillance. Uzi Navot had called it wiping your backside.

She stared out the heavily tinted window of the car. She had spent several years in Switzerland as a young girl and knew the city reasonably well. These were not the Zurich streets she remembered of her youth. These were the gritty, dark streets of the northern districts and the Industrie-Quartier. Ugly warehouses, blackened brick factories, smoking rail yards. There were no pedestrians on the pavements and no passengers in the streetcars. It seemed she was alone in the world with only the

Unimportant One for company. She asked him once more where they were going. He responded with an elbow to Sarah's abdomen that made her cry out for her mother.

He took a long look over his shoulder, then he forced Sarah to the floor and murmured something in Arabic to the driver. She was lost now in darkness. She pushed the pain to one corner of her mind and tried to concentrate on the movement of the car. A right turn. A left. The *thump-thump* of rail tracks. An abrupt stop that made the tires scream. The Unimportant One pulled her back onto the seat and opened the door. When she seized hold of the armrest and refused to let go, he engaged in a brief tug of war before losing patience and giving her a knifelike blow to the kidney that sent charges of pain to every corner of her body.

She screamed in agony and released the armrest. The Unimportant One dragged her from the car and let her fall to the ground. It was cold cement. It seemed they were in a parking garage or the loading dock of a warehouse. She lay there writhing in agony, gazing up at her tormentor through the black gauze of the veil. *The Saudi woman's view of the world.* A voice told her to rise. She tried but could not.

The driver got out of the car and, together with the Unimportant One, lifted her to her feet. She stood there suspended for a moment, her arms spread wide, her body draped in the *abaya,* and waited for another hammer blow to her abdomen. Instead she was deposited into the backseat of a second car. The man seated there was familiar to her. She had seen him first in a manor house in Surrey that did not exist, and a second time at a villa in Saint Bart's that did. "Good evening, Sarah," said Ahmed bin Shafiq. "It's so nice to see you again."

32

ZURICH

IS YOUR NAME REALLY Sarah, or should I call you something else?"

She tried to answer him but was gasping for breath.

"My—name—is—*Sarah.*"

"Then Sarah it will be."

"Why—are—you—doing—this—to—me?"

"Come, come, Sarah."

"Please—let—me—*go!*"

"I'm afraid that's not possible."

She was doubled forward now, with her head between her knees. He grabbed her by the neck and pulled her upright, then lifted the veil and examined the damage to her face. From his expression it was unclear whether he thought they had been too hard on her or too lenient. She gazed back at him. Leather trench coat, cashmere scarf, small round spectacles with tortoiseshell rims: the very picture of a successful Zurich moneyman. His dark eyes radiated a calculating intelligence. His expression was identical to the one he had worn the moment of their first meeting.

"Who are you working for?" he asked benevolently.

"I work"—she coughed violently—"for Zizi."

"Breathe, Sarah. Take long slow breaths."

"Don't—hit—me—anymore."

"I won't," he said. "But you have to tell me what I want to know."

"I don't *know* anything."

"I want to know who you're working for."

"I told you—I work for Zizi."

His face betrayed mild disappointment. "Please, Sarah. Don't make this difficult. Just answer my questions. Tell me the truth, and this entire disagreeable episode will be over."

"You're going to kill me."

"Unfortunately, this is true," he said, as though agreeing with her assessment of the weather. "But if you tell us what we want to know, you'll be spared the knife, and your death will be as painless as possible. If you persist in these lies, your last hours on earth will be a living hell."

His cruelty is limitless, she thought. *He speaks of my beheading but doesn't have the decency to look away.*

"I'm not lying," she said.

"You'll talk, Sarah. Everyone talks. There's no use trying to resist. Please, don't do this to yourself."

"I'm not doing anything. You're the one who's—"

"I want to know who you're working for, Sarah."

"I work for Zizi."

"I want to know who sent you."

"Zizi came for me. He sent me jewels and flowers. He sent me airline tickets and bought me clothing."

"I want to know the name of the man who contacted you on the beach at Saline."

"I don't—"

"I want to know the name of the man who spilled wine on my colleague in Saint-Jean."

"What man?"

"I want to know the name of the girl with the limp who walked by Le Tetou during Zizi's dinner party."

"How would *I* know her name?"

"I want to know why you were watching me at my party. And why you suddenly decided to pin your hair up. And why you were wearing your hair up when you went jogging with Jean-Michel."

She was weeping uncontrollably now. "This is madness!"

"I want to know the names of the three men who followed me on motorcycles later that day. I want to know the names of the two men who came to my villa to kill me. And the name of the man who watched my plane take off."

"I'm telling you the *truth!* My name is Sarah Bancroft. I worked at an art gallery in London. I sold Zizi a painting, and he asked me to come to work for him."

"The van Gogh?"

"Yes!"

"Marguerite Gachet at Her Dressing Table?"

"Yes, you bastard."

"And where did you obtain this painting? Was it acquired on your behalf by your intelligence service?"

"I don't work for an intelligence service. I work for Zizi."

"You're working for the Americans?"

"No."

"For the Jews?"

"No!"

He exhaled heavily, then removed his spectacles and spent a long moment contemplatively polishing them on his cashmere scarf. "You should know that shortly after your departure from Saint Maarten, four men arrived at the airport and boarded a private plane. We recognized them. We assume they are headed here to Zurich. They're Jews, aren't they, Sarah?"

"I don't know what you're talking about."

"Trust me, Sarah. They're Jews. One can always tell."

He examined his spectacles and polished some more. "You should also know that colleagues of these Jews clumsily attempted to follow you tonight after you landed at the airport. Our driver easily dispensed with them. You see, we're professionals, too. They're gone now, Sarah. And you're all alone."

He put on his spectacles again.

"Do you think the so-called professionals for whom you're working would be willing to sacrifice their lives for you? They'd be vomiting their secrets all over the floor to me by now. But you're better than them, aren't you, Sarah? Zizi saw that, too. That's why he made the mistake of hiring you."

"It wasn't a mistake. You're the one making a mistake."

He smiled ruefully. "I'm leaving you now in the hands of my friend Muhammad. He worked for me in Group 205. Is this name familiar to you, Sarah? Group 205? Surely your handlers must have mentioned it to you during your preparation."

"I've never heard it before."

"Muhammad is a professional. He's also a very skilled interrogator. You and Muhammad are going to take a journey together. A night journey. Do you know this term, Sarah? The Night Journey."

Greeted only by the sound of her weeping, he answered his own question.

"It was during the Night Journey that God revealed Quran to the Prophet. Tonight you're going to make a revelation of your own. Tonight you're going to tell my friend Muhammad who you're working for and everything they know about my network. If you tell him quickly, you will be granted a degree of mercy. If you continue with these lies, Muhammad will carve the flesh from your bones and cut off your head. Do you understand me?"

Her stomach convulsed with nausea. Bin Shafiq appeared to be taking pleasure from her fear.

"Do you realize you've been looking at my arm? Did they tell you about my scar? My damaged hand?" Another weary smile. "You've been betrayed, Sarah—betrayed by your handlers."

He opened the door and climbed out, then ducked down and looked at her one more time.

"By the way, you very nearly succeeded. If your friends had managed to kill me on that island, a major operation of ours would have been disrupted."

"I thought you worked for Zizi in Montreal."

"Oh, yes. I nearly forgot." He wound his scarf tightly around his throat. "Muhammad won't find your little lies so amusing, Sarah. Something tells me you're going to have a long and painful night together."

She was silent for a moment. Then she asked: "What operation?"

"Operation? Me? I'm only an investment banker."

She asked him again. "What's the operation? Where are you going to strike?"

"Speak my real name, and I will tell you."

"Your name is Alain al-Nasser."

"No, Sarah. Not my cover name. My *real* name. Say it. Confess your sins, Sarah, and I'll tell you what you want to know."

She began to shake uncontrollably. She tried to form the words but could not summon the courage.

"Say it!" he shouted at her. "Say my name, you bitch."

She lifted her head and looked him directly in the eyes.

"Your—name—is—Ahmed—bin—Shafiq!"

His head snapped back, as if he were avoiding a blow. Then he smiled at her in admiration.

"You're a very brave woman."

"And you're a murderous coward."

"I should kill you myself."

"Tell me what you're going to do."

He hesitated a moment, then treated her to an arrogant smile. "Suffice it to say we have some unfinished business at the Vatican. The crimes of Christianity and the Western world against Muslims will soon be avenged once and for all. But you won't be alive to see this glorious act. You'll be dead by then. Tell Muhammad what you know, Sarah. Make your last hours on earth easy ones."

And with that he turned and walked away. The Unimportant One wrenched her from the back of the car while holding an ether-soaked rag over her nose and mouth. She scratched at him. She flailed. She landed several futile kicks to his cast-iron shins. Then the drug took hold, and she felt herself spiraling toward the ground. Someone caught her. Someone placed her in the trunk of a car. A face appeared briefly and looked down at her, inquisitive and oddly earnest. *The face of Muhammad.* Then the hatch closed, and she was enveloped in darkness. When the car began to move, she passed out.

33

ZUG, SWITZERLAND

GUSTAV SCHMIDT, chief of counterterrorism for the Swiss federal security service, was an unlikely American ally in the war against Islamic extremism. In a country where elected politicians, the press, and most of the population were solidly opposed to the United States and its war on terror, Schmidt had quietly forged personal bonds with his counterparts in Washington, especially Adrian Carter. When Carter needed permission to operate on Swiss soil, Schmidt invariably granted it. When Carter wanted to make an al-Qaeda operative vanish from the Federation, Schmidt usually gave him the green light. And when Carter needed a place to put down a plane, Schmidt regularly granted him landing rights. The private airstrip at Zug, a wealthy industrial city in the heart of the country, was Carter's favorite in Switzerland. Schmidt's, too.

It was shortly after midnight when the Gulfstream V

executive jet sunk out of the clouds and touched down on the snow-dusted runway. Five minutes later, Schmidt was seated across from Carter in the modestly appointed cabin. "We have a situation," Carter said. "To be perfectly honest with you, we don't have a complete picture." He gestured toward his traveling companion. "This is Tom. He's a doctor. We think we'll need his services before the night is over. Relax, Gustav. Have a drink. We may be here awhile."

Carter then looked out the window at the swirling snow and said nothing more. He didn't have to. Schmidt now knew the situation. One of Carter's agents was in trouble, and Carter wasn't at all sure he was going to get the agent back alive. Schmidt opened the brandy and drank alone. At times like these he was glad he had been born Swiss.

A SIMILAR VIGIL was under way at that same moment at the general aviation terminal at Kloten Airport. The man doing the waiting was not a senior Swiss policeman but Moshe, the *bodel* from Paris. At 12:45 A.M., four men emerged from the terminal into the snowstorm. Moshe tapped the horn of his Audi A8, and the four men turned in unison and headed his way. Yaakov, Mikhail, and Eli Lavon climbed in the back. Gabriel sat up front.

"Where is she?"

"Heading south."

"Drive," said Gabriel.

*   *   *

SARAH WOKE to paralyzing cold, her ears ringing with the hiss of tires over wet asphalt. *Where am I now?* she thought, and then she remembered. She was in the trunk of a Mercedes, an unwilling passenger on Muhammad's night journey to oblivion. Slowly, bit by bit, she gathered up the fragments of this day without end and placed them in proper sequence. She saw Zizi in his helicopter, glancing at his wristwatch as he sent her to her death. And Jean-Michel, her traveling companion, catching a few minutes of sleep along the way. And finally, she saw the monster, Ahmed bin Shafiq, warning her that his blood-bath at the Vatican was not yet complete. She heard his voice now; the drumbeat cadence of his questions.

I want to know the name of the man who contacted you on the beach at Saline . . .

He is Yaakov, she thought. *And he is five times the man you are.*

I want to know the name of the girl with the limp who walked by Le Tetou during Zizi's dinner party . . .

She is Dina, she thought. *The avenged remnant.*

I want to know the name of the man who spilled wine on my colleague in Saint-Jean . . .

He is Gabriel, she thought. *And one day very soon he's going to kill you.*

They're gone now, and you're all alone . . .

No, I'm not, she thought. *They're here with me. All of them.*

And in her mind she saw them coming for her through the snowfall. Would they 'arrive before Muhammad bestowed upon her a painless death? Would they come in time to learn the secret that Ahmed bin Shafiq had so arrogantly spit in her face? Sarah knew she could help them. She had information Muhammad wanted—and it was hers to give at whatever pace, and in whatever detail, she desired. *Go slowly*, she thought. *Take all the time in the world.*

She closed her eyes and once again started to lose consciousness. This time it was sleep. She remembered the last thing Gabriel had said to her the night before her departure from London. *Sleep, Sarah*, he had said. *You have a long journey ahead of you.*

WHEN SHE woke next the car was pitching violently. Gone was the hiss of tires moving over wet asphalt. Now it seemed they were plowing through deep snow over a rough track. This was confirmed for her a moment later when the tires lost traction and one of the occupants was forced to climb out and push. When the car stopped again, Sarah heard voices in Arabic and Swiss German, then the deep groan of frozen metal hinges. They drove on for a moment longer, then stopped a third time—the final time, she assumed, because the car's engine immediately went silent.

The trunk flew open. Two unfamiliar faces peered down at her; four hands seized her and lifted her out.

They stood her upright and let go of her, but her knees buckled and she collapsed into the snow. This proved to be a source of great amusement to them, and they stood around laughing for several moments before once again lifting her to her feet.

She looked around. They were in the middle of a large clearing, surrounded by towering fir and pine. There was an A-shaped chalet with a steeply pitched roof and a separate outbuilding of some sort, next to which were parked two four-wheel-drive jeeps. It was snowing heavily. To Sarah, still veiled, it seemed the sky was raining ash.

Muhammad appeared and grunted something in Arabic to the two men holding her upright. They took a step toward the chalet, expecting Sarah to walk with them, but her legs were rigid with cold and would not function. She tried to tell them she was freezing to death but could not speak. There was one benefit to the cold: she had long forgotten the pain of the blows she had taken in her face and abdomen.

They took her by the arms and waist and dragged her. Her legs trailed behind, and her feet carved twin trenches in the snow. Soon they were ablaze with the cold. She tried to remember what shoes she had put on that morning. Flat-soled sandals, she remembered suddenly—the ones Nadia had bought for her in Gustavia to go with the outfit she'd worn to Le Tetou.

They went to the back of the chalet. Here the trees were closer, no more than thirty yards from the structure, and a single frozen sentry was standing watch, smoking a cigarette and stamping his boots against the cold. The outer wall of the house was overhung by the eaves of the roof and stacked with firewood. They dragged her through a doorway, then down a flight of cement stairs. Still unable to walk, Sarah's frozen feet banged on each step. She began to cry in pain, a shivering tremulous wail to which her tormentors paid no heed.

They came to another door, which was tightly closed and secured by a padlock. A guard opened the lock, then the door, then threw a light switch. Muhammad entered the room first. The guards brought Sarah next.

A SMALL square chamber, no more than ten feet on either side. Porcelain-white walls. Photographs. Arab men at Abu Ghraib. Arab men in cages at Guantánamo Bay. A hooded Muslim terrorist holding the severed head of an American hostage. In the center of the room a metal table bolted to the floor. In the center of the table an iron loop. Attached to the loop a pair of handcuffs. Sarah screamed and flailed against them. It was useless, of course. One pinned her arms to the table while the second secured the handcuffs to her wrists. A chair was thrust into the back of her legs. Two hands forced her into it. Muhammad tore the veil from her face and slapped her twice.

*   *   *

"ARE YOU ready to talk?"

"Yes."

"No more lies?"

She shook her head.

"Say it, Sarah. No more lies."

"No—more—lies."

"You're going to tell me everything you know?"

"Every—thing."

"You're cold?"

"Freezing."

"Would you like something warm to drink?"

She nodded.

"Tea? You drink tea, Sarah."

Another nod.

"How do you take your tea, Sarah?"

"You can't—be serious."

"How do you take your tea?"

"With cyanide."

He smiled mirthlessly. "You should be so lucky. We'll have tea, then we'll talk."

THEY ALL THREE exited the room. Muhammad closed the door and put the padlock back into place. Sarah lowered her head to the table and closed her eyes. In her mind an image formed—the image of a clock counting down the minutes to her execution. Muhammad was bringing her tea. Sarah opened the glass cover of her imaginary clock and moved the hands back five minutes.

34

CANTON URI,
SWITZERLAND

THEY BROUGHT THE TEA Arab-style in a small glass. Sarah's hands remained cuffed. To drink she had to lower her head toward the table and slurp noisily while Muhammad gazed at her in revulsion. His own tea remained untouched. It stood between his open notebook and a loaded pistol.

"You can't make me vanish and expect no one to notice," she said.

He looked up and blinked several times rapidly. Sarah, free of the *abaya*, examined him in the harsh light of the interrogation chamber. He was bald to the crown of his angular head, and his remaining hair and beard were cropped to precisely the same length. His dark eyes were partially concealed behind a pair of academic spectacles, which flashed with reflected light each time he looked up from his notepad. His expression was open and strangely earnest for an interrogator, and his face, when he was not screaming or threatening to strike her, was vaguely pleasant. At times he seemed to Sarah like an eager young journalist posing questions to a politician standing at a podium.

"Everyone in London knows I went to the Caribbean with Zizi," she said. "I spent almost two weeks on *Alexandra*. I was seen with him at restaurants on Saint Bart's. I went to the beach with Nadia. There's a record of my departure from Saint Maarten and a record of my arrival in Zurich. You can't just make me disappear in Switzerland. You'll never get away with it."

"But that's not the way it happened," Muhammad said. "You see, shortly after your arrival tonight, you checked into your room at the Dolder Grand Hotel. The clerk examined your passport, as is customary here in Switzerland, and forwarded the information to the Swiss police, as is also customary. In a few hours you will awaken and, after taking coffee in your room, you will go to the hotel gym for your morning workout. Then you will shower and dress for your appointment. A car will collect you at 9:45 and take you to Herr Klarsfeld's residence on the Zurichberg. There you will be seen by several members of Herr Klarsfeld's household staff. After viewing the Manet painting, you will place a call to Mr. al-Bakari in the Caribbean, at which point you will inform him that you cannot reach accord on a sale price. You will return to the Dolder Grand Hotel and check out of your room, then proceed to Kloten Airport, where you will board a commercial flight back to London. You will spend two days relaxing at your apartment in Chelsea, during which time you will make several telephone calls on your phone and make several charges on your credit cards. And then, unfortunately, you will vanish inexplicably."

"Who is she?"

"Suffice it to say she bears a vague resemblance to you, enough so she can travel on your passport and slip in and out of your apartment without attracting suspicion from the neighbors. We have helpers here in Europe, Sarah, helpers with white faces."

"The police will still come after Zizi."

"No one *comes after* Zizi al-Bakari. The police will have questions, of course, and they will be answered in due time by Mr. al-Bakari's lawyers. The matter will be handled quietly and with tremendous discretion. It is one of the great advantages of being a Saudi. We truly are above the law. But back to the matter at hand."

He looked down and tapped the tip of his pen impatiently against the blank page of his notebook.

"You will answer my questions now, Sarah?"

She nodded.

"Say yes, Sarah. I want you to get in the habit of speaking."

"Yes," she said.

"Yes, what?"

"Yes, I'll answer your questions."

"Is your name Sarah Bancroft?"

"Yes."

"Very good. Are the place of birth and date of birth correct on your passport?"

"Yes."

"Was your father really an executive for Citibank?"

"Yes."

"Are your parents now truly divorced?"

"Yes."

"Did you attend Dartmouth University and later pursue graduate studies at the Courtauld Institute in London?"

"Yes."

"Are you the Sarah Bancroft who wrote a well-received dissertation on German Expressionism while earning a PhD from Harvard?"

"I am."

"Were you also working for the Central Intelligence Agency at this time?"

"No."

"When did you join the CIA?"

"I never joined the CIA."

"You're lying, Sarah."

"I'm not lying."

"When did you join the CIA?"

"I'm not CIA."

"Who do you work for, then?"

She was silent.

"Answer the question, Sarah. Who are you working for?"

"You know who I'm working for."

"I want to hear you say it."

"I am working for the intelligence service of the State of Israel."

He removed his eyeglasses and stared at her for a moment.

"Are you telling me the truth, Sarah?"

"Yes."

"I'll be able to tell if you're lying again."

"I know."

"Would you care for some more tea?"

She nodded.

"Answer me, Sarah. Would you like some more tea?"

"Yes, I would like some more tea."

Muhammad leaned back in his chair and slapped his palm on the door of the chamber. It opened immediately and outside Sarah saw two men standing watch. "More tea," Muhammad said to them in English, then turned to a fresh page in his notebook and looked up at her with his eager, open face. Sarah lifted her hand to her imaginary clock and added ten more minutes.

THOUGH SARAH did not know it, the setting of her interrogation was the largely Roman Catholic canton of Uri, in the region of the country the Swiss fondly refer to as Inner Switzerland. The chalet was located in a narrow gorge cut by a tributary of the Reuss River. There was only one road in the gorge and a single slumbering village at the top. Uzi Navot inspected it quickly, then turned around and headed back down the gorge. The Swiss, he knew from experience, were some of the most vigilant people on the planet.

The Saudis had tried to evade him in Zurich, but Navot had been prepared. He had always believed that when tailing a professional who is expecting surveillance, it is best to let him think that he is indeed being followed—and more important, that his countermeasures are working. Navot had sacrificed three of his watchers in northern Zurich in service to that cause. It was Navot himself who had watched the Mercedes with diplomatic plates turn into the warehouse in the Industrie-Quartier, and it was Navot who had followed it out of Zurich twenty minutes later.

His team had regrouped along the shores of the Zürichsee and joined him in the pursuit southward toward Uri. The foul weather had granted them an additional layer of protection, as it did now for Navot, as he climbed out of his car and stole quietly through the dense trees toward the chalet, a gun in his outstretched hands. Thirty minutes later, after conducting a cursory survey of the property and the security, he was back behind the wheel, heading down the gorge to the Reuss River valley. There he parked in a turnout by the riverbank and waited for Gabriel to arrive from Zurich.

"WHO IS YOUR control officer?"

"I don't know his name."

"I'm going to ask you one more time. What is the name of your control officer?"

"I'm telling you, I don't know his name. At least not his real name."

"By what name do you know him?"

Don't give him Gabriel, she thought. She blurted the first that came into her mind.

"He called himself Ben."

"Ben?"

"Yes, Ben."

"You're sure? Ben?"

"It's not his real name. It's just what he called himself."

"How do you know it's *not* his real name?"

She embraced the precision of his inquiry, for it allowed her to add more minutes to her imaginary clock.

"Because he told me it *wasn't* his real name."

"And you believed him?"

"I suppose I had no reason not to."

"When did you meet this man?"

"It was December."

"Where?"

"In Washington."

"What time of day was it?"

"In the evening."

"He came to your house. Your place of work."

"It was after work. I was on the way home."

"Tell me how it happened, Sarah. Tell me everything."

And she did, morsel by morsel, drop by drop.

* * *

"WHERE WAS this house they brought you to?"

"In Georgetown."

"Which street in Georgetown?"

"It was dark. I don't remember."

"Which street in Georgetown, Sarah?"

"It was N Street, I think."

"You think, or you know?"

"It was N Street."

"The address?"

"There was no address on it."

"Which block?"

"I can't remember."

"Was it east of Wisconsin Avenue or west, Sarah?"

"You know Georgetown?"

"East or West?"

"West. Definitely West."

"Which block, Sarah?"

"Between Thirty-third and Thirty-fourth, I think."

"You think?"

"Between Thirty-third and Thirty-fourth."

"Which side of the street?"

"What do you mean?"

"Which side of the street, Sarah? North or south?"

"South. Definitely south."

* * *

IT WAS 2:45 A.M. when Navot spotted the Audi coming up the road at a rate of speed incompatible with the inclement conditions. As it sped past in a blur of blowing snow and road spray, he caught a fleeting glimpse of the four tense-looking men inside. He picked up his phone and dialed. "You just drove by me," he said calmly, then he looked up into the mirror and watched as the Audi nearly crashed turning around. *Easy, Gabriel,* he thought. *Easy.*

"WHO WAS the first to interview you? The CIA man or the Jew?"

"The American."

"What sorts of things did they ask you?"

"We talked in general terms about the war on terrorism."

"For example?"

"He asked me what I thought should be done with terrorists. Should they be brought to America for trial or killed in the field by men in black?"

"Men in black?"

"That's what he called them."

"Meaning special forces? CIA assassins? Navy SEALs?"

"I suppose."

"And what did you tell him?"

"You really want to know?"

"I wouldn't have asked otherwise."

And so she told him, one small spoonful at a time.

*   *   *

THEY STOOD in a circle along the riverbank while Navot quickly told Gabriel everything he knew.

"Are there more guards on the grounds or just the two at the front gate?"

"I don't know."

"How many inside the house?"

"I don't know."

"Did you see where they took her?"

"No."

"Has there been any other traffic on the road?"

"It's a very quiet road."

"It's not enough information, Uzi."

"I did the best I could."

"I know."

"As I see it you have only two options, Gabriel. Option number one: carry out another reconnaissance operation. It will take time. It's not without risk. If they see us coming, the first thing they'll do is kill Sarah."

"Option two?"

"Go straight in. I vote for option two. Only God knows what Sarah's going through in there."

Gabriel looked down at the snow and deliberated a moment. "We go in now," he said. "You, Mikhail, Yaakov, and me."

"Hostage rescue isn't my thing, Gabriel. I'm an agent-runner."

"It's definitely not Eli's thing, and I want at least four

men. Moshe and Eli will stay with the cars. When I send the signal, they'll come up the road and get us."

"When did the Jew come?"

"I can't remember the precise time."

"Approximate?"

"I can't remember. It was about a half hour after I arrived, so that would make it around seven, I suppose."

"And he called himself Ben?"

"Not right away."

"He used another name at first?"

"No. He had no name at first."

"Describe him for me, please."

"He's on the small side."

"Was he thin or fat?"

"Thin."

"Very thin?"

"He was fit."

"Hair?"

"Yes."

"Color?"

"Dark."

"Long or short?"

"Short."

"Was any part of his hair gray?"

"No."

Muhammad calmly laid his pen on his notebook. "You're lying to me, Sarah. If you lie to me again, our conversation will end and we will go about this by other means. Do you understand me?"

She nodded.

"Answer me, Sarah."

"Yes, I understand you."

"Good."

"Now give me a precise description of this Jew who called himself Ben."

35

CANTON URI,
SWITZERLAND

L ET'S RETURN TO THE appearance of his hair. You say
it was short, Sarah? Like mine?"

"A little longer."

"And dark?"

"Yes."

"But it's gray in places, isn't it? At the temples, to
be precise."

"Yes, his temples are gray."

"And now the eyes. They're green, aren't they? Abnormally so."

"His eyes are very green."

"He has a special talent, this man?"

"Many."

"He has the ability to restore paintings?"

"Yes."

"And you're absolutely certain you never heard a
name?"

"I told you. He called himself Ben."

"Yes, I know, but did he ever refer to himself by any other name?"

"No, never."

"You're sure, Sarah?"

"Positive. He called himself Ben."

"It's not his real name, Sarah. His name is Gabriel Allon. And he is a murderer of Palestinians. Now please tell me what happened after he arrived at the house in Georgetown."

THERE WAS a sign at the entrance of the track leading to the chalet. It read PRIVATE. The security gate was three hundred yards into the trees. Gabriel and Navot moved on one side of the track, Mikhail and Yaakov on the other. The snow had been deep along the edge of road coming up the gorge, but in the trees there was much less. Seen through the night-vision goggles, it glowed ghostly luminous green while the trunks of the pine and fir were dark and distinct. Gabriel crept forward, careful to avoid fallen limbs that might have cracked beneath the weight of his step. It was deathly silent in the forest. He was aware of his own heart banging against his rib cage and the sound of Navot's footfalls behind him. He held his Beretta in both hands. He wore no gloves.

Fifteen minutes after entering the trees, he glimpsed the house for the first time. There were lights burning in the ground-floor windows, and a single window was illuminated on the second story. The guards were sheltering in the warmth of one of the jeeps. The engine was running and the headlights were doused. The gate was open.

"Do you have a clean shot, Mikhail?"

"Yes."

"Which one is best from your angle?"

"The driver."

"It's nearly fifty yards, Mikhail. Can you get him cleanly?"

"I can get him."

"A head shot, Mikhail. We need to do it quietly."

"I have the shot."

"Line it up and wait for my signal. We shoot together. And God help us if we miss."

"SO ALLON asked you to help him?"

"Yes."

"And you agreed?"

"Yes."

"Instantly?"

"Yes."

"No hesitation."

"No."

"Why not?"

"Because you're evil. And I hate you."

"Watch your mouth."

"You wanted the truth."

"What happened next?"

"I quit my job at the Phillips Collection and moved to London."

GABRIEL TOOK careful aim at the man in the passenger seat.

"Are you ready, Mikhail?"

"Ready."

"Two shots, on my mark, in five, four, three, *two* . . ."

Gabriel squeezed the trigger twice. Four holes appeared almost simultaneously in the windshield of the jeep. He sprinted up the track through the knee-deep snow, Navot at his heels, and approached the jeep cautiously with the Beretta in his outstretched hands. Mikhail had managed two fatal head shots on the driver, but Gabriel's man had been hit in the cheek and upper chest and was still semiconscious.

Gabriel shot him twice through the passenger-side window, then stood motionless for an instant, scanning the terrain for any sign their presence had been detected. It was Navot who noticed the guard coming out of the trees at the left side of the house and Mikhail who dropped him with a single head shot that sprayed blood and brain tissue across the virgin snow. Gabriel turned and headed across the clearing toward the chalet, with the other three men at his back.

*   *   *

"TELL ME ABOUT this man Julian Isherwood."

"Julian is a dear sweet man."

"He is a Jew?"

"Never came up."

"Julian Isherwood is a longtime agent of Israeli intelligence?"

"I wouldn't know."

"So after leaving the Phillips Collection you went immediately to work as Julian Isherwood's assistant director?"

"That's correct."

"But you were a complete amateur. When were you trained?"

"At night."

"Where?"

"At a country house south of London."

"Where was this country house?"

"Surrey, I think. I never caught the name of the village."

"It was a permanent Israeli safe house?"

"A rental. Very temporary."

"There were other people there besides Allon?"

"Yes."

"They used other people to help train you?"

"Yes."

"Give me some of their names."

"The people who came from Tel Aviv never gave me their names."

"And what about the other members of Allon's London team?"

"What about them?"

"Give me their names."

"Please don't make me do this."

"Give me their names, Sarah."

"Please, don't."

He hit her hard enough to knock her from her chair. She hung there a moment, the handcuffs carving into her wrists, while he screamed at her for names.

"Tell me their names, Sarah. All of them."

"There was a man named Yaakov."

"Who else?"

"Yossi."

"Give me another name, Sarah."

"Eli."

"Another."

"Dina."

"Another."

"Rimona."

"And these were the same people who followed you in Saint-Bart's?"

"Yes."

"Who was the man who first approached you on the beach at Saline?"

"Yaakov."

"Who was the woman who left the message in the bathroom for you at the restaurant in Saline?"

"Rimona."

"Who was the girl with the limp who came to Le Tetou restaurant right before you went to the restroom?"

"Dina."

"They're all Jews, these people."

"Would that come as a surprise to you?"

"And what about you, Sarah? Are you a Jew?"

"No, I'm not a Jew."

"Then why did you help them?"

"Because I hate you."

"Yes, and look what it's gotten you."

THEY ENCOUNTERED one more guard before reaching the chalet. He came from their right, around the corner of the house, and foolishly stepped into the open with his weapon still at his side. Gabriel and Mikhail fired together. The shots were muffled by the silencers, but the guard emitted a single piercing scream as the volley of rounds tore into his chest. Two faces, like figures in a shooting gallery, appeared suddenly in the illuminated windows of the house—one in a ground-floor window directly in front of Gabriel, a second on the upper floor at the peak of the roof. Gabriel took out the man in the first-floor window while Mikhail saw to the one on the second.

They had now lost any remaining element of surprise. Gabriel and Mikhail both reloaded as they sprinted the final thirty yards toward the front door. Yaakov had much experience entering terrorist hideouts in the West Bank and Gaza and led the way. He didn't bother trying the latch. Instead he sprayed a volley of rounds through the center of the door to take out anyone standing on the other side, then shot away the lock and the surrounding wood of the doorjamb. Navot, the largest of the four men, hurled his thick body against the door, and it collapsed inward like a falling domino.

The other three stepped quickly into the small entrance hall. Gabriel covered the space to the left, Yaakov the center, and Mikhail the right. Gabriel, still wearing the night-vision goggles, saw the man he shot though the window lying on the floor in a pool of blood. Yaakov and Mikhail each fired immediately, and Gabriel heard the screams of two more dying men. They moved forward into the chalet, found the steps to the cellar, and headed down. *We'll start there*, Gabriel had said. *Torturers always like to do their work belowground.*

SHE WAS DESCRIBING for him the day of the sale, when there came from the floor above the sound of a disturbance. He silenced her with a brutal slap across her face, then stood up and, with the gun in his hand, moved quickly to the door. A few seconds later she heard shouts and screams and heavy footfalls on the steps. Muhammad turned and leveled the gun at her face. Sarah, still handcuffed to the table, reflexively lowered her head between her arms as he squeezed the trigger twice. In the tiny chamber the gun sounded like artillery. The rounds scorched the air above her head and embedded themselves in the wall at her back.

He screamed at her in rage for having the indecency of choosing life over death and moved a step closer to fire again. Then the door came crashing inward as though it had been blown away by the concussion of a bomb blast. It slammed against Muhammad's back and knocked him to the ground. The gun was still in his hand. He rose onto one knee and leveled it at her once more as two men came flashing through the doorway, their faces hidden by balaclavas and night-vision goggles. They shot Muhammad. They kept shooting him until they had no more rounds to fire.

THEY CUT AWAY the handcuffs and the shackles and spirited her past the tattered bodies of the dead. Outside she climbed childlike into Gabriel's arms. He bore her across the snowy clearing and down the track to the road, where Lavon and Moshe were waiting with the cars. The silence of the forest was shattered by her wailing.

"I had to tell them things."

"I know."

"They hit me. They told me they were going to kill me."

"I know, Sarah. I saw the room."

"They know about you, Gabriel. I tried to—"

"It's all right, Sarah. It's our fault. We let you down."

"I'm sorry, Gabriel. I'm so sorry."

"Please, Sarah. Don't."

"I saw him again."

"Who?"

"Bin Shafiq."

"Where was he?"

"In Zurich. He's not finished, Gabriel."

"What did he say?"

"He's going to hit the Vatican again."

36

ZUG, SWITZERLAND

TWO OF NAVOT'S WATCHERS managed to make it south over the Italian border before the weather closed the mountain passes. The other two went east into Austria. Navot himself joined with Moshe and went to Paris to throw a security net around Hannah Weinberg. Gabriel took Sarah to the private airstrip outside Zug. They sat like lovers as he drove, Gabriel with his arm around her shoulder, Sarah with her wet face pressed against the side of his neck. It was 4:30 when the plane rose into the clouds and disappeared. Carter and Gabriel were not on it.

"All right, Gabriel, I'm listening."

"Sarah saw bin Shafiq in Zurich. He told her he was going to hit the Vatican again."

Carter swore softly beneath his breath.

"Your president is in Rome today, is he not?"

"He is indeed."

"What time is he due at the Vatican?"

"High noon."

Gabriel looked at his wristwatch.

"There's a shuttle between Zurich and Rome that leaves on the hour. If we hurry, we can be on the seven-o'clock plane."

"Drive," said Carter.

Gabriel started the car and headed for Zurich. Carter called CIA Headquarters and asked to be connected to the chief of the U.S. Secret Service.

THE FIRST thirty minutes of the drive Carter spent on the telephone. When the lights of Zurich appeared out of the mist at the northern end of the lake, he hung up the phone and looked at Gabriel.

"Sarah will be on the ground at Ramstein Air Base in less than an hour. She'll be taken to an American military hospital there for a complete examination."

"What does your doctor say?"

"Her condition is as you might expect. Abrasions and contusions to her face. A slight concussion. Damage to her left eye. Deep abdominal bruises. Two cracked ribs. Two broken toes. I wonder why they did that."

"They dragged her down the stairs to the cellar."

"Oh, and the hypothermia. I suppose she got that from riding in the trunk. All in all, things could be a lot worse."

"Make sure you have someone with her," Gabriel

said. "The last thing we need now is Sarah inadvertently spilling our secrets to the doctors at Ramstein."

"Fear not, Gabriel. She's in good hands."

"She says she talked."

"Of course she talked. Hell, I would have talked."

"You should have seen the room."

"Frankly, I'm glad I didn't. That sort of stuff isn't my cup of tea. I sometimes find myself longing for the good old days of the Cold War, when torture and blood weren't part of my business." Carter looked at Gabriel. "I suppose it's always been part of yours, hasn't it?"

Gabriel ignored him. "She told them everything to buy time. The question is, did Muhammad manage to report any of what she told them to his superiors before we arrived?"

"You got his notebook?"

Gabriel tapped the breast pocket of his leather jacket.

"We'll debrief Sarah when she's recovered."

"She might not remember everything she told them. She was filled with drugs."

They drove in silence for a moment. Despite the early hour, there was morning commuter traffic on the road. Industrious Swiss moneymen, thought Gabriel. He wondered how many of them worked for companies linked however tenuously to AAB Holdings of Riyadh, Geneva, and points in between.

"Do you think they're going to let me on this plane, Adrian?"

"Gustav assures me we'll have no problems with our departure."

"Maybe not you, but I have a colorful history here in Zurich."

"You have a colorful history everywhere. Don't worry, Gabriel. They'll let you on the plane."

"You're sure your friend Gustav will keep it quiet?"

"Keep what quiet?" Carter managed a weary smile. "We have a cleanup team en route to Uri as we speak. Gustav will keep the property secured until they arrive. And then . . ." He shrugged. "It will be as if nothing ever happened."

"What are you going to do with the bodies?"

"We have more than secret detention facilities in eastern Europe. They'll get a proper burial, which is more than they deserve. And maybe someday, when this war without end is actually over, we'll be able to tell one of their relatives where they can claim the bones." Carter smoothed his mustache. "You have one, don't you?"

"What's that?"

"A secret cemetery? Somewhere out in the Jordan Valley?"

Gabriel took a long look into his rearview mirror but said nothing.

"How many bodies, Gabriel? Do you remember?"

"Of course I remember."

"How many then? The team needs to know where to look."

Gabriel told him. Two in the four-wheel-drive. Two in the clearing in front of the chalet. One in the first-floor window. One in the second-floor window. Two in the center hall. Two at the bottom of the stairs. And Muhammad.

"Eleven men," Carter said. "We'll run their names. We'll find out who they were and what they were planning. But I think it's safe to assume right now that you took down a major cell tonight, along with a very senior man in bin Shafiq's operation."

"We didn't get the one we wanted."

"Something tells me you'll find him."

"At least two of them were Europeans, and Uzi heard one of them speaking in a Swiss-German accent."

"I'm afraid they'll be buried with the jihadists. I suppose it's how they would have wanted it." Carter glanced at his watch. "Can't you drive any faster?"

"I'm going eighty, Adrian. How much did you tell the Secret Service?"

"I told them we have alarmingly credible evidence that the forces of global jihad are planning to attack the president at the Vatican this afternoon. Heavy emphasis was placed on the words 'alarmingly credible evidence.' Secret Service got the message loud and clear, and I hope to have a moment or two with the president later this morning. He's staying at the ambassador's residence."

"He might want to consider canceling."

"That isn't going to happen," Carter said. "The Vatican is now the most visible symbol in the world of the dangers of Islamic terrorism. This president isn't going to pass up a chance to reinforce his message on that stage."

"He's going to get an earful from Lucchesi."

"He's ready for it," Carter said. "As for security, Secret Service is already making arrangements with the Italians to change the president's travel plans. Coincidentally, they were thinking about it *before* they received my call. Rome is a mess. They're expecting two million people in the streets today."

"How are they going to get him into the Vatican?"

"The motorcade of visiting heads of state usually enters the Holy See through St. Anne's Gate, then heads up the Via Belvedere to the San Damaso Courtyard. He's met there by the commandant of the Swiss Guard and escorted into the Apostolic Palace. The bodyguards of the visiting heads of state have to stay down in the courtyard. Vatican protocol. The head of state goes up alone, protected only by the Guard. I'll let you in on a little secret, though. Secret Service always stashes a couple of men in the official party—nice Catholic boys who want to meet the Holy Father."

"So what sort of changes are you making?"

"The president is going to chopper to the Vatican and land on the Pope's helipad."

"It's in the far western corner, right against the wall. If someone is waiting down on the Viale Vaticano with another missile . . ."

"Secret Service says the area can be secured."

"How many nice Catholic boys are you going to stash in the president's official delegation?"

"More than usual." Carter looked at his watch again. "We should probably enter the airport a few minutes apart. Langley booked us in separate seats."

"You're ashamed of me, Adrian?"

"Never prouder, actually. You and your boys showed a lot of guts going into the chalet."

"We didn't have a choice, Adrian. We never have a choice."

Carter closed his eyes for a moment. "You know, it's possible bin Shafiq was just shooting off his mouth, or bluffing for some reason."

"Why would he bluff, Adrian? He was going to kill her."

37

VATICAN CITY

I T'S A GOOD THING your friend the monsignor asked us to give you a lift," the Carabinieri captain said. "Otherwise you would have never made it from Fiumicino to the Vatican."

Gabriel looked out the window of the helicopter. Rome lay beneath him. The Villa Borghese had been taken over as a staging area by the demonstrators and was now a sea of humanity. The first marchers were spilling from the bottom of the park into the Via Veneto.

"Can you keep them away from the Vatican?"

"We're going to try." The captain pointed out the window. "You see those barricades down there? Our plan is to herd them up the hill into the Janiculum Park. But we're expecting two million protesters. If things get out of control . . ." He gave an Italianate shrug. "I'm glad I don't do riot duty anymore. It could turn into a war zone down there."

The helicopter turned and banked toward the city-state. The dome of the Basilica, partially concealed behind the enormous tarpaulins of the work crews, shone in the bright sunlight, while the Pope's plea for peace fluttered from the façade in the gentle morning breeze. They swept low over the Viale Vaticano, staying over Italian airspace for as long as possible, then slipped over the wall and set down on the papal helipad. Donati, dressed in a black cassock and magenta sash, was waiting there, a plainclothes Swiss Guard at this side. The tall priest's expression was grim as they shook hands briefly and set out across the Vatican Gardens toward the Apostolic Palace.

"How serious is it this time, Gabriel?"

"Very."

"Can you tell me why?"

"The messenger," said Gabriel. "The messenger."

GABRIEL WAITED until they were upstairs in Donati's third-floor office before telling him any more. Donati understood he was being given only part of the story. He was too concerned about the safety of his master to protest.

"I want you by his side until the president leaves the Vatican."

This time Gabriel did not argue.

"You look like you've been through the wringer," Donati said. "When's the last time you slept?"

"I honestly can't remember."

"I'm afraid there's no time for sleep now," Donati said, "but we have to do something about your appearance. I don't suppose you brought a suit with you?"

"I wish I could explain to you just how ridiculous that question sounds."

"You're going to need some proper clothes. The papal protection detail of the Swiss Guard wear suits and ties. I'm sure the commandant can get you reasonably attired."

"There's something I need more than a blue suit, Luigi."

"What's that?"

Gabriel told him.

"The Swiss Guard can get you one of those, too."

Donati picked up the phone and dialed.

THE SAME Swiss Guard who had been at Donati's side on the helipad was waiting for Gabriel in the San Damaso Courtyard ten minutes later. He was equal to Gabriel in height, with square shoulders that filled out his suit jacket and the dense muscular neck of a rugby player. His blond hair was cropped nearly to the scalp of his bullet-shaped head, so that the wire leading into his earpiece was clearly visible.

"Have we met?" Gabriel asked the Guard in German as they set out down the Via Belvedere.

"No, sir."

"You look familiar to me."

"I was one of the Guards who helped you get the Holy Father into the Apostolic Palace after the attack."

"I thought so," said Gabriel. "What's your name?"

"Lance Corporal Erich Müller, sir."

"Which canton are you from, Lance Corporal?"

"Nidwalden, sir. It's a *demi-canton* next to—"

"I know where it is," Gabriel said.

"You know Switzerland, sir."

"Very well."

Just before reaching St. Anne's Gate, they turned right and entered the Swiss Guard barracks. In the reception area a duty officer sat primly behind a half-moon desk. Before him was a bank of closed-circuit television monitors. On the wall behind him hung a crucifix and a row of flags representing each of Switzerland's twenty-six cantons. As Gabriel and Müller walked past, the duty officer made a notation in his logbook. "The Swiss Quarter is tightly controlled," Müller said. "There are three different entry points, but this is the main one."

They left the reception area and turned right. A long dark corridor stretched before them, lined with tiny cell-like quarters for the halberdiers. At the end of the corridor was an archway, and beyond the archway an interior stone courtyard, where a drill sergeant was putting six novices through their paces with wooden rifles. They entered the building on the other side of the courtyard and descended a flight of stone steps to the indoor firing range. It was silent and unoccupied.

"This is where we do our weapons training. The walls are supposed to be soundproof, but sometimes the neighbors complain about the noise."

"The neighbors?"

"The Holy Father doesn't seem to mind, but the cardinal secretary of state is not enamored with the sound of gunfire. We don't shoot on Sundays or Catholic holy days." Müller went over to a metal cabinet and opened the padlock. "Our standard-issue sidearm is a 9mm SIG-Sauer with a fifteen-shot magazine." He glanced over his shoulder at Gabriel as he opened the doors of the cabinet. "It's a Swiss-made weapon. Very accurate . . . and *very* powerful. Would you like to try it out?"

Gabriel nodded. Müller removed a gun, an empty magazine, and a full box of ammunition and carried them over to the range. He started to load the gun, but Gabriel stopped him. "I'll do that. Why don't you see to the target." The Swiss Guard clipped a target to the line and ran it out halfway over the range. "Farther," Gabriel said. "All the way to the end, please." Müller did as he was told. By the time the target had reached the distant wall of the range, Gabriel had loaded fifteen rounds into the magazine and inserted it into the butt of the pistol. "You're quick," Müller remarked. "You must have good hands."

"I've had a lot of practice."

He offered Gabriel protection for his ears and eyes.

"No thanks."

"Rules of the range, sir."

Gabriel turned without warning and opened fire. He kept firing until the gun was empty. Müller reeled in the target while Gabriel ejected the empty magazine and picked up his brass.

"Jesus Christ."

All fifteen shots were grouped in the center of the target's face.

"Do you want to shoot again?" Müller asked.

"I'm fine."

"How about a shoulder holster?"

"That's what pants are for."

"Let me get you an extra magazine."

"Give me two, please. And an extra box of ammo."

HE COLLECTED a parcel of clothing from the commandant's office, then hurried back to the Apostolic Palace. Upstairs on the third floor, Donati showed him to a small guest apartment with a private bathroom and shower. "I stole that razor from the Holy Father," Donati said. "The towels are in the cabinet under the sink."

The president wasn't due for another ninety minutes. Gabriel took his time shaving, then spent several minutes standing beneath the showerhead. The clothing that had been scrounged up by the Swiss Guard fit him surprisingly well, and by eleven o'clock he was walking down the frescoed corridor toward the Pope's private apartment, looking as well as could be expected.

He had made one additional request of Donati before

going to the Swiss Guard barracks: a copy of the final report, prepared jointly by the Italian and Vatican security
services, on the October attack. He read it over a cappuccino and *cornetto* in the Pope's private dining room,
then spent a few minutes flipping round the dial on the
Pope's television, looking for any word of eleven dead
bodies found in a Swiss chalet. There was no mention on
any of the international news channels. He supposed
Carter's team had completed its task.

Donati came for him at 11:45. They walked to the
Belvedere Palace and found an empty office with a good
view of the Gardens. A moment later the trees began to
twist and writhe, then two enormous twin-rotor heli-
copters came into view and descended toward the helipad in the far corner of the city-state. Gabriel felt a bit of
tension drain from his body as he saw the first helicopter
slip safely below the treetops. Five minutes later they
caught their first glimpse of the American president,
striding confidently toward the palace, surrounded by
several dozen heavily armed, nervous-looking Secret Service agents.

"The agents will have to wait down in the Garden,"
Donati said. "The Americans don't like it, but those are
the rules of protocol. Do you know they actually try to
slip Secret Service agents into the official delegation?"

"You don't say."

Donati looked at Gabriel. "Is there something you'd
like to tell me?"

"Yes," Gabriel said. "We should get back to the Apostolic Palace. I'd like to be there before the president arrives."

Donati turned and led the way.

THEY REACHED the Sala Clementina, a soaring frescoed receiving room one floor below the Pope's private apartments, five minutes before the president. The Holy Father had not yet arrived. There was a detachment of ceremonial Swiss Guard standing outside the wide entranceway and several more in plain clothes waiting inside. Two ornate chairs stood at one end of the long rectangular room; at the other was a pack of reporters, photographers, and cameramen. Their collective mood was more disagreeable than usual. The equipment searches and security checks conducted by the Swiss Guard and Secret Service had been far more invasive than usual, and three European camera crews were refused entry because of minor discrepancies concerning their credentials. The press would be allowed to record the first moments of the historic meeting and broadcast the images live to the world, then they would be shepherded out.

Donati went back into the corridor to wait for the Holy Father. Gabriel looked around a moment longer, then went to the front of the room and positioned himself a few feet from the chair reserved for the Pope. For the next two minutes his eyes roamed over the pack of journalists, looking for any signs of agitation or a face that seemed in any way out of place. Then he did the same to the delegation of Curial prelates standing to his left.

Shortly before noon the white-cassocked figure of the Holy Father entered the room, accompanied by Donati, his cardinal secretary of state, and four plainclothes Swiss Guards. Erich Müller, the Guard who had given Gabriel his weapon, was among them. His eyes settled briefly on Gabriel, whom he acknowledged with a quick nod. The Pope walked the length of the room and stopped in front of his ornate chair. Donati, tall and striking in his tailored black cassock and magenta sash, stood at his master's side. He looked briefly at Gabriel, then lifted his gaze toward the entranceway as the president of the United States strode through.

Gabriel quickly scrutinized the president's official delegation. Four Secret Service agents were among them, he reckoned, maybe two or three more. Then his gaze began to sweep the room like a searchlight: the reporters, the Curial prelates, the Swiss Guards, the president and the Holy Father. They were shaking hands now, smiling warmly at each other in the blinding white light of the flashing cameras.

The swiftness of it caught even Gabriel by surprise. Indeed were it not for Donati, he thought later, he might never have seen it coming. Donati's eyes widened suddenly, then he made a sudden lateral movement toward the president. Gabriel turned and saw the gun. The weapon was a SIG-Sauer 9mm—and the hand holding it belonged to Lance Corporal Erich Müller.

Gabriel drew his own gun and started firing, but not before Müller managed to squeeze off two shots. He did not hear the screaming or notice the flashing of the camera lights. He just kept firing until the Swiss Guard lay dead on the marble floor. The Secret Service agents concealed within the American delegation seized the president and hustled him toward the door. Pietro Lucchesi, Bishop of Rome, Pontifex Maximus, and successor to St. Peter, fell to his knees and began to pray over the fallen body of a tall priest in a black cassock.

38

ROME

THERE ARE ROOMS ON the eleventh floor of the Gemelli Clinic that few people know. Spare and spartan, they are the rooms of a priest. In one there is a hospital bed. In another there are couches and chairs. The third contains a private chapel. In the hallway outside the entrance is a desk for the guards. Someone stands watch always, even when the rooms are empty.

Though the hospital bed is reserved for the leader of the world's one billion Roman Catholics, on that evening it was occupied by the leader's trusted private secretary. The street below his window was filled with thousands of faithful. At nine o'clock they had fallen silent to listen to the first *bollettino* from the Vatican Press Office. Monsignor Luigi Donati, it said, had undergone seven hours of surgery to repair the damage inflicted by two 9mm rounds. The monsignor's condition was described as "extremely grave," and the *bollettino* made clear that his survival was very much in doubt. It concluded by saying that the Holy Father was at his side and planned to remain there for the foreseeable future. It did not mention the fact that Gabriel was there, too.

They were seated together on a couch in the sitting room. On the other side of an open connecting door lay Donati, pale and unconscious. A team of doctors and nurses stood round him, their expressions grim. The Holy Father's eyes were closed and he was working the beads of a rosary. A broad smear of blood stained the front of his white cassock. He had refused to change out of it. Gabriel, looking at him now, thought of Shamron and his torn leather jacket. He hoped the Holy Father didn't blame himself for what had happened today.

Gabriel looked at the television. Video of the attack, one of the most dramatic moments ever broadcast live, was flickering on the screen. It had been playing non-stop. Gabriel had watched it at least a dozen times, and he watched again now. He saw Müller lunge from the knot of Swiss Guards, the gun in his outstretched hands. He saw himself, drawing his own gun from the inside of his jacket, and Donati, throwing his long body in front of the president of the United States as Müller opened fire. *A fraction of a second,* he thought. If he'd seen Müller a fraction of a second earlier, he might have been able to fire first. And Donati wouldn't be lying near death on the eleventh floor of the Gemelli Clinic. Gabriel looked at the Pope. His eyes were no longer closed but were fixed on the screen of the television.

"How did he know to step in front of the president instead of me?"

"I suppose he understood that Müller could have killed you countless times if he'd wanted to. Müller was going for the president first, and Luigi understood that."

"In the blink of an eye."

"He's one of the smartest men I've ever met, Holiness." Gabriel looked at Donati. "He saved the president of the United States, and he probably isn't even aware of it."

"Luigi just stopped the bullets," the Pope said, "but you're the one who saved him. If it wasn't for you, we would have never been on alert for something like this. How did you know, Gabriel? How did you know they were going to hit us again today?"

"We'll have to talk about this at a later date. A *much* later date."

"You're in the middle of an operation, aren't you?"

Gabriel was silent.

"Erich Müller, a member of my palace guard . . ." The Pope's voice trailed off. "I still can't believe it. How did they do it, Gabriel? How did they get an assassin into the Swiss Guard?"

"The details are sketchy, Holiness, but it appears Müller was recruited sometime after he left the Swiss army. He didn't have a job waiting for him, so he spent about a year and half traveling around Europe and the Mediterranean. He spent several months in Hamburg, and several more in Amsterdam. He was known to be a frequent participant in anti-American, anti-Israel demonstrations. He may have actually converted to Islam. We believe he was recruited into the terrorist network by a man named Professor Ali Massoudi."

"Massoudi? Really? Good God, Gabriel, but I think Professor Massoudi submitted some of his writings to my special commission on improving ties between Islam and the West. I think he may have actually visited the Vatican at some point."

"Improving ties between Islam and the Church was not part of Professor Massoudi's real agenda, Holiness."

"Obviously," said the Pope. "I suppose we now know who opened the Door of Death for the suicide bombers in October. It was Müller, wasn't it?"

Gabriel nodded and looked at the television as the video of the attack began again.

"I wonder how many people have seen this image today," the Pope said.

"Billions, Holiness."

"Something tells me your days as a *secret* agent are over. Welcome back to the real world, Gabriel."

"It's not a world in which I'm comfortable."

"What are your plans?"

"I have to return to Israel."

"And then?"

"My future is somewhat uncertain."

"As usual," the Pope said. "Francesco Tiepolo tells me you and Chiara have reunited."

"Yes, Holiness. She's in Israel now."

"What are your plans?"

"I have to marry her before she leaves me again."

"Wise man. And then?"

"One step at a time, Holiness."

"Will you allow me to give you one more piece of advice?"

"Of course."

"As of this moment, you are the most famous man in Italy. A national hero. Something tells me the country would welcome you back with open arms. And this time not as Mario Delvecchio."

"We'll cross that bridge when we come to it."

"If I were you, I'd make it a bridge back to Venice."

The Pope gazed silently for a moment through the open door. "I don't know what I'll do if God takes him from me. I can't run the Roman Catholic Church without Luigi Donati."

"I remember the day he came to Jerusalem to see me," Gabriel said. "When we were walking through the Old City, I foolishly described him as a faithless man at the side of a man of great faith. But it took a great deal of faith to step in front of those bullets."

"Luigi Donati is a man of extraordinary faith. He just doesn't realize it sometimes. Now I have to have faith. I have to believe that God will see fit to let me have him a little longer—and that He will now see fit to end this madness."

The next question the Pope asked was the same one he had posed to Gabriel at the end of the attack in October.

"Is it over?"

This time Gabriel gazed at the television and said nothing.

No, Holiness, he thought. *Not quite.*

PART FOUR

THE WITNESS

39

WASHINGTON

THE SENATE SELECT COMMITTEE convened one month after the attempt on the president's life. In their opening statements the ranking members assured the American people that their investigation would be thorough and unsparing, but by the end of the first week senators from both parties were openly frustrated by what they came to regard as a lack of candor by the president's security and intelligence chiefs. The president's men explained in painstaking detail how the forces of global Islamic extremism had managed to penetrate the center of Christendom, and how Professor Ali Massoudi had managed to recruit a young Swiss named Erich Müller and insert him into the Pontifical Swiss Guard. But when it came to who had masterminded the two attacks on the Vatican—and more important, who had footed the bill—the president's men could offer up only informed opinion. Nor could they explain to any of the committee members' satisfaction the presence at the Vatican of one Gabriel Allon, the now-legendary Israeli agent and assassin. After much internal deliberation, the senators decided to subpoena him for themselves. Because he was a foreign national he was under no obligation to obey the summons and, as expected, he steadfastly refused to appear. Three days later he abruptly changed his mind. He would testify, he told them, but only in secret. The senators agreed, and asked him to come to Washington the following Thursday.

HE ENTERED the subterranean hearing room alone. When the committee chairman asked him to stand and state his name for the record, he did so without hesitation.

"And your employer?"

"The prime minister of the State of Israel."

"We have many questions we would like to ask you, Mr. Allon, but we have been told by your ambassador that you will not answer any question that you deem inappropriate."

"That's correct, Mr. Chairman."

"We have also been informed that you wish to read a statement into the record before we begin the questioning."

"That is also correct, Mr. Chairman."

"This statement deals with the country of Saudi Arabia and America's relationship to it."

"Yes, Mr. Chairman."

"Just a reminder, Mr. Allon. While this testimony is being taken in secret, there will still be a transcript made of your remarks."

"I understand, sir."

"Very well. You may proceed."

With that he looked down and began to read his statement. In the far corner of the room, one man visibly winced. *Hercules has come to the United States Senate,* the man thought. *And he's brought a quiver full of arrows dipped in gall.*

"CONGRATULATIONS, GABRIEL," said Adrian Carter. "You just couldn't help yourself, could you? We gave you the stage, and you put it to good use."

"The senators needed to know about the true nature of the Saudi regime and its support for global terrorism. The American people need to know how all those petrodollars are being spent."

"At least you kept Zizi's name out of it."

"I have other plans for Zizi."

"You'd better not. Besides, you need to keep your eye on the ball right now."

"Eye on the ball? What does this mean?"

"It's a sports metaphor, Gabriel. Play any sports?"

"I don't have time for sports."

"You're getting more like Shamron with each passing day."

"I'll take that as a compliment," Gabriel said. "Which ball should I be keeping my eye on?"

"Bin Shafiq." Carter gave Gabriel a sideways glance. "Any sign of him?"

Gabriel shook his head. "You?"

"We may be on to something, actually."

"Anything you want to tell me about?"

"Not yet."

Carter drove across Memorial Bridge and turned onto the George Washington Parkway. They rode in silence for a few minutes. Gabriel looked out the window and admired the view of Georgetown on the other side of the river.

"I saw from your travel itinerary that you're stopping in Rome on your way back to Israel," Carter said. "Planning to undertake another assignment for the Vatican?"

"I just want to spend some time with Donati. When I left Rome, he still wasn't conscious." Gabriel looked at his watch. "Where are you taking me, Adrian?"

"You have a few hours before your flight. There's a little place out in the Virginia horse country where we can have lunch."

"How long before we get there?"

"About an hour."

Gabriel reclined his seat and closed his eyes.

HE WOKE as they entered a small town called The Plains. Carter slowed as he negotiated the tiny central business district; then he crossed a set of old railroad tracks, and once again headed into the countryside. The road was familiar to Gabriel, as was the long gravel drive into which Carter turned two miles later. It ran along the edge of a narrow stream. To the left was a rolling meadow, and at the top of the meadow was a large farmhouse with a tarnished copper roof and a double-decker porch. When Gabriel had last visited the house, the trees had been empty of leaves and the ground covered in snow. Now the dogwoods were in bloom, and the fields were pale green with new spring grass.

A horse came across the pasture toward them at an easy canter, ridden by a woman with golden hair. The swelling in her face had receded, and her features had returned to normal. All except for the smudges of darkness beneath her eyes, thought Gabriel. In Sarah's eyes there were still traces of the nightmare she had endured at the chalet in Canton Uri. She guided the horse expertly alongside the car and peered down at Gabriel. A smile appeared on her face, and for an instant she looked like the same beautiful woman he had seen walking down Q Street in Washington last autumn. Then the smile faded and with two precise jabs of her boot heel she sent the horse galloping across the meadow toward the house.

"She has good days and bad days," Carter said as he watched her go. "But I'm sure you understand that."

"Yes, Adrian, I understand."

"I've always found personal grudges counterproductive in a business like ours, but I'll never forgive Zizi for what he did to her."

"Neither will I," said Gabriel. "And I do hold grudges."

THEY HAD a quiet lunch together in the cool sunlight on the back porch. Afterward Carter saw to the dishes while Gabriel and Sarah set out for a walk through the shadowed woods. A CIA security agent tried to follow them, but Gabriel took the agent's sidearm and sent him back to the house. Sarah wore jodhpurs and riding boots and a fleece jacket. Gabriel was still dressed in the dark-gray suit he had worn to the Senate hearing. He carried the agent's Browning Hi-Power in his right hand.

"Adrian doesn't seem terribly pleased by your performance before the committee."

"He isn't."

"Someone had to deliver the message about our *friends* the Saudis. Who better than you? After all, you saved the president's life."

"No, Sarah, it was *you* who saved the president. Maybe someday the country will find out what a debt they owe you."

"I'm not planning to go public any time soon."

"What are your plans?"

"Adrian didn't tell you? I'm joining the Agency. I figured the art world could survive without one more curator."

"Which side? Operations or Intelligence?"

"Intelligence," she said. "I've had enough fieldwork for a lifetime. Besides, it will never be safe for me out there. Zizi made it very clear to me what happens to people who betray him."

"He has a long reach. What about your security here in America?"

"They're giving me a new name and a new identity. I get to pick the name. I was wondering whether you would allow me to use your mother's name?"

"Irene?" Gabriel smiled. "I'd be honored. She was like you—a remarkably courageous woman. The next time you come to Israel, I'll let you read about what happened to her during the war."

Sarah paused to finger the blossom of a dogwood, then they walked on through the trees.

"And what about you, Gabriel? What are your plans?"

"I think you and I might be moving in opposite directions."

"Meaning?"

"I'm afraid I can't say anything more right now."

She pouted and playfully swatted his arm. "You're not going to start keeping secrets from me now, are you?"

"Now that you're working for the intelligence service of another country, I'm afraid our relationship will have to take on certain . . ." He paused, searching for the right word in English. "Parameters."

"Please, Gabriel. We share a bond that extends far beyond the rules of engagement governing contact between known operatives of other services."

"I see you've started your training."

"Little by little," she said. "It helps to relieve the boredom of living alone on this farm."

"Are you well, Sarah?"

"The days are all right, but the nights are very hard."

"They will be for a long time. Working for the Agency will help, though. Do you know where they're going to put you?"

"The Saudi desk," she said. "I insisted."

The woods shook with the rumble of distant thunder. Sarah asked about Julian Isherwood.

"At the moment his situation is very similar to yours."

"Where have you got him?"

"Sarah."

"Come on, Gabriel."

"He's tucked away in an old house near Land's End in Cornwall."

"And the gallery?"

"It's closed at the moment. Your departure from London caused quite a scandal. The boys at the bar in Green's restaurant miss you very much."

"I miss them, too. But I miss your team more."

"Everyone sends their best." Gabriel hesitated. "They also asked me to apologize to you."

"For what?"

"We let you down, Sarah. It's obvious that we were spotted by bin Shafiq or Zizi's security men."

"Maybe it was my fault." She shrugged. "But it doesn't matter. We all came out alive, and we got eleven of them in that house. *And* we foiled a plot to assassinate the president. Not bad, Gabriel."

There was another rumble of thunder, this one closer. Sarah looked up at the sky.

"I have to ask you a few questions, Sarah. There are some things we need to know before we can close the books on the operation."

Her gaze remained skyward. "You need to know what I told them in that house in Switzerland."

"I know you were filled with drugs. I know you've probably tried to purge it from your memory."

She looked at him and shook her head. "I haven't tried to forget," she said. "In fact, I remember every word."

The first raindrops began to fall. Sarah seemed not to notice. They walked on through the trees, and she told him everything.

CARTER DROVE Gabriel to Dulles Airport and shepherded him through security. They sat together in a special diplomatic lounge and waited for the flight to be called. Carter passed the time by watching the evening news. Gabriel's attention was focused on the man seated on the opposite side of the lounge: Prince Bashir, the Saudi ambassador to the United States.

"Don't even think about it, Gabriel."

"Public confrontations aren't my style, Adrian."

"Maybe not, but Bashir rather enjoys them."

As if on cue the Saudi rose and walked across the lounge. He stood over Gabriel but did not extend his hand. "I hear you made quite a spectacle of yourself on Capitol Hill this morning, Mr. Allon. Jewish lies and propaganda but amusing nonetheless."

"The testimony was supposed to be secret, Bashir."

"Nothing happens in this town that I don't know about. And it's *Prince* Bashir." The ambassador looked at Carter. "Were you responsible for this circus today, Adrian?"

"The senators issued the subpoena, Your Royal Highness. The Agency had nothing to do with it."

"You should have done something to prevent it."

"This isn't Riyadh, Mr. Ambassador."

Bashir glared at Carter, then returned to his seat.

"I guess I won't be eligible for the Saudi retirement plan."

"What?"

"Never mind," said Carter.

Ten minutes later Gabriel's flight was called. Carter walked him to his gate.

"Oh, I nearly forgot something. The president called while you were talking to Sarah. He wanted to say thank you. He said he'll catch you another time."

"Tell him not to worry about it."

"He also said he wanted you to move forward on that matter you discussed on the South Lawn."

"Are you sure?"

"Sure about what?"

"Are you sure the president used those words?"

"Positive," said Carter. "What did you two talk about that night, anyway?"

"Our conversation was private, Adrian, and it will remain so."

"Good man," said Carter.

They shook hands; then Gabriel turned and boarded the plane.

40

TIBERIAS, ISRAEL

THE NEXT NIGHT WAS SHABBAT. Gabriel slept until early afternoon, then showered and dressed and drove with Chiara to the Valley of Jezreel. They stopped briefly at Tel Megiddo to collect Eli Lavon, then continued on to the Sea of Galilee. It was nearly sunset by the time they reached the honey-colored limestone villa perched on a ledge overlooking the sea. Shamron greeted them at the front door. His face looked thin and drawn, and he moved with the help of a cane. It was olive wood and very handsome.

"The prime minister gave it to me this morning when I left the rehabilitation center in Jerusalem. I nearly hit him with it. Gilah thinks it makes me look more distinguished." He showed them inside and looked at Gabriel. "I see you're wearing my jacket. Now that it's clear I'm going to live for a very long time, I'd like it back."

Gabriel removed the coat and hung it on a hook in the

entrance hall. From inside the villa he heard the voice of Gilah calling them to the table for supper. When they entered the dining room she was already starting to light the candles. Yonatan and his wife were there. So were Rimona and her husband. Ronit sat next to her father and tactfully filled his plate from the serving dishes as they were passed round the table. They did not speak of the bin Shafiq operation or the Vatican. Instead they talked about Gabriel's appearance before the American Congress. Judging from Shamron's sour expression, he did not approve. This was made clear to Gabriel after supper, when Shamron led him out onto the terrace to talk in private.

"You were right to reject the subpoena the first time, Gabriel. You should have never changed your mind. The thought of you seated before that congressional committee, even in secret, set back my rehabilitation six months."

"The wellspring of global jihad is Saudi Arabia and Wahhabism," Gabriel said. "The Senate needed to be told that. So did the American people."

"You could have put your thoughts in a secret cable. You didn't have to sit there before them answering questions—like a mere mortal."

They sat down in a pair of comfortable chairs facing the balustrade. A full moon was reflected in the calm surface of the Sea of Galilee, and beyond the lake, black and shapeless, loomed the Golan Heights. Shamron liked it best on his terrace because it faced eastward, toward his enemies. He reached beneath his seat cushion and came out with a silver cigarette case and his old Zippo lighter.

"You shouldn't smoke, Ari."

"I couldn't while I was at Hadassah and the rehabilitation center. This is my first since the night of the attack."

"Mazel tov," said Gabriel bitterly.

"If you breathe a word to Gilah, I'll cane you."

"You think you can fool Gilah? She knows everything."

Shamron brought the topic of conversation back to Gabriel's testimony in Washington.

"Perhaps you had an ulterior motive," Shamron said. "Perhaps you wanted to do more than just tell the American people the truth about their friends the Saudis."

"And what might my ulterior motive have been?"

"After your performance at the Vatican, you were arguably the most famous intelligence officer in the world. And now . . ." Shamron shrugged. "Ours is a business that does not look fondly on notoriety. You've made it nearly impossible for us ever to use you again in a covert capacity."

"I'm not taking the Special Ops job, Ari. Besides, they've already offered it to Uzi."

"Uzi is a fine officer, but he's not *you*."

"Uzi is the reason Sarah Bancroft is alive. He's exactly the right man to lead Special Ops."

"You should have never used an American girl."

"I wish we had two more just like her."

Shamron seemed to have lost interest in his cigarette. He slipped it back into the case and asked Gabriel about his plans.

"I have some unfinished business, starting with the

van Gogh. I promised Hannah Weinberg I'd get it back for her. It's a promise I intend to keep, regardless of my newfound notoriety."

"Do you know where it is?"

Gabriel nodded. "I inserted a beacon into the stretcher during the restoration," he said. "The painting is in Zizi's mansion on the Île de la Cité."

"After everything you've been through with the French, you're planning to steal a painting in Paris?" Shamron shook his head. "It would be easier for you to break into the house of your friend the American president than one of Zizi's mansions."

Gabriel dismissed the old man's concerns with a Shamronian wave of his hand.

"And then?"

Gabriel was silent.

"Ronit has decided to come home," Shamron said, "but I get the feeling you're about to leave us again."

"I haven't made any decisions yet."

"I hope you've made a decision about Chiara."

"We're going to marry as soon as possible."

"When are you planning to break the news to Leah?" Gabriel told him.

"Take Gilah with you," Shamron said. "They spent a great deal of time together when you were in the field. Leah needs a mother at a time like this. Gilah is the ultimate mother."

*   *   *

GABRIEL AND CHIARA spent the night at the villa in a room facing the lake. In the morning they all gathered for breakfast on the sunlit terrace, then went their separate ways. Yonatan headed north to rejoin his unit; Rimona, who had returned to duty at Aman, went south to rejoin hers. Gilah came with Gabriel and Chiara. They dropped Lavon at the dig at Tel Megiddo, then continued on to Jerusalem.

It was late morning when they arrived at the Mount Herzl Psychiatric Hospital. Dr. Bar-Zvi, a rabbinical-looking man with a long beard, was waiting for them in the lobby. They went to his office and spent an hour discussing the best way to tell Leah the news. Her grasp on reality was tenuous at best. For years images of Vienna had played ceaselessly in her memory, like a loop of videotape. Now she tended to drift back and forth between past and present, often within the span of a few seconds. Gabriel felt obligated to tell her the truth but wanted it to be as painless as possible.

"She seems to respond to Gilah," the doctor said. "Perhaps we should talk to her alone before you do." He looked at his watch. "She's outside in the garden right now. It's her favorite place. Why don't we do it there."

SHE WAS SEATED in her wheelchair, in the shade of a stone pine. Her hands, scarred and twisted, held a sprig of olive branch. Her hair, once long and black, was cropped short and nearly all gray. Her eyes remained vacant as Gilah and the doctor spoke. Ten minutes later they left her. Gabriel walked down the garden path and knelt before the wheelchair, holding the remnants of her hand. It was Leah who spoke first.

"Do you love this girl?"

"Yes, Leah, I love her very much."

"You'll be good to her?"

The tears rolled onto his cheeks. "Yes, Leah, I'll be good to her."

She looked away from him. "Look at the snow, Gabriel. Isn't it beautiful?"

"Yes, Leah, it's beautiful."

"God, how I hate this city, but the snow makes it beautiful. The snow absolves Vienna of its sins. Snow falls on Vienna while the missiles rain on Tel Aviv." She looked at him again. "You'll still come visit me?"

"Yes, Leah, I'll visit you."

And then she looked away again. "Make sure Dani is buckled into his seat tightly. The streets are slippery."

"He's fine, Leah. Be careful driving home."

"I'll be careful, Gabriel. Give me a kiss."

Gabriel pressed his lips against the scar tissue on her ruined cheek and closed his eyes.

Leah whispered, "One last kiss."

THE WALLS of Gabriel's bedroom were hung with paintings. There were three paintings by his grandfather—the only surviving works Gabriel had ever been able to find—and more than a dozen by his mother. There was also a portrait, painted in the style of Egon Schiele, that bore no signature. It showed a young man with prematurely gray hair and a gaunt face haunted by the shadow of death. Gabriel had always told Chiara that the painting was a self-portrait. Now, as she lay beside him, he told her the truth.

"When did she paint it?" Chiara asked.

"Right after I returned from the Black September operation."

"She was amazing."

"Yes," said Gabriel, looking at the painting. "She was much better than me."

Chiara was silent for a moment. Then she asked, "How long are we going to stay here?"

"Until we find him."

"And how long is that going to take?"

"Maybe a month. Maybe a year. You know how these things go, Chiara."

"I suppose we're going to need some furniture."

"Why?"

"Because we can't live with only a studio and a bed."

"Yes, we can," he said. "What else do we need?"

41

Paris: August

T HE SECURITY SYSTEM DETECTED the intrusion at 2:38 A.M. It was sensor number 154, located on one of fourteen pairs of French doors leading from the rear garden into the mansion. The system was not connected to a commercial security company or to the Paris police, only to a central station within the mansion, staffed round the clock by a permanent detachment of security men, all former members of the Saudi National Guard.

The first security man arrived at the open French door within fifteen seconds of the silent alarm and was knocked unconscious by one of the six masked intruders. Two more guards arrived ten seconds later, guns drawn, and were shot to death by the same intruder. The fourth guard to arrive on the scene, a twenty-eight-year-old from Jeddah who had no wish to die for the possessions of a billionaire, raised his hands in immediate surrender.

The man with the gun knocked the Saudi to the ground and sat on his chest while he examined the display screen of a small handheld apparatus. Though he wore a balaclava helmet, the Saudi could see his eyes, which were an intense shade of green. Without speaking, the green-eyed man motioned toward the sweeping central staircase. Two members of his team responded by charging upward. Thirty seconds later they returned, carrying a single item. The green-eyed intruder looked down at the Saudi and gazed at him calmly. "Tell Zizi, the next time I come it's for him," he said in perfect Arabic. Then the gun slammed into the side of the Saudi's head, and he blacked out.

THREE NIGHTS LATER the Isaac Weinberg Center for the Study of Anti-Semitism in France opened on the rue des Rosiers in the Marais. Like most matters dealing with the Jews of France, the creation of the center had not been without controversy. The far-right National Party of Jean-Marie Le Pen had raised questions about the source of its funding, while a prominent Islamic cleric had called for a boycott and organized a noisy demonstration the night of the opening reception. Thirty minutes into the party, there was a bomb threat. All of those in attendance, including Hannah Weinberg, the center's creator and director, were shepherded out of the building by a unit of French antiterrorist police and the remainder of the reception canceled.

Later that night she gathered with a few friends for a quiet supper down the street at Jo Goldenberg. It was shortly after ten o'clock when she walked back to her apartment house on the rue Pavée, shadowed by a security agent attached to the Israeli embassy. Upstairs in her flat she unlocked the door at the end of the central corridor and switched on the lights. She stood for a moment, gazing at the painting that hung on the wall above her childhood dresser, then she shut out the lights and went to bed.

42

ISTANBUL: AUGUST

IN THE END IT came down to a business transaction, which both Gabriel and Carter saw as proof of the Divine. Money for information: a Middle East tradition. Twenty million dollars for a life. The source was Carter's, a low-level Saudi prince with cirrhosis of the liver and an addiction to Romanian prostitutes. The money was Gabriel's, though it had once belonged to Zizi al-Bakari. The prince had not been able to supply a name, only a time and a place. The time was the second Monday of August. The place was the Ceylan Inter-Continental Hotel in Istanbul.

He arrived at ten under the name al-Rasheed. He was taller than they remembered. His hair was longish and quite gray, as was his heavy mustache. Despite the sweltering August heat, he wore a long-sleeved shirt and walked with his right hand in his pocket. He refused the bellman's offer of help with his single bag and headed up to his suite, which was on the twenty-fifth floor. His balcony had a commanding view of the Bosphorus, a room with a view having been one of his many demands. Gabriel knew about his demands, just as he knew what room he had been assigned. Money had bought that, too. At 10:09, the man stepped onto his balcony and looked down at the straits. He did not realize that on the street below two men were gazing up at him.

"Is it him, Eli?"

"It's him."

"Are you sure?"

"I'm sure."

Gabriel offered Lavon the mobile phone. Lavon shook his head.

"You do it, Gabriel. I've never been one for the rough stuff."

Gabriel dialed the number. An instant later the balcony was engulfed in a blinding fireball, and the flaming body of Ahmed bin Shafiq came plunging downward through the darkness. Gabriel waited until it hit the street, then slipped the Mercedes into gear and headed to Cannes.

THE RESTAURANT known as La Pizza is one of the most popular in Cannes, and so news that it had been booked for a private party spoiled what had otherwise been a perfect August day. There was a great deal of speculation along the Croisette about the identity of the man re-

sponsible for this outrage. Savvy visitors to the city, however, knew the answer lay in the waters just beyond the
Old Port. *Alexandra*, Abdul Aziz al-Bakari's enormous
private yacht, had come to Cannes that morning, and
everyone knew that Zizi always celebrated his arrival by
commandeering the most popular restaurant in town.

Dinner was scheduled for nine. At 8:55 two large
white launches set out from *Alexandra* and headed into
the port through the sienna light of sunset. The vessels
docked across the street from La Pizza at 8:58 and,
under abnormally intense private security, the party dis-
embarked and headed toward the restaurant. Most of the
tourists who gathered to witness the auspicious arrival
did not know the name Zizi al-Bakari, nor could they
identify a single member of his large entourage. That was
not the case for the three men watching from the grassy
esplanade at the end of the Quai Saint-Pierre.

The entourage remained inside La Pizza for two
hours. Later, in the aftermath, the press would make
much of the fact that no wine was drunk at dinner and
no cigarettes smoked, which was taken as proof of great
religious faith. At 11:06 they emerged from the restaurant and started across the street toward the waiting
launches. Zizi, as was his custom, was near the back of
his entourage, flanked by two men. One was a large Arab
with a round face, small eyes, and a goatee. The other
was a Frenchman dressed in black with his blond hair
drawn back into a ponytail.

One of the men who had watched the arrival of the

party from the esplanade was at that moment seated in the café next door to La Pizza. A heavy-shouldered man with strawberry-blond hair, he pressed a button on his mobile phone as Zizi approached the spot they had selected for his death, and within seconds two motorbikes came roaring along the Quai Saint-Pierre. The riders drew their weapons as they approached and opened fire. Zizi was hit first and mortally wounded. The bodyguards at his side drew their weapons and were instantly killed as well. Then the motorbikes swerved hard to the left and disappeared up the hill into the old city.

The man with strawberry-blond hair stood and walked away. It was his first major undertaking as chief of Special Operations, and it had gone very well. He knew at that moment, however, that the killing would not end in Cannes, for the last thing he had seen as he walked away was Nadia al-Bakari, kneeling over the dead body of her father, screaming for revenge.

AUTHOR'S NOTE

The Messenger is a work of fiction. The names, characters, places, and incidents portrayed in this novel are the product of the author's imagination or have been used fictitiously. Any resemblance to actual persons, living or dead, businesses, companies, events, or locales is entirely coincidental. *Marguerite Gachet at Her Dressing Table* by Vincent van Gogh unfortunately does not exist, though the descriptions of Vincent's final days at Auvers, and his relationship with Dr. Paul Gachet and his daughter, are accurate. Those well acquainted with the quiet backwaters of St. James's know that in Mason's Yard, at the address of the fictitious Isherwood Fine Arts, there stands a gallery owned by the incomparable Patrick Matthiesen, to whom I am forever indebted. The Vatican security procedures described in the pages of this novel are largely fictitious. Visitors to the island of Saint-

Barthélemy will search in vain for the restaurants Le Poivre and Le Tetou.

Sadly, a central aspect of *The Messenger* is inspired by truth: Saudi Arabia's financial and doctrinal support for global Islamic terrorism. The pipeline between Saudi religious charities and Islamic terrorists has been well documented. A very senior U.S. official told me that, after the attacks of 9/11, American officials traveled to Riyadh and demonstrated to the Royal Family how twenty percent of all the money given to Saudi-based Islamic charities ends up in the hands of terrorists. Under American pressure, the Saudi government has put in place tighter controls on the fund-raising activities of the charities. Critics, however, believe these steps to be largely window dressing.

An example of Saudi Arabia's new commitment to stemming the flow of money to terrorist organizations came in April 2002. Eight months after 9/11, with Saudi Arabia besieged by inquiries about its role in the attacks, state-run Saudi television broadcast a telethon that raised more than $100 million to support "Palestinian martyrs," the euphemism for suicide bombers from Hamas, Palestinian Islamic Jihad, and the Al-Aqsa Martyrs Brigade. The telecast featured remarks by Sheikh Saad al-Buraik, a prominent government-sanctioned Saudi cleric, who described the United States as "the root of all wickedness on earth." The Islamic cleric went on to say: "Muslim brothers in Palestine, do not have any mercy, neither compassion on the Jews, their blood, their money, their flesh. Their women are yours to take, legitimately. God made them yours. Why don't you enslave their women? Why don't you wage jihad? Why don't you pillage them?"

ACKNOWLEDGMENTS

This novel, like the previous books in the Gabriel Allon series, could not have been written without the assistance of David Bull, who truly is among the finest art restorers in the world. Several Israeli and American intelligence officers gave me guidance along the way, and for obvious reasons I cannot thank them by name. Jean Becker, known to her legion of admirers as "the center of the universe," and not without good reason, opened many doors for me. My copy editor, Jane Herman, saved me much embarrassment, as did my friend Louis Toscano, who made countless improvements to the manuscript. I consulted hundreds of books, articles, and Web sites, far too many to cite here, but I would be remiss if I did not mention the extraordinary scholarship of Dore Gold, Laurent Murawiec, Gerald Posner, and Derek Fell, whose analysis of Vincent van Gogh's final days at Auvers inspired *Marguerite Gachet at Her Dressing Table*. It goes without saying that none of this would have been possible without the support of the remarkable team of professionals at Putnam: Ivan Held, Marilyn Ducksworth, and especially my editor, Neil Nyren.

We are blessed with many friends, who, at critical points during the writing year, provide much needed perspective and laughter, especially Betsy and Andrew Lack, Elsa Walsh and Bob Woodward, Michael and Leslie Sabourin, and Andrew and Marguerita Pate. My wife, Jamie Gangel, served as a trusted sounding board for my ideas and skillfully edited my early drafts, including some I did not like. She saw the essence of the story, even when it eluded me. Without her care, support, and devotion, *The Messenger* might never have taken flight.

Please read on for an excerpt from
Daniel Silva's exciting novel

THE
SECRET SERVANT

Available from Signet

AMSTERDAM

IT WAS PROFESSOR SOLOMON ROSNER who sounded the first alarm, though his name would never be linked to the affair except in the secure rooms of a drab office building in downtown Tel Aviv. Gabriel Allon, the legendary but wayward son of Israeli Intelligence, would later observe that Rosner was the first asset in the annals of Office history to have proven more useful to them dead than alive. Those who overheard the remark found it uncharacteristically callous but in keeping with the bleak mood that by then had settled over them all.

The backdrop for Rosner's demise was not Israel, where violent death occurs all too frequently, but the normally tranquil quarter of Amsterdam known as the Old Side. The date was the first Friday in December, and the weather was more suited to early spring than to the last days of autumn. It was a day to engage in what the Dutch so fondly refer to as *gezelligheid*, the pursuit of small pleasures: an aimless stroll through the flower stalls of the Bloemenmarkt, a lager or two in a good bar in the

Rembrandtplein, or, for those so inclined, a bit of fine cannabis in the brown coffeehouses of the Haarlemmerstraat. Leave the fretting and the fighting to the hated Americans, stately old Amsterdam murmured that golden late-autumn afternoon. Today we give thanks for having been born blameless and Dutch.

Solomon Rosner did not share the sentiments of his countrymen, but then he seldom did. Though he earned a living as a professor of sociology at the University of Amsterdam, it was Rosner's Center for European Security Studies that occupied the lion's share of his time. His legion of detractors saw evidence of deception in the name, for Rosner served not only as the center's director but was its only scholar in residence. Despite those obvious shortcomings, the center had managed to produce a steady stream of authoritative reports and articles detailing the threat posed to the Netherlands by the rise of militant Islam within its borders. Rosner's last book, *The Islamic Conquest of the West*, had argued that Holland was now under a sustained and systematic assault by jihadist Islam. The goal of this assault, he maintained, was to colonize the Netherlands and turn it into a majority Muslim state, where, in the not too distant future, Islamic law, or *sharia*, would reign supreme. The terrorists and the colonizers were two sides of the same coin, he warned, and unless the government took immediate and drastic action, everything the free-thinking Dutch held dear would soon be swept away.

The Dutch literary press had been predictably appalled. Hysteria, said one reviewer. Racist claptrap, said another. More than one took pains to note that the views expressed in the book were all the more odious given the fact that Rosner's grandparents had been rounded up with a hundred thousand other Dutch Jews and sent off to the gas chambers at Auschwitz. All agreed that what the situation required was not hateful rhetoric like Rosner's but tolerance and dialogue. Rosner stood steadfast in the face of the withering criticism, adopting what one commentator described as the posture of a man with his finger wedged firmly in the dike. Tolerance and dialogue by all means, Rosner responded, but not capitulation. "We Dutch need to put down our Heinekens and hash pipes and wake up," he snapped during an interview on Dutch television. "Otherwise we're going to lose our country."

The book and surrounding controversy had made Rosner the most vilified and, in some quarters, celebrated man in the country. It had also placed him squarely in the sights of Holland's homegrown Islamic extremists. Jihadist Web sites, which Rosner monitored more closely than even the Dutch police did, burned with sacred rage over the book, and more than one forecast his imminent execution. An imam in the neighborhood known as the Oud West instructed his flock that "Rosner the Jew must be dealt with harshly" and pleaded for a martyr to step forward and do the job. The feckless Dutch interior minister had responded by proposing that Rosner go into hiding, an idea Rosner vigorously refused. He then supplied the minister with a list of ten radicals he regarded as potential assassins. The minister accepted the list without question, for he knew that Rosner's sources inside Holland's extremist fringe were in most cases far better than those of the Dutch security services.

At noon on that Friday in December, Rosner was hunched over his computer in the second-floor office of his canal house at Groenburgwal 2A. The house, like Rosner himself, was stubby and wide, and it tilted forward at a precarious angle, which some of the neighbors saw as fitting, given the political views of its occupant. Its one serious drawback was location, for it stood not fifty yards from the bell tower of the Zuiderkirk church. The bells tolled mercilessly each day, beginning at the stroke of noon and ending forty-five minutes later. Rosner, sensitive to interruptions and unwanted noise, had been waging a personal jihad against them for years. Classical music, white-noise machines, soundproof headphones—all had proven useless in the face of the onslaught. Sometimes he wondered why the bells were rung at all. The old church had long ago been turned into a government housing office—a fact that Rosner, a man of considerable faith, saw as a fitting symbol of the Dutch morass. Confronted by an enemy of infinite religious zeal, the secular Dutch had turned their churches into bureaus of the welfare state. *A church without faithful,* thought Rosner, *in a city without God.*

At ten minutes past twelve, he heard a faint knock and looked up to find Sophie Vanderhaus leaning against the doorjamb with a batch of files clutched to her breast. A former student of Rosner's, she had come to work for him after completing a graduate degree on the impact of the Holocaust on postwar Dutch society. She was part secretary and research assistant, part nursemaid and surrogate daughter. She kept his office in order and typed the final drafts of all his reports and articles. The minder of his impossible schedule, she tended to his appalling personal finances. She even saw to his laundry and made certain he remembered to eat. Earlier that morning, she had informed him that she was planning to spend a week in Saint-Maarten over the New Year. Rosner, upon hearing the news, had fallen into a profound depression.

"You have an interview with *De Telegraaf* in an hour," she said. "Maybe you should have something to eat and focus your thoughts."

"Are you suggesting my thoughts lack focus, Sophie?"

"I'm suggesting nothing of the sort. It's just that you've been working on that article since five thirty this morning. You need something more than coffee in your stomach."

"It's not that dreadful reporter who called me a Nazi last year?"

"Do you really think I'd let her near you again?" She entered the office and started straightening his desk. "After the interview with *De Telegraaf*, you go to the NOS studios for an appearance on Radio One. It's a call-in program, so it's sure to be lively. Do try not to make any more enemies, Professor Rosner. It's getting harder and harder to keep track of them all."

"I'll try to behave myself, but I'm afraid my forbearance is now gone forever."

She peered into his coffee cup and pulled a sour face. "Why do you insist on putting out your cigarettes in your coffee?"

"My ashtray was full."

"Try emptying it from time to time." She poured the contents of the ashtray into his rubbish bin and removed the plastic liner. "And don't forget you have the forum this evening at the university."

Rosner frowned. He was not looking forward to the forum. One of the other panelists was the leader of the European Muslim Association, a group that campaigned openly for the imposition of *sharia* in Europe and the destruction of the State of Israel. It promised to be a deeply unpleasant evening.

"I'm afraid I'm coming down with a sudden case of leprosy," he said.

"They'll insist that you come anyway. You're the star of the show."

He stood and stretched his back. "I think I'll go to Café de Doelen for a coffee and something to eat. Why don't you have the reporter from *De Telegraaf* meet me there?"

"Do you really think that's wise, Professor?"

It was common knowledge in Amsterdam that the famous café on the Staalstraat was his favorite haunt. And Rosner was hardly inconspicuous. Indeed, with his shock of white hair and rumpled tweed wardrobe, he was one of the most recognizable figures in Holland. The geniuses in the Dutch police had once suggested he utilize some crude disguise while in public—an idea Rosner had likened to putting a hat and a false mustache on a hippopotamus and calling it a Dutchman.

"I haven't been to the Doelen in months."

"That doesn't mean it's any safer."

"I can't live my life as a prisoner forever, Sophie"—he gestured toward the window—"especially on a day like today. Wait until the last possible minute before you tell the reporter from *De Telegraaf* where I am. That will give me a jump on the jihadists."

"That isn't funny, professor." She could see there was no talking him out of it. She handed him his mobile phone. "At least take this so you can call me in an emergency."

Rosner slipped the phone into his pocket and headed downstairs. In the entry hall, he pulled on his coat and trademark silk scarf and stepped outside. To his left rose the spire of the Zuiderkirk; to his right, fifty yards along a narrow canal lined with small craft, stood a wooden double drawbridge. The Groenburgwal was a quiet street for the Old Side: no bars or cafés, only a single small hotel that never seemed to have more than a handful of guests. Directly opposite Rosner's house was the street's only eyesore: a modern tenement block with a lavender-and-lime-pastel exterior. A trio of housepainters dressed in smudged white coveralls was squatting outside the building in a patch of sunlight.

Rosner glanced at the three faces, committing each to memory, before setting off in the direction of the drawbridge. When a sudden gust of wind stirred the bare tree limbs along the embankment, he paused for a moment to bind his scarf more tightly around his neck and watch a plump Vermeer cloud drift slowly overhead. It was then that he noticed one of the painters walking parallel to him along the opposite side of the canal. Short dark hair, a high flat forehead, a heavy brow over small eyes. Rosner, connoisseur of immigrant faces, judged him to be a Moroccan from the Rif Mountains. They arrived at the drawbridge simultaneously. Rosner paused again, this time to light a cigarette he did not want, and watched with relief as the man turned to the left. When the man disappeared round the next corner, Rosner headed in the opposite direction toward the Doelen.

He took his time making his way down the Staalstraat, now dawdling at the window of his favorite pastry shop to gaze at that day's offerings, now sidestepping to avoid being run down by a pretty girl on a bicycle, now pausing to accept a few words of encouragement from a ruddy-faced admirer. He was about to step through the entrance of the café when he felt a tug at his coat sleeve. In the few remaining seconds he had left to live, he would be tormented by the absurd thought that he might have prevented his own murder had he resisted the impulse to turn around. But he did turn around, because that is what one does on a glorious December afternoon in Amsterdam, when one is summoned in the street by a stranger.

He saw the gun only in the abstract. In the narrow street the shots reverberated like cannon fire. He collapsed onto the cobblestones and watched helplessly as his killer drew a long knife from inside his coveralls. The slaughter was ritual, just as the imams had decreed it should be. No one intervened—hardly surprising, thought Rosner, for intervention would have been intolerant—and no one thought to comfort him as he lay dying. Only the bells spoke to him. *A church without faithful,* they seemed to be saying, *in a city without God.*

From #1 *New York Times*
bestselling author
DANIEL SILVA

The Gabriel Allon series

The Kill Artist
The English Assassin
The Confessor
A Death in Vienna
Prince of Fire
The Messenger
The Secret Servant
Moscow Rules
The Defector

**"Allon is Israel's Jack Bauer...
Thrill factor: Five stars."
—USA Today**

From #1 *New York Times*
bestselling author
DANIEL SILVA

THE SECRET SERVANT

A terrorist plot in London leads Israeli spy
Gabriel Allon on a desperate search for a
kidnapped woman, in a race against time
that will compromise Allon's own
conscience—and life...

**"A textured espionage novel in
the tradition of John le Carré."**

—GQ Online

Available wherever books are sold or at
penguin.com

Gabriel Allon, art restorer and spy, is about to face the greatest challenge of his life. An al-Qaeda suspect is killed in London, and photographs are found on his computer—photographs that lead Israeli intelligence to suspect that al-Qaeda is planning one of its most audacious attacks ever, aimed straight at the heart of the Vatican.

Allon and his colleagues soon find themselves in a deadly duel of wits against one of the most dangerous men in the world—a hunt that will take them across Europe to the Caribbean and back. But for them, there may not be enough of anything: enough time, enough facts, enough luck.

All Allon can do is set his trap—and hope that he is not the one caught in it.

"*The Messenger*'s blood-spattered, true-to-life backdrop pumps up this thrill ride of a story, but its underlying messages about fundamentalism, revenge, oil dependency, and cultural differences are what will keep you awake at night."   —*USA Today*

"Exhibits Silva's usual intelligence, style, and research. . . . Silva uncorks another, even more dramatic climax."   —*The Washington Post Book World*

"The enigmatic Gabriel Allon remains one of the most intriguing heroes of any thriller series, a wonderfully nuanced, endlessly fascinating creation . . . entertaining and well written."
—*The Philadelphia Inquirer*

"Silva [is] the modern-day Robert Ludlum, and his lead character, Gabriel Allon, should remind readers of Jason Bourne (without the amnesia, of course)."
—*The Florida Times-Union*

continued . . .